Mistress of Fashion

Juliette's Story

Mistress of Fashion

Juliette's Story

Ladies of Independent Means Trilogy, Book 1

EVELYN RICHARDSON

CAVEL
PRESS

Kenmore, WA

A Camel Press book published by Epicenter Press

Epicenter Press
6524 NE 181st St.
Suite 2
Kenmore, WA 98028

For more information go to:
www.Camelpress.com
www.Coffeetownpress.com
www.Epicenterpress.com
www.evelynrichardson.net

Cover design by Scott Book
Interior design by Melissa Vail Coffman

Mistress of Fashion: Juliette's Story
Copyright © 2021 by Evelyn Richardson

ISBN: 978-1-60381-617-5 (Trade Paper)
ISBN: 978-1-60381-734-9 (eBook)

Library of Congress Control Number: 2020934865

Printed in the United States of America

To B.—still my romantic hero after 30 years.

*To my sister Madeleine, the world's toughest critic
and the only beta reader I trusted with this book.*

ACKNOWLEDGMENTS

To all those wonderful ladies of the Beau Monde who keep Regency authors honest.

PROLOGUE

NOT BOTHERING TO STIFLE THE YAWN that threatened to overwhelm him as the *corps de ballet* floated onstage, Freddy Claverton, Marquess of Wrothingham, lifted an elegant gold quizzing glass to his eye and gazed hopefully at the surrounding boxes, desperately seeking some sort of diversion. His companions might enjoy ogling the scantily clad limbs of the dancers to their hearts' content, but he had come to the opera to hear Grassini sing the title role in *Gli Orazi e Curiazi*, and the ballet between acts, the only reason the Honorable Herbert Fotheringay and Sir Gerald Ravenel had agreed to accompany him, left Freddy paralyzed with boredom.

The quizzing glass came to a halt in its slow perusal of the assembled multitude as Freddy, gripping it more tightly, gasped and focused all his attention on the box just opposite. "Who *is* that exquisite creature?"

Gerald and Herbert, their own eyes glued to the pulchritudinous display in front of them, remained oblivious to their friend's obvious astonishment.

"I say, Herbie," Freddy plucked at his friend's sleeve of the finest dark blue Bath superfine, "who *is* that vision of elegance?"

"Eh? What did you say, Freddy?" The Honorable Herbert reluctantly tore his eyes away from the stage.

"Her!" Freddy waved his quizzing glass in the direction of the beautiful *incognita*.

"How should I know?"

"What do you mean, *How should I know?* You know every pretty face in town, and if you don't, you have only to ask your mother or your sisters and they do."

"You been in the sun too long, old fellow?" Herbert regarded him with indulgent exasperation. "That box belongs to Mrs. Gerrard and there is a different delicious morsel occupying it every week. It could be any one of Mrs. Gerrard's's lovely inhabitants."

"Most exclusive seraglio in the whole of London," Sir Gerald offered helpfully. "Best selection in the entire country—clever, charming, and every single one of them a stunner. Well," he waved an authoritative hand at the box where an admiring crowd was rapidly forming, "take a look for yourself. Just goes to show, doesn't it? I mean, if people are ignoring all the dancers on stage for one woman in a box, there has to be a reason for it."

"Most definitely."

Freddy's tone of hushed reverence was more than the other two could take. "Touched in the upper works." Herbert shook his head sadly.

"Besotted." Gerald agreed. "Never seen him look like that at a woman—a waistcoat perhaps and a snuff box at Rundell and Bridges but never a woman."

"I *must* meet her! Do you know anyone who can introduce me?"

"I say again, *You been in the sun, old fellow*?" Herbert spoke with the controlled patience of a rider dealing with a restive horse. "That's what she's in the box for, to be *introduced*."

"Oh." Revelation dawned on the marquess' cherubic countenance. "But there are so many other fellows there already, and . . ."

"You're a duke's son and rich as Croesus," Sir Gerald patted him comfortingly on the shoulder, "and in this sort of, er, *encounter*, that is all that matters. The moment you introduce yourself she'll know that. She's a high flyer—all Helen Gerrard's ladies are high flyers—and she has been well taught. Believe me, they know the entire lineage, income, and all the properties of everyone who walks through the exclusive portals of their establishment."

"Very well," the Honorable Herbert sighed, rising reluctantly from his seat, "I shall accompany you, but that means you will not be allowed to leave the *young lady's* box until you have arranged an assignation."

"I will, if she will have me." Freddy, his eyes still glued to the box, was utterly oblivious to the look that passed between his two companions. Freddy Claverton with a ladybird? They would be regaling their cronies with this little tidbit for weeks.

Following in Herbert's wake, Freddy himself was beginning to realize just how radical a departure this was from his own comfortable little routine—snug bachelor quarters in Mount Street, afternoons spent closeted with his tailor, strolling down Bond Street, or driving in the park, or evenings at the theater with a convivial group or at Brooks's with nothing more strenuous in any of it than the usual Wednesday evening spent accompanying his mother and sister to Almack's or, possibly, escorting his formidable fiancé, Lady Lavinia Harcourt, and her mother to a concert at the Hanover Square Rooms. Now, suddenly he was about to disrupt that reassuringly familiar pattern by visiting a high flyer in her box at the opera!

Ruthlessly he shoved aside the million implications and complications that rushed into his head as, metaphorically clinging to his friend's coattails, he entered the box. This was no time to second-guess himself. He had made up his mind as to what he wanted, and nothing was going to stop him now.

"Delighted to make your acquaintance." Herbert's voice floated mistily around Freddy's ears as he gazed raptly at the vision in front of him, a symphony of large blue eyes, delicate blond curls, and shimmering silk draped over an ethereal figure so languid and graceful it seemed to have been poured into the velvet chair in front of him.

"Mademoiselle Juliette Fanchon," the clipped matronly accents of the vision's companion finally penetrated Freddy's fog.

"Mademoiselle Fanchon." Past master of the elegant leg, Freddy executed his most beautiful bow as he bent over the slim white hand presented to him. "Mademoiselle Fanchon, I would be most," Freddy took a deep fortifying breath as he tried desperately to ignore the rakish Corinthians hovering at the back of the box—fine looking fellows with broad shoulders, muscular legs, and scores of demi-reps in their past—and concentrated instead on the angel in front of him.

Buck up, Freddy, old boy. Father's a duke, you're rich as Croesus, females like that sort of thing. "Er, yes, Mademoiselle Fanchon, I do hope you are enjoying the singing. Grassini is superb. Mr. Waters was most fortunate to engage her when Catalani refused to agree to his terms, but there is no one quite like Catalani, don't you agree?"

"There is not, is there, my lord, though it is most unusual to find a gentleman who actually knows enough about her singing, or anyone else's, to appreciate it much less make comparisons."

"Oh, there is no question that Catalani is the best, even if one takes into account Naldi or Mrs. Billington." Was it just wishful thinking on his part, or did those dark blue eyes shine more approvingly on him as he uttered these sentiments?

"Ahem," a purposeful voice grated in Freddy's ear, reminding him that even though it felt to him as though he and Mademoiselle Fanchon were the only two people in the box, they were not, and Freddy had come to this box for a particular reason. "But I should not be distracting you from one of the best singers the Continent has to offer. Perhaps I may call on you later, some time when you are free to discuss . . . or we could . . . ."

"That would be lovely, my lord. Tonight perhaps? After the performance."

"Tonight?" Freddy's somewhat fluty voice rose to what could only be called a squeak.

"Why yes, my lord." There was a twinkle in Mademoiselle's glorious eyes, but it was a kind twinkle. "That is, if you are not otherwise engaged?"

"Me? Oh no, nothing else to do, eh, Herbert?"

"Nothing except call on Mademoiselle Fanchon, old boy."

Freddy was trapped, a victim of his own success. "Yes," he gulped. "I would like that, if, that is . . ."

"I look forward to your visit." The twinkle deepened into an enchanting smile that revealed pearly teeth, and an irresistible dimple hovering at the corner of delicately sculpted lips.

The breath Freddy had been holding from the moment he had entered the box, escaped in a sigh of relief as he bowed and turned to head out the door."

"Shall I give you my direction?" The musical voice was warmed by the faintest hint of gentle laughter.

"Oh, I . . . ."

"I shall see that he gets there, Mademoiselle Fanchon, if I have to carry him myself." The Honorable Herbert swept an elaborate leg himself as he shoved his bemused companion through the door of the box and into the crowd promenading outside.

"There! See, was that so difficult?"

"Nnnnno, ... but she is so lovely and . . ."

"Freddy!" The Honorable Herbert's patience was wearing thin and he did not bother to hide his exasperation this time. "Mademoiselle Fanchon is a professional at this sort of thing. *You* do not have to *be* or *do* anything except pay handsomely. It is up to her to make it all come out right."

Freddy brightened perceptibly. "Well, in that case, I am for it. It does make things a good deal easier, in a comfortable sort of way—paying, I mean. Not like having to come up to scratch for a female who might demand . . . well . . . anything."

"Precisely." Herbert repressed a shudder as the image of the bracket-faced Lady Lavinia, promised to Freddy since birth, rose before him. "And Mrs. Gerrard's was created with just that sort of thing in mind—a man's comfort, that is."

CHAPTER 1

JULIETTE SANK BACK AGAINST THE VELVET squabs of Mrs. Gerrard's elegant town carriage reveling in the peace and quiet after the crowd at the opera. It had been the usual, the box filled with fashionable men as eager to be seen flirting with the ladies of Mrs. Gerrard's as they were to impress the ladies themselves. And in the boxes around them, women of the *haut ton* were doing their level best to ignore the ladies as though they did not exist at all despite all the masculine attention they were attracting. It was the same everywhere; Juliette and her companions were completely invisible to the women and utterly desirable to the men of the fashionable world. Still, she would not have traded places with any one of the self-satisfied peeresses so studiously avoiding her for Juliette knew very well that while even wealthy peeresses had to do the bidding of husbands, brothers, fathers, mothers; she, Juliette was answerable to no one but herself. Yes, she worked at Mrs. Gerrard's, but she earned her keep, paid her own way, and made her own decisions; to someone who had been fighting for independence since the moment she could walk, it meant a great deal, no matter how much scorn she saw in those rigidly averted faces. Yes, it had been a usual night at the opera, but if Juliette were guessing correctly, and she usually did, having experienced far too much of the world than a gently born young woman should, it was the second part of her evening that was going to prove interesting. Smiling at the footman who handed her from the carriage, she thanked her *companion*, Mrs. Taylor, for accompanying her and hurried to her chamber to await further events.

Immediately, there was a rap on the door and Helen appeared, elegant as usual in white satin gown whose spring green bodice and dangling emerald earrings exactly matched the color of her enigmatic eyes. Taking a seat opposite

Juliette's, she glanced around the room in her coolly appraising way. "Mrs. Taylor tells me you made quite an impression on the Marquess of Wrothingham this evening." Mrs. Gerrard's proprietress nodded approvingly. "The Clavertons are as wealthy and powerful as any family in the land; you have done very well indeed, but then I always knew you would from the moment I met you. Starving and ill as you were, you had the presence and manners of a duchess, not surprising considering your upbringing. "Still Freddy Claverton is something of an anomaly and utterly lacking in the self-assured arrogance usually associated with dukes' sons or leaders of the *ton*. Despite his exquisite manners, he is rumored to be shy and that can be dangerously seductive to women such as we who are not used to kindness. Guard your heart, if you have any of it left."

"I will, Helen." Juliette stifled a sigh. Somehow the self-effacing gentleman who had been impressed with her knowledge of the opera hardly seemed like a threat, but Helen was right, of course; it would not do for a lady from Mrs. Gerrard's to care about one of her patrons. It seemed such a discouragingly cynical way to view humanity, not that humanity had been anything but cynical in its relations with her, but somehow Juliette could not look at things that way, preferring a more pragmatic, less hardhearted view of the world. Helen did, however, and it was this cynicism and strong-mindedness that made her, the owner of the establishment, a power to be reckoned with, and fierce protectress of all who called it home. For that home and for that protection Juliette would do anything in her limited power to repay her, and if that meant not falling in love with the Marquess of Wrothingham, then certainly she would not fall in love with the Marquess of Wrothingham.

"I know I do not need to warn you, it is just that love," Helen wrinkled her patrician nose in disgust, "or even attraction, can be such a powerful thing, not that I have ever felt it, mind you, but I have seen others become utterly foolish in its grip. Now, I imagine his lordship has arrived. I shall give you some time to collect yourself and send him up."

Juliette stared into the fire as Helen closed the door. No, she had never been in love, nor was she ever likely to be. She had only one passion in her life and that was her art and her dream. One day she would be the premier modiste in London, in all of England. But that was for the future. Right now she had a shy, exquisitely attired gentleman on his way up to see her.

The glint of light on a quizzing glass had first caught her attention she had surveyed the crowd from Mrs. Gerrard's box at the opera. While everyone else's eyes had been glued to the *corps de ballet*, the owner of the quizzing glass was surveying the audience until his gaze had fallen on her. She had practically felt his gasp of amazement, even from that great distance, and could not help chuckling to herself. Even after a year at Mrs. Gerrard's, she had not gotten used to the admiration. It was not that she had not been admired before, but then it was because she was the well—brought—up daughter of one of France's most distinguished families, it had nothing to do with her person and everything to do with her heritage. The admiration she received these days was all for her and for her alone, from her carefully arranged blond curls to the dark blue eyes she kept bright and sparkling, no matter what she was feeling, and a dimple that she had been taught to use to deadly effect when she smiled.

In this case the admiration seemed to have rendered the poor gentleman speechless the moment he entered her box so that his friends had to do all the talking for him. There had been something ineffably sweet in that deference which was at odds with his modish costume and elegant bow. Usually gentleman who considered themselves tulips of the *ton* affected a bored, worldly air and a waspish wit so completely the opposite of the lively interest she had seen in his eyes. It was such an unusual contrast that Juliette could not help but be intrigued. And the admiration she had seen in his amiable blue eyes had nothing to do with lust. She couldn't quite place it, but the more she considered it, the more it seemed like the admiration of a connoisseur enjoying a beautiful painting or an exquisite piece of porcelain. And now he was here.

"His lordship, the Marquess of Wrothingham," the maid ushered a slightly portly blond gentleman whose diffident air belied his height.

"You came, my lord!" Juliette rose from her chair next to the fireplace.

"Of course I came." Freddy reddened slightly this time. "The moment I caught sight of you I had to come."

There was so much awe in his voice, she could not help blushing in return. "I am glad. I was hoping you would, but I could not be sure."

"How could I stay away? I had to know."

"Had to know?"

"Yes. Your gown. Is it? I mean, it must be, but how can it be . . . .Lyons silk?"

Many men had said many things to Juliette during her time at Mrs. Gerrard's, extravagant things, naughty things, seductive things, but no one had come remotely close to this! The woman whose manners had been drummed into her by her mother and her nurse before she could walk, and who had been schooled in sparkling repartee by the proprietress of London's most popular and exclusive brothel was utterly at a loss for words.

"It is absolutely exquisite, the dress I mean; only Lyons silk catches the light in just that way."

Juliette giggled. She could not help it, he was so intent, so earnest, and such a dear. Then, hastily pressing one slim hand to her lips she was instantly contrite. "Oh dear, I *am* sorry. I should not laugh, but it was just that it was, well, so unexpected."

Freddy grinned back. "Well, is it?"

Recollecting herself, she tilted her head provocatively. "You could help me take it off and see for yourself."

His look of pure horror was even more amusing than his question, but instead of laughing at him, she found her heart going out to him for his awkwardness, and she patted his hand reassuringly. "Yes, as a matter of fact, it *is* Lyons silk; it's the gold threads in it you know that shimmer in the light."

"I knew it!" He breathed triumphantly. "But how? We are only just invading France now; surely there has not yet been time for anyone to send silk back to London?"

A shadow crossed her face. "No, this is from long ago, a dress of my moth . . . er, a *friend*. The material seemed too beautiful to waste."

Freddy nodded, reverently stroking the hem of her skirt that she held up for him to examine. "Whoever re-made it for you is an artist indeed. The stitching is so fine and the cut is unlike any I have seen. This deep—beaded border and the flower garlands at the hem are most original, clever too, for the weight of it makes the material drape well and highlights an elegant figure when in motion. You are fortunate indeed in your mantua maker. Who is it, if I might ask?"

Juliette regarded him soberly for a moment. Could she trust him? There was genuine interest in the bright blue eyes looking so earnestly into hers, and nothing but kindness in the boyishly rounded face, still, he was the son of a duke and moved in the very highest circles of the *ton*. Helen had told her so.

Comprehension dawned in his eyes and the interest in his face warmed to sympathy. "You really *are* French, are you not?"

Juliette nodded dumbly.

"I thought so. You speak without a trace of an accent, but there is a lilt in your voice that can only have come to someone born speaking that most civilized of languages. And your taste—no English woman is so naturally elegant. French people do not live in England out of choice. Who would? The food alone is enough to . . . ," Freddy shook his head in disgust. "Then again, any, er *friend* who once possessed a gown of Lyons silk could not have been too popular with the good citizens of the glorious new republic. No, I would say," his frown revealed that deduction did not come easily to someone who preferred to occupy his mind with waistcoats and snuff boxes, "I would say that you and your family left your native land in rather a hurry some time ago and have taken up the needle to defray expenses ever since." He smiled triumphantly. "Aha! That's it! I've guessed it, haven't I?"

He looked so pleased with himself that Juliette could not help smiling, even though her heart was breaking into a thousand pieces as it always did when the past caught up with her.

Now it was Freddy's turn to grow somber as he saw the shadows darken eyes that glistened with a hint of tears. "But that is not all, is it?" He asked gently.

Again Juliette shook her head.

He took both her hands in his. "And that does not explain how you got here."

"Nnnnnno."

"Did *you* make this most exquisite of gowns?"

"Ye . . . yes," she gulped. "I . . . it was my design and I . . . er . . . already had the silk . . . and the lace . . ."

Freddy examined the lace, which was also beautifully done, but in his enthusiasm over the silk he had entirely overlooked it.

". . . so, I made it up according to my own ideas. It was something to do and I like . . . I like to sew."

This last declaration was made defiantly, as though it had been uttered many times before over the course of a short young life.

"And you do it brilliantly, I might add. Too brilliantly not to do more. Did you never think of becoming a mantua maker yourself?"

The stricken look in her eyes, quickly hidden though it was, spoke volumes, and even before she opened her mouth he forestalled her. "I am sorry, that was dreadfully impertinent of me; my enthusiasm for your talent makes me forget my manners."

But the relief of it, being treated with respect and admiration for something other than her beautiful face and enticing figure was too much, and with a silent apology to her employer, Juliette began her story.

"I was working for a mantua maker, a fine one in Bond Street, but then one day I caught the eye of a . . . a . . . *gentleman* who was there with his wife. I tried to avoid his . . . his *notice*, but it was no use and soon his attentions became so, so . . . *obvious* that I was let go. With my reputation compromised I could find no one to hire me, and soon my savings were entirely gone. I was quite desperate when one of my former employer's customers, a singer at the opera, told me about Helen." It was not a precisely accurate description of the disaster that had brought her to Mrs. Gerrard's, but Juliette felt sure this exquisite, well—brought—up gentleman did not want to hear a tale of rape and suffering.

"Helen? The formidable woman who welcomed me to this establishment?"

Juliette nodded. "She is really the kindest person you can imagine, though she would not be best pleased to know I am boring you with my story when I should be *entertaining* you. But really, she has been wonderful to me. She has taken me in, cared for me, set me on my feet again . . ."

"Reminds me of the Mater. Starchy old woman, fierce as a Tatar, always watching you to see you don't put a foot wrong, but if she cares about you she would do anything for you, and you don't want to say a word against any of her children, not to her face anyway, even if it is your own brother." Freddy shuddered at the memory.

"Exactly. At any rate, that is why I am not a mantua maker, but," she lifted her chin proudly, "I am in charge of creating all the gowns for the ladies here at Mrs. Gerrard's. And I teach them sewing and fine needlework."

"You teach them needlework?" Freddy's experience with the sort of women who inhabited Mrs. Gerrard's was less than none, but he didn't think that lessons in needlework constituted a normal occupation for those sorts of people.

"Yes, we all teach one another something," Juliette continued, her natural vivacity returning as she warmed to her theme. "Helen, Mrs. Gerrard, wants us to better ourselves. She sees our stay here as a stepping stone to financial independence and our chosen way of life. I also teach French. Grace teaches us singing and the pianoforte, Dora explains household accounts, and Helen gives us instruction in the rest—reading, writing, sums, history, and Latin and Greek if we wish."

"Latin and Greek!" Freddy could not help thinking that the classics would have stuck in his mind a great deal better if he had studied them in this establishment instead of having them beaten into him by the cadaverous tutor at Claverton.

"Only if we wish it." Juliette chuckled. "There are not a lot of us who do, as you can imagine."

"I dare say." Freddy, whose own memory of both languages was extremely hazy, not to mention unfortunate, could only gaze in admiration at someone who clearly relished the opportunity to study them. "But I still maintain that your talent is wasted here. Why you could cast all of Bond Street in the shade if you'd a mind to . . . and the blunt to do it, of course."

A thought struck him, so blindingly simple and perfect that he could visualize it even before he opened his mouth to propose it. "I say, I *do* have the blunt! I could set you up in a shop of your own, that is, of course, if you would allow me to discuss the designs and fabrics."

Juliette was touched. His blue eyes blazed with such generous enthusiasm that she did not have the heart to destroy it. Smiling, she shook her head. "It takes a very great deal of blunt, I am afraid. Besides, I owe my life to Helen; I could not simply leave her like this."

"But you said she wanted you to better yourselves, to gain financial independence . . ."

She stopped his lips with one slim finger. "But then I would be dependent on you."

"Oh." Freddy knew all about that sort of dependence. The Pater was always trying to control his son's behavior with the proper application of funds, not that he could keep him in penury—the estate willed to Freddy by his maternal grandmother kept him comfortably plump in the pocket, but the hard-living duke, continually disappointed by what he termed is first—born's *namby—pamby* ways, was constantly offering him bribes to indulge in more manly pursuits, to tie the knot with his dragon of a fianceé, and to produce a nursery full of heirs to the vast Claverton properties. "Yes, well, I see." He was cast down, but only for a moment and then his natural optimism asserted itself, "But it could be sort of a loan. You are bound to be a success and then you could pay me back in no time."

"You are very kind, but I do not see how it is to be done." Juliette stifled a regretful sigh for it really was a most attractive proposition as well as a chance to show Madame Celeste, better known as Sally Brimblecombe in her humbler days, that turning away Juliette Fanchon from her Bond Street establishment without character out of a false sense of respectability had been a big mistake. Then, mindful of the woman who had saved her from Sally Brimblecombe's nearly fatal stupidity, she added, "But you could come visit me here and we could discuss designs and fabrics and trimmings to your heart's content."

"By Jove, that is a brilliant thought! What a clever thing you are!" Freddy took both her hands in his, planting a grateful kiss on the backs of each one. "Of course Mrs. Gerrard will send me the bill. What a bang-up idea! When can we start?"

Juliette chuckled; never had a lover been more to her liking, though the life of a demi-rep had not been so bad as she expected it to be when desperation had driven her to Helen Gerrard's doorstep. "Whenever you like."

"Famous! I shall just speak to Mrs. Gerrard on my way out." And snatching up his curly brimmed beaver, Freddy executed an elegant, if hasty bow and dashed down the stairs.

Hearing voices in the drawing room, he concluded that the proprietress was busy with other guests so he continued on his exuberantly precipitous exit, too bemused to notice that one of the guests had looked up from his cards as Freddy bounded by. For the briefest of moments the impassive face of the veteran card player broke into an expression of utter astonishment, hastily stifled, then all his attention reverted to the cards in front of him

CHAPTER 2

"COULDN'T BELIEVE IT MYSELF," the card player confided to the Duke of Claverton the next evening in the gaming room at White's.

"Freddy?" The duke's bushy black brows rose incredulously. "Sure it wasn't Adrian, or even John, for God's sake?"

"No, the cravat was too high for John; he's too much of a sober sides—Vicar of St. George's and all that. And last time I saw Adrian he was in his regimentals. Bound to wear them all the time now; there's not a woman alive as can resist a man in uniform these days, especially someone who has been in the Peninsula. No, it was definitely Freddy."

A slow smile of satisfaction spread across the duke's florid features as he rubbed his chin thoughtfully. "You don't say . . ."

Lord Wolverton nodded vigorously. "I do say! Most impressive. Helen Gerrard, that is to say, Gerrard's, don't admit just anyone."

"Well, almost anyone, eh Alfred? After all, *you* were there." The duke poked his friend in the ribs. They'd been together since Eton and were closer to one another than they were to their own brothers.

"And, God's truth, that's what he told me," the Duke repeated the story later that day to his youngest son, Major Lord Adrian of his majesty's First Life Guards, who had just happened to stop by the family pile in Grosvenor Square to present his regards to his mother and offer to take his sister for a ride in the park.

"Freddy?" Lord Adrian was less visibly taken aback by the news than his parent had been, but that was to be expected. There was very little that could surprise someone who had spent the last year and a half trying to outwit Napoleon's cavalry. He was, however, intrigued. Freddy had never in his life demonstrated the least interest in any female, his fiancée excepted, and in her case, what he exhibited was closer to aversion than interest which was completely understandable. In Freddy's younger brother's opinion, the kindest thing that could be said about Lady Lavinia Harcourt was that she was an antidote. It wasn't that she was ugly, for she was, in fact, quite handsome in her own sort of way; it was just that if there were any joy or laughter in a room, it died the moment she entered it. Make no mistake about it, Adrian honored his eldest brother for knowing his duty—after all, Clavertons had been marrying Harcourts since the beginning of time or, at the very least, since the Conquest, but he pitied him with all his heart.

It was sympathy, therefore, as much as curiosity that prompted Lord Adrian to stroll down St. James's the next day and into the square that was dominated on one side by Mrs. Gerrard's discreetly elegant façade.

As luck would have it, his brother, who was at that moment visiting Juliette in her bedchamber overlooking the square, happened to carry some of her design sketches over to the window for a closer look in better light just as Adrian rounded the corner. The flash of scarlet caught Freddy's eye. "I say, it's Adrian!" In an instant, Freddy was bounding down the stairs leaving Juliette frantically grasping the sketches he had dropped into her lap.

She barely had time to wonder at her guest's odd behavior when he reappeared on the threshold, his round face beaming, tugging the sleeve of a tall broad shouldered gentleman in uniform.

All the breath squeezed from Juliette's body as she gazed up at the living breathing incarnation of the blessed Saint Michel as pictured in her precious book of the saints, one of the few things kept when her family had fled France. It was all there—the magnificent physique, boldly determined features, eyes filled with fire, compassion, and sorrow—all that was lacking was the flaming lance and the glorious white wings.

"My brother, Major Lord Adrian Claverton of His Majesty's First Life Guards," Freddy announced proudly, "Miss Juliette Fanchon."

The vision disappeared as a very real man bent over her hand, his eyes as blue as Freddy's, only darker, and twinkling with amusement at the absurdity of the entire situation. The reality was more overwhelming than the vision. The vision took her breath away. The man made her heart pound and her head dizzy in a way no man—not the flowers of France's nobility nor the most dashing members of London's *ton*—had ever made her feel before, In fact, no man had ever really affected her—until now.

"Mademoiselle Fanchon is a most talented *artiste*," Freddy continued by way of introduction, "with exquisite taste and an impeccable sense of design and fashion, and she has been so kind as to let me consult with her on her creations." He waved an airy hand toward the sketches Juliette was still clutching convulsively in her lap.

"I see." But Adrian did not see at all, just felt, that the woman in front of him was the embodiment of all he had dreamt of and longed for during the battle weary months in the Peninsula. She was beauty, grace, gentleness, and a wisdom mixed with both sorrow and humor that glowed in the dark—fringed sapphire eyes. She was the woman of his dreams, not that he'd had any dreams until now—and she belonged to Freddy.

Drawing a deep steadying breath, Adrian summoned up the devastating smile and charming manners that had been captivating female hearts, old and young, since he had grown out of short coats. "My brother is fortunate indeed in having such a . . ." What was she? Mistress? *Fille de joie?* Friend? Confidante? "mentor." Whatever she was, she was responsible for a look of—what was it—happiness? tenderness?—on his brother's face that Adrian had never seen before. Poor old Freddy who was so tied to his duty as heir to the dukedom he had never been able simply to enjoy life; and he, Adrian should rejoice that Freddy was finally able to do so. But how could he, when he, wanted her to smile at him instead of Freddy? "I am afraid that Freddy's own exquisite taste goes largely unappreciated in our family, crude country squires that we are. Father may be a duke, but, unlike your French *ducs*, those few that are left, he is more concerned with hunting, sport, and other *manly* occupations than he is with taste and culture, or anything remotely resembling refinement, eh, Freddy?"

The look on Freddy's face told it all, and once again, Juliette felt herself oddly sorry for someone whose fortunate life was so very different from her own. "The Marquess' encouragement has been so important to me. His kindness means everythi..he is kindness itself."

"I am delighted to hear my brother is at last getting the appreciation he deserves. And you are correct in thinking he is a kind and chivalrous man." Adrian believed every word he uttered. He loved his brother, but why did it suddenly cost him so much to articulate what he had always felt? Was it because he wanted that grateful smile, that happy glow in her eyes for himself, the son who, his father never lost an opportunity to point out was twice the man his eldest brother was? Perhaps she didn't like men like him—an unnerving thought—and Major Lord Adrian Claverton of Majesty's First Life Guards never suffered unnerving thoughts, especially where the female sex was concerned.

Suddenly the elegant bed chamber seemed hot and suffocating, as if the other two occupants had sucked up all the air in it between them. "I am charmed to make your acquaintance, Mademoiselle Fanchon, but please do not let me intrude. I can see that you and my brother were in the middle of . . ." And what had they been in the middle of? Had Freddy been losing himself in those glorious eyes so deep with sympathy and understanding that a man could drown in them, or kissing lips as delicate and inviting as a fresh summer berry? Or had he been tracing the tantalizing line of her neck as it curved into her shoulder reveling in the warmth of the silken flesh? God, he had to stop, had to get out of there before his imagination ran even more wild than it already was.

"Not to worry, old boy, Mademoiselle Fanchon and I were nearly finished." Freddy's cheery voice was ridiculously at odds with his brother's desperate thoughts. "If you don't mind, Mademoiselle, I shall just toddle along with my brother now, but I shall be back tomorrow. I am eager to see the trimmings you decide upon." He turned to Adrian. "You have no notion what clever things she does with even the simplest of ruchings, so inventive yet so perfect as to seem obvious after she has drawn them when they weren't at all that way before she put pencil to paper." Freddy beamed at Juliette as he leaned over to kiss her cheek.

If Adrian's mouth had not suddenly gone dry at the thought of kissing that soft smooth flesh, he would have seen that the expression on his brother's face was nothing more than avuncular, if not fatherly pride, but he was too absorbed in his own disturbing feelings to have the least concern for Freddy's.

Adrian was not the only one suffering disturbing feelings. Juliette, who had been so sure that any feelings she might have harbored had been destroyed long ago, was suddenly aware that her calm detachment towards everything except her art was not so pervasive as she had assumed. A pair of intense blue eyes and a hand that had briefly held hers in a strong and comforting clasp had utterly destroyed that illusion.

Hundreds of men had looked into Juliette Fanchon's eyes, and hundreds of men had bent over her hand, but none of them had caused her to experience anything so much as the barest awareness of contact. A *fille de joie* never felt anything, at least anyone who was any good at it, and she was very good at it. Everyone knew that being a professional was all about reading a man's desires and fulfilling them, and nothing about oneself. One had to concentrate; one could not be distracted by such trivial things as the touch of another human being.

But Juliette was well and truly distracted now. Her drawings slipped from her lap as she leaned toward the window to catch a glimpse of broad shoulders under a red tunic, the sun glinting on dark blond hair as Major Lord Adrian Claverton turned to respond to some remark from his brother walking next to him, the arresting profile with its square jaw, masterful nose, and high forehead all bespeaking the intensity that radiated from him, an intensity that had somehow turned her into a quivering mass of jelly. How could that be? She had been born to an unbending lineage of soldiers who never flinched and great ladies who were the essence of iron control under their refined and elegant exteriors, people who never felt anything except the duty and pride that was owed an illustrious name was now a mass of unnamable yearning.

Non! She could not feel. She would not feel, that in one glance, one touch, this man had seen down into her very soul, understood her as no one else had ever done before, not even her beloved brother, Auguste. And in the end, Auguste had not understood her very well either: he had joined the others in advising her to settle with one of the self-satisfied courtiers of their exclusive circle, then headed off to war, more interested in *la gloire* than his little sister or his aging parents, just as his father had left his wife and two young children with no thought for anything except that same *gloire* and burnishing the family honor which, it seemed, could only be won on the field of battle. Not only was Major Lord Adrian Claverton a man who had caused her a momentary lapse in composure, he was a soldier, and not to be trusted where feelings of any sort were involved.

But just for once in her life, it would be nice to indulge in a dream. *Non!* Juliette gathered her drawings and examined them critically, going over in her mind every design detail she had discussed with Freddy. *This* was her dream, her dresses, and the life she would make with them, not some dashing, impossibly handsome soldier who, along with his fashion-mad brother had disappeared down the street and out of view.

CHAPTER 3

THE TWO BROTHERS SAUNTERED TOWARDS ST. James's Street in companionable silence, each absorbed in his own thoughts. Freddy's were filled with visions of ruchings and blond lace while Adrian's held but one, an enchanting mouth whose lips promised a thousand tender delights to the lucky fellow they smiled on and a pair of speaking blue eyes. He could have been that lucky fellow; after all, Mademoiselle Fanchon *was* a resident of Mrs. Gerrard's. If only his brother had not found her first, a matter of honor that meant he could never be anything more to her than the brother of her admirer.

Being Freddy's brother had meant a lot of things to Adrian over the years: knowing that Claverton, the ancient house with all its treasures and traditions would not be his adult home, having no real established place in the world, income only at the whim of his father who, it could not be denied, had been more than happy to purchase his commission in the Life Guards and more than happy to brag to his cronies at White's of his son's exploits in the Peninsula. It had also meant he had freedom that poor Freddy as heir, never had. No one had worried when Adrian had fallen from the beech tree and broken his arm, and hardly anyone had noticed when he had been ill with a fever. But every childhood illness or mishap of Freddy's had been cause for alarm, at least on his mother's part, the duke being very much of the mind that unfortunate occurrences were a perfect opportunity to prove one's superiority by ignoring them which poor Freddy, delicate child that he had been, never could. And Adrian had been blessedly untroubled by the matchmaking schemes of predatory mamas and their equally marriage-minded daughters. No one was the least bit interested in a younger son, and that had left him to sow all the wild oats that he had wished to. Adrian could not help grinning at that thought. In fact, he had actually been *expected* to sow the wild oats in the family.

Yes, all in all, being Freddy's brother had been a liberating and adventurous experience, and in time he'd grown to be grateful to his elder brother for having to bear all the weight of expectations and responsibilities while Adrian could hare off to the Peninsula with his comrades to court danger, adventure, and glory slaying the Corsican monster. Yes, he had been grateful to Freddy—until now.

Now he was weary, weary of long marches over inhospitable terrain, weary of living with pain, death, and constant danger, sick to death of heat and dust and poverty stricken people, eyes filled with despair over the loss of what little they had possessed, and for what?

Adrian and his brothers—in—arms never spoke such thoughts, never alluded to them in the slightest way. There was no need; they saw it all in one another's tired eyes and weather-beaten faces, lined by sun and hardship. And there was certainly no one at home among the adoring crowds clustered around the red-coated conquerors who wanted to hear such things. No there was no comfort to be had there, but that didn't stop him from seeking solace and comfort all the same; the solace of freshly plowed fields waiting for the warmth of the spring sun to turn them green with the promise of new crops, for bare trees to burst into snowy blossoms that predicted a sustaining harvest at the end of a summer filled with birdsong, and sheep grazing contentedly in fields tended for centuries by sturdy, dependable souls who were as much a part of the ritual of life as the seasons themselves. He was looking for the peace of a gentle rain that filled the brooks where he longed to fish and immerse himself in the quiet rhythm of unchanging daily life until he felt peaceful with himself once again.

Oh, it had been all the challenge and excitement that he had hoped when he left for the Peninsula—furious charges that tested him to the limits of his strength and endurance, danger so ever-present and intense he had no time to wonder whether he had the courage to face it. It had been the test of his manhood that he had craved, but now that he had proven himself, the need had fallen away, leaving a much greater need in its place. It was a need so compelling he had not even been able articulate it to himself until the moment he had looked into Juliette Fanchon's eyes, and then, for a moment, he had caught a glimmer of what it might be.

But for Adrian, glancing at his brother's amiably rounded features now clouded over with thought, that glimmer would remain just that and nothing more because Juliette belonged to Freddy. Still, he consoled himself, he had at least seen a glimmer which was more than he had before, and maybe if Freddy invited him to join him and Juliette again, as he had today, Adrian might get enough of an idea of what that glimmer was to pursue it on his own elsewhere.

While two of the Claverton brothers were reflecting on their visit to Mrs. Gerrard's, the third was spending an uncomfortable moment with his irate parent in the gloomy library of Claverton House, Grosvenor Square. This was exceedingly ironic, John thought as he endured the duke's famous glower, because his father had absolutely no use for that particular room or the books that adorned its walls except as a place where he could be assured of his wife's absence. On the other hand, John desperately coveted every one of the leather bound volumes his father so studiously ignored.

"I promised the bishop that you will wait on him tomorrow and now you tell me you are too busy visiting the sick to spare the time to advance your career? Have care lad, your noble connections will only take you so far and then you must make a push for yourself. If you do not pay attention, you'll end up as a rector for the rest of your days."

John sighed inwardly. It was the same conversation they'd had over and over again since he'd left Oxford. "Which is all that I really care to be, Father."

"Nonsense!" The duke's fist slammed down on the ancient desk in front of him. "Whelps! I have raised nothing but whelps, and not a man to stand up among you," the duke shouted, conveniently forgetting for the moment his youngest son's military exploits that so frequently peppered his conversations. You and Freddy, namby—pamby, the both of you! Why, until Wolverton told me your brother is a regular at Mrs. Gerrard's I had begun to doubt Freddy was a man at all. You, at least, can ride and play a decent hand of cards, but . . ."

"Mrs. Gerrard's?" John had heard the note of pride in his father's voice and, being the cleverest of the duke's sons, not to mention a superb card player, saw his opening and took it. The distraction worked like a charm.

"Yes. Can you believe it? Likely Lady Lavinia drove him to it because he doesn't have enough bottom to do something like that on his own. What I wouldn't give to see her face when she finds out." The duke took a moment to savor the picture of the starchy Lady Lavinia Harcourt learning of her fianceé latest interest. She would be mad as a wet hen, and a good thing too. Freddy was far too biddable as it was, and if he weren't careful he'd spend the rest of his life under that cat's paw.

"It doesn't bear thinking of." There was not much John and his father agreed upon, but a hearty dislike of Freddy's fiancée was one of them. "I shall have to call on Freddy myself soon." Having successfully turned his father's thoughts away from the bishop, John rose to go.

"And I am sorry for it, such a kill-joy as that woman is, but Harcourts have married Clavertons since the beginning of time and that is all there is too it." The duke had never stopped being grateful for the lack of female Harcourts in his generation. "Freddy," the duke began, glowering again as he realized how easily he had been lured off track, "at least knows his duty to his family."

"And Adrian knows his, so there is hope that in time I shall know mine." John flashed a surprisingly charming smile and made his exit before the duke could warm to his theme.

Striding briskly back to the rectory, John tried to push resentful thoughts from his mind. He had embarked on what he had hoped to be a promising career at Oxford, expecting all the while to take over one of the livings in his father's gift, when the duke had suddenly awakened to the fact that his second son's formal education had finished. Naturally the duke had several excellent livings on his vast estates, any one of which he could have bestowed on his son, but what was a simple country vicar, compared to a bishop or even an arch-bishop? Clavertons did *not* become simple country vicars, no matter how much they might wish to. Without even bothering to consult his son, the duke had spoken to friends and within a short period of time announced to John that he was to be installed as rector of Saint George's, Hanover Square.

Any other young man would have been exultant, but John had felt the golden manacles closing around his wrists. As a boy he had concerned himself deeply with the affairs of his father's tenants and the villagers within Claverton's parish, urging Cook and the housekeeper to share the bounty of the estate's gardens, hot houses, and home farm with poor widows and orphans, the aged and the infirm, convincing the steward to hire those that everyone else had long given up on. He had dreamed of the day when he could offer spiritual as well as material solace to those suffering and in need.

Providing weekly sermons to bored members of a fashionable congregation who viewed the church simply as a place to conduct marriages and baptisms was not what John had in mind. There was nothing for it, but to acquiesce to his father's will. He needed a living and if his father would not give him one of his own, then he was forced to take what others would give; never mind that any other of his brothers in the cloth would have traded him more than gladly for such a prestigious post.

A brisk walk in the fresh air did him good, and by the time John had reached his own lodgings in Grosvenor Street he was calm enough to retreat to his own library where the books crammed on the shelves were truly appreciated and lost himself in reading *The Lives of the Puritans*.

After an inspiring hour or so, Lord John managed to put most of his father's customary rant out of his mind, as he had done so many times before, but one small piece of the conversation remained stuck in his head—Freddy's patronage of Mrs. Gerrard's. As someone concerned with the plight of the poor and disadvantaged, John was more aware than most of London's Upper Ten Thousand of London's vast array of bawdy houses and the unfortunate crea-tures who inhabited them. A brothel was a brothel, whether its doors opened onto St. James's Square or the Piazza at Covent Garden and, try as he would,

John simply could not picture Freddy crossing the threshold of such a place, much less becoming a regular customer as the duke seemed to think he was.

Finally, curiosity got the better of him and he managed to include St. James's Square in his daily routine, passing by Mrs. Gerrard's discreet portals at various times in the hopes of catching sight of his brother entering or exiting its elegant portals.

What was his astonishment when little over a week after his interview with the duke, he saw not one, but both of his brothers descending the steps to make their way leisurely down St. James's so deep in conversation they would not have noticed him even if he hadn't taken the precaution of stepping hastily back into the shadows of a neighboring building.

The intent conversation and the purposeful pace did not suggest the bearing of two men who had been indulging in the pleasures of the flesh, nor did the hour—three o'clock in the afternoon—seem at all like the time to pay a visit to one's inamorata.

Born with an inquiring mind and active intelligence, Lord John was not about to let such a mystery go unexplained, and before he knew what he was about, he was ringing the bell of the oddly venerable—looking establishment.

This first impression was not dispelled when an imposing butler answered the door and, upon hearing his name, conducted him to a drawing room of such subtle and restrained elegance that John at first though he had mistakenly entered the wrong establishment. The trill of female laughter soon reassured him that his original assumptions had been correct, and he was about to settle into the proffered chair and await the butler's promise of refreshments and the mistress of the house when an exceedingly odd sound began to emanate from the direction in which he had heard the laughter.

Was it? Could it be? John strained his ears. Yes! It was the sound of female voices reciting Latin declensions! Overcome with astonishment, he edged cautiously toward the sound, glancing quickly on either side of the drawing room doorway before crossing the hall and sidling towards the door where the voice continued to recite "*amo, amas, amant.*"

Flattening himself against the wall, he peered cautiously around the door frame. Only years of rigidly correct upbringing kept him from gasping at the scene before him. Several young ladies in white smocks sat facing a slim, auburn haired instructress who frowned critically as her pupils chanted the words.

"Excellent. I do believe you have all got it correct so we may move along to another more useful word. Love is all very well for dreamers and poets, but the verb *to be* is far more essential and much for difficult to master"

The rest of her advice was interrupted by the sound of approaching footsteps and John ducked back into the drawing room seconds before the butler re-appeared. "Mrs. Gerrard will be with you directly, sir, but in the meantime she begs you to make yourself comfortable." He set down a tray of tea and biscuits.

John barely had time to take a swallow of tea before the fellow was back. "Mrs. Gerrard will see you now. I am to take you to her office."

Office? What sort of bawdy house proprietress had an office? John followed docilely trying to get another peek into the *schoolroom* as he climbed the stairs, but it was too far down the hall to see. The next floor was as elegant as the first, but the room at the back where he was announced in stentorian tones was completely at odds with all the others. Here there were no damask covered walls, no elegant chairs, only a serviceable desk and floor-to-ceiling book shelves crammed with an impressive array of titles, chiefly history, the classics and an enviable collection of mathematics.

This time his upbringing could not save him. John's jaw dropped as he perused the titles enviously. There were a number here that he himself had been longing to read and he found himself wondering if their owner . . . .

"I see you are interested in my *Treatise on Algebra in Practice and Theory.* The author makes some intriguing observations, but in general I found it disappointing."

The same low musical voice he had heard instructing the *students* brought John crashing back to reality. "I beg your pardon," he felt his face go hot, like a schoolboy caught in a prank, "it is just that I have been longing to read it myself."

"Then you have an interest in mathematics, my lord?"

He looked at her in surprise. Who was this woman who read mathematical treatises and appeared to recognize Lord John Claverton in the rector of St. George's Hanover Square? She certainly looked more like a governess than an abbess, not that he knew any abbesses, but she looked like an extremely fashionable governess dressed in a dark yellow three quarter length tunic whose correct name Freddy would undoubtedly know, over a lighter yellow dress which set off the rich auburn curls peeping out from a modishly demure cap. The startling green eyes regarding him with tolerant amusement were alive with intelligence and something else so faint and shadowy that a lesser man would never have seen it, but Lord John was first and foremost the shepherd of his earthly flock, a vicar of God who took the spiritual well-being of his parishioners seriously despite their obvious lack of interest and he recognized in Mrs. Gerrard a soul who had suffered much despite the air of self-confidence and worldly sophistication.

"Yes I do. If find its predictability quite comforting in a world filled with confusion and misery."

This time she really looked at him. The cynical glint disappeared and the tiniest of smiles hovered at the corner of her delicately sculpted lips. "Hmm,

I should have thought a man of the cloth would have looked to God for such things." She tilted her head, raising a quizzical eyebrow. Then the smile deepened. "But perhaps you also enjoy a good hand of cards, my lord."

"I do." Lord John could not help smiling in return. And for some quite inexplicable reason, he suddenly found himself thinking that he would like nothing better than to match wits at the card table with this very intriguing woman.

CHAPTER 4

T HE SMILE TRANSFORMED HIS FACE COMPLETELY from earnest and intro-
spective to charming and surprisingly sympathetic. When the butler had
told Helen that the rector of St. George's was in her drawing room, she had
reacted reflexively, instructing the butler to deny him. She had suffered the
reforming zeal of men of the cloth often enough to know that she did not want
to do so again. But then, standing at the head of her little class, she had caught
sight of a slight movement in the hall and had looked up to discover him glancing furtively into the *schoolroom*. He had only peeked around the corner for a
moment, but it was enough for her to register the lively curiosity of his expression and something that almost looked like approval in his eyes. Intrigued, she
had changed her mind and immediately agreed to meet him in her office even
though, sitting down behind her desk a few minutes later, she was already telling herself it was a bad decision.

"Am I quite mistaken, or did I just hear you instructing a class in Latin a
moment ago?"

Her visitor's voice broke into Helen's momentary fit of abstraction. "You
are not mistaken," she replied, a trifle defensively. Then, looking him full in the
face, she realized she need not have felt that way. His eyes were like his brother,
Freddy's—utterly guileless and filled with nothing but friendly interest, only
Lord John's were darker. He exuded a sense of purpose that was lacking in
Freddy but so like that of his younger brother Major Lord Adrian. Helen had
only met Adrian in passing, but she had been immediately struck by the force
of the man's character. There was something about all three Clavertons that set
them apart from the rest of her *patrons* and most of their peers—call it passion, interest, curiosity—the brothers all appeared to look at the world with an

alertness unfettered by the usual prejudices, as men guided by their own hearts and minds rather than fashion, and it put her oddly at ease with them, she who had vowed never to trust a man ever again.

"I expect you are wondering how Latin can be of any possible use to my . . . er . . . *students.*"

"Not at all. There is nothing better for clearing the mind and organizing one's thoughts, except possibly mathematics, but it is a rare person who would agree with me on that head."

Helen glanced sharply at him, but there was not a trace of irony in his expression, nothing, in fact, except a lively and sympathetic interest.

"I had not expected to discover an educational establishment here," he admitted. "I know that Freddy is a regular visitor, and his aversion to all things educational is legendary. Tell me, what else to you teach?"

"Some arithmetic, nothing of interest, to be sure, mostly household accounts, ledgers, that sort of thing, and needlework, drawing, music, French, reading, writing, some history."

"And Latin. Your students are fortunate indeed, not many girls are considered worth the trouble of teaching Latin."

"I want them to make their own ways in the world, to be independent so they never have to . . . have to . . . ." It had been years since Helen Gerrard had found herself at a loss for words. Her composure, her armor against the world, never deserted her, even in the most trying of circumstances, but suddenly faced with genuine concern and understanding, she found her exquisitely constructed, icily sophisticated shell cracking into a million pieces under the warmth of his obvious sympathy. She clamped her lips shut to keep from exposing the vulnerable person inside that shell.

"Suffer again," he finished quietly.

Helen's eyes widened in surprise as she stared him full in the face, all thoughts of rearranging her features into their customary inscrutability forgotten.

She nodded. "In fact, I want them to thrive and to invest their money as I have invested mine so that their money gives them power, so that nothing will stop them from dreaming their dreams and realizing those dreams. I have seen what my own investments have done to make a difference and to improve this city by offering a refuge and education to those tossed aside by society. I want the same thing for them."

Why was she telling him all this? Sharing with this man dreams she hardly dared admit to herself? There was something about his quiet way of listening—curious and accepting—that made her want to confide in him.

"I should like to help," he ventured softly, so softly that at first she was not sure he had even spoken. "You are teaching them the skills to become independent and self-sufficient, but who is helping their souls become that way?"

Helen had to admit that she had never thought of such a thing. She had won back her life through a combination of hard work, intelligence, pure stubbornness, and a little luck that had allowed her to buy her freedom from having to depend on anyone. But had she won back her soul? She was not so sure of that. The soul that had been so badly bruised she was not sure it would ever fully recover still wanted to punish the men who had destroyed it, and the only way she could win even a part of it back was to create an establishment so exclusive that only a select few gained admittance and to charge them exorbitant sums for a fleeting moment of pleasure to be had there.

"I could help, you know," John continued, just as softly, "by showing them that even though they may have been cast out by a hypocritical society, they are not cast out from the human race."

She wanted to believe him, but too many men of the cloth had preached patronizingly to her about God's grace without ever having been in desperate enough need of it themselves for her to take them seriously. Even her own father, kindly village vicar that he had been, had not understood true misery of hopelessness; in fact, neither had she when her father was alive.

John saw the cynicism creep back into those amazing green eyes. "It is not that I am such an authority on God's grace as I am something of an authority on the human heart," he fixed her with what appeared to be a pleading smile, and it occurred to her that perhaps there was another soul almost as desperately in need of saving as hers, "a knowledge I have learned through countless conversations with unhappy souls, most of whom appear so prosperous and secure in their lives that it would be unthinkable for them to know a moment's doubt, but when faced with the fear of the great beyond, and in the presence of a sympathetic listener they reveal more confusion and misery than anyone could possibly guess."

Helen smiled at his eagerness. Clearly the rector of St. George's was desperately seeking his own type of spiritual fulfillment and not finding it amongst the fashionable membership of his parish; she liked him better for it. In fact, she liked him very much. He would be good for her girls, and maybe even for her. "Very well then, my lord, but we must first begin by playing cards, you and I, and then, when the girls are accustomed to your presence you may begin to help them. After all they have been through they do not trust easily, especially men."

He rose and held out his hand. "You are a wise woman, Mrs. Gerrard and, I think, a very good one. Let us see if you are equally good at playing cards."

"Better!"

He laughed. "Then I *do* look forward to our first game."

"Are you free this evening, my lord?"

John found the challenging sparkle in her eyes more seductive than the most coquettish of glances. "I am, and I look forward to matching wits with you."

"Good. I shall expect you at eight o'clock before my regular players appear, a treat for the penance I pay spending an entire evening trying not to win every hand."

John smiled as he sketched a bow. "Until this evening, then."

"And there goes a most intriguing man," Helen remarked thoughtfully as Juliette appeared in the doorway. "Yes, I can see there is something on your mind. Best to speak and get it over with."

"It is Lord Freddy," Juliette began tentatively. "In addition to his usual time he wishes to visit me at Lord Huntley's accustomed hour. Lord Huntley is a regular; on the other hand, Lord Freddy is a most important customer and . . . ."

"You like him very well." Helen smiled, gesturing to the chair recently vacated by Lord John. "You must keep your next appointment with Lord Huntley. We are an establishment noted for its integrity as well as its quality, but I shall talk to Lord Huntley and see if he might not enjoy Grace's company as much as yours. Perhaps he has a taste for music I had not previously discovered, in which case, Grace's musical abilities would be most attractive."

The wrinkled on Juliette's brow smoothed out. "Thank you. I *knew* you would have a solution."

"Of course, but mind you, Juliette," Helen fixed her protégé with a stern gaze, "do not forget that Lord Freddy is a customer, not a friend. No falling in love with him, no matter how interested he appears to be."

"No ma'am. I know very well that it is my skill at dressmaking, not my person that intrigues him."

Helen chuckled. "Yes, I suppose, after all, your heart is quite safe with that one, no matter how much he calls on you, but you know what I mean. I am only thinking of your welfare."

Juliette nodded as her employer's eyes softened with concern, eyes that customarily held a cynically clear-eyed view of the world, but looked with such warmth and understanding on those fortunate enough to escape into her protection.

Juliette would never forget her introduction to Helen Gerrard. She had stood before the dark solid desk willing herself not to faint from hunger and the paralyzing weakness that had overwhelmed her since her agonizing miscarriage the week before. Nothing in her pale hollow cheeks, haunted eyes, scrawny frame and lifeless hair suggested that anyone, much less a customer to Mrs. Gerrard's would find her anything but repulsive. But Helen, after inviting her to sit down and eat the first full meal she had been able to eat in months, had waited until she had finished everything before her and then, smiling gently, had begged her to share her pathetic story.

It had all come spilling out in a rush. Juliette did not even know why she, always so proudly withdrawn and discreetly well mannered, was suddenly sharing the most intimate and sorry details of a life gone horridly wrong with the woman who sat silently listening behind her desk. There had been something about her, a quiet strength, softened by a genuine interest that was both reassuring and inspiring. As she talked, Juliette sensed that this was a woman who had endured the same humiliation and despair and had survived, more than survived; she had survived and emerged triumphant, and she wanted the same thing for Juliette.

"I beg your pardon," Juliette gasped as she had finished the sad little tale. "I don't know what came over me. There is not the least reason for you to hear all this."

"Ah, but there is every reason in the world." The sympathetic glow in the watchful eyes had burst into a green flame whose intensity was distinctly at odds with the self-possessed figure behind the desk. "Olivia sent you to me for a reason. Yes, she did it out of the kindness of her own heart, but she also knew that what you needed more than food and lodging was Mrs. Gerrard's."

Juliette had stared at her rescuer. When she had shown up on Olivia Child's doorstep, Juliette had been too demoralized to think or to act; she had been driven by some primal sense that the opera singer, who had been her special patroness at Madame Celeste's would care about the disaster that had befallen her and would somehow, miraculously, know what to do.

CHAPTER 5

A ND OLIVIA *HAD* KNOWN JUST WHAT TO DO. "My dear, whatever has happened to you?" she exclaimed bundling Juliette straight off to her own bed chamber and sending the maid scurrying off for hot milk and a basin of warm water.

"I wondered when I didn't see you at Madame Celeste's and they were most uncommunicative when I asked after you which immediately confirmed my suspicions that something untoward had occurred, but try as I would I could not discover what had become of you."

Juliette nodded miserably. "I know." In her pride and despair she had covered her tracks too well and certainly Madame Celeste, who had thrown her out in a passion the minute she had discovered her employee's unfortunate condition, would never have told anyone what had happened.

"I always thought you were different from the others in Madame's establishment, quite apart from your obvious talent, of course," Olivia continued, handing her the mug of hot milk the maid had brought. Your accent and your bearing betray someone too well brought up to know that most seamstresses are considered little better than the women who ply their trade in Covent Garden and therefore fair game for the men who accompany their wives and mistresses on their visits to the modiste. In fact, it is virtually the only reason any man takes an interest in such a feminine establishment."

Again Juliette nodded miserably. "I thought the seamstresses were there to learn a trade at which they could earn a living, but no matter how much I showed I was willing to learn and work hard, others thought differently and then . . . Lord . . ." Juliette could not go on. The horror of Lady Talbot's husband returning late one evening when she was all alone in the shop and forcing himself on her was something she refused to think of.

"And then the inevitable happened," Olivia concluded matter-of-factly, not bothering to tell her erstwhile guest that even if fate in the form of Lord . . . had not intervened, Madame Celeste would not have tolerated competition for long from a truly talented seamstress with a desire to learn the trade.

"I prayed that nothing would happen, but it did and Madame Celeste knew almost immediately that I was pregnant and . . .

"Because it happens all the time."

". . . and she turned me out. I tried to find work elsewhere, but no would take me and then I got sick and . . .

"Lost the baby and ran out of the money you had saved up for food and lodging."

Juliette nodded dumbly. "I remembered how kind you had been to me when I was at Madame Celeste's and I thought that maybe if I could find you I could ask if perhaps you could use a maid or a scullery maid, or . . . anything, something I could do to work for you," she ended on a sob that broke Olivia's heart.

Olivia herself had been nearly that desperate once, but her talent had saved her and a childhood spent on the streets of London had given her a toughness that had protected her until her talent had been recognized and eventually re-warded. This poor girl had only talent; her lovely manners and obviously gen-teel roots were working very much against her.

"Here." Olivia handed Juliette a basin of water, soap and a cloth. "You would not believe how much better one feels after washing one's face."

Juliette rubbed the warm wet cloth over her face, reveling in the scent of lavender. Hot tears pricked her eyelids. "Almost respectable now," she finished up with a watery smile.

"Almost respectable indeed." Olivia nodded encouragingly. This girl had spirit and an ethereal beauty that would only grow more radiant with a little rest and good solid food, and this brought to mind another woman of spirit, her friend Helen Gerrard, also beautiful, genteel, and with an unfortunate past. Olivia's household was not in need of anyone, but Helen's was. Perhaps this girl would find a place there, perhaps not, but Olivia would leave that to Helen to decide.

"I have a friend who might need someone," was all she said, "but first you must rest and get better, and then we shall call on her."

And so it was that a week after arriving at Olivia's Juliette had sat facing Helen very much as she was sitting facing her now, while Helen had told her about her establishment.

"No one becomes a *Cyprian* because they want to," Helen had explained, "at least no one I know. We have all had that most private and special part of us taken without our consent so that it has been ruined and lost to us forever, but in the course of things we have all of us learned that what was special to us and now is lost, continues to be special to men, and many of them will pay a great deal of money to have it again and again. I see you do not believe me. Let me assure you that every woman in my establishment lives in greater luxury and earns more in one evening than a junior cleric or a civil servant makes in an entire year. Think of it. Is it so very different from being married to a man your parents would have chosen for you as a husband? In either case you lie with a stranger in order to be clothed and fed, a stranger with complete control over your pin money. How much better to be able to choose with whom you lie—for no woman at in my establishment is forced to be with someone repugnant to her—and spend your earnings on what you wish or, better yet, and what I teach all my girls to do, save them and invest them so you will never again have to depend on anyone but yourself for a roof over your head or food on your table even when you are too old or too ill to be of interest to anyone."

The weak-jawed image of the vain and self-important Comte de Montmorency rose before Juliette as Helen alluded to her parents' choice of husband, and she could not help thinking there was a good deal of truth in what the establishment's proprietress said. A wedding night with her parents' chosen husband would have been no less horrific, no less revolting and no more truly consensual than her forced encounter with Lord Talbot. Juliette's father had turned a deaf an ear to Juliette's pleas that she did not want to marry the Comte de Montmorency as Lord Talbot had to hers begging him to leave her alone, and even her mother had viewed Juliette as nothing so much as a prize to be traded for social advancement in the inner circle of the exiled king of France. Juliette had shuddered at the thought of becoming a *fille de joie*. Her parents would have died of the horror, but then, her parents had disowned her for wanting to earn what she had thought were honest wages as a seamstress, wages that would have paid for nourishing food and medicine for her ailing mother and her rapidly aging father. Far better, they had thought, to starve upon the pittance her mother received working on her exquisite embroidery in the atelier with other exiled aristocrats than to stoop to a trade. But yet, these same parents, too proud to have their daughter earning enough to live on, would willingly have traded her into bondage with a hopeless idiot whose more important social connections gave him access to a life only slightly more comfortable than their own.

"And do not forget," Helen Gerrard continued, "you *are* providing a comforting womanly presence for our *guests*, the same comforting womanly presence any good wife should provide her husband, which their wives so demonstrably do *not* do or they would not be such regular visitors to our establishment. You will soon discover that many of our *guests* come here simply to relax and talk, to find the ease of companionship they do not find in their own homes, sadly enough."

In the end, Helen, as Juliette had soon come to think of Mrs. Gerrard's' proprietress, had been entirely correct. Her first *guest* had been a self-effacing peer from the country compensating for a necessary visit to the capital by a bit of self-indulgence at Mrs. Gerrard's. He had been so awed by Juliette's beauty, sophistication, and French accent that he had treated her with a reverential courtesy she had never experienced from any other man. Checking up on her later, Helen had nodded encouragingly as Juliette recounted their evening, but the hint of slyness in her smile confirmed Juliette's suspicions that Sir Walter had been very carefully selected for the newest member of the establishment. It was surprising after that how easy it had been to shut her mind to the more intimate details of her new profession and concentrate on the purely social and most important aspects, being a charming hostess to men desperate for true feminine companionship.

Also surprising were the other members of the establishment. At Madame Celeste's the seamstresses had worked in jealous silence under the watchful eye of Madame, each one determined not to let any other get a better assignment or to work on a gown for a customer more wealthy or more important. At Mrs. Gerrard's everyone had been friendly and welcoming from the first day when the maid had led Juliette upstairs to the exquisitely furnished blue damask bedchamber. "For me?" Juliette had gasped observing in pleased surprise the cheerful fire at one end of the room flanked by two comfortable bergere chairs, the handsome dressing table and looking glass along one wall and the luxuri-ous bed with embroidered silk hangings opposite the fireplace at the other end.

"The mistress always does everything in the best of taste." The maid smiled shyly. "And she spares no expense on the comforts of everyone, patrons and members of the household alike."

Juliette turned her attention from the luxurious surroundings to her guide. She was a slight, homely little thing, but there was a glow of health and an air of self-possessed contentment that made her attractive in spite of the plainness of her features. "Mrs. Gerrard is a good mistress, then?"

"The best. She does aught she can to help poor girls in need. When she found me begging for a bit of bread outside the church, didn't she up and bring me here? Of course I am not pretty or genteel enough to be one of her ladies like Dora or Grace or . . ." she blushed fiercely, "you, but she found a place for me just the same, and I have been here ever since."

"And how long ago was that?"

"Nigh on three years. And she has taught me to read and write and dress hair and clean lace and . . . and soon I shall be a proper ladies' maid." Her eyes shone at the prospect of achieving this ultimate triumph.

"And I shall teach you to sew the straightest seam and mend the finest lace, and even speak French, if you like, so that you will be the most sought after of ladies' maids in all of London, if you like." Juliette could not say what had prompted this sudden offer, but there was something touchingly appealing about this girl and her admiration for her mistress that made Juliette want to contribute to the realization of her dream. "And what is your name?"

"Rose, miss."

"Well then, Rose, I shall ask permission from Mrs. Gerrard and if it is agreeable to her, we shall find a time to teach you all that I learned at Madame Celeste's."

"Ooooooh. Thank you ever so much, Miss Juliette."

"It is *Mademoiselle* Juliette. Her French air of fashion and sophistication will give us all extra *cachet* in the eyes of our customers." A voice in the doorway made them both turn to find Helen smiling approvingly. "And it is an excellent idea. In fact," the proprietress' shrewd gaze took in Juliette's simple, but elegant cambric walking dress whose softly falling frill formed the perfect frame for her slim white neck and whose deep flounces allowed just a tantalizing glimpse of a slender ankle, "I think it would be an excellent idea to have her direct the making of *all* our gowns, for despite her recent unfortunate experiences, she is the picture of elegance." And with another brief smile Helen disappeared as quickly and quietly as she had appeared.

And that had been the beginning of Juliette's days at Mrs. Gerrard's, days so full of shopping for muslins, silks, laces, and ribbons, cutting and fitting, that she was too busy to stop and reflect on the strange turn her life had taken depositing her on the doorstep of Helen Gerrard's select establishment.

In many ways, with all the fittings and stitching, it was no different from Madame Celeste's, except that Juliette was allowed to give her imagination free rein and there were no envious or suspicious eyes monitoring her every move, nor were her companions yoked together in uneasy and mistrustful vigilance of one another; in fact it was quite the opposite. The ladies at Mrs. Gerrard's had all welcomed Juliette with the openness of a happy family eager to share good fortune with those in need.

Her very first evening Juliette had been served her dinner on a tray in her room, "For the mistress wants you to rest and regain your strength as quickly as possible," Rose explained setting the tray on a low table in front of the fire.

"But that does not mean you have to dine alone . . . if you do not mind company?" Juliette glanced up to see a tall dark-haired woman hovering tentatively in the doorway.

"No. Please come in." Juliette gestured to the chair opposite.

"I am Grace," the visitor sank into the chair, her dark blue eyes filled with a mixture of curiosity and sympathy that made Juliette feel she was already half way to making a new friend. "Helen says you are exhausted and we are not to tire you with company until you are well, but I . . . well, I know what it is like to be a stranger here in such an . . . er . . . *unusual* place so I wanted to be the first of us to welcome you and to tell you that it will be all right, even though it may not seem so at this particular moment."

"Thank you." The lump in Juliette's throat made it impossible to say anything more, but her visitor, well aware of the riot of emotions overwhelming the newest member of their group, chatted blithely on until Juliette recovered her composure. "Helen tells me that Olivia sent you. Olivia is the reason I am here too. My father," a slight shadow, quickly banished, clouded the beautiful features "was leader of the orchestra for Olivia's opera company. He never was the same after my mother died, and I am afraid he took to drink which ruined his career as a professor of music and very nearly cost him the job he finally found with the orchestra except, . . . except," she swallowed hard, "for the manager who forced himself on me as payment for keeping my father on. There was nothing I could do but keep giving in to his . . . er . . . *demands*. We had nowhere to go. My mother's family had cast her off when she married father, and his family would have nothing to do with him after he refused a commission in the army to pursue his music. Neither one of them cared about that because they were so happy together. We were so happy together in our little house in Oxford until she died. Olivia knew what was happening with the manager. I could tell from her special kindness to me that she had been forced into the same sort of difficult situation once herself, but then when Father died, I was cast off with nowhere to go. I did not have Olivia's talent, not yet at any rate. She had become friendly with Helen who always attended her performances and she knew Helen would take care of me. And Helen has."

Grace leaned forward to pat Juliette's hand. "I have been happy here and so will you. You may not think it now, and it seems odd to say it, but it's the respect one gets here that helps us heal. It makes a great difference, you will see. But now," she smiled rather sheepishly, "I have a favor to ask."

"A favor?"

"Yes. Helen says you are French."

Juliette nodded cautiously, not yet ready to share her wretched story with a stranger.

"Well then, I should like you to teach me French. Mama had started, for she had been taught by a French governess and was quite fluent, but that was long ago and I hardly remember anything now." Grace turned to look out the window, but not before Juliette caught the rapid blinking of thick dark lashes that told her she was not the only one with painful memories.

CHAPTER 6

A ND SO, JULIETTE MADE HER FIRST FRIEND at Mrs. Gerrard's. Others quickly followed. After Grace came Dora, the irrepressible daughter of an inn-
keeper who had lost his establishment in spite of his daughter's sacrificing her
virtue to his creditor. Juliette found her optimistically down-to-earth personal-
ity and her fierce determination to clear her father's name refreshingly bracing
and inspiring. "I am not one of Helen's fine ladies like you," Dora confided
cheerfully, but every once in a while, a gentleman just wants a tumble in the hay
with a country lass. I am the country lass."

But there were no flies on Dora whose tough cleverness was far more suited
to the accounting and household management Mrs. Gerrard insisted they all
learn than Juliette's or Grace's more dreamy intelligence. There was Clarissa,
the former Bath solicitor's daughter whose new stepfather's unwelcome attentions had caused her mother to cast her out of the house with only the clothes
on her back and nowhere to go except London where no work was to be found
without references. And then there was Jane whose parents' death in a carriage
accident had left her to the tender mercies of her resentful drunken brother
and his salacious friends.

Each one's story was as desperate and pathetic as the last until their paths
had eventually crossed that of Helen Gerrard, rescuer, governess, and hard-
headed stepmother to them all. It was a fiercely protective stepmother who
now sat across the desk from Juliette, fixing her with a quelling look. "Yes Lord
Freddy may visit at Lord Huntley's usual hour as well as his own, but I have
told you before, and I tell you again, there is no such thing as love. Lord Freddy
may be all that is kind, charming, and enthusiastically generous, but do not for
one minute think he cares about you. You will only hurt yourself if you allow

yourself to believe that love or even kindness from men is anything but an invention of the poets."

"I know." Certainly there had been no one in Juliette's close knit émigré community who had made her believe in that romantic idea; all the men she had known, despite their slavish *courtoisie* were woefully deficient in the fire and character that so distinguished the heroes of her beloved Chretien de Troyes. If they possessed any spark of passion at all, it was confined to their dress and their toilette. Unbidden, the face of Freddy's brother, alive with suppressed energy and intensity simmering just beneath the surface of a cool exterior rose in her mind. Now *there* was a man one could picture as Lancelot or Tristan, a man who would dare all for his beloved. Juliette smiled at her own weakness. She was doing exactly what Helen was warning her against, confusing poetry with real life. Major Lord Adrian Claverton was no more like Lancelot or Tristan than she was. He was simply Freddy's brother. And even Freddy, kind and generous as he had been to her, did not care about her; it was her talent and her creations that made him seek her company and kept him coming back again and again. "I know that there is no such thing as love, but it is still very nice to be appreciated."

"Very true, and such appreciation of one's actual talents is far more lasting and far more valuable than any love could be, which is why I want all of you—Grace, Dora, Clarissa, the rest—to develop them while you are here so that when you leave you will be able to rely on them and your earnings from here to support you. Then you will never have to delude yourselves into believing in love or marriage because you won't need them. And while you are here, you can comfort yourself with the thought that those who seek you out do so simply because of who you are and not because they are being forced to by their family's or society's expectations." Helen's eyes twinkled and one corner of her mouth rose in her usual ironic smile. "In fact, it could be said that in a number of ways, we live far more honestly than our more *respectable* sisters in the fashionable world."

Even while she nodded thoughtfully, Juliette could not help acknowledging to herself that it did hurt when she encountered the disdainful looks in those *respectable* women's eyes, if they looked at her at all. Most of the time, they simply averted their gaze, refusing to recognize that she even existed, much less that she had once shared the same hopes and dreams, the same sense of her own essential goodness as they did, had once felt secure of her place in the world, if not necessarily satisfied with it.

Helen saw the shadow cross her face and it tore at her heart. No matter how many times she saw that look, she never got used to it, was never able to harden herself against that loss, no matter how rich or successful she or her girls became. "It is difficult, lonely, even," she admitted reaching across the desk to pat

Juliette's hand, "but there is also freedom. We have no one's expectations to live up to now except our own."

"You are right, of course," Juliette rose, smiling apologetically at her momentary lapse, "and that means I must be on my way to Harding and Howell to look for some jaconet muslin for Grace's walking dress."

Helen rose too, happy to see Juliette's resilient spirit reasserting itself. She could only help her girls so much, but then it was up to them to reclaim their lives. Hers was the most exclusive establishment in London, but very few people, if any, recognized that its rigorous standards had far less to do with beauty or background than with spirit. Spirit could make a plain woman attractive and enticing, an uneducated one clever and interesting, and even the most unfortunate, determined to improve herself. Yes, Juliette had spirit in abundance, and some day she would, as others had done before her, take back her life, make it hers again, and, as Helen had predicted, live up to no one's expectations but her own.

Meanwhile, in Grosvenor Square, Freddy was finding himself falling miserably short, as usual, of someone else's expectations.

"I cannot believe you cannot find the time to escort Mama and me to the concert at the Royal Philharmonic Society!" Lady Lavinia Harcourt's words might suggest surprise and disbelief, but the patent resignation in her elegantly modulated tones implied that it was exactly what she had expected all along. Her well-bred features would not, of course, betray emotion of any kind, but her dark brown eyes were decidedly frosty as they surveyed her fiancé with barely suppressed annoyance.

"I . . . I am sorry, Lavinia," the hapless Freddy stammered, "But a longstanding engagement . . ."

One haughty eyebrow rose a fraction of an inch.

". . . with my brother."

"Surely Lord John would tell you that an enlightening evening of the very best music is better for one's soul than . . ."

"My *other* brother." Freddy ran a desperate finger inside the excruciatingly high collar, a gesture that would have caused his valet to faint if he had seen it. They had spent a good part of the morning tying and re-tying cravats which now lay in a heap of brilliant white on his dressing table.

"Lord Adrian." Lavinia snorted delicately. "Surely the sort of companionship he can provide can be had at any time."

"He has just come back from the wars, Lavinia, where there was little amusement of any sort to be had, and certainly not the opera," Freddy replied more firmly this time, hoping fervently that Adrian would consent to the sudden invitation. In fact, Freddy was the only member of the family with the least interest in music, but surely *The Beggars' Opera*, now being played at Covent

Garden, would provide enough entertainment that even someone who was tone deaf could enjoy it. Besides, Mrs. Gerrard's had a box at Covent Garden, so an evening of delightful companionship could always be found there.

"The opera!" Lady Lavinia snorted again. "Vulgar spectacle, women disporting themselves on stage in the most ridiculous manner. Even Basil enjoys the opera." Since Lady Lavinia's brother was notorious for his ruinous pursuit of opera dancers—he least disreputable trait of his questionable character—any interest on the part of her fiancé, no matter how legitimate, was unlikely to find favor in her eyes. "Really, Freddy, I *do* wish you would consult me before making such engagements."

"Well I would, of course . . . I mean, I do in general, but since this is my brother I didn't think it was important."

Somehow his placating tone and hopeful smile only served to irritate her further. "One would think that someone to whom one has been betrothed since birth would merit the first consideration in all your plans."

"One would think. I am sorry, Lavinia." Freddy refrained from pointing out that being betrothed to someone since birth made them fade into one's daily background like a family heirloom or a distant cousin, familiar, but unremarkable, like a twinge of an arm broken in childhood, something to which one had accustomed oneself because there was nothing to be done about it, but which occasionally forced one to recognize and deal with it. Ordinarily, he managed to avoid this particular part of his family background, but in this case he had been caught by his fiancée and her mother coming to call on his mother just as he was leaving.

"Come Mama." His fiancée smoothed her green kid gloves, redoubling her grip on her matching parasol before marching to the door, "Clearly the Duchess is engaged and we have other calls to make. "Good day, Freddy."

She left him, as she often did, feeling hopelessly inadequate, more inadequate than even his father made him feel, which was saying something. And he could not help wondering, for the hundredth time, if it would be better or worse when they were married and she had him totally under her supervision, when he would not have time enough alone to make what she considered to be mistakes.

The butler handed him his curly brimmed beaver, and, consoling himself with the prospect of an afternoon choosing snuff boxes at Rundell and Bridges and an evening at the opera in more congenial company, Freddy, as he had been doing for most of his life, put all thoughts of his fiancée completely out of his mind as he stepped out into the sunshine and sauntered towards Bond Street.

CHAPTER 7

"**Y**OU BEST HAVE ME COME WITH YOU," Dora warned Juliette and Grace when she overheard them discussing the trip to the linen drapers. "Just because Harding and Howell is one of the finest establishments in town does not mean that they won't charge you more than they should. Intelligence is all very well and good," she smiled at the indignant look on both their faces, "and both of you are exceedingly clever at all those things well brought up young ladies should know—French, music, dancing and such—but they will do you no good when faced with a hard headed merchant."

"You forget, Dora, that none of us has been a well—brought—up young *lady* in quite some time," Juliette retorted. "And I have been wearing my fingers to the bone for years working with the finest jaconet muslins, cambrics, sarsnets, satins and any other material you can name. Believe me, I am quite comfortable in my ability to select nothing but the very best quality to be had."

"The best quality, yes, but not the best price. You must admit you were raised to be a lady, gracious and agreeable, which means you haven't the least notion how to drive a hard bargain, much less argue with a merchant, a person whose existence your parents would never even have allowed you to acknowledge. And Grace is no better than you. Come, ladies, let us go and I will show you how it is done."

The shop in Pall Mall was thronged with customers standing at the counters while harassed clerks pulled down swathes of material from the bolts stored in cubbyholes that reached from floor to ceiling behind them. It was nearly half an hour before they were served, giving them ample time to observe the others ahead of them; a large imperious mother whose two retiring daughters obviously bore the brunt of her domineering ways, two bracket-faced spinsters who began haranguing the clerk even before being invited to take a seat at the counter, and a haughty, expensively clad woman accompanied by her equally haughty maid.

Surveying the competition with satisfaction, Dora smiled pleasantly at the young man who, making a quick swipe at his dripping brow with a none-too-clean handkerchief, asked how he could serve them. "We've come to look at a number of things, but we'll begin with some muslin I think. That checked on there." She pointed to a bolt a little above his head.

He climbed up and pulled out a length for the ladies to examine. Bowing to Juliette's superior knowledge, Dora passed the swag of fabric to her.

"Very fine," Juliette ran it between her fingers, "Madras, I think."

"Precisely, Madam, and at seven shillings a yard, an excellent price."

"Seven shillings. Hmm." Dora looked thoughtful. "And if one were buying a great quantity of it, twenty yards, perhaps? It might be a trifle less, say six shillings, sixpence?"

The clerk swallowed hard and Dora favored him with a friendly smile. "I quite see that it is not your decision to make, so if you would like to show us some silks and satins while you consult with the proprietor, I certainly understand. Ours is a large female establishment, you see, so we have a great deal to purchase. A rose satin for you, Grace, and blue for you, Juliette?"

"We are the exclusive purveyors of the Queen's silk, woven right here in Spitalfields, madam," the clerk volunteered proudly.

Juliette thought a moment. "No, sarsnet, drapes a good deal better."

"We shall need at least ten yards of each," Dora nodded "and then . . . but go along and speak with the proprietor while we check our list to make sure we do not forget anything." Dora pulled a long sheet of paper from her reticule making sure the clerk had an excellent view of the pile of gold coins nestled around the list.

"Ah . . . that won't be necessary, I am sure, Madam," the clerk eyed the list which was considerable. "I feel certain that six shillings sixpence would be agreeable for such a large quantity of material."

"And cambric," Dora continued as though he had not uttered a word, "enough for handkerchiefs and a quantity of shifts, twenty at least, I should think, don't you, Grace?"

"Oh at the very least."

"Lawn," Juliette broke in.

"What?" Into her bargaining full swing, Dora was momentarily thrown off her stride.

"Lawn for the shifts."

"Oh." Dora's quick eyes caught the clerk nodding in agreement. It was only the tiniest of nods, but she was quick to take advantage of his dawning respect.

"Of course and . . ."

"And that must be all for the moment. As it is, there will not be room in the carriage. We shall have to send a footman to fetch the rest," Grace finished for her.

"You are quite right," Dora winked discreetly at Grace, "I was letting my enthusiasm run away with me." Dora pulled out a handful of guineas, laying them on the counter. "In the future, please direct the bill to Mrs. Gerrard, St. James' Square."

"Yes, Madam. With pleasure, Madam."

The clerk hurried out from behind the counter to escort them to their carriage.

"So you see," taking her seat in the carriage Dora glanced back through the shop's large windows at the imperious mother and daughter and the bracket- faced spinsters still waiting to conclude their transactions, "that is how it is done. Respectability is not everything; they are paying dearly for their respectability, their every haughty *my good man*, by being kept waiting while we have saved ourselves a great deal of money *and* commanded the clerk's devoted attention. I must say, Grace, you did well to mention the carriage, and you, Juliette, despite your unfortunately genteel upbringing, were a great help. I did not think you would know how to strike a good bargain."

"No, but my mother never accepted anything but the very best, and she made sure I never did either," Juliette replied, thinking that if the Comtesse de Fournoy had possessed even a tenth of Dora's practical skills they would have had more than one candle in the evenings and a great deal more food on the table.

"Well, together we three make a formidable but enchanting trio," Dora linked her arms in theirs, "and there is not a tradesman alive who could take advantage of us. Now, I think we should reward ourselves for saving so much money by treating ourselves to some ices at Gunters."

Their carriage soon joined all the other fashionable equipages thronging the east side of Berkeley Square as waiters dodged in and out of traffic taking orders. Eventually they gained the door, and a few minutes later, savoring her exquisite sorbet as she surveyed the elegant shop, Juliette could not help reflecting that her life since meeting Helen Gerrard was in fact far more luxurious, more interesting, and certainly much more comfortable than it had ever been before—just not respectable, as Dora had pointed out. Here she was at one of London's most fashionable establishments, beautifully dressed, enjoying a treat she never could have afforded at any other time in her life with two real friends, and all of them would soon return by carriage to St. James' Square where their creature comforts and their welfare were taken care of to a degree that none of them had ever experienced in their tumultuous lives. Why then, did she even think about respectability, wistfully or not?

"It's not that we want to be like them," Grace spoke softly as if reading

Juliette's thoughts, "so much as we do not want to have them look down on us as though they are so much better than we are, as though we are nothing at all." She glanced over at a group of starchy matrons who were surveying the crowd with smug superiority.

Juliette nodded. "It is something like that."

"When for all we know," Grace continued thoughtfully, "they could be going home to husbands who are perfect brutes, who make their lives a misery in spite of respectability, which is one thing we do not have to tolerate. Helen is extraordinarily discerning where men are concerned and accepts only the most gentlemanly of clientele. And for our parts, any time we spend with our patrons is fleeting, not like a marriage where one is a prisoner for life if one's partner is not to one's liking."

"Quite true." In reality, Juliette's life *was* in fact more pleasant than most of her former peers; it was just difficult to cast off the rigid code of thinking in which she had been raised where honor and the glory of the family name was all-consuming, even at the expense of creature comforts, friendship, or love itself. It was what had made the Comte de Fournoy too proud to accept a comfortable salary teaching history or another offer to manage the vast estate of a former friend—his angry refusal of this well meant kindness had cost him not only a decent income, but the friendship as well. And his pride had also cost him his daughter when, sick and tired of being hungry, cold, and bored, she had opted to earn her living doing something she loved. But there was still that unconscious part of herself that told Juliette she no longer belonged, even as the conscious part of her had long ago rejected the utterly useless and unrealistic standards by which her society had judged the world.

Chapter 8

"**M**ADEMOISELLE JULIETTE!" Freddy's cheery voice broke into these somber reflections, and Juliette looked up to see the Marquess of Wrothingham, resplendent in biscuit-colored pantaloons, exquisitely fitted coat of dark blue Bath superfine, pale figured waistcoat and a starched cravat that was a miracle of intricate folds. It was not the dazzling elegance of his attire, however, that made her breath catch in her throat, but the gentleman next to him smiling at her as though they were the only two people in the room, as though he had been thinking about her as much as she had been thinking about him ever since Freddy had introduced them.

Major Lord Adrian Claverton was every bit as magnificent as she remembered, but then, a uniform did a lot for a man. Juliette chided herself for being so impressionable; after all, her father had also looked magnificent in his uniform, but what good had he been after the battle was won? With the revolution over, the Comte de Fournoy had retired to live on *la gloire*, imposing his code of honor on his family while his wife and daughter eked out a pittance making lace and doing fine embroidery with their fellow émigrés reliving the old days as they plied their needles. Soldiers were all well and good during a war, but Juliette had yet to see one who knew what to do off the battlefield. And now Dora was poking her in the ribs, unobtrusively enough, but there was no mistaking the message.

The Comtesse de Fournoy would have been appalled at her daughter's lack of *politesse*. Gathering her wits about her, Juliette introduced the Marquess and his brother to her companions.

"How fortunate we are to run into you." Freddy included all three in his elegant bow. "We have been taking advantage of the fineness of the day with a stroll in the park, very tame stuff for my brother, I assure you, but he kindly consented to grant me his company—it has been so long since we have seen one another. But we did not see you in the park. How could we have missed such a lovely trio?"

"Because we had more important things to do, my lord," Dora favored him with her saucy grin. "We were shopping."

"Shopping!" Freddy's eyes lit up as he turned to Juliette. "Have you decided on the trimmings for the dress? Was it the blond lace or silver lamé?"

"Both."

"Both!"

Juliette chuckled. "It may sound a trifle over done, but it will add more weight to the skirt so that it enhances the figure while at the same time calling attention to elegantly shod feet which are too often neglected."

"Daring, very daring. I told you she was a bold thinker, did I not, Adrian?" He appealed to his brother whose eyes had never wavered from Juliette's face since they entered the shop.

"Indeed you did, but to my mind it appears more the passion of creative genius than boldness for boldness' sake. I would wager that when Mademoiselle Juliette is designing, she is so carried away by her inspiration that she is oblivious to everything around her." His smile was as dazzling as his uniform, but no matter how much it warmed her, it also made Juliette wary. He was simply too magnificent to be real.

"It is true." Dora who had been slyly observing Adrian admire her friend, agreed. "One can always tell when Juliette is thinking about a dress. She gets a faraway look in her eyes and it is as though there is no one else in the room— much the way Grace looks when she is practicing her music."

"Which is why we both need our practical Dora here, to keep us firmly anchored in reality." Grace smiled fondly at her companion.

"Music?" Freddy's attention was immediately diverted to her other friend, just as Dora had intended. "You are musical?"

"Our Grace will be a famous opera singer some day soon, mark my words."

"And *our* Dora is far too partial to her friends, as you see, but yes, my lord, it is my greatest dream."

"Do you attend the opera often?"

"As much as possible. Juliette and I are usually to be found there every Tuesday and Saturday night."

"Have you heard Grassini lately?"

"Most assuredly, my lord."

"And do you think she will ever equal Naldi? Of course she cannot aspire to Catalani's artistry, but . . ."

"But she does have a certain something that sets her apart. I agree." Grace frowned thoughtfully as she struggled to articulate just what that particular something was.

With his brother fairly embarked in a discussion of his other passion besides fashion and snuff boxes, Adrian seized the opportunity to take a seat next to Juliette. "Freddy tells me that it is your dream to open a shop of your own and become London's premier modiste. Now *that* is bold." He liked the way she raised her chin which, in any other circumstances could have been called delicate, but now looked decidedly firm. And he liked the way she looked him straight in the eye, something, he thought bemusedly, no other woman, except his sister, had ever done before.

"It is not a dream, my lord, it is a *plan*."

"Oho, you *are* bold indeed, as Freddy says. But I gather you know what you are getting into and all the work that your *plan* entails. Freddy mentioned that you worked for one of London's most fashionable modistes before . . ." Realizing the infelicitous nature of his conclusion, Adrian paused in confusion. What was it about her unflinchingly direct gaze with its sparkle of pride, self-awareness, and humor that robbed him of his usual glibness and made him as tongue-tied as a schoolboy?

"Before I became a *fille de joie*, you mean?"

He swallowed hard, his face hot with an embarrassment he had not experienced since had been dressed down by the colonel of his regiment in his days as a raw subaltern.

"No need to dress it up in fine linen," she replied tranquilly, but her eyes were definitely laughing at him "it was my choice."

Adrian looked at her curiously. Was that pride in her voice? The woman who set her sights on becoming the premier artiste of fashion for the *ton* was proud of being a . . . . being . . .

Again, she seemed to find humor in his discomfort, but her smile was kind enough as she explained. "It was not something I sought out; I was employed as a seamstress until I was let go because of an *unfortunate incident* which was *not* my choice, but then I met Helen who gave me a chance to win back my dream, er plan, and I took it. And that *was* my choice."

Adrian nodded, his blue eyes suddenly serious in his lean tanned face. "The *unfortunate incident* had nothing to do with your work or your talent with a needle, I collect."

The sudden change from charming soldier to intent listener caught Juliette off guard. Usually men as handsome and self-assured as the major preferred to talk about themselves, rarely, if ever, evincing the slightest interest in anyone but themselves. "You are correct, it was not."

He waited silently for her to continue and Juliette, realizing that he really *was* interested, or curious, at any rate, continued. "Let us just say that the life

Helen Gerrard has given me has restored my self-respect in an odd sort of way, and where I was once a victim of a man's desires, I am now the mistress of them." A faint smile curved the delicate lips. "I expect that sounds rather odd to speak of *self-respect* in those terms, but at least now the choice is mine."

"If you will but tell me who did this to you I will make sure he never dares show his face in this town again."

His matter-or-fact, almost conversational tone made the offer all the more convincing, but the steely glint in his eyes reminded Juliette, not that she had forgotten, that Major Lord Adrian Claverton was not some glibly fashionable man of the *ton* or a dandy who shot at Manton's, fenced at Angelo's, but had never done anything more dangerous than take a high fence in the hunting field. No, Major Lord Adrian Claverton was a warrior, and at the moment, every inch of him spoke of a warrior's deadly purpose, and all because a *fille de joie* had been mistreated.

A warm tide of gratitude, and something else she could not quite name swept over her leaving her inexplicably shy and tongue-tied, then her practical French nature and the exquisite manners instilled in her since birth came to her rescue. "You are too kind, my lord, but all that is in the past now, best to forget."

For a moment she had allowed herself to picture Lord Talbot on his knees begging for mercy, the point of the major's saber pressed to his throat, crying and begging as she had once cried and begged, but no, she had vowed never to think of Lord Talbot ever again and she hastily banished the image.

"*I* cannot forget. No one, especially someone as lovely and gentle as you, should have to suffer at the hands of another."

"You are wrong about that." She corrected Adrian with a fierceness that surprised him. "Refusing to forget condemns one to a life of suffering, to living the indignity over and over again."

She might be speaking to him, but Adrian could tell from the faraway look in her eyes and throb of passion in her voice that Juliette was really answering to someone else, someone in her past, someone who had once meant a great deal to her, but now was long gone, and he was seized with a sudden longing to revisit that past and change it for her, wipe away that faint shadow of—was it sadness, regret, loss—that haunted the corners of her eyes despite her brave words.

Adrian shook his head slowly. He must be all about in the head. He had given up trying to right the wrongs of the world ages ago. Nothing he had done in the Peninsula, not his most death-defying charge, his fiercest attacks, had been able to change the misery that had stalked the citizens suffering under Napoleon's rapacious occupation. To be sure, the tyrant had eventually been routed, but at what cost? They had freed the citizens well enough, leaving death, destruction, and famine in their wake. Yes, he was through with helping people, through with leaving them worse off than before he had come to rescue them.

"Major?" It was Juliette's turn to wonder at the demons haunting her companion. What thoughts was he powerless to keep at bay? What nightmares had robbed his handsome face of its easy smile and the crinkle of laugh lines around his eyes, eyes that had changed in an instant from boldly admiring to acutely observant, and now empty and remote? Juliette frowned thoughtfully; on the one hand it was flattering to be the object of such intense interest, but on the other, it was strangely disconcerting. Most men were more than content to admire her, enjoy her, and nothing more; this one wanted to know her, and intimacy such as that she shared only with a few, very few, of her closest companions, none of them men, and certainly none of them some dashing here-again-there-again glory-seeking soldier.

Adrian suddenly realized that she was regarding him curiously, no, *warily*, was a better word. Waiting for a reply, he had been so lost in his own bitter reflections that he had quite forgotten his surroundings; they both had—the light chatter, a trill of laughter here and there, the faint tinkle of silverware were completely at odds with the somber worlds both of them had just been inhabiting. "I beg your pardon. Perhaps you are right, it is best to forget the past. On the other hand, if we do that, we are condemned to ignorance, never to learn from our mistakes and, worse yet, likely to repeat them in the future."

Juliette wondered just what experiences had clearly cost him so dearly, experiences whose recollection darkened his eyes with pain. Perhaps, after all, he was more than just a dashing here-again-there-again glory-seeking soldier. Perhaps he truly would understand . . . but no, Helen had warned her that such thoughts could lead one down dangerous paths, paths that made one vulnerable to a handsome face and attentive manners, paths that robbed one of one's dearly bought independence and ripped away the fragile control one had finally won over one's life. "Learn from our mistakes, yes, dwell on them, no."

Again, there was such a wealth of conviction in her words that Adrian knew it was not simple philosophical reflection, but bitter experience that had led her to this conclusion.

"As I am sure you will agree," she continued. "There must be a great deal that you have learned from your experiences fighting in the Peninsula which, I would venture to guess, you would just as soon put completely out of your mind."

Adrian stared at her. Was she a witch? Everyone else he had encountered since returning home simply assumed he wanted to relive his heroic exploits. Friends, flirts, parents, family, all of them, were constantly begging him to regale them with stories of valor and glory. How little they knew; there might have been valor aplenty, but there was no glory, and how little they cared to hear about anything else. But no, he saw the understanding in her eyes and the tiny smile that tugged at the corners of her mouth because she knew she was right. No, she was not a witch, just a woman who observed closely and cared deeply.

Without thinking what he was doing, Adrian reached out and took her hand, raising it to his lips, inhaling the delicate scent of rosewater and feeling a sudden peace washed over him, a peace he hadn't known since he had left university. "Sweet oblivion," he murmured raising one mobile eyebrow. "You are indeed a mind reader. But how did you know?"

Juliette chuckled. "Nothing so mysterious as that, my lord. It is just that you are here in a pastry shop with your brother and three ladies instead of reminiscing with your fellow officers on guard duty. In my experience most soldiers ask nothing better than to seek out glory at the expense of all else and, having done so, they continue to forget everything else in re-living it again and again with their comrades-in-arms"

And somehow this simple observation and this logical deduction made her more endearing and entrancing than if she had been able to read his mind after all. On the other hand, he could not help wondering—and he hated himself for doing so, for Major Lord Adrian Claverton never competed for a woman's attention—who these other soldiers were who had given her such a disquietingly unflattering opinion of them. Surely she did not consider him one of them, or did she? Surely he was not like that? He had joined the army to fight against the Corsican monster threatening to conquer the world, not simply to cover himself with glory . . . hadn't he? Would Mademoiselle Juliette have condemned his younger self as a glory hunter? He knew better now.

"Good heavens, the time!" Grace's voice brought both of them back to the reality of the pastry shop and their companions. "Jane will be wondering what has become of me and her pianoforte lesson."

Freddy rose reluctantly. "We have taken your attention for too long, but we really could not help it; your company was too charming."

Dora laughed, patting him fondly on the arm, "It is not as though we shan't be enjoying your company later. You *are* coming to see how the trimming looks on the new dress, are you not?"

Freddy brightened. "Of course. Until then, my dears," and with a graceful bow and a wave of his hand he led them out to their waiting carriage.

CHAPTER 9

"A LOVELY TRIO OF LADYBIRDS," a silky voice hissed in Freddy's ear. "I don't believe I recognize any of them. You must introduce me."

Freddy whirled around to discover Lord Basil Harcourt at his elbow, a knowing look in his close-set pale gray eyes and a feral smile curling his thin lips. "Didn't know you were there or I would have." Freddy reluctantly acknowledged his fiancée's brother. "They are friends of . . . ."

"Mine. Just came to town," Adrian supplied, misliking Basil's sly expression. The worst that could be said of Lady Lavinia Harcourt was that she was a humorless, sanctimonious, overbearing young woman convinced of the natural superiority conveyed on her by her ancient lineage. But her brother, Basil, was something entirely different altogether, a thoroughly nasty piece of work whose association with an equally nasty set of companions kept him skirting the edges of outright scandal. No one had actually accused Lord Basil of anything, but the rumors of heavy play in the metropolis' most unsavory gambling hells clung to him like a particularly noxious odor, and most of polite society vigorously shunned his company.

"Recently come to town, have they?" Ignoring Adrian, Basil fixed his eyes on Freddy, his smile widening to reveal tiny sharp teeth that made him look even more than ever like a hungry cat waiting to pounce.

"As have I, you may recall." There was no mistaking the menace in Adrian's voice now as he moved forward to tower over Basil. "And one of the things I missed most in the Peninsula was Mr. Gunter's refreshing ices which is why I convinced Freddy to join me after several hours admiring the very fine horseflesh at Tattersall's. But you must excuse us, we have a great deal of catching up to do and calls to make before the opera this evening." He cast a knowing look at his brother who nodded vigorously. "Good to see you in such fine fettle." Adrian's tone, which barely avoided the contemptuous, still managed to convey surprise at the continued existence of someone whose lifestyle didn't bear close examination and, taking his brother's arm firmly in his, strolled off in the direction of Grosvenor Square.

"But I thought we were going back to Tatt's," Freddy protested under his breath.

"We are, but he is likely to follow us there. He won't if he thinks we are going to call on Mama. We shall stop in and then go to Tatt's."

"Oh." Not for the first time, Freddy found himself admiring his younger brother's resourcefulness. As the dutiful eldest son and heir, Freddy had, had little time, and even less inclination to fall into scrapes as a child, but on the rare occasion when he had, it had always been Adrian who had come to his rescue, manufacturing an appropriate excuse so quickly that it left his brother speechless, always a good thing when explanations were being demanded.

"Thank you." Freddy heaved a sigh of relief as they turned the corner and were well out of Basil's sight. "I cannot believe he is the brother of someone who is the very soul of propriety." His brother's carefully bland expression said all there was to say. "I mean, whatever you may think of her, Lavinia is extremely well bred and would never set a foot wrong while Basil . . . ." Freddy sighed heavily as the none-too-happy vision of the future rose before him " . . . well Basil is . . . rather a loose screw."

"Decidedly." Privately Adrian thought there was a great deal of similarity in the brother and sister's thoroughgoing selfishness and determined pursuit of their own ends regardless of the feelings of the rest of the world, but he was certainly not about to share that particular opinion with poor Freddy.

But even Adrian had underestimated the unsavory appetites of his future brother-in-law which apparently included a love of intrigue and a taste for pretty women who were quite above his touch, for that very evening Basil suddenly appeared at Freddy's side as he handed Juliette into her carriage after the opera.

"So *that* is the reason you could not escort Lavinia to the Academy of Ancient Music this evening. I *thought* it was more than a love of music that compelled your presence at the opera, and certainly it was not your brother's burning desire to hear Grassini sing." Basil's wolfish smile left Freddy grasping helplessly for a reply, any reply. Even Adrian was momentarily bereft of speech.

"What *I* think," Basil continued silkily, "Is that it would be best if Lavinia did not hear a word of this—has a nasty temper, my sister Lavvy, would make you miserable for weeks. *I* think it would be best if I were to keep mum about our, er little *encounter.* What do you say to a small loan to tide me over until next quarter day? I seem to have come up short at the table last night, nasty streak of bad luck."

"Ah, er, oh, certainly." Freddy ignored Adrian's quiet pressure on his arm. "You may call on me tomorrow, but in the meantime . . ."

"In the meantime, you have an appointment at a most exclusive establishment that owns the carriage that just left, an establishment where I very much crave an introduction only you can give me, eh *brother*?"

"Well, I don't know, Freddy began doubtfully. "It is not up to me, and Hel . . . er, Mrs. Gerrard, is very set in her ways."

"But I feel she must hold a soft spot for you, eh Freddy? Everyone does, heir to a dukedom and all. I feel certain you could smooth the way for me, *if* you did not want Lavinia to know about your *other interest* of course. What do you say we put it to the test right now?" And grabbing Freddy's other arm in a surprisingly vicelike grip for one whose whole appearance spoke of many unhealthy nights spent at the gaming table, Basil led them off in the direction of St. James' Square.

Helen, seated at the card table, was gazing dispassionately at the hand in front of her when the footman's discreet cough made her look up to see him glance meaningfully in the direction of the parlor at the back which doubled as the school room. Regretfully she excused herself and followed him to the hallway.

"Gentlemen to see you ma'am. It's his lordship, his brother and . . . .*another* gentleman."

There was only one *his lordship*, Freddy having won the hearts of all Mrs. Gerrard's inhabitants with his easygoing charm, genuine interest in their lives, and his kindness to Juliette. His lordship's brother was also becoming a standard fixture, and since Helen had just left his lordship's other brother at the card table it left *another gentleman* to be the cause of the footman's concern.

One look at Freddy's expression, which resembled nothing so much as a trapped animal, and Helen was instantly on the alert.

"Good evening, madam." Freddy's bow was as practiced as ever, but his blue eyes, usually beaming with guileless good humor, were troubled. "May I introduce to you my brother-in-law to be, Lord Basil Harcourt."

Helen nodded coolly at the visitor. No need of Freddy's hesitant attitude or the disdainful distance Lord Adrian left between himself and their companion to warn her; this customer had havey-cavey written all over him. "Good evening, my lord." Rapidly reviewing which of her ladies was available that moment, Helen heaved an inward sigh of relief. Dora, with her no nonsense attitude should be more than a match for someone who had clearly blackmailed his way into her exclusive establishment. Helen would see to it that Dora was forewarned and then keep a watchful eye out, making sure that the usually generous amount of spirituous beverages supplied to her guests was kept to a minimum with this one.

"Good evening, madam." Basil's oily smile did nothing to dispel the general air of unease hanging thick in the room. "My *brother*, here, assure me you have a quantity of delightful young ladybirds to share their *company* with an interested gentleman."

"The marquess is too kind." Helen shot a reassuring smile at the miserable Freddy. "All of our young ladies are delightful, but I think you will find Dora particularly to your liking."

A maid appeared the instant Helen rang to conduct Basil to Dora's chamber leaving Helen alone with the two brothers. Laying a kindly hand on Freddy's arm, she arched one delicate dark brow. "An unfortunate encounter, I gather?"

Freddy nodded unhappily. "I do apologize. Even Adrian could think of no way to extricate ourselves."

Helen nodded sagely. "These things happen. Do not distress yourself, my lord, here we take such things in stride and Dora knows what she is about. Now go see Juliette; she is longing to discuss the opera with you and show you her latest design. Forget all about your, er, *companion*. He will be taken care of. The disdainful shrug of her elegant shoulders managed to convey both sympathy and agreement that Freddy's soon-to-be relative was a nasty piece of work.

For once, Helen, relentlessly realistic as she usually was, was mistaken, for not half an hour later a stifled scream, a crash, and a loud oath interrupted the quiet concentration of the card players in the drawing room. Beckoning to the footman, Helen excused herself and ran upstairs to find a small crowd gathered around the door to Dora's chamber.

Grace and Clarissa, faces pale with concern, hovered anxiously in the hall with Juliette while inside Freddy was solicitously handing a glass of water to a shaken and disheveled Dora. Adrian, his face taut with disgust, blue eyes icy with fury, held a struggling Basil by the collar.

"My goodness," Helen managed to gasp. "What . . ."

"Nothing to concern yourself about, ma'am." Adrian, still holding Basil at arm's length, began to walk him toward the door. "Vermin, prevalent as they are, sometimes even make their way into the very best of establishments, but immediate elimination usually solves the problem and offers a telling example to others. This particular specimen is well aware that if he ever shows his face in the vicinity or has any contact with any of the inhabitants of this house, he will find himself challenged to a duel . . . a *fatal* duel." He spoke calmly enough, conversationally even, but there was no mistaking the deadly undertone, nor the tightening grip on Basil's collar which left the man gasping for breath, or the very ugly bruise beginning to stain one side of the prisoner's face.

"Now I feel sure, Mrs. Gerrard, you have two strong men who can conduct him safely to his chambers."

"Of course." Helen sent the maid scurrying to find the butler and alert the coachman, and in no short order Basil was firmly escorted down the back stairs and into Mrs. Gerrard's carriage, but not before had had snarled over his shoulder to the little group clustered around Dora, "You will pay for this—all of you!"

"I am so very sorry. I should not have let him convince me . . . ." Freddy turned to Helen.

"Force you, more like; men like that never ask, much less convince, they just take what they want. I am sure you had no choice in the matter, my lord."

While Freddy was apologizing to the establishment's proprietress and Adrian, clenching and unclenching his fists, was watching out the window to see that the unwelcome visitor was thoroughly dispatched, a tall, soberly clad individual materialized at Dora's side to offer her another glass of water and a clean handkerchief. "Here, I thought you might have need of both of these." Lord John smiled at her kindly as he checked discreetly to be sure that the red marks on her throat were beginning to fade.

Thank you," she sighed, pressing the handkerchief to her lips. I shall be all right. It was just the shock, you know."

He nodded, but with such a wealth of sympathy and compassion in his eyes that unexpected tears pricked her own. What was wrong with her? Dora Barlowe had seen a sight worse than this, endured more indignity in her life than this nasty bit of humanity; why would she feel like crying now when she hadn't shed a tear since the age of eight when her mother had died?

Looking away from Helen to see how Dora was doing, Freddy came to a dead stop, his jaw dropping. "John?"

And hearing the note of incredulity in his brother's voice, Adrian turned from the window where he had confirmed Basil's unceremonious eviction. "And *what*, may I ask, is the rector of St. George's Hanover Square doing at Mrs. Gerrard's?" Raising one quizzical eyebrow he strode over to his brother who gave Dora's shoulder a reassuring squeeze and an encouraging smile as she stared at him in considerable consternation.

"Availing himself of the best card partner in all of London, and that includes White's and Brooks's." The blue eyes so much like his brothers' were limpidly innocent as John nodded guilelessly to Freddy and Adrian, both of whom were transfixed with astonishment at the discovery of their sober, studious brother obviously feeling quite at home in London's most notorious, albeit exclusive, bawdy house.

"You, you . . . are a priest?" Dora finally found her voice.

"Well, yes, I am." There was a slightly apologetic note in John's voice as he waved away the little group of onlookers and Helen, fully comprehending the meaningful look he shot at her, cleared them efficiently from the hallway, shutting the door to Dora's chamber as they dispersed.

CHAPTER 10

DORA LOOKED AT JOHN HELPLESSLY, her big brown eyes swimming in tears. "What you must think of me, Father," she whispered dropping her head in her hands.

"What *I* think is that you were the victim of a most unhappy circumstance, just as you were victim of an unhappy circumstance that brought you here in the first place," he answered softly as he gently pushed her down into a chair and took a seat next to her.

"My . . . my mother would be so ashamed. She was a God-fearing woman, went to church every Sunday. So did I until . . . until . . . I couldn't anymore." Her voice suspended in a sob as she dabbed furiously at the tears running down her cheeks.

"And why couldn't you?"

"Because . . . because of the life I am leading . . . my mother would call it a life of sin."

It was the barest of whispers, but it was loud enough to break his heart. "And who did our Savior care more about than the sinners of this word, Dora? Who was one of his most devoted companions but Mary Magdalen? Only those who have suffered as you have can fully understand the true nature of his love and forgiveness."

She lifted her head up. "Oh, if only I could believe you, I would feel so comforted."

He smiled at the faint glimmer of hope he saw in her eyes. "Of course you can believe me. I would never mislead you. But," he smiled gently, "I can understand that someone as accustomed to hard bargaining as Mrs. Gerrard tells me you are, will need a great deal of convincing, eh? If you were to come to Sunday service you would see. And you would also see how many others there are who need convincing too."

"Oh no! I could never go to church, not after . . . not with all those *respectable* people."

Once again, John's heart twisted painfully in his chest as he thought of his complacent parishioners, half asleep in their pews, nodding from the excesses of the previous evening, without a care for their mortal souls, comparing them with this poor girl who, against her will, had been shoved into an existence that had made her give up on her own mortal soul. "I think I can fix that."

Dora stared at him. The glimmer of hope was growing stronger.

"I imagine you are not the only one here who feels the way you do. What if I were to come and offer holy services here, just for you and the rest of your friends?" John mentally consigned the certain horrified reactions of his superiors to the rubbish heap. Saving souls was saving souls, and doing God's work was doing it wherever it was most needed.

"Oh, if only you could!" she breathed.

"And why couldn't' I? I am sure Hel . . . er, Mrs. Gerrard would give me her permission to use the schoolroom. Surely you could leave off lessons one day a week?"

"Oh Father!" She clasped her hands together, her soft round face almost childish as she smiled joyfully at him.

"Then we are agreed. I will talk to Mrs. Gerrard. You will insure that I have a congregation, and now you will forget about this," he pointed to the angry red welts darkening her slender throat. It was none of your doing, and my brothers will make sure he never comes near you or this place again. Gentle soul, my brother Freddy, but he cannot bear meanness, and Adrian . . . well Adrian, no one Adrian sees behaving badly is ever allowed to forget it. A passionate fellow that Adrian, one who has been righting the wrongs of the world since he was six when he made my father get rid of a surly groom who was beating the stable boys, not to mention the horses."

"And you, my lord, are cut out of the same bolt of cloth, I think—saving lost souls wherever you may find them." Dora had regained her composure by now, and the teasing sparkle was back in her eyes.

"I try, Miss Dora, I try, but the world is a dangerous and challenging place—as you know."

She nodded, smiling, "Which is why I am glad we have the Claverton brothers on our side."

John laughed and patted her shoulder. "That's the spirit. And I think I speak for both Freddy and Adrian when I say we are glad to be of service."

"You are too kind, all of you." Her brow wrinkled thoughtfully as though she were about to ask something and then thought better of it, but John, acute observer of human nature that he was thought he could guess. "And you are wondering why we are this way?"

Again she nodded.

"This time I cannot speak for Freddy and Adrian, but for myself I would say that I want a purpose in my life, to do something meaningful, to prove myself worthy of existence; I would venture a guess that it is the same for my brothers. Our reward is to feel that we have attained this purpose in helping people. And then," he flashed a smile of disarming sweetness," we also reap the benefit of enjoying some very charming company."

Seeing the skepticism in her eyes, he hastened to add, "It is not what you think. You are a most congenial and interesting group, and I expect that Freddy and Adrian find, as do I, that the atmosphere at here is infinitely more relaxing, and far more genuine than most of the drawing rooms we might find ourselves visiting—not to mention the best hand of cards I have yet to discover."

"Hel . . . Mrs. Gerrard is very clever, isn't she?"

"Veeery clever. Even at university I encountered few minds as quick as hers, and none with such a deep understanding of mathematics. But, more importantly, I think she is a good person, someone who actively and courageously works for the betterment of others—a rare creature indeed." He should not have been surprised at Dora's gratified smile for he was well aware of all that Helen tried to do to improve the lives of her ladies, but it pleased him to see that they understood and appreciated her efforts, just as it touched him to realize exactly how important it was to people like Dora to have the validation of Helen's worth from a member of the outside world. Mrs. Gerrard's was a rare place indeed, and the more he discovered that, the more John wanted to help. "You will speak to Mrs. Gerrard and the others about my performing the service?"

She nodded, and he rose to take his leave. "Good. I shall await your word. In the meantime, put this unfortunate incident out of your mind. And," he grinned," you might find that Turner's Imperial Lotion soothes your neck. It can be found at Allans', I believe." With a quick, encouraging smile he was gone leaving them both feeling better than either one of them had felt in quite some time.

Despite the improvement in his mood, John was still left with the original question of what had drawn Freddy and Adrian to Mrs. Gerrard's in the first place. Freddy was certainly not the sort to seek out the sort of liaison offered there and Adrian, who spent most of his time fending off the lures cast in his direction, had no need.

He found his brothers enjoying a cup of tea with Helen who glanced up anxiously as John entered her office. "She will be fine." He smiled reassuringly. "It was the shock . . . and the suspicion that somehow she had brought the situation upon herself that is causing her pain, but I think I have convinced her that it is not her fault and has nothing to do with her."

Helen nodded solemnly, her elegant emerald eardrops glinting in the candlelight.

"Basil is a very bad man, always was. I should have . . ." Freddy broke off unhappily as Adrian gripped his shoulder.

"There was nothing you could do, Freddy, he had us trapped. And he won't dare to show his face in town for quite some time."

There was an implacability in Adrian's voice that even John found a little unnerving. When had his younger brother turned from an adventure-mad boy into . . . into this man to be reckoned with? He supposed it was only natural that Adrian's time in the Peninsula would have changed him, but still it was something of a shock to realize that his scapegrace younger brother was a man of drive as well as passion. The classically handsome face whose winning smile could charm anyone, even a cook whose tarts had just been stolen, had hardened into features whose lean tanned lines betrayed an intensity of purpose utterly lacking in other men of the *ton*. The gaze that had once held a lazy lurking smile was now direct and searching, betraying how much it had witnessed and how much it had endured. Looking at him, John suddenly felt a rush of pride in this soldier brother who, whatever his original reasons for joining the cavalry—glory, adventure, the chance to prove himself in foreign lands—had defended his country and freed Europe from the grip of a tyrant.

"I think you are correct, my lord," Helen agreed, "and thank you for making certain that she knows she did nothing wrong. Only a coward hurts a helpless woman; only a weakling takes advantage of the powerless, and such a person, when faced with someone who possesses true strength and courage, avoids all possibility of further confrontation and exposure of his weakness."

"In general, what my brother says is true," Adrian looked thoughtful for a moment, "but if I may be so bold as to make a suggestion?"

"Certainly, my lord."

"Having a second footman to help evict other, er *poorly behaved* clients might not be amiss."

Helen tilted her head, a tiny speculative smile tugging at the corner of her mouth. "And why, Major Lord Adrian, do I have the distinct feeling you have just the person to recommend to me?"

"It is fortunate we live in these enlightened times, for in days gone by you would have been burned as a witch, Mrs. Gerrard." And indeed, there was an unnervingly knowing look in the enigmatic green eyes whose slightly exotic tilt at the corners only added an air of mystery to her inscrutable expression. "But, in fact you are correct, I do, my batman. His wife has died, leaving him with a young daughter to care for, and as I now have more need of a valet than a bat-man . . ." he flashed a winsome smile. "He is a handsome chap, tall and infinitely resourceful—can find something to eat in an absolute desert—not that you would be needing that, but he would be quite an addition to your household."

"Oh very well," she chuckled. "Send him around. What is his name?"

"Tom. Tom Sandys, and I would be forever in your debt, madam." With a flourish, Adrian leaned forward and raised her hand to his lips.

"Be off with you, my lord, you are too charming for your own good."

"I say, Adrian." Freddy, who had been brooding over his cup of tea, suddenly came to life. Could you go check on Mademoiselle Juliette? I fear the unpleasantness may have upset her and I have something further to discuss with Mrs. Gerrard."

"But of course!" Adrian was out of the room before his brother could set down his tea cup.

CHAPTER 11

HE FOUND JULIETTE SITTING IN FRONT OF THE FIRE in her chamber determinedly stitching together the bodice of Grace's blue satin dress. Her attention was fixed on the task in front of her, but Adrian could see that her hands were shaking.

She had taken up her work hoping that the regular rhythm of her needle and thread poking through the cloth and the smooth comforting feel of the satin between her fingers would slow the heavy beating of her heart and calm her ragged breathing as she tried to put the whole nasty episode out of her mind.

"Mademoiselle Juliette." Adrian knelt in front of her, gathering her hands into his, looking up into eyes that were dark with pain in her white face.

"The needle, my lord."

"What?"

"Be careful lest you prick yourself on my needle."

"Oh." Gently he removed it from her nerveless grasp and stuck it safely into the blue satin, then gathered her hands back in his. "You mustn't worry; he will not be back again, I swear to it." Adrian pulled her hands tight against his chest, willing away the fear and trembling that made his heart ache more painfully than it had during his entire time in the Peninsula.

"It is not that I am afraid of him. It is just remembering . . . .the utter powerlessness, the brutality . . . how one person could subject another . . . someone who is not even an enemy . . . to such indignity . . ." Seeing the red marks on Dora's throat had brought it all back to her in a rush, the remorseless hands grabbing her breasts, forcing themselves between her legs, tearing at her clothes, all the while holding her prisoner while she had struggled helplessly. The words were spilling out of her now in great gasps and she could not stop. Somehow those warm hands, so firm and steady, yet gentle and reassuring, the hardness of his broad chest, made her feel safe, protected, and infinitely cared for in a way she had not known since she was a child in her mother's arms comforted after a fall, and just as she had done then, Juliette burst into tears, now that she was safe, now that someone was watching over her.

"My poor girl." Oblivious to the satin sliding from her lap, Adrian pulled her into his arms, her soft hair brushing against his chin and the tear drenched cheeks pressing confidingly against his neck like a small child. Every sob that shook the delicate shoulders pierced him with the tenderness and the pathos of it all. And yet, at the same time, an odd sense of peace stole over him. He was helping, really helping someone at last. After all that time hurting people for what he had hoped was the greater good of the world he was now truly making something better.

Adrian smiled to himself as the sobs subsided and Juliette looked up at him, blue eyes enormous, still sparkling with the last of the tears that clung to the long dark lashes.

"I do beg your pardon. I don't know what came over me."

"You have been shamefully treated; that is what came over you."

"I know," she lifted her chin proudly, "but I do not give in to the hurt he forced on me; that would be letting him have his way with me all over again. I *never* let anyone have their way with me!"

"That I can well believe," Adrian grinned in earnest at a sudden vision of a two-year-old Juliette stomping her foot and refusing to do her mother's bidding. The stubborn set of her jaw told him all he needed to know about the steel within the delectably soft exterior. Mademoiselle Juliette might look all that was lovely, delicate, and yielding, but there was a challenging spark in her eyes that belied the charming exterior.

"I fought," she added unnecessarily, "but he took me by surprise and he was so much bigger than I."

"I wish I had been there."

She smiled at that, gripping his hands tightly. "I do too. You were magnificent today. I wish I could be like that—making bad men afraid."

He chuckled. "You *are* like that. I am very afraid of you and I am not even bad."

The blue eyes opened wide. "Afraid of me? How could you be afraid of me?"

"You are so elegant, so beautiful, who would not be afraid of someone so perfect?"

Juliette studied him for a long moment, but his eyes were deadly serious now, devoid of the teasing twinkle that had been there just moments ago. He actually thought that of her, former seamstress and fallen woman? "But ....but ... what are you afraid of?"

"I don't know . . . of not measuring up, not being good enough." *Of* wanting *to hold you in my arms forever. Of being one of those braggart soldiers you
dismiss so scornfully.*

"Good enough? For me? But that's absurd!"

"Why is it absurd? You are all that is beautiful, graceful, charming, and
intelligent."

"And talented," Freddy, who had paused in the doorway at the sight of
his brother on his knees in front of Juliette, remarked, an unusually thoughtful expression clouding his ordinarily sunny features. "I beg your pardon,
Mademoiselle Juliette, I would have come immediately to check on you, but I
wished to assure Mrs. Gerrard that though Lord Basil, by the purest circumstance, is an acquaintance of mine, I do, by no means, recommend him in any
way, nor do I approve of his character, if he can be said to have one. And then I
made a suggestion for the draperies in the drawing room—blue swags over buff
sub-curtains arranged in a simple Greek mantle form would lend more texture
and color to the room, don't you think? White transparent veils underneath
that would let in the light at the same time, maintaining privacy and softening
the harsh glare of direct sunlight—so unbecoming to all but the most youthful
and beautiful among us, don't you agree?"

"Ah . . . oh." Juliette retrieved her hands from Adrian's as she struggled to
arrange a riot of emotions into some semblance of coherent speech. "I would
have to draw it first to make sure I understand the concept, but yes . . . I think
. . . What do you think, my lord?" She turned to Adrian who, by now, had risen
from his knees and was gazing at his brother with fond bemusement.

"I think that Freddy is never wrong about such things, eh, Freddy?"

Freddy beamed. "Not usually. But, I say, Mademoiselle, are you feeling quite
the thing? You are still looking a little pale."

"Mademoiselle Juliette has recovered her composure, I think." Adrian's eyes
were warm with approval, and something else that brought a sudden hot flush
to Juliette's ashen cheeks. "It was a momentary weakness brought on by a natural disgust for brutish behavior which would be offensive to anyone so unfortunate as to witness it. Is that not so, Mademoiselle?"

Juliette nodded. "But I am fine now, thank you, my lord." She managed
to summon up a reassuring smile for Freddy, but what she really wanted
was for Adrian to take her in his arms again and hold her safe against him.
She had felt her entire body relax, surrounded by his strength, and as the
rigidity had seeped out of her, she realized that since the day she had left
her parents' house, which had actually been a few threadbare rooms off
Manchester Square, she had been constantly wary and tense, never letting
up her guard for a moment. And, after all, what had that watchfulness gotten her? Nothing! It still had not saved her from being caught off guard

alone at night in Madame Celeste's workroom by a man who would stop at nothing to get what he wanted. She gritted her teeth as the remembered rage flowed back into her veins.

Watching her, Adrian saw her jaw tighten as her lips compressed into a tight line. It was only for a moment, an unconscious gesture quickly banished, but it was enough to make his own blood boil as he imagined what she must be feeling. "I think that perhaps I can help, Mademoiselle."

"Help? How? I mean, I do not need any help now. Hel . . . Mrs. Gerrard has helped me. She has given me, given all of us a home."

"But even she, for all her good intentions, all that she has done to save you all, could not protect Dora," he prompted gently.

"What can *you* do?"

"What can I do?" Adrian was not at all sure he liked the implication that, compared to the manifold talents and abilities of Helen Gerrard, a mere soldier in His Majesty's First Life Guards, experienced officer though he might be, had very little to offer. "I can teach you to box."

"Box!"

"And why not? You and all the others here would be well served if you knew how to weave and duck from an opponent's assault, not to mention being able to plant a facer when necessary."

"But . . . but . . ." Juliette struggled to grasp the concept. "I was grabbed from behind."

"Ah, then, you drop like a stone from your assailant's grasp and kick him in the shins."

Freddy eyed his brother with misgiving. "Where did you learn that maneuver, not at Gentleman Jackson's surely."

"Eton. Or, well, rather, John taught me when one of the older boys was making my life miserable. Think how much better it would make you feel, Mademoiselle Juliette, if you too had the skill *to make bad men afraid.*"

He truly was in earnest, and the more Juliette considered it, the more she liked the sound of it.

"Women *do* box, you know, not often, but I have heard of pugilistic contests between women—even between women and men. Please, at least think about it, Mademoiselle. I do not want you ever to feel afraid again . . . you, or anyone else here."

His voice was a caress, tender and reassuring, and his eyes were so full of concern that she could have wept. It had been so long that anyone had cared for her—not that Major Lord Adrian Claverton, third son of one of England's wealthiest dukes could care for a *fille de joie*, but for the moment, at least, Juliette wanted to believe it. A dimple hovered at the corner of her mouth as she smiled up at him. "Well then, if you truly think you can teach me *to make bad men afraid*, I would like that very much, my lord. And, I would be forever in your debt."

The thought of Juliette, with her provocative and soft pink lips being forever in his debt made Adrian's throat go dry, and he suddenly felt there was not enough air in the room to clear his head of this dangerously enchanting vision. Taking her hand in his, he pressed it to his lips. "I promise you I shall do so, once I have secured Mrs. Gerrard's permission, or course, which I mean to do directly."

And with that, he was gone, leaving Juliette and his brother staring after him.

CHAPTER 12

HELEN HAD NOT YET RETURNED TO the card players in the drawing room when Adrian sought her out in her office where, much to his surprise, he found his other brother deep in conversation with her.

"Only if they wish it, my lord," Helen was saying.

John grinned, brushing back a thick lock of hair that had fallen across his forehead in a way that made him look more like a mischievous schoolboy than the rector of London's most fashionable church. "Believe me, Madam, I have enough unwilling parishioners as it is; I have no intention of adding any more."

"What? Saving souls again?" Adrian breezed into the room. "He will not be happy until he has comforted all the lost and miserable of the land, or London, at the very least, but since he has been forced to take on a parish where no one is lost and no one is miserable, that leaves only John to be lost and miserable."

But Helen, seeing the warmth in Adrian's smile and the pride in his eyes, was not fooled. Nor was she surprised when he patted John's shoulder. "And if it were not for you, brother, Dora would still be hiding away in her chamber instead of picking herself up and marching herself down here." Adrian waved a hand to point to Dora hovering in the doorway.

"Do come in, Dora. What is one more in a crowded room? But be quick about it for Lord John and I must get back to our card game."

"Yes, Helen." An uncharacteristic shyness suddenly seemed to have taken a hold of the normally ebullient Dora. "It is just that his lordship . . . .well you see . . . he offered to come here of a Sunday and conduct services and . . . oh please, could he? I have talked to the others and they would like it ever so much. It would be sort of like the lessons you give us only . . . .could we, please?"

Even Helen, who had suffered more than her share of pathos in her life, was touched by the eagerness in Dora's voice and the hope lighting up her face. If the Reverend Lord John Claverton never did anything else in his life, he could die a contented man knowing what he had just done for the ladies of Mrs. Gerrard's. But Helen had a reputation to maintain as a hard-headed thinker and an even tougher businesswoman. Tilting her head to one side, she considered the proposition carefully. "And when would this be?"

"Right after he is through with services in his church, around dinner time. We could skip dinner so no time was wasted."

"Hmmm."

Surreptitiously watching the exchange, John suppressed a grin. He had played cards with Helen long enough to read her every expression, even down to the twitch of an eyelid, which was generally the very most she revealed of what she was thinking, and he knew that this moment of deliberation was purely for show—a clever woman, Helen Gerrard. In fact, he could not ever remember having known anyone cleverer.

At last she nodded. "Yes, I think that can be arranged. What do you say, my lord, are you ready to take on another congregation?"

"Most certainly. If they will have me." He winked at Dora.

"Very well, then. Now come along; we have deserted the card table far too long. Let's go relieve my guests of some more of their fortunes." She rose from her chair and sailed from her office, as regal as any monarch in Christendom, leaving the others to follow in her wake.

Not being the card player his brother was, Adrian sauntered off to his rooms in the Albany wishing with all his heart that it was he instead of Freddy cozily ensconced in Juliette's chamber.

It would have surprised him to know, as he sat sipping a glass of brandy in front of his own fire some time later berating himself for acting like a lovelorn schoolboy, that he was the topic of discussion in that very chamber he longed to inhabit.

"Fine fellow, Adrian," Freddy observed as he picked up a roll of blond lace from the chair opposite Juliette and sat down.

Juliette nodded, glad that her mouth was too full of pins she was using to hold the bodice together to reply. The less she thought about Major Lord Adrian Claverton, the better. He was taking up far too much of her thoughts as it was already.

"Seems to be rather taken with you, Mademoiselle Juliette, from what I can see, and Adrian is rarely taken with any woman—quite the other way around. I often accuse him of joining the cavalry simply to get away from all those females chasing after him"

"I could not say." Juliette's eyes were riveted on her stitching—in and out, in and out –she tried to match her ragged breathing to the smooth rhythm of her needle, but she could do nothing about the delicate flush that warmed her cheeks, revealing to her guest all that he needed to know.

Freddy smiled to himself. Good! She was as interested in his brother as he was in her. Adrian deserved a bit of distraction after all the hardships he had endured in the Peninsula and he, Freddy, was going to see that he got them. And, there was no time like the present. "I say, Mademoiselle," Freddy leaned forward conspiratorially, "I do not suppose you would like to help me out in that quarter, would you?"

This time Juliette did look up from her sewing.

"As I said, Adrian is a bang-up brother, but at the moment, he is a bit at sixes and sevens, what with nothing useful to do in London after all the action he is accustomed to. You saw him today; he needs to be active, and dancing attendance on my sister and my mother at Almack's is not it, nor is sitting around swapping stories with his fellow officers. If I could say that you never have seen the sights of London, that you needed to get out in order to take your mind off things, he would feel a bit more the thing—being useful, you know, just until he gets his peacetime bearings. What do you say, Mademoiselle?"

"You would not mind?" Freddy had always been an unconventional customer, but asking her to amuse another man, even though it was his brother, was unconventional in the extreme.

"Oh no. I should be most indebted to you, and it would not cut into our time with these." He reached over to pick up some rough sketches that had fallen to the floor along with the lace and studied them carefully. "I do like the way this is cut closer to the body, and pink satin drawn back to reveal the white underneath will be completely becoming to even the most unfortunate of figures."

"The mention of *unfortunate figures* unhappily brought one to mind. Freddy shuddered at the thought. "Last month I escorted Lady Lavinia Harcourt and her mother to an exhibit at the Egyptian Hall which, I daresay, you would greatly enjoy it. I shall suggest it to Adrian, and since I have already seen it, it is only natural that I ask him to take you." Freddy's smile of triumph at his own cleverness quickly dispelled the gloomy look induced by the thought of his fiancée, but not before Juliette had seen it and guessed what it might mean.

"Lady Lavinia enjoyed it, did she?"

"My fiancée never enjoys anything. No, I shouldn't say that. She *appreciates* things, if they are of an improving nature, and the Egyptian Hall provided enough of an improving nature for her to approve of it." Freddy fell silent for a moment seeming to stare blindly at the drawing in front of him. "She ought to wear more color like this satin, if it were a deeper rose, but she insists on white, you know." He sighed heavily. "Then again, if I married her, she would not feel compelled to wear white."

"This engagement is of a longstanding nature, I take it."

Freddy nodded lugubriously. "Since birth." Then, seeming to think better of himself, he continued. "Don't take me wrong, she is not a bad sort of person, great deal of character, fine old family, except for Basil of course, ancient title and estates . . ." estates, he did not add, that were mortgaged to the hilt, ". . . it's just that she . . . .she . . . is so very *rigorous*." This time the sigh was heartfelt to the point of being gusty.

Juliette reached over to pat his hand. She did not like seeing anyone unhappy, but somehow the expression of misery seemed more out of place, and therefore even more touching, on Freddy's cheerful open countenance. At least she was not condemned to spend the rest of her life with someone who made her unhappy. Lord Talbot might have ruined her dreams of a marriage and children, but, in reality, marriage most likely would have been to a man of her parents' choosing to whom she felt entirely indifferent, and that would have been if she were lucky, because most of the young men her parents favored were so self-absorbed and frivolous as to be the objects of her undying scorn. Better to be alone and lonely than to be tied for all eternity to someone she could not even respect or like. Poor Freddy!

"But perhaps when you have a family? She may retire to the country and . . . ."

"And she will ride roughshod over them too. Won't even know my own children, I won't," he replied morosely, then drew himself up. "Beg your pardon, shocking bad form to be so blue devilled with such a charming companion. And I am not married yet. With any luck, someone in the family will die and she'll have to go into mourning—got several great aunts whose health is not in the best of states. At any rate, there is no point in ruining my time here, though, come to think of it, I must go. Promised Fotheringay I would join him at Brooks's. Has a new snuff box he wants my opinion on. I shall see you tomorrow. In the meantime you'll think on what I said about Adrian, won't you?"

Oh, she would think about Lord Adrian, Juliette acknowledged to herself. There was absolutely no doubt about that.

CHAPTER 13

F REDDY WAS SO PLEASED WITH HIS IDEA for throwing Adrian and Juliette together that he was up betimes the next morning, but when he strolled over to his brother's chambers, it was to be met with the news that Adrian had already left.

"Guard duty?"

"No, my lord," Wilson, doubling for the moment as both Adrian's valet and butler, replied thoughtfully, "he did not say, though he did mention walking around St. James' Square to clear his head."

"Must be going to Brooks's eventually. Ah well then, I shall just toddle on to Brooks's myself. Thank you, Wilson." Freddy mulled over this interesting bit of information as he strolled back down Piccadilly, but none of the possible scenarios he conjured up came close to reality.

"You wish to teach the ladies to box?" Even Helen, unflappable though she was, could not quite hide her astonishment as Adrian put forth his proposal.

"Well, Mademoiselle Ju . . . er Miss Dora, seemed rather shaken up by the incident with Basil and I thought that knowing how to defend herself might have spared her the unpleasantness, not that even looking at a miserable toad like Basil is an unpleasant enough experience in and of itself." The emerald eyes surveying him held a twinkle of amusement now though the rest of Helen's expression remained as inscrutable as ever. "I just thought that it might make a difference to everyone here if they felt secure in the knowledge that they could stand up to bullies like Basil." Adrian heaved an inward sigh of relief as Helen nodded thoughtfully and the gleam of amusement was replaced with genuine interest. Adrian's commanding officer made even seasoned warriors like Adrian quake, but compared to the redoubtable proprietress, the man was no more threatening than the tabby cat sunning itself on the cobblestones in the street below.

"It might just do," Helen gently tapped her pencil on the account book in front of her as she considered his proposal. "All of us have cursed our own helplessness in the face of men intent on taking advantage of us. Being able to wipe out that memory with the knowledge it would never happen again would go a long way to gaining back some of our pride and self-respect. Then too, a familiarity with the Fancy will certainly hold conversational appeal for some of our more sporting-mad guests. Yes," she laid down the pencil with a decisive thunk, "I think it an excellent idea, my lord. When can you begin?"

"Whenever you like."

"We shall have to devise a suitable costume, something that allows for freedom of movement while remaining discreet, but Juliette will think of something." Noting his eager expression, at the mention of Juliette's name, though quickly banished, Helen continued smoothly, "but I should say that sometime next week would be as good a time as any to begin. We shall fit it in before our lessons, I should think. There is nothing like vigorous exercise to sharpen the mind."

For a moment, she sounded to Adrian more like his first governess than the proprietress of an exclusive bawdy house, and the usual glint of ironic amusement in her expression was briefly clouded with, could it have been regret? The impression was so fleeting as to make Adrian doubt its existence, but it stayed with him as he rose to take his leave and head for the gracefully curving stairway. Pausing in the doorway, he turned around, "I don't suppose that Mademoiselle Juliette is available . . . I mean . . . since I am here I thought I would give her my regards."

"I *am* sorry, Mademoiselle Juliette is engaged at the moment, but I will tell her that you asked after her." In fact the only thing engaging Mademoiselle Juliette at the moment was the ruching she was sewing onto Grace's gown, but the look in the handsome soldier's eyes made Helen distinctly uneasy. It was admiration, and something else that gave her pause, something that did not belong in her establishment, or any of their lives, and she deemed it best to nip it in the bud before anyone was hurt. Far better to remind him now what Juliette did for a living than to have that reverent look deepening into more dangerous feelings that would be inevitably destroyed by bitter disillusionment.

"Of course." The faintest tinge of red crept along his cheekbones, deepening his Peninsular tan. "And I would be grateful if you would tell her I asked after her."

Helen bowed regally. He was a magnificent young man and she hated to be the one responsible for the fleeting bleak look that darkened sharp blue eyes, eyes that had seen too much already, she wagered, but it was better to force reality on him now rather than later. Yes, she hated to do it, hated not being able to hope that he cared about her sweet Juliette who deserved more than anyone to have a handsome young soldier care for her as he appeared to want to, but the years had forced Helen to become a realist. Romantic dreams were for other people. Self-sufficiency and independence were the goals that sustained them here. Still, it was nice, for the moment, to have her suspicions confirmed that this gallant young man cherished tender feelings toward Juliette.

Helen had reckoned without Freddy, however, whose hopes for his brother's happiness were not so grounded in the harsh realities of life. He caught up with his brother just as Adrian, filled with a renewed sense of purpose and the heady sense of having something to look forward to, turned the corner of St. James' heading towards Gentlemen Jackson's Bond Street boxing rooms to brush up on his technique.

"Hallo, Adrian. You're up betimes this morning."

"One might say the same thing of you with a good deal more accuracy, old fellow. I am *always* up betimes." Alerted by the false heartiness of Freddy's greeting, Adrian eyed him curiously.

"Oh. Anyone would be up betimes on a day like today, fineness of the weather and all that."

Since Freddy never indulged in any activity that had any remote dependence on the weather except possibly a tame drive through the park in his showy curricle, Adrian's curiosity deepened into the suspicion that this encounter was not entirely accidental. "And where were *you* headed this fine day?" Adrian linked his arm with his brother's as he steered him towards Bond Street.

"Actually, looking for you, old fellow."

This time, there was no mistaking the conscious look in Freddy's eyes. Adrian smiled. "Happy to oblige, whatever you were going to ask me to do, that is."

"No, nothing like that, wouldn't take advantage of you for the world . . . but the fact is . . . I *do* have something of a suggestion."

Adrian's right eyebrow rose higher. "And that would be?"

"The fact is that the other day, Lady Lavinia was speaking of the Egyptian Hall and . . .

The eyebrow dove from a quizzical tilt into a ferocious frown.

"Good Heavens, man! Never think that I would ask *anyone*, especially my own brother to sacrifi . . . well, never mind. It's just that it sounded like the sort of place that Mademoiselle Juliette might enjoy, what with her interest in antiquities and all."

"Interest in antiquities?" Adrian's mind reeled. Even for Freddy, this was a bit obtuse.

"Well, she told me she enjoys her lessons in Latin and Greek, so it would seem to me that those sorts of things interest her. Besides, I would hazard a guess that even though she lives in London, she has not had the opportunity to take in any of its attractions."

"And you thought I might show them to her?"

"Well . . . yes." Freddy tugged ever so gently at his exquisitely constructed cravat which, until this moment had not been tied all that tightly, but now, meeting his brother's gaze, it felt entirely too constricting. There was something altogether too knowing about his younger brother. Adrian was far too awake on every suit for his more simple-minded brother to try anything but the most direct approach. "Well, the thing of it is, I *like* Mademoiselle Juliette well enough—we have a bang-up time talking fashion and trimmings, but well . . . the thing of it is, I ain't all that much of a ladies' man," Freddy admitted uncomfortably. "But," pleased with his own cleverness, he brightened considerably, "you are!"

"And?" Adrian tried unsuccessfully to dampen the bubble of hope that began to rise within him.

"And I think it would be the very thing if you were to escort her around. Show her all the things she's missed. Give her a chance to experience all the amusements London has to offer. She'll enjoy that, and she likes you, that's clear enough."

The bubble of hope threatened to overwhelm him, and for a moment, Major Lord Adrian Claverton, admirer of scores of women in several countries, had difficulty breathing. She liked him! And Freddy apparently didn't care. In fact, the more Adrian studied his brother's guileless countenance, the more he thought Freddy looked quite pleased with himself, rather like a cat who had caught a mouse.

"I may not have so much in the brain box as you, but I've got eyes in my head, you know." Freddy flicked an invisible piece of fluff from his exquisitely cut coat of dark blue Bath superfine.

"Well, old fellow, if you don't mind . . ."

"Of course I don't mind. I suggested it!"

"That you did."

Adrian grinned. Freddy might not, as he said *have so much in the brain box* as his two younger brothers, but he had a certain intuition about people and, seeing the pleased expression on his face, Adrian suddenly realized that Freddy had sensed a great deal more than even Adrian himself had about the irresistible attraction between him and Mademoiselle Juliette and, in his usual kindhearted way, was doing his best to promote the happiness of two people he cared about. Still, a dog-in-the-mangerish thought would intrude that he wished it had been Adrian who had dreamt up the excursion to amuse Juliette rather than Freddy.

"Well, I must be off, promised to take a look at Fotheringay's new snuff box." Freddy hoped that Juliette and Adrian didn't become intimate so quickly that they discovered how many times Freddy invoked Fotheringay's new snuff box as an excuse to leave in a hurry.

But Adrian wasn't even listening. Giving his brother a parting clap on the shoulder, he turned the corner and headed up Bond Street, whistling in a most unfashionable manner as he went.

CHAPTER 14

THE BOXING LESSONS COMMENCED a little less than a week later when Adrian and John, whom he had commandeered for purposes of demonstration, met with five oddly clad inhabitants of Mrs. Gerrard's. Juliette had devised a costume, modeled on bathing costumes she had once seen in Brighton when the family were guests of the Comte D'Artois, who had taken lodgings there for the season. If the Comte and Comtesse de Fournoy had been disapproving then of sea bathing in England's most fashionable seaside resort, which they had, they would have been horrified beyond words at the boxing. But then, they had been horrified beyond words at their daughter's going off to work for a fashionable modiste in order to earn a living wage.

And look where *that* had gotten her! Juliette glanced around the light-filled room with its furniture pushed to one side, the carpet rolled up, and two scions of England's highest nobility, clad only in breeches and shirts, facing one another in the center.

From the sidelines Juliette scrutinized the two men as Adrian explained the rudiments of the sport, emphasizing the importance of good footwork and the critical nature of balance in delivering an accurate and effective punch. Major Lord Adrian Claverton in uniform was impressive, but clad only in breeches and a fine linen shirt he quite took her breath away. There was something about the naturalness and informality of the attire that transformed him into a real living breathing man instead of a soldier that made her want to run her hand over the hard muscles rippling under the thin fabric of his shirt. The square shoulders emphasized the broad planes of his chest which narrowed to a slim waist and long powerful legs—all in all a magnificent specimen of an athletic man in perfect condition that made her want to gaze at him forever. The sight of skin and a sprinkling of gold hair visible at the open neck of his shirt made her mouth go dry and her heart pound. Glancing quickly around the room, Juliette chucked to herself as she saw that she was not the only one affected this way. Dora, suddenly aware that she had been gaping at their instructor, shut her mouth with an almost audible snap and Grace, her pale faced flushed to a becoming pink, wiped on hand slowly across her brow, her gaze never wavering from their instructor.

From his position facing Adrian, John had ample opportunity to witness his brother's effect on the ladies and it amused him that even in this worldly group, Adrian inspired considerable interest. He saw Juliette's hand fly involuntarily to her lips and he stifled a grin, but not before she saw it. Smiling, he shook his head ever so slightly and was rewarded by an answering grin and yet, all the while, she seemed quite unaware of the fact that Adrian only had eyes for her. Oh, he hid it well enough, looking at each one of his prospective pupils in turn as he spoke, but John had been observing congregations from his pulpit for too long not to know where people's real attention was focused. So, Freddy was right, Adrian *was* attracted to the beautiful Mademoiselle Juliette, and, if the blush deepening her already rosy complexion were any indication, she was equally attracted to his brother. Good! Adrian needed the distraction of a beautiful and charming woman after the wasteland of war that had been his recent life.

"Now that I have explained the importance of keeping the left foot forward, knees bent, and the weight on the right, you can think about delivering a punch with all the weight of your body behind it and then advancing with the left foot. My brother will demonstrate, and at the same time I shall show you how to defend yourselves since, I, as the youngest brother, am a great deal better at defense than he is." Adrian grinned wickedly as he neatly parried John's punch. "See? That is how it is done. Now I would like you to pair off among yourselves and I shall walk around and observe."

But when the girls had paired off, Juliette was left alone, and not by chance, John thought as he saw how quickly they had claimed their partners. "Here," he gave Adrian a gentle push towards Juliette, "you can be Mademoiselle Juliette's partner while *I* walk around and observe."

Adrian, who had looked at everyone *but* Juliette, could no longer avoid it. His mouth went dry at the sight of her slender figure draped in a white cambric shift over matching pantalettes. In fact, more of her was covered than any other time he had seen her, but the looseness of the clothing somehow emphasized the body beneath it more fully than the most revealing gown, and the stark plainness provided a contrast that showed how very beautiful she really was.

Swallowing hard, he held up his fists. "Now, put your left foot forward, toes of that foot and the other turned slightly to the right. Good! Now raise your fists as I showed you, and tuck your chin slightly behind the left shoulder.

But that gesture displayed so much satiny skin, the delicate vulnerable line of her jaw, and the long slim neck that it was all Adrian could do not to think about grabbing the slender wrists and lifting them high over her head while he pressed his mouth to the sweet-scented flesh of her neck. Swallowing hard, he brought himself back to the matter at hand. "Now I shall defend myself while you attempt to get in under my guard and land a punch." The little wrinkle between her brows was utterly adorable and he could not help chuckling. "Don't worry, you can't hurt you."

Not surprisingly, she was light on her feet, but she was also swift, hovering around him like an intense fairy, her eyes dark with concentration making her utterly captivating. Suddenly, she untucked her chin to look up at him opening her lips into a smile so devastating it quite took his breath away. The next moment he heard a crack and realized with sudden bemusement that it was the sound of her fist hitting his jaw.

Adrian shook his head in astonishment. "Where did you learn to move like that?" The others, quickly smothering smiles, tried desperately not to laugh, and he couldn't blame them; she had gotten in under his guard so quickly and skillfully he still didn't know how she had done it.

"My brother. He taught me how to fence. The footwork is quite the opposite, but the principle is the same, *non*?"

"Your brother?" This beautiful creature who looked like some celestial being from an enchanted world had a brother? And what brother would let a sister become a . . . . no, he was not even going to think about it.

"Yes, he served under the Comte D'A . . ." Juliette clapped a hand to her mouth in dismay. "Yes. Many, many years ago." She clamped her lips shut with a determined expression that told him he would learn no more if it, no matter how much he pressed.

"But how did you do it?" He knew how. That beautiful smile had distracted him and she had used that moment to get under his guard.

"We too have our weapons, my lord." This time the mischievous smile didn't blind him; it frightened him. Did she see how irresistible she was to him, and was she warning him against her, telling him that she could belong to no man because she belonged to all men? Adrian felt as though he had been punched in the stomach instead of the jaw. All the wind went out of him and a cold chill splintered through his entire body.

Watching him, Juliette saw the amusement drain from his expression as the handsome features grew rigid, the smile distant, and the eyes empty of all expression. Gone was that secret smile he seemed to reserve just for her. What had she done? What terrible thing was he thinking? "My lord?" She reached out a tentative hand to touch his sleeve, trying to ignore the sinewy strength of the arm beneath it. Oh to feel that arm around her! She would never feel alone or afraid again.

He shook his head as the color came back into his face. "A neophyte delivers a perfect blow to someone who has been boxing with Gentleman Jackson for years and you wonder if something is amiss? My dear girl, my pride is shattered; that is what is amiss." He smiled down at her, but it was not the special smile of before. It was the genial smile he showed to everyone. Adrian had himself well in hand now, explaining to the rest of them how it had happened, the importance of pressing any advantage when you had one, but Juliette felt the distance between them, a distance that had not been there before, a distance that hurt far more than it should have even though she had purposely created it.

The rest of the lesson passed without incident. Adrian and John walked among the pairs of women adjusting an arm here pointing to an improperly weighted foot there, adjuring another to turn both feet slightly to the right, but in general they were pleased with their efforts. "Very good, ladies. I think you have the general idea." Adrian concluded the lesson. "But you must practice the footwork and the balance which are crucial whether you are attacking or defending. And always follow through with the punch; do not hesitate to go after your opponent."

"Never fear, my lord," Dora assured him with a wide grin. We are Mrs. Gerrard's ladies; we've all got the heart; we simply lacked the science. Nothing will stop us now, will it ladies?"

They all nodded vigorously, eyes sparkling, cheeks flushed, and Adrian, despite the soberness of his reflections, could not help smiling in return. It felt good to have done something for a change. And if he could save even one of them from what Dora had suffered, it was well worth the effort, never mind what he was suffering now as he watched Juliette chatting gaily with her fellow students without a thought for their instructor.

CHAPTER 15

Bteased Dora about the ferocity of her punch and complimented Grace on her agility. Always she was conscious of Adrian watching them, watching her, his eyes dark with some unfathomable emotion, his face utterly inscrutable. And she was also aware that she was not the only one carefully observing Adrian; as Lord John stood in one corner with Helen discussing the morning's lesson, his eyes kept straying towards his brother, and the hint of a frown wrinkling his scholar's brow told Juliette that he was as aware as she of his brother's somber expression.

Unlike Juliette, however, John taxed Adrian with it the moment they descended Mrs. Gerrard's steps into the pale sunshine where the faintest touch of green in the center of the square promised that Spring was on its way. "Out with it, man."

Adrian did not even bother to dissemble. His brother John had always possessed an uncanny ability to read minds, and an even uncannier one of being able to get straight at the root of the problem. "She is so beautiful," it was more a sigh than a statement, "so elegant and graceful, yet spirited and bold. One cannot help being captivated." He fell silent, examining the thousand thoughts and feelings roiling inside him, then smiled ruefully into the gray-blue eyes fixed so sympathetically on him, "I do not like the fact that there are others who feel the same way I do. I understand how it happened, how she came to be . . . to be . . . what she is. She did it to win her independence, to take back control over her life. I know that she has dreams of leaving this existence far behind, that she will become something different someday, have her own business. She is too talented, too dedicated not to succeed and fulfill her dreams, but in the meantime . . . ."

"In the meantime she is one of Mrs. Gerrard's ladies."

"Exactly!" Adrian nodded unhappily. "The most exclusive seraglio in all of London, perhaps the world. I should be glad that it is Mrs. Gerrard's where she is admired by only a very select few, and yet . . . She reminded me of it today, calling attention to the power of a woman's ways."

"I think it is not the attentions of other men that bothers you. What man would not want others to agree with him that the woman he admires so intensely is admired with equal intensity by his fellows? The question really is, how does the object of his admiration feel about those other admiring men, and how does she feel about you? And," John held up an admonitory hand as Adrian opened his mouth to reply, "does she feel the same way about you that you feel about her? That, my boy, is the age old question and one that would torment you whether Mademoiselle Juliette were a member of an ancient and respected family, which actually I suspect she might be—not English though— with a house in Grosvenor Square, an enormous estate in the country, and a constant presence at Almack's or an inhabitant of Mrs. Gerrard's. Furthermore, I would venture to guess that if she took the trouble to remind you of what she is, then she cares enough about you that she does not want you to let your admiration blind you to the reality of her situation. She is protecting you because she does not want you hurt."

Adrian was silent for a moment. It was a rather lowering thought that a member of His Majesty's Life Guards was being protected from himself by a chit of a girl—a beautiful girl, but still a girl. Than he brightened. "Do you really think so? That she does care, I mean?"

"Yes I do, but I also think that her devotion to Hel . . . er, Mrs. Gerrard, and her practical nature will keep her from letting it go any further than that. And you should have care, if you are as concerned about her happiness as you appear to be, that you do nothing to make her life more difficult than it is." John's tone was gentle enough, but there was a wealth of concern in his eyes that warned his brother how very seriously he viewed the matter.

John, for all his passion for ministering to the suffering of humanity and saving the souls of the lost, was a supreme realist, more so than his hot-headed brother, and Adrian was forced to accept the truth of what he said, even though he did not want to. He wanted to give Mademoiselle Juliette all the happiness and carefree enjoyment of life that had been stolen from her, and protect her from anything that threatened it further. Surely someone who had suffered as she had and worked as hard as she deserved someone looking out for that happiness, not to mention her safety and welfare.

Adrian wanted to know everything about her, what she liked to do most of all in the world, what foods were her favorite, which songs pleased her most, what flowers she preferred, did she like horses or dogs, or both, walking in the park or the country or reading by the fire. Did she have a family beside the brother she had inadvertently mentioned? What had happened to them? Adrian wanted to know it all, to share it all, to fix it all, to right the wrongs that had been committed and wipe away the shadows that lingered in the depths of those sapphire eyes even when she laughed. But he could not, as John had hinted, he could not ask for all that because it would not bring her happiness, only more pain, just as his exploits in the Peninsula, no matter how well intentioned or heroic, had only brought more desolation and destruction to the people he had come to help.

Or would it? Freddy, on the other hand, seemed to think it would not, or at least that there would be no harm in a few simple excursions, purely for amusement and diversion, of course. Freddy seemed to think that any attention Adrian paid to Mademoiselle Juliette might serve to remedy some of the shortcomings of her unfortunate past rather than recall them. Which of his two brothers was right? And why was it Freddy always the one who seemed to be able to help her to share her artistic passion with her and make her laugh, not Adrian?

There was only one way to find out, one way to address the issue, the only away Adrian had ever dealt with any issue, by plunging into it headlong. And besides, that was what he wanted to do anyway, bring a smile to Mademoiselle Juliette's face, a sparkle to her eyes, and a laugh to her voice. And there was no time like the present. The moment he returned to his quarters he would send a note around inviting her to accompany him to the exhibits at the Egyptian Hall.

Little did Adrian know that at that very moment, the merits of the Egyptian Hall were being hotly debated in the ruthlessly elegant drawing room of a slim house in Brook Street.

"You *promised*, Basil, that you would escort Mama and me," Lady Lavinia fixed her brother with a minatory eye, "and now, the only time you have called on us in eons . . . to beg for more money from Papa, no doubt. What is it, Basil, under the hatches again?"

"No need to be so vulgar, dear sister. It don't become you."

"And it doesn't become the heir of Harcourt to frequent every low gambling hell the city has to offer."

"If my sister were married and off our father's hands, maybe our father would have more blunt to spare to keep his only son and heir plump enough in the pocket that he didn't have to make up the difference until next quarter day at the gambling table. But no, termagant that she is, she cannot even bring her fiancée since birth up to scratch and is not like to, now that her shrewish temper has sent him into the very comforting arms of the ladies of Mrs. Gerrard's."

"Of what?"

"Have care, sister dear," Basil wagged an admonitory finger at her, "Freddy may be too weak to stand up to his father or go against family tradition, but even *he*, easygoing fool that he is, doesn't relish living under the cat's paw, and that lovely little armful he is now visiting at Mrs. Gerrard's won't be encouraging him to do so any time soon, believe me."

"Now it is *you* who is being impossibly vulgar, Basil. I cannot believe that you, low as you are, would bring up such things in a lady's presence, much less her own drawing room."

"Not a lady, my dear sister, you are not gentle or gracious enough to be called that despite your title." Basil flashed his cat-like smile as his sister's unbecomingly angular features grew even more hatchet-like. "And you ignore such things at your peril. Mademoiselle Juliette may be below your notice, but she ain't below ruining your life if you are not careful. You aren't *that* much of a catch, you know, Lavvy. You've the devil's own temper and family tradition is only family tradition, which is not much compared to what a little lovebird like Mademoiselle Juliette has to offer. One look at her in the box at the opera, I hear, and your Freddy was her slave."

"You are disgusting and I do not have to listen to this! Forget about escorting Mama and me to the Egyptian Hall for believe me, I would not be seen there with such a vulgar person even if you were the last man on earth!"

Basil's grin grew wider. "And here I thought you had already dragooned poor Freddy into taking you, but once is not enough, eh Lavvy? But I know you'll still think of some way to bend me to your will"

It was not fair, Lavinia thought for the thousandth time as, striving for dignity, she stalked upstairs to Lady Harcourt's dressing room. *She* was the eldest. *She* should have been born a boy, the one to carry on the Harcourt name with distinction and honor. *She* was the only one with the energy, the determination, and the ambition it took to restore the Harcourts to their former glory. *She* was the one who knew every inch of the estate, every hamlet, every cottage, and every tenant's name while Basil who, if he ever left town at all, confined his visits to their estate to coincide with the races at Newmarket and those not so much for the horses as the odds to be had. She was left with nothing but marriage to further the family fortunes, and even then, it would not be the Harcourt name to which she brought glory, but to the Clavertons. And who were the Clavertons but opportunistic upstarts, brought to prominence by those equally opportunistic upstarts, the Tudors! At least her sons would have Harcourt blood in their veins to make up for the Claverton's inferior breeding, and their mother would raise them to have the proper respect for their heritage. They would learn to conduct themselves with all the propriety and distinction that was due to ancestors who had fought with the Conqueror himself. Basil, miserable worm that he was, was right about one thing, it was time to get started on raising those sons, and there was no time like the present.

"Mama," she marched into the room where Lady Harcourt and her maid were critically surveying several shawls laid out for their owner's perusal, "we *must* invite Wrothingham and his parents to dine with us. We haven't seen them this age, and Freddy . . ."

"But Lavinia dear, we see them all the time in the country, and dinner parties are too fatiguing, all that conversation. Besides, you know Cook is getting older and crosser every year. All those courses—better by far to have a ball where everyone amuses themselves instead of our having to humor them. Now, which do you think? The primrose Kasmir or the lemon-colored silk?"

"I don't know, Mama. What's to the purpose, you will only be wearing it in your own drawing room. Whichever will keep you the warmest." Lavinia's mother spent most of her days on her own couch working her exquisite embroidery in an endless array of fire screens, landscapes in colored silks, and other far less useful articles.

"Oh," Lady Harcourt's hand hovered over yet another shawl, "perhaps a paisley?"

Biting her lip to stifle a stinging retort, Lavinia took a deep calming breath. "But Mama, the Clavertons will think it odd that we do not invite them to dinner. *I* shall talk to Cook. *I* shall see to *everything*. You need not lift a finger." *As was usually the case*, she thought grimly.

"Very well, dear." Lady Harcourt sighed.

"And I shall arrange it for a Tuesday so that Freddy will be bound to escort us to the opera afterward," she announced, her previous dislike of the opera immediately forgotten. "Yes, I think that will do very well indeed. I shall just consult with Cook while you write the invitation." Smiling triumphantly, Lavinia headed off to the nether regions to browbeat the redoubtable Mrs. Timms into agreement while Lady Harcourt, envisioning the coming battle, reached for her vinaigrette.

CHAPTER 16

L ADY LAVINIA PREVAILED, AS SHE USUALLY DID, and the very next Tuesday found Freddy, the duke and the duchess, and an impossibly bored Basil in the Harcourt's dining parlor partaking of a surprisingly elegant dinner. Surveying the turbot with lobster sauce being served him by the footman, Basil remarked laconically, "I can see my sister has done the ordering of the dinner-turtle soup and now this? Undoubtedly the *supreme de volaille* I see being brought in is *aux truffes*. Heaven knows what Cook was threatened with to produce this, though I wager, Your Grace, prefers more solid British fare at your table. You, on the other hand," he smiled slyly at Freddy, I am sure have the most sophisticated of palates. You are fortunate indeed to be getting as discriminating a hostess as Lavvy for your wife."

Freddy was saved from having to do anything more than nod as his father, encouraged to speak on a topic dear to his heart, expounded on the virtues of good plain English food unadulterated with Frenchified sauces and jellies. "There is nothing that ruins a fine piece of British beef so much as covering up the good honest taste with herbs and what not, eh, Basil?" The duke winked broadly as he made short work of his turbot, despite its offending sauce.

In fact, Lady Harcourt need not have worried about the conversational exertions she would be called upon to make since there were no conversations to speak of, the duke and the earl concentrating on the food in front of them and Basil surveying the party with and ironic air, ready to pounce with a cynical observation when called upon, which he wasn't, and Lavinia watching the footmen with an eagle eye to insure they carried out their duties to the letter as befitted the household. It was left to poor Freddy to hazard a few conjectures as to the likelihood of the good weather continuing and the possibility that Lady Harcourt might enjoy some upcoming drives in the park despite her indifferent health.

At last the duke and the earl declared themselves satisfied, the ladies repaired to the drawing room where the duchess was called upon to admire Lady Harcourt's newly complete fire screen before the duchess, Freddy, and Lady Lavinia, and her mother, with Basil tagging along, headed off to the theater.

The Beggar's Opera was not one of Freddy's favorites, and he had already seen it once with Adrian but, feeling guilty that he had neglected his fiancée as much as she claimed he had, he considered himself lucky escaping with the simple penance of escorting her to something that fell below his usual standards. He brightened considerably as he caught sight of Juliette, Grace, and Mrs. Taylor ensconced in the box opposite, and comforted himself with the prospect of comparing notes with them later over one of the snug little suppers that Helen never failed to produce, no matter what time one showed up at her establishment.

The lifting of Freddy's gloom was not lost on Basil who immediately took advantage of it by pointing out the box and its fair occupants *sotto voce* to his sister at the first opportunity.

"Oh do be quiet, Basil! I fail to see why you should think it would be of any interest to me *who* is sitting in that box." Lavinia opened her fan with an irritated snap and waved it gently in front of her face to signify her utter lack of interest. But Basil knew his sister, and he soon saw her beady, close-set eyes darting surreptitiously over her fan in the direction of the box. Smirking, he settled back in his seat, content with the havoc he had wrought before opening his mouth to wreak some more. "Quite a delicious armful." The smirk grew broader as, settling back further in his seat, he crossed his arms over his chest and watched his sister's thin arched brows flatten into what could not have been called anything else, but a ferocious scowl.

"Nonsense! She hasn't nearly enough character to manage Freddy," Lavinia responded tartly before, too late, she realized she had been drawn into a conversation that was utterly beneath her notice. If there was one thing she knew about Freddy, it was that he was ridiculously soft. He simply lacked the spine to take his true place in society. To be sure, no one knew how better to tie a cravat, select a waistcoat or a snuff box, and his manners could be counted on to be exquisite in even the most trying of situations; they simply lacked decisiveness which meant that he was beloved by hostesses, servants, and retainers everywhere and not feared in the least by any one of them which was why he would have no more need for someone as smiling and sweetly yielding as the dainty young woman in the box than he would for a cart horse. He needed someone to assert his authority, to help him take his rightful place in the world as the future Duke of Roxburgh, and no one was more suited to that role than Lady Lavinia Harcourt, Lavvy thought with a good deal of satisfaction.

Candlelight gleamed on golden curls as the woman in the box gracefully turned her head toward the stage below. As her gaze swept the theater, it paused momentarily on Freddy before returning to the men clustered around her and her companions. It was the briefest of looks, filled with innocent curiosity, but Lavinia's blood ran cold with rage and something else that might have been fear, if Lady Lavinia Harcourt feared anything at all, which she did not.

Meanwhile, totally oblivious to the drama unfolding around him, Freddy chatted happily with the countess about the grotto she was having built at Harcourt.

"Nothing too dramatic, you know, but some place cool and refreshing where one can repair after a stroll on a hot summer's day."

"Or simply sit and admire the prospect of Harcourt's magnificent gardens and the fields beyond," Freddy, to whom any sort of physical exertion was anathema, nodded approvingly.

The curtain rose and everyone's attention focused more or less on stage, or at least enough to provide a diversion from all previous conversations. For her part, Lavinia ruthlessly focused her concentration on the scene before her though later during Freddy's futile attempt to discuss the performance with her, it seemed as though she had been completely oblivious to the entire thing.

Juliette, however, *had* paid attention to the action on stage, despite the admirers crowding the box. Like Freddy, she preferred Italian opera, but music of any kind soothed and inspired her. She could see, glancing from time to time at the box opposite, that Freddy felt the same way, though he seemed to be the only one in his box paying even the slightest attention to what was happening on stage. She recognized the despicable Basil and a woman whose features, though far more strongly carved than Freddy's, must be his mother. The woman on the other side of Freddy who seemed to be doing her level best to ignore Basil must be the fiancée, Lady Lavinia Harcourt, while the faded woman with a family resemblance to both Lady Lavinia and Basil could only be their mother. When Juliette looked up during the entr'acte to find herself the victim of the young woman's furious glare, she was sure of the woman's identity, and felt even sorrier for poor Freddy who asked for nothing more in life than to be left alone to enjoy beautiful things.

This woman with her basilisk stare, high bridged nose, and determined mouth would never allow him to do that. This woman wanted him to *be* someone, to become the Duke of Roxburgh the way the Duke of Roxburgh was supposed to be—a force to be reckoned with, and a mate worthy of the future Duchess of Roxburgh. Poor Freddy! She was not unhandsome, this Lady Lavinia. Her features, though strong, were regular enough to be attractive in an angular sort of way, but the determination in the compressed lips and the bold jaw did not bode well for anyone who did not immediately fall in line with the lady's wishes—not a comfortable sort of person at all. No wonder Freddy regularly sought out the congenial atmosphere at Mrs. Gerrard's whether or not Juliette was available to see him.

"I *beg* your pardon, my lord, I was not attending." Juliette caught her name as it was repeated for what must have been the second or third time.

"Yes you were attending, but it was not to me." Lord Huntley grinned good naturedly. "But I do not mind; you are so very lovely that I am as content to look at you as I am to converse with you."

"No." Juliette was contrite. "It was very ill mannered of me to ignore you."

"We are at the opera, after all. It *is* permissible to let your attention wander to the performance on stage once in a while, though you would hardly know it to look at everyone else."

"But still . . ."

"You know me, Mademoiselle Juliette, I consider it an honor just to be seen with you. You have no idea how the fellows look up to me now."

She laughed. "Really?"

"Really." He raised her hand and pressed his lips against the soft white skin.

In the pit below, another observer drew a sharp breath. Lord Adrian Claverton was not a devotee of the opera, but he, knowing that his oldest brother had been dragooned into attending it with his fiancée, had dropped by Mrs. Gerrard's, ostensibly to join in a hand of cards with his other brother and Helen Gerrard, an intention that had dissipated immediately when he learned of Juliette's absence. So he had taken himself off to the opera in the hopes of catching sight of her there, but now that he had, he wished he hadn't come. She was so beautiful—like an angel glowing above him in the light of the chandeliers, an angel who had scores of other earthly admirers. In the back of his mind he knew this, had always known this, but he had not realized until now that it would bother him quite so much.

Rivals of any sort had never bothered Adrian before. Even during his most desperate flirtations, he had been more amused than annoyed by the competition, flattered that so many others desired someone who clearly preferred him. Now he was seized with the irrational and desperate desire to be everything for Juliette, to give her everything so she would lack for nothing and need no one except him—not even Freddy. And, being a man of action who suffered few illusions about himself, he quickly took himself to task. *Well, Adrian, my lad, if you want to be the only one in her life, then it is time to make yourself the only one in her life.*

CHAPTER 17

THE VERY NEXT DAY ADRIAN SET ABOUT following his own advice, and Freddy's as well. After all, it had been Freddy who suggested that he show Juliette the sights of London. Of course he hadn't asked Adrian to steal Juliette away from him, but barely acknowledging his motives to himself, Adrian realized he was setting out to do just that. It was not that he did not want her to enjoy Freddy's company, it was just that watching Juliette's expressive face as she reveled in the music and the singing at the opera had made Adrian happier than he could ever remember. There was an inner glow about her—call it energy, or optimism, or sheer resilience—that made him want to warm his tattered soul with it. He longed to be near her with an ache that was almost physical and utterly inexplicable, to reach out and touch that soft skin, bury his hands in the silky blond curls, and inhale the scent of her warm flesh, to feel intoxicated and comforted all at the same time.

Adrian's first impulse, which took more than his usual self-control to restrain, was to dash over to Mrs. Gerrard's first thing the next morning and ask Mademoiselle Juliette in person if she would join him on an excursion to the Egyptian Hall. Someone as sweet and kind would as Juliette not have the heart to say no to a person's face.

But no one, especially a young woman who had been at the opera and lord knows what else afterwards, would be up at the early morning hour Adrian wanted to see her so he contented himself with exercising off his impatience in a long ride in the park and a hearty breakfast of eggs and a rasher of bacon before sitting down to dash off a very civil invitation that revealed none of his burning eagerness to see her. Then there was nothing to do, but wait.

Fortunately for Adrian, a young woman who had spent much of her young life earning her way in the world was up betimes and wrote back a reply within an hour of receiving the invitation. With a whoop, Adrian was out of his chair where he had been forcing himself to sit reading *The Times* with as much patience as he could muster. "She'll have me, Wilson! I'm off," he shouted shrugging into his jacket as he rushed out the door, giving his servant no time to do anything but nod and observe sagely to himself, "He has it bad this time, does Master Adrian," before returning to polishing the buttons on the jacket he had just finished brushing.

Somehow, Mademoiselle Juliette in broad daylight, her slim hand resting gently on his arm was more ravishing than Mademoiselle Juliette at the opera or in a boxing lesson, or discussing sketches with Freddy. All those other times her mind had been focused on the task at hand, the blue eyes intent with concentration. Now, in a deceptively simple white muslin walking dress, her face framed by the deep ruffles at the neck and a jaunty bonnet of straw-colored satin, she looked absurdly youthful, like a child on a pleasure outing, eyes sparkling with anticipation and a spring in her step so energetic that it might be called a bounce. Her anticipation was as infectious as it was palpable and Adrian could not help thinking how pleasant it was to be doing something with someone who made no effort to conceal her delight, in contrast to the world-weary boredom cultivated by his peers. Not all his peers Adrian amended swiftly; actually Freddy was another one who relished life—a well sung opera, an exquisitely tied cravat or fanciful waistcoat, a beautiful snuff box—which was why Adrian sought him out so often even though Adrian's interests—horses, saving the world, managing his own snug estate to which he would soon return—were vastly different from his brother's.

The unnerving thought that someone who shared Freddy's delight in beauty might be bored by someone interested in horses, saving the world and managing his own estate was ruthlessly squelched.

"It is so kind of you to invite me. I have been longing to see the Egyptian Hall, especially the Roman Gallery."

Adrian couldn't help smiling at Juliette's eagerness. "Freddy told me you were quite the classical scholar."

"Me? Good heavens no. It is just that I enjoy my lessons in Latin and Greek, which I suspect Freddy did not."

"No." Adrian cast his mind back to the schoolroom at Claverton and the stern faced Reverend Thaddeus Wharton. "None of us did . . . well John, but he's different."

Juliette nodded. "My brother loathed lessons too. He . . ." Auguste! She clamped her lips shut. How could she have brought him up when they hadn't seen one another in years, and now, twice she had mentioned him to this virtual stranger who was so very easy to talk to that she forgot everything, including her resolve never to allude to the past. Recovering quickly Juliette continued "It is a rare boy that does not; they have so many enjoyable alternatives whereas girls have only needlework."

"Your brother, the soldier?"

The blue eyes widened in alarm. "How did you know he was a soldier?"

He hadn't. It had been a lucky guess following her reference to her fencing lessons, but apparently he had hit the mark. "You told me during the boxing lesson."

The alarm deepened to panic now. She hoped that he had forgotten, even if she had not. "I . . . I did? I never meant . . . oh dear."

"My dear girl," Adrian took her gloved hand in his, "there is no reason to take on so. Your secrets are safe with me. Believe me, I would die to keep them that way." And oddly enough, looking into those haunted eyes, he meant it. John had been right, there was a great deal more to Mademoiselle Juliette's past than she let on. The proud, graceful bearing, the elegant movements, her refined speech all pointed to a gentle, cultured background. There was a more tragic story than just being forced by economic necessity into becoming an inhabitant of Mrs. Gerrard's.

His clasp was strong and reassuring, his voice deep with conviction. Juliette had no trouble believing every word he said, dramatic as it might sound. He *was* her Saint Michel come to save her. She had no idea why she felt this absolute conviction; dozens of men made promises to her every day, promises that were no more substantial than the soft breeze caressing her cheek or the pale spring sunshine just beginning to break through silvery gray clouds, yet this man told her he would die to keep her secrets and she believed him. He, a son of one of England's most noble families was vowing to protect the honor of a *fille de joie*. No, she told herself, she was not just a *fille de joie*, she was Juliette de Fournoy, and proud of it, not so much of the noble heritage that obsessed her parents, but of her talent and ambition, and her strength and resilience. A golden bubble of happiness rose inside her, and for the first time in longer than she could remember, she felt hopeful. No, it was more than that, she felt good about herself again and he had given that to her. Rashly and generously he had offered himself to a mere Cyprian without a moment of hesitation. No one in her life, not her parents, not even Auguste, had ever wanted to do anything for her until this relative stranger offered her everything. How could she not want to be part of him?

It was not until that moment that Juliette realized all she had lost, the depth of the shame she felt, no matter how well buried, no matter how widely shared with her friends at Mrs. Gerrard's, a shame that had always hovered below the surface, dulling her own self-respect. But now, with a few simple words, this man had given it back to her, this man who was so committed to protecting what he saw as her honor, that he offered to die for it. Juliette felt the sting of tears in her eyes as she struggled to swallow the lump in her throat.

"Mademoiselle?" His voice was incredibly gentle, like a mother's soft caress on her baby's cheek. "What is it? Have I upset you? Believe me, I had no . . ."

"No," she blinked rapidly, trying desperately to stem the tears that threatened to overwhelm her. "No, my lord, you have not upset me, only made me so very . . . happy. Your kindness . . . you have no idea . . . ." Juliette fought to regain her voice suspended by the feelings washing over her. "Your concern means more to me than I can say, more than you can possibly know. Thank you." Regaining her composure, she clasped the hand covering hers and smiled up at him.

But Adrian was not satisfied. The hurt and anguish in her eyes, though quickly banished, had been too deep and Adrian wanted to fix that. Speaking softly, so as not to alarm her further, and almost as though he were talking to himself, he added, "I know if it were my sister, I would *always* love her, *always* want to see her, no matter what had happened to her. Families are stronger than one thinks. Look at mine. The Pater never has a good word to say about Freddy—always going on about his namby-pamby ways, but let anyone agree with him and they will have their head taken off. I would imagine that yours is no different."

"I have no family."

The statement was so matter-or-fact that it sent a chill down his spine. How dreadful to have the break so final, so irrevocable, that anyone else hearing her speak would assume them to be dead, but the pain he had glimpsed in her eyes was too raw to have been caused by death. Death brought sorrow and loss; what he had seen was the hurt, anger, and despair one felt toward the living. And just like that, Adrian made it his goal in life to discover just who Mademoiselle Juliette Fanchon really was and fix it all for her.

The rest of that afternoon he learned, not surprisingly, that she was a charming companion with boundless curiosity and an enthusiasm for learning new things. "It is incredible to me," she declared, examining the carefully gathered artifacts gathered for their viewing, "what with all the wars and one empire conquering another only to fall into decay and be conquered in turn that we have anything left of the civilizations that have gone before us, and yet, in spite of all the history we learn and the proof we have of the glory of civilizations gone by, we feel certain that ours will last where others have not."

"And apparently you do not subscribe to this view of ours as the final lasting civilization?" Adrian paused by a column whose jagged edges spoke more of wanton human destruction than the ravages of time and natural decay.

"No. Nor do I think it a good thing to think that way, for how are we to grow and improve if we feel secure in the belief that our culture will last forever?"

"Then you believe that such change and upheaval are good, that peace and serenity bring stagnation and complacency." He cocked a skeptical eyebrow.

"Noooo ... well, not precisely." Juliette bit her lip. He had her there. She had seen first-hand how the supreme assurance of her parents' breed and generation had lulled them into a false sense of security, blinded them to the reality of their destructive society and dulled their energy and creativity until disaster had struck their supposedly serene world. At the same time, such a state of affairs had given rise, not to improvement of that society, but to the worst excesses of the revolution and a war that engulfed the entire continent.

"Peace and security also give men, and *women*," he flashed her a quick smile, "the time to think and create. After all," he pointed to the magnificent statues of Isis and Osiris, "it was the relative stability of the Egyptian empire that gave rise to the mighty pyramids."

"And yet," Juliette tilted her head provocatively, "for all your talk of peace and its benefits, you are a warrior." *And a magnificent looking warrior at that*, she could not help adding to herself.

"Which is precisely why I am a warrior, to oppose those who would make war, and to secure peace and prosperity for everyone."

The blue eyes were deadly serious now and the teasing note had vanished. Yes, he was her avenging angel come to save mankind from itself. "And what will become of you now that you have done that?"

"Oh. I shall farm."

"Farm?" Try as she would, Juliette could not imagine the bold and fiery Major Lord Adrian Claverton as a farmer.

"Yes, I have an estate near Newmarket, now being looked after by an excellent steward, but soon Caesar and I shall put ourselves out to pasture and raise the best racing studs to be found in all of England."

"Caesar?"

"My horse, and a more trusty comrade in arms you'll not find anywhere."

The warmth in his voice when he spoke of his equine companion tugged at her heart. This was a man who cared deeply about the welfare of others just as he was making it his concern that she enjoy a fine Spring day.

"Raising horses in the country; it sounds heavenly."

Adrian laughed. "A fashionable creature such as yourself, Mademoiselle Juliette, would be bored within a fortnight—no Gunter's, no opera, no linen drapers of any quality to speak of."

Not if I had someone to share it with, a tiny voice whispered in her head, *to talk long walks in the countryside, to make a garden and watch it grow.* "Perhaps, but I would venture to say that people who live there do not find it boring at all," she countered lightly, or at least, she hoped it sounded that way.

"No," he agreed, "it is those who live in the country that make us the nation we are; they feed and clothe us, keep alive the sturdy ancient ways that sustain us, nurture that stubborn independence that is so peculiarly British."

"And it was the thought of them that sustained you fighting in a foreign land?"

"How did you know?" He gripped the gloved hand in his with an intensity that was almost painful.

"Your eyes told me that, even though we are looking at the menagerie of stuffed wild animals, you were seeing something very different."

"Very different indeed," he whispered, raising her hand to his lips. His eyes bore into her very soul, filled with questions and a longing so palpable it scorched her. Involuntarily, her other hand rose to touch his lean brown cheek then checked as she remembered where she was, with a man in a very popular public place.

They stood transfixed for what seemed like forever to Juliette. The world disappeared around them as they gazed at one another, too overwhelmed by dreams that were too beautiful to dream, until the spell was broken by an irritated, well-bred voice. "Really, Basil, we have only just come. There is no need to hurry so."

"Lavinia!" Adrian hissed. "Come." And tucking Juliette's hand firmly under his arm, he led her out into the sunshine and the crowd on Piccadilly.

"I beg your pardon," he slowed his brisk pace to a more companionable stroll, "but that woman casts a damper everywhere she goes, a regular Medusa. One look at her and everything turns to stone. I cannot imagine what threat she held over Basil's head to make him escort her here."

The picture of Basil's battered face, ruthlessly suppressed, rose before her. Major Lord Adrian Claverton was a protector and defender of the innocent, but she had seen the anger in his eyes before he mastered it.

"And yet, it is a fascinating exhibition," she continued. She too was good at hiding her feelings.

"It is not the place, but the company that makes all the difference."

Again, the look that accompanied this observation turned her bones to water. What was it about this particular man that affected her so, touched places in her soul no one had ever touched before? If she were not careful she could end up breaking the one inviolable rule at Mrs. Gerrard's: *never fall in love.* Love? Juliette drew a sharp breath. Was that what this was, the glorious sense of excitement and possibility, and at the same time a sudden feeling of peace and security as if she had arrived home after a long and dangerous journey? Somehow being with Lord Adrian made her feel sheltered from every disaster, shielded from everything that haunted her from the past. And it was all an illusion, a wonderful glorious illusion, but an illusion, nevertheless, conjured up by her own, never-acknowledged longing for something she could never have—a home with a loving husband and a family. Ruthlessly, Juliette thrust this glorious vision aside. "I imagine, now that you have spent time with your family you are longing to get back to your estate."

CHAPTER 18

WHETHER OR NOT ADRIAN WAS TRULY LONGING to get back to his estate quickly became a moot point, thanks to a certain ambitious Corsican who chose that particular moment to land on a beach at Golfe Juan and begin his triumphal march toward the French capital.

"Damn and blast!" Adrian muttered when a messenger, sent by his father, whose political connections made him one of the first to know of Napoleon's return, relayed the news. Throwing on his jacket, Adrian abandoned the glass of port he had been nursing in front of the fire, not to mention tantalizing thoughts of Juliette and sundrenched days in the country. "I'm off to headquarters," he shouted over his shoulder to Wilson as he charged down the stairs and headed off to Portman Square.

In no time at all, the news was everywhere. Even Jeanne, Juliette's nurse, and the only one from the small émigré community who loved her former charge enough to be privy to her secrets, arrived at Mrs. Gerrard's wild-eyed and out of breath. "I know you do not like me to visit you here, Mademoiselle," the gaunt-cheeked older woman apologized, "but I could not waste the time arranging another meeting place. Poor Madame and Monsieur, they were only waiting for the weather to improve before returning to the chateau Auguste has been readying for their arrival. Now he will have to go fight *le Monstre* and once again their hopes and dreams are only so much dust."

Ever since Bonaparte had been packed off to Elba, the Comte and Comtesse de Fournoy, along with all their compatriots, had been in a fever of anticipation at returning to their homeland. In their monthly meetings in the park Jeanne had kept her former charge abreast of the news. "It will be like the old days, Mademoiselle," the faithful retainer had announced happily, her lined face looking almost youthful in her joy at the news of the Corsican monster's defeat.

Juliette had not had the heart to warn her that after more than two decades of revolutionary rule, the world had changed considerably, but then she had never been able to convince her parents of that irrevocable change and they certainly had more intellectual resources at their disposal than did simple, loyal Jeanne who risked everything by keeping in touch with her disgraced *petit chou*.

Juliette never knew just exactly how Jeanne had managed to track her down at Olivia's and finally to Mrs. Gerrard's, but she was aware that servants had a vast network of contacts and access to information that even someone like Juliette who worked for her living, could not breach. At first she had been defensive and guilt-stricken by the sadness in her old nurse's eyes when she had finally run Juliette to ground at Mrs. Gerrard's, but then, she had slowly come to realize that the sadness rose from compassion rather than condemnation, and that the servant's very presence was proof of her continuing love for her charge, which had always led Juliette to ask herself the same question over and over again. If a servant could feel this way, how could her own mother not? How could her own mother turn her own daughter out on the street into a world of strangers without a backward glance?

"I do not know what to do, Mademoiselle," Jeanne's voice broke into Juliette's reflections. "They cannot stand the loss of everything all over again. The Monsieur, he has a will of iron, but he is old, and the Madame, well she is becoming frail and needs the luxuries she was accustomed to. I am afraid this will kill them both."

Juliette refrained from retorting that two people who had survived the loss of a daughter would very likely survive the loss of unrealistic expectations, but Jeanne would never believe her, much less understand. She looked into the servant's eyes, eyes that were starting to betray the dimness of age, and saw the plea in them, faint though it was.

"What? What would you have me do?"

"If you could but come home, take care of them, reassure them that the English milord you told me about and his fellow soldiers will beat *le Monstre* back forever this time."

Juliette snorted. "They would not listen, Jeanne. They would never let me cross their threshold; you know that!" *And I would never cross it myself or give them the time of day ever again,* she muttered to herself, even as she realized that her own pride and stubbornness were more than equal to her parents'. But then, she had been born into a different generation. Nothing had been taken from her, and she could feel only impatience with people who did nothing to improve the harsh lot they were constantly complaining about. Her mother might sigh for the beeswax candles that had once lighted their chateau by the hundreds, but she scorned her daughter for working to earn them. The Comtesse might bemoan their lack of heat and their cramped quarters, but she had dismissed her daughter for disgracing the family by taking up a real occupation to support them instead of picking up a few pennies here and there working on embroidery in the atelier of respectable émigrés. Oh yes, Juliette too had her pride, and it consisted of being able to earn her keep and set some money aside to provide for her own future instead of waiting for the old ways of life to return, which everyone knew they never would.

"They are different now, Mademoiselle, frailer, worn down by years of making do and worrying about your brother fighting under foreign masters to defeat *le Monstre*."

Auguste, their pride and joy, their good child who had kept the family honor intact because a man could earn his keep without disgracing his family, especially if he were a soldier. Juliette shook her head. "You know they would both rather die than accept me back. The best I can do, the only thing I can do, is to tell you what Major Lord Adrian Claverton has assured me, on the few occasions he has spoken to me about his service in Spain which is that Wellington is as good a general as Napoleon, if not better. Tell *Maman* and *Papa* . . ." Juliette stumbled over their names, her eyes stinging with unexpected tears, " . . . tell them to go join their king in exile, for assuredly, the English will not let anyone but Louis rule France, and *Maman* and *Papa* will have their home at last."

Jeanne was forced to be satisfied with that. Smiling bleakly, she patted her former charge's cheek with a careworn hand. "I will do as you suggest, Mademoiselle. I only hope you are right. And I hope the English milord . . ."

" . . . has already gone to join his regiment, I am sure," Juliette finished briskly. "Take care, Jeanne."

Juliette smiled encouragingly as the servant took her leave, but the smile faded as soon as she closed the door to her chamber. In fact, she had no idea if Adrian had gone to headquarters or not, but in her experience with soldiers, at least her father and her brother, they forgot everything—wives, children, sisters—at the first hint of battle. Obviously Adrian, despite his patent admiration, despite his clear enjoyment of her company, was one of those, and not so devoted to her that he would not forget all about Juliette Fanchon the moment the chance for glory and adventure appeared. Despite his sympathy and understanding, he was a man after all and just like the other men she knew, her father and her brother, he would undoubtedly find war more compelling than a woman or a family.

For years Auguste had been her playmate and closest friend, giving her the love her parents had not. Oh, the Comte and Comtesse had been proud of their beautiful daughter with her exquisite manners, graceful carriage and sprightly conversation, but never in their lives had they shown that they cared for her. It had been Auguste and Jeanne who had comforted her when she had fallen and skinned her knee. It was Auguste who had carved an awkward wooden doll, the only toy she had ever had. Auguste had shared his stories of school-boy pranks at the Abbe de Broglie's academy and taught her how to fight with swords, even listened to her dreams of being a great modiste, but the moment he had been old enough to fight for real, he had gone off to win back his country without a second thought for the lonely sister he was leaving behind. Now it was clear that Major Lord Adrian Claverton was going to do the same thing. Juliette sighed gently and picked up her sketchbook to work on her latest idea of a carriage dress for Dora.

Lord Adrian had been a lovely dream anyway, something out of the normal pattern of existence, someone who was interested in her, someone more inter-ested in amusing her and tending to her comforts rather than the other way around—a novelty in Juliette's life. Helen was right to be concerned for Juliette's happiness. It was far too seductive a situation to continue, one that could lead to dangerous hopes and dreams, impossible hopes and dreams for someone like Juliette.

"May we come in?" Grace and Dora peeped around the edge of her door.

"But of course."

"Dora told me you were working on something very à la mode for her, may I see?"

Juliette handed them the sketchbook. "Beautiful!" Grace breathed.

"But practical, like our Dora here. I have designed the barouche wrap to be eye-catching with its heavy embroidery, but when it is removed, and if one exchanges the bonnet for a cap, one has a simple half dress that suits many purposes."

"You are indeed a genius. And I shan't be the least surprised if it catches the eye of a certain someone who is too busy to idle away his hours on promenades in the park."

Grace's saucy smile was not lost on Juliette who turned quickly enough to catch the unflappable Dora stifling a self-conscious little smile without much success. "Why Dora, can it be some young man has actually made an impres-sion on your jaded, critical soul?"

"Juliette, you *know* Helen will not allow us having thoughts like that; it makes us weak and forgetful of our independence!"

"Nevertheless," Grace smiled knowingly, "a certain handsome new footman *does* seem to have won approval rather quickly from someone usually account-ed to be a very tough customer indeed."

"Oh Grace, always full of imagination and daydreams. It will get you into trouble one day." Dora shook her head, but there was no denying the sparkle in her eyes or the faint tinge of red on her cheek.

"It's Tom Sandy's, Major Lord Adrian's former batman, as handsome as they come and so devoted to his little Alice. Who would not have a soft spot for a poor widowed soldier and devoted father?" Grace laid a hand on Dora's shoulder. "I was only teasing, you know, but it is clear that he admires you too, and not just because you are pretty. Anyone can see he likes your boundless energy, not to mention your way with household accounts."

"Well he won't be admiring them for long if old Boney has his way. I expect Lord Adrian will be wanting his batman back again soon, and then what will become of Alice?" Somber now, Dora gazed out the window where the trees in the square seemed to have become full and green overnight.

"We'll think of something, some reason to keep her here with us. It's time she learned needlework, and if she is clever at it, I could use her hemming handkerchiefs and chemises." Juliette pointed to a work basket overflowing with just those sorts of projects.

"Do you really think Lord Adrian will have to go fight?"

"It is not a case of having to, Dora. Men, soldiers like Lord Adrian, live to throw themselves into a glorious cause, and what cause could be more glorious than saving all of Europe?" Juliette had not meant to sound cynical, but she could see that she had shocked her friends. They, however, had not seen a father ride off to war, sure of the rightness of his cause and the inevitability of victory, only to return a bitter and broken man. They had not pleaded with an adored brother to stay at home and care for his loved ones only to see him ride off gaily to fruitless years of following one leader after another in the hopes of conquering the unconquerable conqueror, only to have that conqueror rise again, more swiftly and powerfully than before. Lord knew where Auguste was now. The last she had heard, he and his fellow officers had been with Wellington in the Peninsula, but then all contact had been cut off with her parents and even Jeanne was not sure of details except that he had been trying to win back the family estate.

"But surely, that is a noble thing, is it not?"

"Of course it is." Seeing genuine concern for her in Grace's eyes, Juliette relented. "It's just that it can be rather tiresome, all that questing for honor and glory." *And worrisome*, a tiny little voice, too strong to be ignored, echoed in her head and in her heart.

CHAPTER 19

B UT JULIETTE WAS WRONG. She had not been forgotten. In fact, Adrian's first thought, once he had confirmed the news of Napoleon's victorious march towards Paris, was of her and savoring every moment in her company before the inevitable happened and he was sent off to put a stop to the Corsican's boundless ambition once again.

Juliette had barely finished uttering her disparaging words when Rose appeared bearing a note addressed to Mademoiselle Fanchon in a dashing masculine script.

Grace nodded sagely to Dora. "Freddy is far too artistic to write so bold a scrawl, and Lord Huntley far too self-effacing, besides which, Helen has steered Lord Huntley towards Grace now that the Claverton brothers are taking up so much of Juliette's time and attention."

"Judging from her expression, I would say you are quite correct. See how she colors up? It is an assignation, I am sure, with the handsome major."

"The two of you make a great deal too much of it. You are nothing more than common gossips." Juliette shook her head in disgust. "It is nothing like an assignation. He merely writes to ask if I would like to accompany him to the British Museum."

Dora laughed outright. "And when a man selects an outing intended to appeal to a lady's mind rather than her heart, he is well and truly on his way to being in love, for why else, if he were not in love with her, would he waste time on her intellect, I ask you?"

"She is right you know," Grace nodded, smiling.

Juliette sighed in bemused resignation. There was nothing she could say to convince them otherwise, nor did she actually want to, for in her heart of hearts, so deeply buried that she could not even admit it to herself, she wanted them to be right. She wanted to be accepted . . . no, she wanted to be appreciated as a person, a thinking person, not just an object, a refined and beautiful object, but an object, nevertheless.

Adrian's expression when he came to collect her told her all she needed to know, that Grace and Dora were right; he *was* looking forward to her company, not just feasting his eyes on her face and figure. And oddly enough, in the grip of a perverse whim that she could not quite explain, Juliette had dressed in her plainest attire, a white twilled sarsnet pelisse trimmed only with white satin and worn over a simple white cambric walking dress, the only color in her ensemble being sandals and gloves of green kid and a matching green ribbon on her bonnet.

"I hope you do not mind riding in my curricle, a remnant of my salad days, I admit, but the weather is so fine I thought you might enjoy it. I have sent my groom on ahead to take care of the horses so that Rose, that is your maid's name is it not, can sit in his seat." Adrian grinned, almost sheepishly, it seemed to Juliette. "I thought she might enjoy it, and I did not want you seen riding alone with a man in an open carriage."

"How very dashing," Rose murmured at the back as Adrian, having helped her in as well, took his own seat.

And how very kind. Juliette marveled to herself at the irony of his caring about the reputation of someone who, at best, would be labeled a *fashionable impure* by the rest of the world.

"I thought, having visited the Egyptian Hall, you might appreciate the real thing." Adrian maneuvered skillfully around a wagon whose weary horse looked askance at the fashionable bays pulling the elegant equipage.

"So you have your doubts as to the authenticity of the marvels we saw at the Egyptian Hall?"

Adrian chuckled. "Let us just say, that my time spent soldiering has turned me into something of a cynic."

"How sad. We shall have to do something about that. Cynicism in one so young—tragic."

Privately, Adrian thought that a smile so charming, accompanied by an enchanting dimple and a mischievous glint in the eyes smiling up at him could go a long way into turning him into a believer in infinite possibilities—beauty happiness, the goodness of life, even love itself—but he thrust these feelings to the back of his mind. It was too soon even to think of such things. She had already been hurt so much in her short life, and his future, not to mention the future of all of Europe, was decidedly uncertain at this particular moment. No, best not to think about anything except the fineness of the day and the pleasure of the outing and savor the moment as it should be savored—to its very fullest.

Adrian's groom hurried to the horses' heads as the curricle entered the court in front of Montague House's imposing façade and stopped in front of the shallow steps. Adrian jumped down, handed the reins to the groom and, with a gallant flourish, led Juliette into the main hall.

"Oh!" Mistress and maid could not help exclaiming at the sheer vastness of the place, and their guide, eager to show Juliette all the wonders inside, was forced to wait with as much patience as he could muster as they took it all in—the long stairway fading into the distance with three enormous giraffes standing guard at the top.

"There is so much to see, so many treasures all gathered in one place. One could live here and still never see them all." Juliette's hand tightened on Adrian's arm as she gazed, wide-eyed around her. "But I do admit to a longing to see Sir William Hamilton's vases most of all, though of course there are the Townley marbles, the Rosetta stone . . ." her voice trailed off at the sheer richness of it all.

"You seem remarkably well informed, Mademoiselle, and decisive too," Adrian raised a quizzical brow, calling attention to the thin white scar just below it.

"I am," the dimple reappeared at the corner of her mouth. "I purchased a copy of *The New Picture of London* in preparation for our outing so I would not waste a minute of time."

"Your time or mine? And here I was counting on impressing you with my worldly knowledge as I guided you expertly through the exhibits."

"Let us call it *our* time, shall we?"

"A good answer, Mademoiselle, clever, yet diplomatic. It is easy to understand why you are so sought after . . . quite apart from your obvious beauty, of course."

"Oh beauty," she dismissed it with a shrug, "anyone can have beauty; that is simply a matter of style and taste."

"For you, perhaps. Tell that to my sister, though, and you will be dismissed as a madwoman."

"Your sister is not beautiful? How could one belong to a family of three splendid brothers and not be beautiful? *Non*," the blond curls danced around her face as she shook her head.

"Try convincing her of that. *She* will not believe *you*. Her last modiste called her a *great gawky thing* before throwing up her hands in despair and leaving. And Lavinia hints at it, ever so delicately, of course, by calling her an *Amazon* in a funning sort of voice."

An Amazon, Juliette thought, was still better than being the mean-eyed, hatchet-faced woman she had seen at the opera. "Then it was the modiste who was at fault, not your sister. It is up to the modiste to make the patron attractive, not the other way around."

"Spoken like a true artist." He found the sparkle in Juliette's eyes, the intensity in her voice, and the determined set of her chin which betrayed a passion that was compellingly attractive and, Adrian realized with some surprise, unique among all the women he had ever known. Oh they had been passionate enough in a variety of ways, ranging from smashed Sevres figurines to languorous caresses to intimately acrobatic positions that even he, athlete that he was, had found challenging, but none of them had been passionate about something other than themselves and their relationship to him. Juliette's passion was pure, inspiring, and, to Adrian, who had his own causes that drove him, utterly irresistible.

Studying him out of the corner of her eye, Juliette wondered just what was going on behind that handsome face with the eyes that missed nothing. "Just ask Freddy, I am sure he would agree with me."

"I am sure he would." Adrian rubbed his jaw thoughtfully, "And I am sure he would be the first to ask you to work your magic with Georgie, unless he has already?"

She shook her head.

"Well then it is only a matter of time before he does." Adrian could not help feeling slightly gleeful that for once had stolen a march on Freddy and made a mental note to broach the subject with his brother later. "I am sure the two of you would get along famously."

"We would?"

"Certainly. Georgie is a no-nonsense sort of person just like you."

"I am?"

"Well of course you are. What other sort of woman would read a guidebook when she has been invited by a gentleman to tour a museum?" Her independence rankled, but Adrian was not about to admit it to himself, much less let on to Mademoiselle Juliette that it had affected him in the least. "And why is it, by the way, that you particularly wish to see the vases first?"

"The drapery."

"The what?"

"The drapery." Juliette rather enjoyed his complete befuddlement. It was so rare that she truly felt she had any advantage over anyone that she could not help reveling in the moment. Oh yes, the gentlemen who visited her were completely at the mercy of their physical urges, so, in that sense, she had the advantage, but this was different and she found herself savoring the power, just the tiniest bit, fleeting though it might be. Then she took pity on him. "Yes. The Greeks were known for their drapery, or, I should say, their simplicity of dress whose drapery is one of its major ornaments. Capture the art of drapery and one captures the art of fit and movement—the keys to making any garment becoming to anyone."

"I stand corrected, Mademoiselle Juliette. And here I thought this was a simple pleasure expedition. Do you ever do anything just for the pure fun of it?'

The ripple of her laughter floated through the hall. "No, my lord, never."

"Well then," Clasping her chin with his long lean fingers he tilted it, forcing her to look up at him, "you should."

Blue eyes held blue eyes for one long breathless moment, then he released her to slide that hand down her arm to cup her elbow, his fingers warm and strong though the material of her pelisse and her dress. "Come along then, let us see what wonders await."

CHAPTER 20

TOURING THE MUSEUM WAS A GLORIOUS DISTRACTION from Juliette's routine and Adrian's uncertain future, from life itself, and they enjoyed it immensely, wandering like children from room to room, gazing in awe as new treasures appeared before their eyes at every turn. No one else was in the galleries, and even Rose, trailing behind wrapped in her own awed silence, ceased to exist. They laughed and teased, pointed and discovered, much the way Adrian and his brothers had roaming the woods and fields, streams and ponds of Claverton.

From Sir William Hamilton's vases they sauntered through the Townley marbles, pausing for Juliette to admire the Townley Venus. "More draperies," Adrian murmured wickedly, eyeing the statue's perfect breasts. "Of a graceful, but *minimal* nature."

Juliette refused to be drawn. "Not all women are similarly endowed, hence the need for more complete clothing than this goddess, not to mention a skillful modiste."

Adrian grinned, "No one could say you are not single-minded!"

But as they strolled around the circular room admiring the magnificent Discobolus from all angles, Juliette sensed Adrian's attention wandering elsewhere. "What is it? Oh dear," she clapped a hand to her mouth, "there is something else you wish to see. *Imbecile!*"

Adrian looked up in some dismay, but since the epithet he had clearly been meant for herself he smiled, banishing the dark thoughts that had been haunting him. "I admit I would like to see the Rosetta Stone." How easily the lie came when her happiness was involved.

"But of course! *Ah que je suis bete!* I am sorry. I have been selfish looking only at all those things I wanted to see."

He took her hands into his, smoothing the soft leather of her gloves with his thumbs, "Do not distress yourself, Mademoiselle. You cannot know how happy it makes me to see your delight in these treasures."

The warmth of his touch, even through her gloves, moved her in a way no one else's ever had. It felt so right, so natural, as though somehow she was where she belonged, hand in hand with him. Her mind dismissed that thought as absurd as quickly as the rest of her body knew it was meant to be. "Ah, ah," she cleared her throat, fighting to regain her composure. "It is one positive thing that has come out of this war, *non*?"

"How so?"

"Well, it has advanced our knowledge of the history of mankind, and even though the French were forced to hand it over to the British when they lost Egypt, it was collaboration between British and French scholars that brought about the translation of the Demotic text."

"Once again, Mademoiselle, you are way ahead of me. You are indeed a paragon of learning." Adrian was not sure whether he was charmed or frustrated by her superior knowledge.

"Pooh, not so much as you might think. I had all that from Lord John only a few days ago."

"My brother?" Adrian wished he had something clever to contribute to this conversation, to this entire outing, instead of echoing her stupidly like some naïve schoolboy.

"Yes," she continued serenely, clearly enjoying his discomfiture. "When he was giving us holy service, well, after, to be exact, I mentioned our excursion and, since he is a friend of Mr. Young who has been working on the Demotic text, he told me about it."

First Freddy, then John. His brothers seemed always to be one step ahead of him lately and, much as Adrian liked and yes, even admired, his brothers, he wished that in this particular case they were nowhere around. Forcing himself to adopt an expression of polite interest, he continued, "So John performed church services, did he?"

"Yes, it was ever so kind of him, though I believe it was actually Dora who put the thought into his head. You have no idea . . ." Juliette paused for a moment, picturing the ladies of Mrs. Gerrard's on their knees in reverent silence, some of them with tears running down their cheeks as John had spoken the dear familiar words from the *Book of Common Prayer*, "no idea how much it means to everyone. He is indeed a good man, a Godly man. We are so grateful to him."

"And you?" Try as he would, Adrian could not quell the dog-in-the- mangerish thoughts clambering in his head; he only hoped they didn't show.

"I . . . I . . . thought it was very kind of him."

And then it occurred to him that, of course, she was probably Catholic. "It must have been difficult for your fam . . . er . . . you to find a place to worship all these years."

"Not necessarily. A great number of French priests fled to England during the revolution, you know."

And if he had thought he would discover anything further about her family by asking her that question, Adrian scolded himself, he was fair and far off. She was much too cool a customer to fall for it and, blast it, it only made him admire her all the more.

"But your brother did invite me to join them in spite of our differences in religion." And it had proved a solace to her as well as the other girls. Despite the lack of incense and a service spoken in English instead of Latin, the solemn incantations, the mumbled prayers of the others, inaudible at first, then louder as they felt the comforting power of the words wash over them, Juliette had been transported back to the Spanish Chapel in Manchester Square, kneeling between her parents, her rosary in her hands, with Auguste on the other side of her father, his mind clearly someplace far more adventurous than the chapel's dim interior. It had felt so real that it had been something of a shock when, opening her eyes after a prayer, she had seen Dora next to her instead of the Comtesse de Fournoy.

Juliette had not admitted anything about her past or her family, but Adrian could tell from the faraway look in her eyes that she was thinking of them. And then it occurred to him how he might discover more about the true identity of Mademoiselle Juliette Fanchon. While it was true that many priests and many families had escaped from France during the revolution, it still had not been all *that* many. How many of them had had a daughter Juliette's age and a son who was a soldier serving with the Comte d'Artois? Surely a priest would know—the *right* priest would know—and he was willing to bet that John, who had wide-ranging charitable and scholarly interests, might know just which priest to ask. Adrian resolved to speak to his brother right after he had completed another important task he had set for himself.

It was not so uncommon for dashing military men to frequent one of London's most celebrated book sellers, the clerk at Hatchards' told himself when Adrian strode into the shop the next morning, but more often than not they were purchasing books of poetry or the latest novel to give to a young lady or, possibly, just possibly, a book of military history for themselves. They certainly did not ask for something as rare or scholarly, not to mention valuable as Tischbein's engravings of Sir William Hamilton's Greek vases.

The clerk examined Major Lord Adrian Claverton more closely. Certainly he looked like one of those devil-may-care lunkheads who, when not riding into the fray without regard for life, limb, or much of anything else, spent their days hanging about Tattersall's arguing the finer points of equine bloodlines or beating one another to a pulp at Jackson's or shooting at Manton's.

Correctly interpreting the clerk's skeptical stare, Adrian flipped critically through the volume the clerk was eventually able to unearth. "I don't suppose you have all four volumes?"

Again, the clerk's eyes registered a hint of surprise. "No, sir, just the one."

"Well then, I suppose I must make the best of it."

"We do have Mr. Kirk's one volume rendition which is a good deal less . . ."

Adrian, who was not about to give the insolent puppy the least bit of satisfaction by betraying in any way the careful coaching he had been given by his brother John, a frequenter of Hatchards' and any number of other book sellers catering to the scholarly crowd, cut him off with an impatient wave of the hand. "I prefer the Tischbein, thank you."

Having procured the precious folio, Adrian tucked it carefully under his arm, making his way as quickly as possible along Piccadilly towards St. James' Square. The odds of finding Mademoiselle Juliette *at home* were slim to none, but Adrian was too excited by his purchase to wait. He only wished he could see her face when she received it, but if he couldn't, no matter, he simply wanted her to have it as soon as possible so she would know he was thinking of her.

As luck would have it, when Adrian reached the square he saw Juliette and Rose approaching from the other side. But even as he was assuring himself that the two ladies were in fact Juliette and Rose and not just apparitions of an overactive imagination where Juliette was concerned, he caught a movement out of the corner of his eye, a carriage coming from King Street at an unusually fast pace for such a short street whose only entrance and exit was the square. Even as he registered this, the carriage picked up speed as it rounded the corner and Adrian broke into a run, catching up with Juliette just in time to push her to safety as the carriage careened over the curb at the exact spot where she had just been standing. Barely keeping from turning over, the carriage righted itself and clattered around the square and out towards Jermyn Street and anonymity.

CHAPTER 21

"MADEMOISELLE JULIETTE, ARE YOU ALL RIGHT?" Naturally Adrian's first concern was for her though a part of him wished he had gotten a better look at the carriage whose sudden and suspicious appearance and equally sudden disappearance seemed far from accidental.

"Ye . . . yes." Struggling to catch her breath, more from the surprise of it all rather than shock or fright, Juliette was having some difficulty reconstructing the sequence of events that had taken her from a brisk stroll in the park to being swept into Major Lord Adrian Claverton's arms and thrust against the iron railings in front of Mrs. Gerrard's. In fact, she was still clasped in his arms, and finding it remarkably reassuring, when, unfortunately, he recollected himself and, gently setting her away from him, scanned her face anxiously, his eyes dark with concern.

Summoning up a tremulous smile, she gently touched his cheek. "Truly, I am quite all right, thanks to you, and no thanks to the driver who should know better than to take a turn like that at such a speed."

"Thank God you are unhurt." But there was no sign of relief, no lessening of concern in his steady gaze. In fact, it seemed to deepen, darkening into anger, as he stood there his hand on her arms, warm and strong even through her pelisse.

"My lord?" Ever so gently, Juliette traced the fine white scar that running up his cheek to just below the eye as she looked at him curiously. "I am safe now, thanks to you. There is no further cause for alarm. I fear you have been on the battlefield too long." She had seen him go to that dark place before, just as she herself was sometimes dragged unwillingly back to the past. It gave them a kinship, but at the same time, it made her uneasy.

He captured the hand gently caressing his cheek, her touch burning his skin far more than the sabre cut ever had, and brought it to his lips. "Fortunately I have, and it has kept my senses alert enough to recognize danger almost before it starts, and even in the most peaceful of settings." He glanced around the now serene square.

Her eyes were soft with sorrow. "I know, and I am grateful, but at the same time it makes me sad that you still see danger everywhere."

"And you do not?" He gathered her other hand in his, pressing both of them to his chest as though he would again pull her into the safety of his arms.

Her pupils widened, and the soft lips opened, but no sound came out. For a moment they stood there, to all intents and purposes the only people in the world, bound together by pasts filled with danger and pain. A soft sigh escaped her as her lips curved into a rueful smile of acknowledgment. "Touché, my lord, but I only use my wariness to make me cautious, not suspicious. There is a difference, you know."

He was about to respond in his own defense, but Rose, who had been trailing some paces behind her mistress, recovered from her own shock and hurried forward, oblivious to everything except Juliette's safety, even to Lord Adrian staring down at her with his heart in his eyes. "Miss Juliette, Miss Juliette, you are not hurt?"

"No Rose, I am quite unhurt, thanks to the Major here."

"Oh. Rose suddenly attuned to her surroundings, blushed furiously. "My lord, I do beg your pardon for bursting in . . ."

"It is quite all right."

Rose's blush deepened as she felt the full effects of the Major's devastating smile and, desperate to regain her composure, she cast her eyes to the pavement where the folio, wrapped in paper and string, lay forgotten. "Oh my goodness," she stooped to retrieve it, "a package.

"Why thank you, Rose." Adrian took it from her nerveless grasp. "I had quite forgotten it in all the excitement." Dusting it off with his handkerchief, he handed it to Juliette.

"For me?"

"For you." In a million years he would never forget the look of surprise and delight as she took the package from him. She had no idea what it was, and, according to most women he knew, the best, the most expensive gifts usually came in small packages, but she did not care. The sheer excitement of receiving a present shone in her eyes.

"Here." Adrian held out his hand. "It is rather awkward. I can carry it inside for you."

"Then by all means, let us go inside!" Completely forgetting her near escape, Juliette led the way up the steps where Tom Sandys stood smiling and holding the door. "Mademoiselle Juliette, my lord." His smile remained, but Adrian could read the question in his eyes. "Later, Tom, we shall talk later."

"Very good, my lord."

They proceeded to the drawing room where Juliette seated herself at a small table as Adrian placed the package in front of her.

"May I open it?"

"Of course!" Again the eagerness in her face tore at his heart.

Carefully, but obviously fighting the urge to tear off the wrappings she untied the string and pulled back the paper. The slender fingers trembling with anticipation were nothing like those he had seen wielding a needle with such deft assurance. "Oh!" One hand flew to her lips as, recognizing it instantly for what it was, she gazed in astonishment, and once again, Adrian was forced to acknowledge that this *fille de joie* was a great deal better informed and better educated than the youngest son of the Duke of Roxburgh.

"How exquisite!" Juliette opened the pages to a drawing of a young girl dancing and ran her hand reverently down the page. "And how very thoughtful of you, my lord." A smile tugged at one corner of her mouth making her dimples dance, "And exceedingly clever of you as well to know just how much I would enjoy it."

Suddenly Adrian did feel rather clever, and inordinately proud of himself, but Mademoiselle Juliette had that effect on people. She had it on Freddy, for example, and one admirer in particular he had noticed in her box that night at the opera. A more cynical man would have told himself that making men feel pleased with themselves was the stock in trade for the Mademoiselle Juliettes of the world, but Adrian, despite his experience with women and the world, was not a cynic, nor did he believe that the smile in her eyes was anything but genuine, or anything but the very special smile she reserved just for him. It was too open, too full of pure and unadulterated joy to be anything else. And that joy lifted his own spirits despite his own dark suspicions concerning the barely averted accident, despite the threat of war hanging over him.

Smiling in return, he took her hands in his. "I could not help myself, Mademoiselle, I wanted you to have something to remember me . . . er, our trip to the museum, and I thought you might like to refer to some of these drawings when you are making your own designs."

"How . . ." Juliette struggled to capture a thousand thoughts and feelings without being able to articulate a single one. "How perfect," she finished simply, but her face told it all, and she could see in his eyes that he understood everything she wanted to say. "Thank you." She reached across the table to take his hands in her own, hands that were so much like the man—beautifully shaped with long lean fingers, strong and tanned and capable of holding a powerful horse in check or gently stroking her palm as they were doing now, comforting, caressing, and with an intimacy that brought the blood rushing to her cheeks. How absurd it was. Men did more than this to her every day and she never felt anything, but it was the tenderness, the closeness that nearly overset her, she who had not only been taught at a tender age, but also had severely schooled herself never to lose her composure ever!

"It is the most wonderful gift, and I should like to stay here looking at it with you, but I promised Dora I would have the finishing touches on her new carriage dress completed in time for a ride in the park this afternoon." Rising, Juliette tucked the book under her arm, as elegantly as she could and headed for the door. "I assure you I shall spend a great many happy hours studying these designs." *And thinking of you*, she could not help adding to herself as she tried to make what was a barefaced cowardly escape look like a graceful exit.

But Adrian was not fooled in the least—the faint flush on her cheeks betrayed her—and, congratulating himself once again on being so clever, accepted his somewhat abrupt dismissal with aplomb, before going off to find Tom Sandys.

The footman was still at his post by the front door. "My lord?"

"What is this *my lord*, Tom? No *Major, sir*? You have gotten very fine in your powdered wig and knee breeches, not too fine, I hope, to deal with the likes of a poor soldier, your former master, for example?"

The former batman grinned. "No, my . . . er . . . Major, sir."

"Not getting soft are you in all your finery and this comfortable berth, are you?"

The grin widened. "No, Major, sir, though, if I may say so, I am most grateful to you for finding me a place where I can be with my little Alice."

"And I hope she is doing well. 'Tis a sad thing for a girl to lose her mother."

"She is doing very well, thank you, sir. The ladies are being ever so kind, making sure she knows her letters and learns her needlework."

Adrian nodded sagely. "I thought as much. And you, Tom, not finding the work too tame?"

"Well, sir, it is certainly quieter, as you must be finding it yourself, sir."

"Not for long, though, Tom, not for long." Adrian gazed off over the square for a moment, then fixed him with a keen look. "What do you say, will you come with me?"

"Wherever you wish, sir."

Adrian was silent for a moment, more touched than he could say by the man's instant and unhesitating reply. "I am afraid it won't be pretty, but I expect it will be short. I shall clear it with Mrs. Gerrard and make sure that Alice is taken care of. It would not feel right to head off to what might just be the greatest battle in history without you."

"Much obliged. Thank you, sir. You just give me the word."

"As soon as I have it. But in the meantime," Adrian moved a little back in the hall and lowered his voice, "you didn't happen to see the little incident before you opened the door to Mademoiselle Juliette, did you?"

"No, sir, though I did hear a carriage moving powerful fast around the square."

"It was moving *powerful fast*, too fast. I am sorry you did not get a look at it, for I am sure it was up to no good."

"In St. James' Square?"

"Yes, even in St. James' Square. Evil lurks everywhere, Tom. It narrowly missed knocking Mademoiselle Juliette down, and no, in spite of the high esteem in which you hold the square, it was *not* an accident, of that I am certain."

"But Mademoiselle Juliette looked well enough to me."

"That was because she had me to pull her out of the way and because *she* thought it was an accident."

"You always was a quick one, sir." The footman shook his head admiringly.

"Quick enough to save her; not quick enough to see anything that would help me identify the carriage, its driver, or its owner."

"But I am sure that someone somewhere saw something. I could try to find out, if you like, sir."

"And you, Tom, were always clever! Yes, I would like it, and the sooner the better."

"Straightaway, sir. I shall just ask Mrs. Gerrard. But why would anyone want to hurt Mademoiselle Juliette?"

"Precisely. There is no obvious reason, which leads me to believe her life is in danger."

"You don't say! Does Mrs. Gerrard know?"

"I doubt it, or Mademoiselle Juliette would have been less inclined to think it an accident. But Mrs. Gerrard will soon find out, if you will be so good as to discover if Mrs. Gerrard is free to see me."

Chapter 22

Helen was free, and she welcomed Adrian with a warm smile, but the green eyes remained alert and one slim eyebrow shot up questioningly as Tom ushered him into her office. "My lord, this is an unexpected pleasure. Before I send him for some refreshment, may I thank you for bringing us Mr. Sandys whom we already find an invaluable member of our staff, not to mention Alice."

"I am glad to hear you are pleased." Adrian took the proffered chair as Tom shut the door quietly behind him. "Unfortunately, given the dire turn of events, I may have to beg your indulgence and ask for him back, for a little while, at least."

Helen nodded somberly. "Of course. Do you know when you are leaving?"

He shook his head. "No, but it is only a matter of weeks before the whole world joins the Duke and the others in Brussels."

"We shall miss him. He has quickly become a popular presence in our . . . er . . . *household*. The ladies feel safer with him here and, of course, his imposing person lends us consequence, always important. And we adore Alice, such a good girl and so eager to help."

"So he tells me, for which we both are most grateful, your taking her in."

She cocked her head giving him her half ironic, half measuring stare, her lips crooking slightly into the enigmatic smile. "And you, my lord, are a very good and generous man, I think."

Adrian felt his face grow warm under her scrutiny. He rubbed his cheek, tracing the line of his scar. "I would not go so far as to say that . . ."

"But you are here about something else besides Tom Sandys," she continued smoothly.

As always, he was struck with her uncanny ability to read minds. "Well, yes, in fact, I am."

"And how may I be of assistance?"

"I don't know that you can. But today as I was walking toward the square with a . . ." Adrian felt the flush rising in his cheeks, ". . . a present for Mademoiselle Juliette, a carriage came around the corner fast and nearly hit her."

"Except that you pulled her to safety. Tom told me, but I could have guessed that. Odd that a carriage could have got up that much speed in the square."

"Exactly!" Adrian knew that Helen Gerrard was no fool, and if she agreed with him that there was something havey-cavey about the entire situation, then there was.

"I don't suppose you were able to get much of a look at the carriage?"

"No, curse it."

"I doubt it was there by accident, which must mean someone either in this establishment or keeping a very close eye on it from elsewhere, is sharing information about Mademoiselle Juliette's comings and goings . . . if Mademoiselle Juliette, and not just any of Mrs. Gerrard's' residents was the intended victim. I shall keep my eyes and ears open and see what I can discover."

Damn, but the lady was clever! No wonder John enjoyed playing cards with her, and why hadn't Adrian thought of the obvious, that someone had to let others know when Mademoiselle Juliette, or anyone from Mrs. Gerrard's, would be in a position to be a victim of a runaway carriage?

Helen rose, "I thank you for your quick action in preventing an injury to Mademoiselle Juliette and, quite possibly, saving her life." Oddly moved at the thought, she found herself fighting the urge to invite him upstairs to assure himself of Juliette's well-being. It was against all her principles to encourage romantic notions in her girls, or her customers, but Helen was no proof against the anguish and frustration she saw in her visitor's face. Placing one slim hand on the scarlet clad shoulder, she continued, not unkindly, "Naturally, my lord, you are concerned with Mademoiselle Juliette's welfare, and I assure you we shall do our utmost to see that she is well cared for, that any possible ill effects she might have suffered will be attended to. I shall make sure that she rests after what must have been a shock, even though she considers it to be a simple mishap."

The green eyes, though guarded, and far too knowing, were sympathetic, and for that, little though it was, Adrian was grateful. "Thank you, Mrs. Gerrard. Knowing she is so well cared for and watched over relieves me a good deal." He rose to take his leave. "And, if I might, I should like to call in a few days to assure myself of her well-being?"

"Certainly, my lord. Until then, we shall see what further information can be discovered. Shall we not?"

"Indeed we shall." He was forced to be satisfied for the moment with the simple promise of investigation because, for the moment, it was all he had to offer, but given even the slightest lead, the tiniest scrap of information, he vowed to pursue it until he found the answers he sought.

True to her word, Helen did go upstairs to see Juliette who was not, as she had told Adrian, working on Dora's carriage dress at all. In fact, no needlework of any kind, sketchbooks, or even bits of trimming or scraps of material were to be seen anywhere.

Instead, she sat by the window, the book of drawings in her lap, flipping slowly through the etchings, a dreamy expression on her face that told the establishment's proprietress everything about the giver and nothing about the gift. Juliette's hands might be gently turning the pages, smoothing them abstractedly with her fingers, but her eyes were fixed, unseeing, on the window next to her, and her smile was clearly not for the pictures in her lap or the blue sky visible through the window.

"I hear you nearly suffered an accident today. How very fortunate that Lord Adrian was by and acted so quickly."

"Yes." Juliette came to with a start, "It was *incroyable*! One minute Rose and I were walking along enjoying the sunshine, and the next there was a carriage nearly oversetting itself on the turn, but before I was even aware of what was happening, the Major had pulled me to safety." The dreamy smile widened and the faraway look in the blue eyes turned into something Helen did not want to identify. So much for being unnerved by a brush with death! She supposed it was better that Juliette had not been so terrorized by the runaway carriage that she would not always be looking backward over her shoulder for any other attack on her person, if indeed it was she who had been the intended victim. On the other hand, the alternative, falling in love with a heroic, unattainable young man who had just saved her life, was more upsetting and, quite possibly, more hopeless.

"Then you are quite unharmed?"

"Oh yes." The real concern in her employer's voice brought Juliette back to reality. "There is no need to worry. I did not suffer the smallest scratch." To her person, anyway—her heart, when she had looked into Adrian's eyes so full of tender concern, was a different matter altogether. "The Major was so very quick thinking and acting. I never was in any danger."

We'll see about that, Helen thought grimly. "And Rose?"

"She is unhurt as well for she was a good deal behind me, having stopped to tighten her boot as we rounded the corner. We had been for a walk in the park, you see and one of her laces was loose."

"Ah, well, I am glad that you are unharmed, and I will leave you to your . . .", she pointed to the book in Juliette's lap.

"Oh, Lord Adrian was so kind as to purchase a folio of Tischbein's plates of the vases we saw at the museum that I admired so much."

"That was very kind indeed." Helen did her best to contain her surprise for she, like Adrian's brother John, was very well aware of the uniqueness and the expense of such a gift. "I am sure you will enjoy it."

Juliette blushed in spite of herself. "I plan to make use of the drawings for my designs. You will see, my Greek creations will soon be all the rage."

"I am sure they will," Helen responded dryly as she closed the door behind her. Clearly there was nothing useful to be learned about the incident from Juliette, but Rose was another matter. She had been several paces behind Juliette and might have a better idea of exactly what had happened.

But Rose's concern for her mistress, and her admiration for the Major's brave rescue had utterly overwhelmed her critical faculties. "No ma'am, I did not see a thing. All of a sudden, here was this great carriage and his lordship throwing himself in front of Mademoiselle Juliette. Risked his life for her, he did! And then there was Mademoiselle Juliette all shocked at the dreadful possibility of what might have happened if the Major had not been there and, no ma'am, I did not see the carriage as it went on its way."

"It must have been very sudden indeed, both the coming and the going," Helen nodded, more firmly convinced than ever that the Major was right. It had been no accident.

"Oh yes ma'am, in the blink of an eye and I am that grateful the Major was there to save her."

"So am I, Rose, so am I." And Helen, her mind entertaining a hundred disturbing possibilities, retired to her office to think and to plan her next steps for getting to the bottom of the affair. Was someone hoping to strike at Mr. Gerrard's, or just at Mademoiselle Juliette and why?

CHAPTER 23

FACED WITH TWO MYSTERIES—who had made an attempt on Mademoiselle Juliette's life, and the question of Mademoiselle Juliette's true identity— Adrian chose to concentrate on the more easily solved, though the least unnerving of the two—the true identity of Mademoiselle Juliette, and he directed his steps to the rectory of St. George's Hanover Square.

Taking a little time for himself away from parish duties, which were far too light for his liking, John was buried deep in *A Treatise on Algebra in Practice and Theory* when his butler interrupted him, "It is Major Lord Adrian here to see you, my lord."

"My brother?" It was not that the Claverton brothers were not close, but they ordinarily moved in very different circles, their paths usually crossing at the family mansion in Grosvenor Square or, more recently, Mrs. Gerrard's.

"Adrian! What brings you here? Is something amiss?" Trying not to examine his brother too closely, John gestured to a chair. "Do sit down. Now, out with it."

Adrian did not even bother to wonder how John knew he needed help. Yes, it was not like him to call at the rectory, but the lively understanding in his brother's eyes told him that, once again, John knew to a fair degree of accuracy what he was thinking. In anyone else, it would have been unnerving, but in John, it was always reassuring and often saved a good deal of embarrassing explanation.

"It is Mademoiselle Juliette."

"Naturally." Adrian ignored the wealth of implication in his brother's tone and plunged ahead with his story. "A carriage very nearly mowed her down today and I do *not* think it was an accident. Of course I am having Tom investigate the carriage, but I thought that another approach to finding the answer might be to discover who she really is."

"Quite possibly." John's words might agree with what Adrian suggested, but the enigmatic smile told him that he was not fooled. He knew Adrian simply wanted to know more about Mademoiselle Juliette, accident or no accident.

"I know you were helping some of the émigré priests and I thought that perhaps you might know one whose connections with the French community would help him identify her."

"The Abbe Carron is someone whose work among the poor and aged in Somers Town I admire greatly, and I have communicated with him from time to time. He also established a school for émigrés, daughters as well as sons. The last I heard, he had returned to France after Napoleon's defeat, but who knows if perhaps he has returned to London, given the recent, unfortunate events. I shall see what I can do."

"Thank you." Adrian wrung his brother's hand, struck all over again by the kindness in his eyes. The people of Reverend Lord John Claverton's parish were fortunate indeed!

John was as good as his word, and not a week later was calling on the venerable Abbe at his Spartan chamber at the Church of St. Aloysius. The Abbe was now living in Kensington where he had taken up residence so as not to disrupt those who had taken over his work in Somers Town, but he had agreed to meet John in his former quarters for old time's sake.

"I am sorry for the unhappy circumstances behind your return, Father, but am glad to see you safely back among us. You have been greatly missed."

"It is kind of you to say, but there was much work to be done in France as well, all those years without the comfort of their priests. Ah well, as you say, there is work to be done here." The Abbe waved a thin hand toward the window-overlooking the parish. He had aged enormously since the last time John had seen him, the lines of care and sympathy more deeply etched than ever in his face, the long nose even more sharply drawn. But the eyes were alert and bright as ever and they were now fixed on John with a barely discernible glint of humor. "But you are not here to talk of the recent unfortunate events, *non*?"

"You are entirely correct, Father, I am here to ask your help."

"My help? The rector of St. George's and a milord in his own right needs my help? This is interesting indeed!" Some of the Abbe's former energy seemed to return as he leaned forward in the heavy oak chair.

"Yes. I know that you have not only worked among the poor in your own parish, but through your school and its associations, you are well acquainted with much of the émigré community. I have recently made the acquaintance of someone who was once a part of that community, but is . . . but is, er . . . no longer."

"Someone in unhappy circumstances?" The Abbe probed gently.

"One might say so. On the other hand, one might not, depending on what her previous circumstances had been."

"Ahem. And may one know the name of this unfortunate, if, that is, you wish to know her story, as I presume you do."

"She calls herself Mademoiselle Juliette . . . Mademoiselle Juliette Fanchon. The name, I feel certain, is assumed, though perhaps not all of it. I was wondering if I were to describe a lovely blond young woman of roughly twenty-five, cultured, intelligent, well educated, whose brother is a soldier with the Comte d'Artois, if you might know such a person, a person who claims she has no family."

"Hmmm." The Abbe stared thoughtfully at the crucifix on the wall opposite him for some time. "I am sure it has occurred to you that if this young person says she has no family, there is good reason to say so. She may be protecting someone near and dear to her, someone who might be in danger if she were to reveal her identity."

"I had thought of that, but my brother, who knows her better, swears that is not the reason; it is something else—an unhappy occurrence, some misunderstanding possibly arising from her present circumstances—that may have caused a rift with her family."

The Abbe was silent for some time thinking, then nodding slowly, he seemed to arrive at a discovery and a decision at the same time. "Perhaps I may be able to help you, but you must promise not to act on this until I say that it is possible."

"Of course, Father."

"There was a girl at the school, a bright, eager, and," he smiled gently, "somewhat headstrong girl. Her brother attended a school more prestigious than ours, one more *appropriate* to his social standing, but ours was the only school for girls so she came to ours. The daughter of the Comte de Fournoy was not too good for us even though the son was. Mademoiselle Juliette," again he smiled reminiscently, "always chafing against the many rules circumscribing the existence of a proper young lady. Always wanting to *do* something, never content with just *being* the lovely young girl that she was, the perfect ornament to the house of Fournoy. When she left school, I saw no more of her. I assumed she would be married soon to some eligible son in her parents' circle, but that never happened or I would have heard. One day when I was in Manchester Square visiting old friends, I stopped in at the Spanish chapel on, what is it you English call it, a *whim*, and asked about her. The Comte de Fournoy and his family were devoted members of the congregation. I was told that she had died—so sad. She had been so full of life and wit and *espieglerie*. It seemed so tragic, so unnecessary, but *le bon Dieu* has his own ways. But now," the Abbe shook his head, "perhaps *le bon Dieu* had nothing to do with it, and that is even sadder. How can I help?"

John was just as lost as the Abbe. "I do not know, Father, not at the moment, but when things become clearer . . . if it is she . . . I will call on you. Is there any way we would know for sure it is Mademoiselle Juliette?"

"Hmmm. She always wore a cross, very old, very intricate design. Like this." He crossed to his desk, drew out a sheet of paper and drew. "But if she has fallen on hard times, perhaps she no longer has it. Aha! I have it! One day she was playing with the other girls and, being more daring that the others, climbed a tree and fell. Fortunately nothing was broken, but she cut herself, here." He pointed to his left temple. "It bled dreadfully and everyone was most alarmed, but not Juliette. She never cried at all and held her handkerchief to it until the bleeding stopped. It was, after all, not very deep but it left a scar, a crescent moon scar. The other girls felt sorry for her, having this blemish, but personally, I think she was rather proud of it."

"From the little I know of her, I would say it sounds exactly like Mademoiselle Juliette." It was John's turn to smile. "Thank you, Father." He rose and held out his hand. "You have been a great help."

"The little one, she is all right?"

"Yes, she is well cared for and, I hope, will be better cared for soon."

"*Grace a Dieu.* I am relieved to hear it, but you will let me know if there is anything more I can do."

"I shall, Father, or even if there is not, I shall let you know, when it is time, when . . . .*if* she wants to reconcile with her . . . .er . . . her past."

"May *le bon Dieu* favor you with his blessings, my lord. You are a good man, but not a happy one, I think?"

John stared into the kindly old eyes. "And why do you say that, Father?"

"You would like to be doing more of this," he again gestured to the world outside his windows, "God's work. But for now, you are forced to fight for the crumbs that fall your way while you are tied to your wealthy parish, crumbs like the one you brought me today."

"Precisely." John grinned.

"I wish you luck, my friend, and better fortune to the young woman whose cause you have taken up. If I hear more, I shall let you know."

"Do you know where the Comte de Fournoy can be found, if this young woman is his daughter?"

"Yes, they made their home in Manchester Square and I know personally that they were not among those who returned to France when the Corsican was beaten the first time. The Comtesse's health was too frail and they were waiting for their son to find them suitable quarters before attempting such a journey. Fortunately, he had not quite completed preparations for their arrival.

Undoubtedly he, as a soldier, a member of the Bourbon Cavalry that fought with Wellington in the Peninsula if I recall, has joined the Allied forces in Belgium. It is an enormous force I am told, and this time I hope they beat the Corsican for once and for all. On my brief return home after he was exiled I saw what has happened to France under his rule—shops open on Sundays, no parish priests, and still the poor and desperate in need of help. Ah, bah! It takes a good deal of faith to believe the world can truly become better, does it not, my friend?"

"It does indeed. Thank you, Father. And may you continue with your good works, wherever you find yourself, in London or in France."

John could not resist strolling through Manchester Square on his way back to the rectory. Trying to appear as casual as possible, he took a turn around the square, but saw no one except a few obvious tradesmen and servants. He had not actually expected to discover anything, he was a man of God, after all, whose mind was supposed to be on higher things. Adrian was the soldier, far more suited to reconnaissance than John, and since Adrian was the one who wanted the information, John would leave that task up to him.

CHAPTER 24

RECONNAISSANCE OF QUITE A DIFFERENT SORT was being carried on at Mrs. Gerrard's, much to the indignation of Dora who, opening the door to her chamber the very afternoon following Lord John's visit to the Abbe Carron, discovered Daisy, the most recently hired maid, with one ear pressed to Juliette's door. "You little sneak!" Dora seized the astonished maid by her other ear and marched her towards the staircase. "Whatever do you think you are doing spying on Mademoiselle Juliette? Just wait until Mrs. Gerrard learns what a snake-in-the-grass she has allowed under her roof!"

"I . . . I weren't spying!" Daisy twisted, struggling fruitlessly to free herself from Dora's grip as she stumbled down the stairs behind her.

"No, you were eavesdropping to be precise, but it's all the same," Dora snapped, "it's dishonest, wicked, and it won't be tolerated, believe you me!" Barely stopping to knock at the door of Helen's office, she flung it open so hard it banged against the wall.

"Dear me," Helen glanced up from her account books "something seems to be amiss."

"This little slyboots," Dora thrust the cowering maid in front of her, "was listening at Mademoiselle Juliette's door."

"I . . . I . . ?" Under Helen's relentless gaze, the girl began to sob so noisily and helplessly that chamber doors opened and heads popped out before Dora could shut the door to Helen's office, and even as she reached for the door knob, Juliette and Grace, followed by Freddy, appeared on the threshold, their expressions betraying varying degrees of curiosity and dismay.

"'Tis nothing." Helen spoke calmly. "Go back to your chambers. Daisy and I are merely discussing her duties."

Exchanging glances, Juliette and Grace headed back up the staircase, but Freddy, still clutching the plates from *Ackermann's Repository* he had been discussing with Juliette, remained, a worried look crumpling his boyishly rounded features. "Not to thrust a spoke in your wheel, but if I can be of any assistance . . . ." He glanced anxiously at Helen. "I think I heard what this is about," he continued in a rush, "and I know Adrian mentioned something to me about the near accident with Mademoiselle Juliette . . . rather suspicious . . ." he faltered into silence as Helen, frowning thoughtfully, turned back to the girl in front of her.

"Out with it, my girl, all of it, or you shall find yourself in a much worse position than being turned away without a reference. They are now providing straw for the inmates at Bridewell to sleep on and flogging has been abolished, but it still is rather an unpleasant abode."

If possible, Daisy grew even more pale than she had been before. "No, please, Mrs. Gerrard, I will tell you anything you want to hear."

"Not anything I want to hear, but the truth, Daisy." Helen's icy green eyes continued to bore into the unfortunate maid's, but her voice softened somewhat.

"Well," Daisy gulped, wiping her streaming eyes with her sleeve, "I were just returning through the square with a package of ribbon Miss Juliette had sent me to fetch when this gentleman stopped me and asked me if I wanted to do him a favor for his master. He were ever so respectful and he said as how his master had a great admiration for Miss Juliette, but were ever so shy and would I be ever so helpful and tell him when Miss Juliette was likely to go out for a walk."

"And then he offered you money which made you even more eager to oblige his master," Dora added dryly.

"Well . . . , yes, he did offer . . . er"

"More than a guinea I'll guess." Dora's expression grew even more ironic.

"Well yes, but Miss Dora, Mrs. Gerrard, my mother is sickly and I need the money." Poor Daisy glanced desperately from Dora to Helen and back again.

"Go on," Helen prompted gently. "What did the man who accosted you look like?"

"Well, he spoke ever so gentlemanlike, and he wore a dark jacket . . . he seemed most appreciative when I told him I would try . . . and he had ever such a nice smile."

"Not only a sneak, but empty-headed as well!" Dora folded her arms across her chest in disgust.

"And how were you to convey this information?" Helen leaned forward in her chair. "Think. Is there anything more you can remember about him?"

"No nothing," Daisy gulped as tears began to flow again, "just that I was to walk out in the square every day about noon and he would find me and get his answer. Please Madam, I didn't think there was no harm in it. Miss Juliette has lots of admirers and . . ."

"It is not so much what you did as it is the way you went about it, Daisy. It was dishonest. I cannot have anyone in my employ that I cannot trust completely, and it is the same for Dora and the others here. They do not want a sneak and a tattletale in their midst."

"Oh no, Madam, please do not let me go. My mother, it will kill her!" The frantic girl sank into a chair, sobbing hysterically.

"I might be able to help." Freddy spoke up quietly after a moment, but no one seemed to hear him.

Helen twisted the emerald ring on her finger as she frowned mercilessly at her account book. She hated to toss the poor girl out onto the street. After all, wasn't her avowed mission to rescue poor helpless, souls? But dishonesty, even when one was in the most dire of circumstances was not to be tolerated, or was it if the girl's mother were truly ill and truly dependent on her? With a burden like that, how honest would Helen herself be?

Dora had no such qualms. Striding straight out of the door in disgust, she slammed it shut behind her, snapping Helen out of her reverie. "Er, what did you say?"

"I said I might be able to help. I have an estate, you see," Freddy continued hastily, somewhat unnerved by the blank look on Helen's face, a face that rarely revealed anything except complete ironic composure, "actually a rather snug little estate in Cornwall that has an empty cottage, just the right size for two people, and Mrs. Fellowes, the housekeeper, could use an extra hand."

"Ah." Helen's lips curved into an approving smile. "An excellent suggestion. I expect time spent in fresh air and among decent country folk would be most beneficial to both Daisy and her mother. As always, my lord, you are the soul of kindness."

"Oh, 'tis nothing." Freddy's face grew pink, but he looked highly gratified, nevertheless. "Er, thank you."

"Cornwall!" Daisy wailed as though it were darkest Africa, "but that . . . .that's in the country!"

"Precisely. And with any luck, you will find some sturdy young farmer who will make a decent woman out of you. Now you will stay here and help in the kitchen until the Marquess makes the necessary arrangements for your removal. Cook will keep a weather eye on you until then, and you may count yourself fortunate to have met with as kind a gentleman as the Marquess of Wrothingham. There is not a finer gentleman in the kingdom, believe me. Now be off with you!"

"Yes, Madam." The girl scuttled off leaving Freddy and Helen to ponder the original question.

"Adrian swore it was no accident," Freddy rubbed his chin thoughtfully, "and this proves him correct. But it would be best if Mademoiselle Juliette were kept out of this, best for her to think it was simply an accident, no need to cause her any worry. Adrian will get to the bottom of it—good man, Adrian."

Helen nodded, resolving to have a serious talk with the Major as soon as possible, and before Daisy was sent off to her new home. If anyone could help Daisy recall further, more useful details of the man who had hired her, it would be Lord Adrian with his winning smile and his charming way of making a woman, any woman, feel as though she were the most intriguing, most attractive creature in the world.

But even Adrian, smile reassuringly though he would, was not able to help Daisy recall much more than she had already told them. "He were a nice spoken gentleman," she kept insisting, but beyond that, she could remember nothing. Everything else about the man—his height, his hair, his complexion, everything thing was *middling*. "I am that sorry, my lord, but I don't remember nothing else." Daisy's protuberant lower lip was taking on a decidedly stubborn look.

"Nor should you be expected to." Adrian smiled soothingly as he directed a sharp glance at Helen. "After all, you were just a messenger of sorts, doing a favor. Hardly the kind of thing one comments to memory."

"Yeees."

"But perhaps you could remember him if you saw him again?"

"Oh yes, my lord." Daisy nodded vigorously.

"And then you could give him one last message and warn him that you are returning to the country with your mother."

"But I won't be *returning*, my lord, 'cause I never been to the country. I don't even know if I *like* the country. In fact I am sure I *won't* like the country."

"Nevertheless, you will *tell* the gentleman you are returning to the country. Is that understood?"

"Yes, my lord." Recognizing an order when she heard it, Daisy cut short her wail of protest and nodded dutifully.

"That is all then, you may go."

Utterly subdued, she looked at Helen who nodded. "Well," she snorted in disgust as the wretched girl slunk out the door, "we are no better off than we were before."

"Actually, we are. Tom Sandys may be a strapping fellow, but he knows how to fade into the scenery when he needs to. He'll keep an eye on Daisy and then follow the fellow to his master, a master whose identity I am beginning to suspect already."

"Surely not Basil Harcourt, not after the dressing down you gave him before? He wouldn't dare."

"No, he wouldn't dare himself, but a nasty weak coward such as he is quite likely to be dangerously infuriated by a threat he cannot handle and therefore all the more likely to employ others to make mischief for him. This time, however, I shall threaten him with more than a duel."

"What could be more threatening than a duel with you?"

"The gallows." Adrian smiled grimly as he went off in search of his former batman.

CHAPTER 25

B UT TOM SANDYS, SKILLED THOUGH HE WAS at making himself invisible, was able to report nothing more than following his quarry to a gambling hell in Covent Garden where he had met another *gentleman* who defied description. "He were a gentleman, but just barely," the shamefaced Sandys reported. "'Twere so dark in there I could hardly get a look at his face and there were two nasty brutish porters at the door who began to look askance at me when I didn't sit right down at a table, so, not wanting to call attention to myself, I left."

"Thank you, Tom. You did the best you could." Adrian gave his batman a reassuring pat on the arm. "It is now up to me, and, as I have had my suspicions all along, I shall simply call on Lord Basil himself, proof or no proof."

In fact, Adrian did not much care whether he had proof or not. Someone had tried to harm Juliette, and Lord Basil Harcourt, as the scum of the earth who had attacked Dora, needed a talking to, even if he had, had nothing to do with the attack on Juliette; and if he had, so much the better. It felt good to be able to do something about it; therefore, he wasted no time in making his way to Cavendish Square just as Basil, bleary-eyed after a night at the gaming tables with a few choice spirits, staggered unsteadily up the front steps to his lodgings.

"Basil! Glad you are here as I want a word with you." Seizing his collar, Adrian dragged his befuddled quarry through the door and up the stairs to his chambers where he deposited him none too gently in a chair next to the cold dark fireplace.

"Word with me?" Basil rubbed his eyes, struggling to come to his senses. "Whatever for?"

"To tell you that if you ever lay a hand on Mademoiselle Juliette, no . . . if you ever come near . . . if you ever show your face in St. James' Square again, you are worse than a dead man."

"You can't do that! Why some of the best games to be had are in houses there."

"Nevertheless," Adrian's jaw tightened, "you will now avoid them at all costs."

"You can't do that. I have a right to go wherever I want. This is England, after all, not some Byzantine . . ."

"You will not show your face for fear of being arrested for attempted murder."

"Murder! I never tried to murder anyone in my life!"

"I suppose you were just trying to frighten Mademoiselle Juliette by sending a carriage careening into her which, given the way the fool who drove it managed his team, might just as well have been murder."

"I did nothing of the sort! Why would I want to hurt her?" Basil shut his jawing with a snap, shifting uneasily in his chair.

"Then you do know Mademoiselle Juliette!" Adrian exclaimed triumphant, narrowing his eyes to fix his future brother-in-law with a cold blue stare that could have nailed him to the wall. "Then you will understand that if anything so much as a leaf from a tree she walks under happens to brush her shoulder as it falls I will have you in the dock so fast your head will spin."

"But I did nothing to Mademoiselle Juliette . . . or anyone else."

"It doesn't matter. I am warning you that if you *do*, you will be facing a hangman's noose. The Harcourts may be a more ancient family than the Clavertons, but they are not nearly so well connected, and the Clavertons can put those connections to good use when necessary, brother-in-law be damned! Have I made myself clear?"

Too bemused to come up with a suitable reply, or any reply at all, for that matter, Basil nodded.

"Good." Adrian turned on his heel and stalked back down the stairs. It had taken all the self-control he possessed not to thrash Basil within an inch of his life then and there, but despite the pent-up rage that demanded he do something visible, something real, he knew in his mind that his thirst for vengeance would be better served by justice later. His rash feelings conquered, he congratulated himself on action taken, but as he reached the bottom stair, he again heard a soft voice saying *but I use that sense to make me cautious, not suspicious* and the nagging suspicion that Mademoiselle Juliette might not have been best pleased with his hotheaded reaction began to take hold. There was nothing naïve about Mademoiselle Juliette, but there was an innate kindness, a gentleness about her, that warmed his soul, a kindness and gentleness he suspected might not totally approve of his condemning Basil out of hand, no matter how much of a loose screw he might be.

With a slightly self-conscious shrug of his shoulders, Adrian set off towards

Portman Square. There was bound to be news from the continent at head-quarters, and even if there were not, he could be sure to find others waiting as tensely and expectantly as he.

More often than not, Adrian found the bloodthirsty enthusiasm of his fellow cavalrymen simpleminded, but in this particular moment of self-doubt, he rather welcomed it. And they welcomed him with their usual gusto. "Adrian, old fellow, about time you showed your face around here!" Captain Henry Braxton gave him a hearty clap on the back that would have knocked a smaller man flat. "Not long now and we'll have a chance to redeem ourselves."

"Not that it was our fault we didn't cover ourselves with glory at Vittoria—that damned ravine, eh, Henry?"

"Exactly." Henry grinned, slung an arm around Adrian's shoulder and led him into headquarters. "Look who's here, lads, the master of the saber himself! Time for those Frogs to start being sorry they started it up all over again—gives us a chance to show that we can really ride over the enemy!"

And slowly, but surely, Adrian was drawn back into the familiar world of battle order and discussions of provisioning, transport and, of course, the endless talk of horses, the part of cavalry life dearest to his heart.

Oddly enough, it was talk of horses that dominated his very next meeting with Juliette. Having tired pretty quickly of endless speculations as to their probable departure date and countless boasts of glorious deeds to come and battle honors to be won, Adrian stopped by Mrs. Gerrard's later on in the afternoon in the hopes that Juliette would be free for a walk in the park, or a moment of conversation on some topic other than the monumental struggle to come.

As luck would have it, she was in the drawing room poring over the engravings he had given her. Entranced by the picture she made sitting at a table by the window, the sunlight turning the golden curls into a halo that lit up her delicate features, Adrian held up a silencing hand as Tom Sandys opened his mouth to announce him. Just for a moment he wanted to enjoy the picture as slim white fingers smoothed the pages flat sending shivers chasing down his spine. Oh to feel their soft warmth tracing his lips as they traced the frame of the etching, to have those eyes fixed on his face with the intensity they studied the drawing!

Leaning forward, Juliette sighed with pleasure, her soft lower lip caught ever so gently in her teeth as she dwelt on the sweeping flow of the drapery.

It was as much as Adrian could do to keep himself from pulling her into his arms and covering those invitingly delicate lips with kisses.

Then suddenly, as if sensing his presence, she looked up and smiled. "Major!" Setting aside the engravings she rose gracefully, hurrying forward, hands outstretched, her lovely smile lighting her face.

Adrian fought for breath. What was it about her that her smile could make him feel as though he had just been hit in the chest with a cannonball? Was it the joy, the warmth, the gladness at seeing him? Never in his life had he ever felt anything like this. Whatever it was, it was irresistible, and he never wanted to let it go. He wanted to keep it for himself, for always. Major Lord Adrian Claverton, soldier, adventurer, who had never had an *always* in his entire life suddenly found himself wanting that more than anything in the world just at that particular moment in time when *never* was hovering threateningly on the very near horizon.

"Thank you again for the book. It is absolutely beautiful, and I have already put it to good use." Juliette pointed to her open sketchbook which he had not even noticed.

"I am so glad you are enjoying it, Mademoiselle. I wish all my gifts were such happy choices. Believe me when I say if there is anything you wish, you have but to ask.

"Well," Juliette tilted her head to one side, the dimple on the right corner of her mouth flashing bewitchingly while Adrian tried unsuccessfully to ignore a stab of disappointment. She was just like every other woman after all, except possibly his mother and his sister; give a woman something and she only wanted more. He should have known better. Not only was she a woman, but she was a woman from Mrs. Gerrard's.

"If you truly mean that, and if you would be so kind, I should like to meet your horse."

"My, my whaaaaat?"

Juliette burst into laughter, not just a provocative trill of an attractive woman, but serious gasping-for-breath laughter. The look of utter bewilderment on the major's face was beyond description. "You are a cavalry officer, are you not? It has been my experience, limited thought it might be, that cavalry officers come with horses."

Still too befuddled to speak, Adrian nodded dumbly.

"I have also heard it said that a cavalry officer is only as good as his horse.

Adrian nodded again, looking a little less bewildered, but only slightly.

"Then, as we know a great battle is coming in which you are about to take part, I would like to meet the other half of Major Lord Adrian Claverton of his Majesty's First Life Guards."

"Caesar," Adrian gasped at last, "you would like to meet Caesar!"

"Yes, I would, if that is his name. I have a great deal to say to him on the matter of bringing you both home safe and sound."

Juliette's tone was playful, but the blue eyes were deadly serious and dark with worry. Adrian was completely at a loss. At one moment he had been thinking she was no better than any other blood-sucking harpy, and the next she was telling him she was worried about him in battle, enough so to wish to inspect Caesar. What a woman! He shook his head in admiration. And Caesar *should* meet her. Why had he not thought of it before? Caesar had a nose for a good female and no patience with a bad one. Why he had seen right through Lady Mary Featherstonaugh when Adrian had not, categorically rejecting the lumps of sugar the dashing young lady had plied him with in an attempt to worm her way into his master's good graces. And he absolutely detested Lady Lavinia Harcourt which, by itself, showed him to be a horse of remarkably discriminating taste.

"He would be delighted to meet you, Mademoiselle Juliette." Having recovered his aplomb, Adrian sketched a bow with a flourish that would have done Freddy proud. "We exercise regularly in the park in the morning when it is quiet, if, perchance, you might happen to be there."

"Perchance I might." Both dimples appeared now at the corners of that delicious mouth as Juliette held out her hand. "But now I must excuse myself."

Adrian raised her hand to his lips inhaling the warmth and her special scent. The softness against his mouth made him long to continue on up her arm to the creamy skin of her neck and press it just under the delicate curve of her ear. Doing his best to stifle the sigh of longing, he gently released her hand, placing it carefully back at her side. "Until some happy morning, then."

"Some happy morning," Juliette echoed, and the knot of desire that seemed to be twisting him mercilessly inside loosened just the slightest bit when he saw her eyes widen with the same pent up longing and caught the shallow rise and fall of her breasts beneath the thin muslin of her gown, a rise and fall that was a great deal faster than it had been just moments ago.

Good! She was not indifferent. And he was, Adrian thought as he clattered downstairs, totally infatuated, captivated, as head-over-heels as any schoolboy, and glad of it. Whistling tunelessly, he headed off to the stables to see Caesar and inform him of the momentous event coming his way, an event that had little to do with Napoleon Bonaparte and everything to do with a certain enchanting young woman.

Chapter 26

"**W**HATEVER HAS GOTTEN INTO YOU to take a drive in the park at this ungodly hour?" Grace grumbled as John coachman handed her into Helen's elegant barouche. And if you tell me it is the fresh air and the beauty of a spring morning, I shall do you a mischief. Why could you not ask Dora to accompany you? She is a country girl and revels in such things."

"It *is* the fresh air and the beauty of this particular spring morning. And Dora is showing Tom, who is soon to leave for the continent, a better way to clean gold braid," Juliette added with a significant look.

"And someone else is likely to be in the park, or had better be, or you won't get me to give up my singing practice ever again. You know morning is the only time I have uninterrupted time at the pianoforte."

"I know. And I promise I shall make it up to you." Juliette tried to look contrite and failed. The day was too lovely and the prospect of seeing Adrian and Caesar too happy for her to be anything but excited.

Seeing the expectant joy in her friend's face, Grace gave up trying to make her feel guilty and took pleasure herself in the fineness of the day and the never diminishing thrill of having a well sprung carriage at one's disposal, not to mention a fire in her bed chamber, reliable and excellent income, and warm companionship. "Did Lord Adrian ask you to meet him?"

"Not in so many words, but when I asked to be introduced to his horse, he told me that they were to be found in the park every morning. And," Juliette's voice suddenly caught in her throat, "there he is!" Major Lord Adrian Claverton on foot was a magnificent specimen of humanity, but Major Lord Adrian Claverton on horseback was absolutely breathtaking!

"Oh my!" Even Grace's eyes were glued to the pair as waving, Adrian trotted toward their carriage.

But before he was near enough to exchange greetings, another horse and rider suddenly appeared from another path and joined them. Juliette was unprepared for the sudden stab of envy at the easy familiarity between the two riders, nor could she dismiss the feeling as curiosity; it was envy pure and simple, as she gazed at the figure of a woman on the other horse, a young and vivacious woman who seemed to be not just familiar with the major, but on excellent terms. And what was worse, he seemed not only to be on excellent terms with her, but also suddenly to be avoiding the barouche which, until a minute ago, had been his goal.

Leaning forward, Grace gently squeezed Juliette's hand, the sympathy in her eyes making the entire scene even harder to bear.

Then suddenly the woman broke away and headed straight toward them with Adrian in determined pursuit. She arrived breathless, just seconds before he caught up with her. "Adrian will tell you I am a sad creature with not the least notion how to go on, but I did want to meet you. You *are* Mademoiselle Juliette are you not?"

"Ah, er yes, I am, but you have the advantage of me, I am afraid. You are?"

"Lady Georgiana Claverton," Adrian supplied ruefully, riding up behind her, "and a more hoydenish, ill-behaved . . ."

". . . but loving sister, it would be hard to find." Georgiana finished triumphantly with such a friendly open smile that it was impossible to resist smiling back.

And Juliette did smile back even though Adrian was frowning at his sister like a thundercloud, an expression Juliette had never seen before. Her heart sank. He admired her, enjoyed her company, but he did not want her to meet his sister.

"Adrian, you are not my keeper," Georgiana protested, and his expression softened.

"No, you are right, I am not," he sighed, then, brightening, added, "And thank heavens for that!"

Juliette's first instinct was to tease him, but, taking pity on him instead, she turned to Lady Georgiana to ask the question Adrian did not seem able to articulate. "But how did you know my name?"

"Oh, one hears things," Georgiana responded airily.

Juliette raised a skeptical eyebrow and Adrian's sister flushed ever so slightly. "Well, ...one *discovers* things, if you will, and the other day I *overheard* Freddy asking Adrian if he were going to call on you, I mean, Mademoiselle Juliette and then I recalled Lady Mary Featherstonaugh asking me about the woman Adrian was escorting to the British Museum, and I put two and two together and began to wonder about you. "You see," Georgiana smiled apologetically at Juliette, "Adrian never favors any woman over another so I was quite dying to see what sort of woman he did favor enough to take to a museum, and now I have found out!" She threw a triumphant glance at her brother. "And I must say, she is very pretty Adrian, and looks to be far nicer than Lady Mary who is forever throwing herself at you. Do you ever go to Almack's? I would love to have a friend to talk to. It is ever so boring there, one sees the same people over and over. The unmarried women only talk about the eligible men, and everyone else about the latest scandal. You look as though you would have something more interesting to say."

The rapidity of Lady Georgiana's thought processes caught Juliette off guard. "Why, why, thank you, I think. But . . . ah . . . no, I do not go to Almack's. Actually, I do not frequent the same circles as you do."

"Well, you should. You are far more fashionable and far better spoken than anyone I know, or anyone I have seen there."

Despite his increasing uneasiness with the entire situation, Adrian could not suppress a grin. Georgie was young and pretty, but otherwise she sounded just like his mother and would undoubtedly eventually become another ferociously plain-spoken duchess or countess in her own right some day.

"Again, thank you, but I do not think it is likely to happen."

"Well, I shall just invite you. There!" Georgie smiled triumphantly at her own cleverness.

For once in his life, Adrian, who, as a handsome, charming son of one of England's most powerful peers had pretty much been able to carry on forever blithely ignoring social niceties, was caught. On the one hand, it was the duty of every brother to protect his sister's reputation, and befriending a denizen of Mrs. Gerrard's would go a fair way towards threatening Georgie's, or at least causing comment. On the other hand, Juliette was just the sort of person Georgie needed as a friend—intelligent, resourceful, independent—and vice versa, and, according to John, with as good a pedigree as Georgie's. On yet another hand, society would notice and talk which would do neither of them any good. But on another hand (Adrian realized he had long ago run out of hands) Georgie was bound to ruin her reputation anyway.

"It is indeed very kind of you, but I truly mean that we move in vastly different spheres. I am . . ." Juliette could not help glancing at Adrian, and what she saw in his eyes made her own prickle with hot tears of gratitude and her heart swell with something more than gratitude, something akin to love. Unlike any man she could think of, except, perhaps, John and Freddy, his eyes held no alarm, no warning, his brow was not furrowed in disapproval, nor did he avoid her gaze, but held it instead with the same steady respect as if she were from his and his sister's sphere instead of the one to which she had fallen. "I am a dressmaker, you see."

Georgie's eyes flew open. "You are? Famous! And all the more reason we should become friends. Mama despairs of my ever having the least bit of style, but I cannot be bothered with all the prodding and poking and people talking about you as though you were some kind of horse. Actually not as nicely as they would talk about a horse. *Her ladyship is rather large-boned to carry this look well. Her ladyship's shoulders are rather too broad for the latest fashion in sleeves. "Tis a pity her ladyship is too fair for the newest shade of....*Ugh! I detest it! I don't want to be looked at! I want to be comfortable, what *they* say is all the rage is invariably so constricting that one is barely capable of even the tiniest movement."

Juliette laughed. "That is because they are trying to make you fit the style. Now *I* create the style that fits the person."

"You do? How very clever of you! Ah . . ." comprehension dawned in Georgie's animated face, "and *that* is, of course, why Freddy likes you. He was asking Adrian if he were going to see you which means that he knows you and likes you too, which, of course he would. Freddy is absolutely devoted to fashion of all sorts."

But Juliette, following Georgie's line of reasoning, hoped it wouldn't prompt her to ask the next logical question which was why Adrian, whose military calling, was quite the antithesis of all things fashionable, was also interested in a mere dressmaker. In fact, she often wondered that herself, but looking up into blue eyes dancing with merriment, sympathy, and something more than that, Juliette knew why. And just for one moment, she allowed herself to revel in the joy that flooded through her, making her mouth go dry, her breath catch in her throat, and her knees tremble, even though she was sitting down.

But Juliette had guessed wrong, and the next remark was even more disconcerting than she could have imagined. "If Freddy and Adrian visit you at your shop, then so shall I!"

Juliette looked desperately toward Adrian, but all he did was smile, and it struck her with something of a shock, that he trusted her to reply, trusted her completely, as he would a friend. Juliette couldn't remember when she'd had a friend, except for Grace and Dora and the others at Mrs. Gerrard's. And a man? She had never even thought of having a man as a friend, but now it seemed she did, and the thought of that was almost as gratifying as the thought of other things that made her throat go dry, her breath quicken, and her knees tremble. "I do not have a shop . . . yet," she added firmly. "For the moment, I call on my patronesses at their own establishments."

"Then you must call on me, and if you can make me look *just the thing*, you will be so sought after you will have to open a shop!" Once again, Georgie grinned at her own cleverness, and was opening her mouth to embark on a series of questions when there was a loud *harrumph!* From behind her. "Oh," she glanced over her shoulder at her groom. "That is Ned reminding me that Mama said I must be home in an hour—the dancing master is coming."

She looked so tragic that Juliette could not help laughing.

"It is no laughing matter. He is very French and very critical of *these clumsy English girls with the feet of horses*. Oh," she raised a gloved hand to her mouth, "I *do* beg your pardon. You are French, are you not? Yes, I can see you are! Fashionable, pretty, and," she sighed gloomily, "undoubtedly light on your feet. Well, no matter, soon I will have you take me in hand and then I too shall feel pretty and graceful." And with a cheery wave, she was off like a shot, galloping across the park with poor Ned trailing behind her.

"My sister . . ."

"Is charming, my lord, and . . ."

"Completely out of control." Adrian shook his head. "But I do not fault her entirely; she misses the country desperately. Here she has no one to talk to who is interested in the things that are important to her, and she finds the social life, fussy, confining, and dull."

"Dull!" Juliette and Grace echoed, and Adrian chuckled.

"Like her brothers, she likes to *do* things, to be useful. The life of a drawing room ornament is not her style."

"No, I can see it would not be." And Juliette, who occasionally admitted to a pang of envy towards the women she saw who were that very thing, felt a rush of sympathy for Lady Georgiana Claverton who, if she had known what Juliette Fanchon truly was, denizen of Mrs. Gerrard's, *fille de joie*, would have been shocked and horrified, but then again, Juliette reflected, remembering Lady Georgiana's cheery, direct manner, maybe she wouldn't be. Maybe she would be as uncensorious and accepting as her brothers were.

"But we are here for Juliette to meet your horse," Grace broke into the unspoken conversation between Adrian and Juliette which seemed likely to go on for quite some time with them staring at one another as though the rest of the world had ceased to exist.

"Of course!" Adrian started guiltily, and sprang off his horse, leading him over so he could hand Juliette down from the carriage.

"Caesar," she whispered softly, looking up into the large dark eyes. "A magnificent name for a magnificent animal." Pulling off her glove, she dug into her pocket and pulled out a cloth wrapped around several pieces of apple. "It is permitted?"

Adrian nodded, oddly touched by the gesture. Had she had a horse in her past, one that made her know just how to impress his?

Caesar lowered his head, took the offered treat delicately, munched it, and softly snuffled, making the blond curls escaping from her bonnet dance in the sunshine.

Smiling, she stroked his nose, continuing her conversation as though no one else was there. "You must take great care of yourself and Lord Adrian,

Caesar. I know you have always done so, but there is a battle coming like no other battle before, and I am so afraid for both of you."

Adrian heard the tears in her voice and his own eyes misted as his heart turned over in his chest. Odd how he had never thought of anyone's being afraid for his life before when he had ridden into battle. He'd risked his life a number of times, but it had never occurred to worry about himself or those he might be leaving behind. Now, all of a sudden, Adrian could think of nothing else, and he was consumed with a desperate longing to show her what it meant to him, a desperate need to hold her, to love her, to claim her as his friend, his love, his soulmate while he still had time. But how was he to do that? How was he to make her understand what it all meant, to prove to her that he was different from all the other men who had known and admired her?

Juliette's low laughter broke into his reverie. "So like a man, always greedy for more in in spite of your dignified bearing." She shook her head as Caesar nosed her pockets for more bits of apple.

"Caesar, that is a Mademoiselle Juliette creation, I'll have you know," Adrian took his horse sternly to task, "and not to be trifled with." He turned to hand Juliette back into the carriage. "I am afraid we must go before our manners deteriorate entirely, but I hope I may call on you later, Mademoiselle?" *And say what? Do what?* a little voice nagged him, but he ignored it as he lost himself in the warmth of her smile.

"Oh yes! Please do."

CHAPTER 27

"A ND NOW, NOT ONLY HIS BROTHER, BUT HIS SISTER and his horse adore you. If the man weren't besotted before, he is utterly lost now." Grace smoothed her lemon kid gloves, then opened her parasol whose dappled shade did nothing to hide the sly smile hovering around the corners of her mouth.

"Oh no, Lord Adrian is just an acquaintance. He has been very kindly escorting me to the British Museum, the Egyptian Hall . . . ."

"And saving your life! Save your flummery for someone else; I am more than seven, you know. Besides, what is wrong with his being besotted by you? It is perfectly natural, entirely understandable and . . ." Grace tilted her parasol casting its shade on Juliette and making her blush even more noticeable. "quite clearly reciprocated."

"Is it so obvious?"

Grace patted her hand, "Only to the knowledgeable and the very, very observant."

"It is nothing. He is going away soon."

"No need to defend yourself to me."

"But Helen is always warning us against . . . *becoming fond* of our customers."

Grace snorted. "Lord Adrian is not a customer . . . that I know of."

"No . . . no, he is not, but Freddy is."

This time Grace tossed her head as she snorted. "In a manner of speaking. Freddy is a customer of the entire establishment, a place he feels comfortable both with himself and with us."

And it was true. They returned from their drive to find the subject of their conversation in the drawing room showing swatches of material for drapes to Helen while John waited patiently to begin their daily hand of cards.

Taking pity on him, Juliette pulled off her gloves and took the samples over to the window to examine them while Grace disposed of her gloves and parasol and sat down at the pianoforte. At the first tinkling notes, John took his place at the card table while Freddy, who had begun to debate the rival merits of the samples with Juliette, looked up. "Mademoiselle Juliette tells me that you sing as well as play, Miss Owen."

"I do, my lord."

"I had no idea you were so musical though Mademoiselle Juliette did tell me that you were giving pianoforte lessons. I did not realize you sang. If you would be so kind as to sing for us, I am sure we would enjoy it, wouldn't we?" He cast an anxious glance at the card players.

"I am sure we would." Helen's eyes glinted with amusement. "Do be so kind as to favor us with one of your *songs*, Grace."

"Certainly, madam." And with only the briefest of instrumental introductions, Grace launched into *Der Holle Rache in Herze.*

At the first notes of Mozart's famous aria, Freddy's head, which had been bent over the samples, snapped back with such force that Juliette had to stuff a hand into her mouth to keep from laughing outright. His jaw dropped and his eyes grew round with astonishment as he groped for the arm of the nearest chair, sinking slowly into it, a beatific expression settling over his chubby features as he remained transfixed until the last note died away.

"Miss Owen, you are a treasure beyond belief! What range, what agility, what style! You hit the high F without the least effort in the world. You will make Catalani and Grassini look to their laurels. *One of Grace's songs*, Mrs. Gerrard, you sly thing! You knew all along what talent you were hiding here! This woman," Freddy strode over to raise Grace's hand to his lips, "is a miracle of musical talent and utterly enchanting! We must make sure her talent is given its proper arena."

"Precisely." Helen nodded complacently before going back to her cards.

"Mademoiselle Juliette, did you know too?"

Juliette chuckled and nodded.

"Astounding! This place is a hive of hidden talent, a veritable Mount Parnassus. I cannot believe I am so fortunate to have come upon it. But Miss Owen, another one of your *songs*, I beg of you."

"But of course my lord, do you have any requests?"

"This angel of music asks *me* if I have any requests." Freddy rolled his eyes toward the ceiling. "I am in heaven! But not so much in heaven that I am deprived of my critical faculties. If you can sing *Der Holl Rache* with such style, can you do *Martern Aller Arten?*"

Again the shy proud smile hovered around Grace's lips as she again took her place at the pianoforte. "But of course, my lord."

"A miracle," Freddy breathed, shaking his head as he sank back into his chair. "It was a most blessed day I saw you in the box at the opera, Mademoiselle Juliette."

Juliette nodded and went back to examining the samples. Truly, it had been a blessed day for each one of them when Freddy had discovered Mrs. Gerrard's. Even Lord John looked happier and more relaxed as he took up his hand of cards. Juliette had felt the frustration that furrowed his brow, hunched his shoulders and tightened his aristocratic features into harsh angles when she had first met him and she had delighted in seeing these outward signs of a restless and unhappy soul melt away as he administered holy services and gave comfort and counsel to Helen's little band. It was clear that, in the house on St. James' Square at least, Lord John was following his true calling and it brought joy to her heart to see it.

But in giving a haven of sorts to a collection of lost souls, Mrs. Gerrard's had gained its own modicum of happiness. Since the brothers Claverton had begun to frequent its exclusive portals, its residents all seemed to have absorbed some of their energy and transformed it into a more optimistic outlook on their own lives, from Dora whose ebullient spirits had always kept them going even while her eyes were clouded with her own dark memories, who now glowed with happiness when Tom Sandys smiled at her or when she instructed Alice on the principles of household management, to Grace, beaming at the praise of a true opera connoisseur. Even Helen's harsh, cynical edges had softened as she argued mathematical theorems with Lord John, or watched him, her face impassive, but her eyes sparkling, over a hand of cards. And then there was Adrian, who had made one person at Mrs. Gerrard's feel as though she mattered, feel as though the pain and shame in her life were so irrelevant as not to have existed. Adrian who, with his interest and admiration, had turned back time and transformed her into a young girl again, the girl who had dreamed of happiness and love before they had been so rudely taken away. Adrian, whom she could not wait to see again, even though it had only been a few hours since she had seen him last.

Juliette did not have long to wait. Adrian, after putting in the briefest of appearances at headquarters, long enough to learn the latest plans for removal to the continent, hurried over to Mrs. Gerrard's early the next afternoon while most of London's fashionable world were still in their beds or just taking their morning chocolate which, given that it was well past noon, could hardly be called *morning* chocolate.

He found Juliette bent over her needlework, the sunlight streaming in from the window behind her turning her blond curls to a golden halo. As Rose opened her mouth to announce him, he put a finger to his lips, overcome with a desire just to stare at her, to take in every exquisite detail from the slender fingers so skillful and deliberate in their work to the soft delicate curve of her neck, a neck he longed to trail with slow silken kisses. He found Juliette's total absorption in her work fascinating, compelling, even. No other woman of his acquaintance had ever demonstrated a strong interest in anything, and very few men either, if the truth were told. It bespoke a passion in her that matched his own, a passion that had always set him apart from his bored, world-weary contemporaries, a passion that had often left him isolated and, yes, lonely, until he had discovered that passion in her, and seeing it there had felt oddly like coming home. But, he wondered, could she feel the same passion towards a person that she felt towards her work? That was the question. After all that Juliette had suffered, would she even allow herself to care about anything or anyone except her work?

A wave of longing swept over Adrian, paralyzing in its intensity, as he realized with devastating certainty that he wanted her to care about him, and, even more appalling, he did not have the vaguest notion as to how to go about making it happen. His mouth went dry and he felt his heart pounding at the mere thought of it. And then, sensing his presence, Juliette looked up and smiled and he forgot everything, everything but the welcome in her eyes.

"Mademoiselle Juliette." Adrian sank to his knees beside her chair and, cupping her chin in his hands, devoured her face with his eyes, committing every feature to memory—the slender expressive eyebrows, the short, straight nose and determined chin, the dimples that hovered at either corner of a mouth made for laughter or . . . kissing. With a sigh of desperation that was precisely what he found himself doing, gently at first, but then, as he felt her lips, soft and lush, open underneath his, with a hunger he hadn't known was there. He longed for her, wanted her in so many ways and now, he realized he always had wanted her from the moment he had first seen her, but now he would be leaving, perhaps never to see her again.

His hands slid up the smooth column of her neck to bury themselves in the soft curls, pulling her closer so he could taste her more deeply, craving her the way a man lost in a desert craved water. He felt the sigh of her breath against his lips and almost died at the sweetness of it as, looking down into her half-closed eyes, he gathered her into his arms feeling her soft and warm and infinitely precious against his chest. The long dark lashes swept upward and Adrian found himself staring into her eyes, the blue depths filled with an expression he had never seen before. Had he done something wrong? Did she not feel the same indefinable connection with him that he felt with her? Surely . . . surely, everything his heart and soul were telling him couldn't be wrong?

A slow smile curved the soft lips so close to his. "I am glad it was you," Juliette sighed.

"Me?"

"Who gave me my first kiss."

"What . . . ?"

The smile deepened as she laughed outright. "I am sorry. It is probably not done . . . laughing at such a time, I mean, well, you have no idea how comical you look."

Comical was the last word Adrian would have used to describe his feelings at that particular moment.

Taking pity on him, Juliette reached up to stroke his cheek with a gentle hand. "I know you are thinking that what I am telling you is what you English call a *bouncer*, but in truth, I never *have* been kissed. Other things," her eyes darkened, "yes, but not a kiss. Kissing is for the soul, to be shared only by people who share theirs with someone else; the rest," she shrugged, "is just animal appetite, and never mine."

"Never yours?" Adrian felt an unexpected bubble of happiness rising in him. He had never allowed himself to admit that he cared about the others she had been with, never allowed himself to think that it mattered—after all, he had always known, and she had always been completely forthright about her *profession*—but now, hearing her words, he knew it mattered very much that the others had meant nothing to her. He wanted to be the only one, the only person who had ever made her feel the way he felt, the confusing mixture of tenderness and desire, of longing and companionship, of utter trust and hope, yes hope, that in the vast and careless world, he had found a soulmate.

"*Never* mine." She reached up and kissed him gently on the lips. Her eyes were smiling now, a special smile, just for him, a smile that filled him with a joy he had never known, a joy so sweet he was afraid to believe it could last even as he longed for it to stay with him forever.

"We *filles de joie* have our standards, you know," she explained at last. "What has already been taken from us, well," again she shrugged, "That has already been taken, but we guard that part of ourselves that is still our own, our hearts. Those we do not give, so we do not kiss lightly, if at all."

"And . . ." Adrian, his mind reeling, could not keep himself from asking, "and no one, er, remarks on this?"

Her lips curled scornfully. "They are men. What do they care about love if their . . . er . . . *urges* are satisfied?"

"Oh." He digested this unflattering bit of information for a moment, then, "Does this mean I am *not* a man?"

"Oh you are a man, to be sure." Her voice, low and husky, sent sparks of hot desire shooting through his veins, and the soft feelings of tenderness burst into a passion so intense that he could barely breathe from aching for her. He had no idea he had been holding himself so closely in check until he knew, without a doubt, that she wanted him—no, more than that, *cared* about him. Now, watching the pulse fluttering at the base of her soft white neck, the flush heating her cheeks, and the swelling of her parted lips, he knew. Oh yes, he knew. And with a groan, Adrian pulled her to him, devouring her mouth with his.

For a moment, Juliette was too overwhelmed to respond, or to do anything except let the tide of unexpected, never before experienced emotions and sensations, wash over her. For all her experience at Mrs. Gerrard's, she had never felt anything before. No man's touch had felt any different from any other's, nor had it ever been more than the superficial contact of skin against skin. But at the first brush of Adrian's lips against hers, something had stirred deep within her, uncoiling from her very center and rising slowly, sensuously, until her entire being was aflame with a nameless longing that seemed impossible to satisfy, as though she were dying from a thirst that would never be quenched, and, looking into his eyes as they burned dark with that same unquenchable longing, she knew that he was as much at the mercy of this longing as she was. Only together, could they overcome the tide of desire sweeping over them. Only by giving in to it together did they have any hope of surviving it, of saving their souls or finding peace or happiness ever again.

Oddly enough, for someone who had clung so fiercely to her independence as the only means of self-preservation, Juliette was not afraid. She who had kept herself aloof from all her customers, protecting her heart from everything, safe from further hurt and destruction in its frozen state of isolation, now welcomed the irresistible magnetism of a kindred spirit, and instead of fighting it, she opened her soul to it as she reached up to trace his jaw with her hands before sliding them up to pull his head closer as she savored the sweet discovery of shared desire.

CHAPTER 28

TIME AND SPACE FELL AWAY, and Juliette, carried along by a wave of happiness, lost all sense of everything except Adrian—the smell of him, the feel of him, the comfort of him, and, most surprising of all, a strange tingling of some new unnamable feeling akin to excitement. It was as though she had come alive after being dead during all those years of pain and struggle. How strange that for all her fight to save her soul, only now, seeing herself reflected with tenderness and desire in someone else's eyes, could she be sure that she had won it back.

His lips, warm and firm, moved against hers, lovingly, teasingly, savoring them and evoking responses in her she had never known existed. Sighing, she opened her mouth to him, overcome by longing and the sweetness of it all, aching to be closer, to be one with him. As she wrapped her arms around his neck, he slid his hands slowly down to her waist, pulling her to him so she could feel his heart beating in the broad muscled chest, and the strength in his thighs against hers, so solid and comforting, yet exuding an attraction so powerful she was helpless to resist. So this is what it felt like to want a man!

Slowly, she raised heavy eyelids, hardly daring to open them for fear it was all a wonderful dream that would fade away the moment she looked, but what she saw took her breath away. Adrian, his hair slightly tousled in a way that made him look both irresistibly roguish and adorably boyish, smiled down at her, his face alight with tenderness and happiness, his whole heart in his eyes. So this was what it felt like to love a man!

Juliette knew she should be horrified. Helen's cardinal rule, in fact her only rule, other than that they were to cultivate themselves, act like ladies at all times, and become independent and self-supporting, was never to fall in love, and at the moment, Juliette very much feared she was about to break it. Perhaps it was not quite love, but something very much like. The arms holding her, muscles taut under the deceptively elegant red jacket, felt strong and protective, ready to shield her, as he already had, from the dangers of the world. The lips, now tracing the line of her neck, sending tingles of fire shooting through her with each caress, were loving and arousing all at the same time, and the hands, cradling her hips, melting her very bones, seemed to know her body, its every curve, its every sensation more intimately than she did herself, worshipping it at the same time as they inflamed it with the fervor of an adoring acolyte.

"Ah Juliette, my beautiful girl." Adrian's breath, soft and warm in her ear, sent waves of desire crashing through her. A miracle! It was a miracle that she could feel such things after all she had been through, that a man's touch, once so invasive, humiliating, and disgusting, could now feel so . . . so . . . perfect. Juliette's eyes stung with tears of gratitude, and her throat clogged with the inexpressible wonder of it all.

"Juliette." Sensing the change, Adrian tilted her chin so he could look deep into her eyes, his own now dark with anxiety rather than passion. "Juliette, my love, what is it? Please tell me I have not hurt . . . not offended . . ."

"No, no," she managed a watery smile as she reached up to touch his cheek. "It is just . . . 0just that I am so . . ." she struggled for a word, but there was none in English, or even in French, to describe the riot of emotion. The liquid fire pulsing through her was healing, purifying, and, like the phoenix, she was rising from the ashes of despair and loneliness into a new person, fully alive to the pleasures and happiness the world had to offer. " It is just that I am . . . I am happy."

The surprise and wonder in her voice nearly broke Adrian's heart. Happiness. It was such a simple thing, but she, so lovely, so unassuming and hard-working, had been robbed of it. More than anything, he wanted to give it back to her, to make sure that she was never anything but happy for the rest of her life.

"Mademoiselle, . . . oh, I beg your pardon!" Alice hovered awkwardly in the doorway, clutching the doorknob in one hand and a parcel wrapped in brown paper in the other. She was poised to flee, but Juliette looked up and smiled at her. "I am so sorry, Mademoiselle, but the door was open and you did ask me to bring the lace for Miss Grace's gown as quickly as possible and I did knock, but . . ." Her face crimson, Alice began to back out of the room.

Juliette gently disengaged herself from Adrian's arms. "It's all right, Alice, I did ask you to bring it to me immediately. Thank you."

"Yes, Mademoiselle." The girl ducked her head and was gone.

"A very good girl, Alice, always eager to please and so ready to learn, such a help to us all. She will miss her father when he joins again, and she was just getting to know him." *And I shall miss you*, Juliette thought sadly. And missing him was the least of it. From the lowest street-sweeper to the smallest climbing boy, everyone in London, and all of England, knew that the battle of all battles was to be fought very soon, that troops from nations all over Europe were massing for what everyone hoped would be the last battle against the seemingly invincible Corsican.

"And Tom will miss her, as I shall miss you, Juliette. I came to tell you that I expect our orders are likely to come today. In fact, I am just on my way back to headquarters where we expect to be called away at any minute, but I wanted to see you first, to beg you to save all your time for me before I go."

"*All* my time, Monsieur?" She lifted a coquettishly skeptical eyebrow, but she was smiling all the same. "You are greedy, my lord, very greedy."

Adrian pulled her back into his arms, burying his face in the soft curve of her neck. "Yes," he whispered, his breath warm against her skin, "I am. You have no idea how I crave . . ." it was his turn to cock a teasing eyebrow, "your . . . ah . . . *company.*"

The responding heat flooded Juliette making her blush. Was it a blush of self-consciousness or desire, pure and simple? She did not know which, both emotions being so unfamiliar, but somehow so utterly natural where Adrian was concerned. When he smiled at her, she felt like the most beautiful, most special, most admired, and most desired woman in the world. Surely she did not deserve to feel that way, and surely she wanted to, oh, how desperately she wanted to be that woman.

"Very well, sirrah," she allowed herself to consider for a moment, or at least, appear to do so. "Since you are a soldier about to defend us from le Monstre, I suppose that special considerations can be made, but . . ."

He stopped her mouth with a kiss so full of hunger and passion that it took her breath away. But then, ever since Juliette had laid her eyes on Major Lord Adrian Claverton, he had been taking her breath away on a regular basis. What was it about the man, the aura of daring and intensity, the dashing good looks, or simply the fact that by some gift of fate he seemed to be equally drawn to her? Whatever it was, there was no resisting it, even if she had wanted to.

"Then I shall see you at the opera this evening, and perhaps later? "He flashed a smile as irresistible as it was provocative.

Juliette laughed. "Very well, my lord, until this evening." *And perhaps later.* What was she doing? Had she lost her senses? Perhaps she had, but while cold self-protective reason told her she was making a mistake to let her heart rule her head, a little voice inside her pointed out that it might be her very last chance to see Major Lord Adrian Claverton ever, her last chance at happiness.

Adrian took both her hands in his, lifting them to his lips, then pressing them to his heart. The laughing devilry in his eyes was gone, replaced with a seriousness she had never seen before. "Until this evening, Mademoiselle, and then for as long as we have." Placing her hands gently back by her sides, he bent to kiss her forehead, and then he was gone, and she heard him on the stairs, taking them at what sounded like two at a time.

Craning her neck toward the window, she watched him stride briskly around the corner onto King Street as he headed towards Portman Square. There was an energy about him that gave her pause despite his ardent words. Yes, at the moment he was enamored of her, but what happened when he was once again called into action. Would the chance for fame and glory, the chance to prove himself in what was bound to be the ultimate test for every soldier in every army converging in Belgium wipe all thought of her from his mind? Juliette did not like to think so, but she remembered her father when Auguste had left to join the Bourbon Cavalry Corps in the Peninsula. For days, both before and after his son had left, he had talked about soldiering as the only possible life of honor, reliving his own exploits with a faraway look in his eyes that told her more clearly than if he had spoken the words that during his years in the army, nothing else but honor had existed for him, not his wife, not his children, not even his ancestral home. They all paled in comparison to *la gloire*. How much did Adrian, with what his brother John had referred to as Adrian's *passion to right the wrongs of the world* resemble her father? While it was true that wishing to right the wrongs of the world was not quite the same thing as seeking *la gloire*, it could just as surely dominate a man's life to the exclusion of all else.

Helen would tell her to guard her heart against such a man, but then, Helen told them all to guard their hearts against everyone except one another. Still there was truth in what Helen said. Sighing, Juliette slowly opened the packet of lace Alice had brought her. It was a risk, allowing herself to care, but then she had already lost her heart to Major Lord Adrian Claverton, she might as well enjoy it for the little time they had left.

CHAPTER 29

IN A DARKLY ORNATE DRAWING ROOM in Grosvenor Square, a risk of another sort was being attempted. "I do not want to go to Madame Celeste's, Mama," Lady Georgiana Claverton declared firmly, her lower lip sticking out slightly, just as it had done when, as a two year old, she had stomped her foot defying Nurse to give her a bath.

"But of course you will, my dear," the Duchess, long inured to her daughter's stubbornness, replied smoothly. "Otherwise, you will have nothing to wear."

"But I detest that place. They all laugh at me behind my back, roll their eyes and despair of me as being so hopelessly awkward and unfashionable that nothing can be done."

"And since when did any Claverton pay the least attention to what anyone else has to say, especially a pack of seamstresses?" The Duchess raised her dark eyebrows scornfully. Her children, all fashionably fair, had gotten their coloring from their father, but her daughter had inherited her mother's determined nose and jaw which made her handsome and distinctive rather than pretty. Not that Georgiana cared, her mother thought ruefully; the only things that brought a sparkle of interest to her bright blue eyes were horses and everything related to them, but very little else. Her mother could sympathize; after all, in her day, she had been much like Georgiana, but that did not mean she did not have her duty as a mother.

"What if I know of another modiste, one who understands me and can appreciate the sort of person I am?" Georgie smiled slyly

"What? How would you know such a person? As it is, I have to drag you to Bond Street."

"I don't, but Freddy does," Georgie responded serenely

"Freddy would!"

"Mama, please, if I can have Mademoiselle Juliette as my modiste, then I shall be happy to undergo hours of fittings, but I will *not* go to Madame Celeste's anymore!"

"Very well." The Duchess sighed. It was not her general principle to give in, but in truth, she had as little fondness for Madame Celeste's hoity-toity ways as her daughter, and she was too astounded that Georgiana showed an interest in any modiste to argue. "Talk to Freddy about it then. I must tend to the puppies."

Though she would never admit so much to her daughter, the Duchess of Roxburgh was in London under as much duress as Georgie was, being equally as fond of the country and country pursuits as her daughter, but the Duchess' passion was dogs, and at that very moment her favorite spaniel was in a delicate condition which, despite its being perfectly natural, commanded all of the Duchess' attention.

Georgie took the opportunity of broaching her plan to Freddy the next evening at Almack's when he asked her to stand up for the waltz. "Mama asked me to," he explained at her look of surprise at his stooping so low as to dance with his sister. "Says you need some improvement before you stand up with a real partner. Ouch! My foot! Georgie, doesn't your dancing master teach you anything?"

"Yes," she smiled sheepishly, but I am afraid I wasn't attending. You see, Atalanta has been favoring her right foreleg and . . ."

"Georgie! This is an assembly, not a stable!"

"I know, but I hate having people stare at me and . . ."

"And don't hang your head! You are a Claverton, for heaven's sake. Oh! . . ." he barely refrained from clapping a hand to his mouth in horror, "and now I sound like Mama!"

"You do." Georgie grinned. "And speaking of Mama, she has given me permission to choose my own modiste, and I choose Mademoiselle Juliette, only I don't know her direction. Will you take me there?"

This time Freddy had his hand half way to his mouth before his exquisite manners came to the rescue. They did not, however, prevent him from coming to a dead stop in the middle of the floor. "What! Whaaaaat do you know about Mademoiselle Juliette?"

"That she is a very clever modiste and will come to Claverton House to work instead of my having to be poked and prodded and be on show in front of a gaggle of smirking seamstresses in some horrid shop."

Freddy could not help wondering how many women in London would have given their right arms to be admitted to Madame Celeste's *horrid shop* for poking and prodding.

"I met her, you know," Georgie added, misliking her brother's bemused expression. Freddy was a dear, but too easily distracted. One could start off a conversation with him on a perfectly unexceptionable topic, such as the races at Newmarket, only to find that his mind had wandered off to the most fashionable color for carriage dresses or the superiority of mull muslin to jaconet for trimming on a walking dress.

"You met her!" The acute discomfort in Freddy's expression turned to abject horror.

"Yes. Adrian and I ran into her in the park. I must say, she is quite lovely, and ever so nice. She says that one shouldn't force a person into a style because it is à la mode, but choose one that is most flattering to that person. A very good scheme, I think, and a clever one too; then one doesn't end up looking like everyone else."

But she had lost him. Freddy was searching frantically for some idea, any idea, to keep the project from going any further. Mademoiselle Juliette absolutely could *not* show up at Claverton House. Lavinia was bound to find out, bound to make inquiries, all in the interests of doing the best for the Claverton name, and then there would be hell to pay, for Lavinia would put the worst possible interpretation on the situation and make them all miserable. And while it was true that she made them all miserable anyway, Freddy didn't want her making them any more miserable, and he certainly didn't want her making Mademoiselle Juliette miserable at all. She was too sweet and kind and had suffered too much as it was.

"Ah . . . certainly I will speak to Mademoiselle Juliette, but since, as you say, you have already met her, perhaps we can save some time by having her sketch out some possible designs for your perusal and then you can discuss them with her," he suggested, his mind working furiously to develop a plan for an unexceptionable meeting place that was not Claverton House and definitely *not* Mrs. Gerrard's. The Claverton brothers might be in a fair way to calling it a second home, but there was no possible way, by no stretch of the imagination that a Claverton sister could.

Georgie beamed. "Famous! Thank you, Freddy. I knew I could count on you."

Which, thought Freddy gloomily, was perhaps the first time that anyone in his family had ever felt that way and he was, more likely than not, going to be unable to deliver on his promise. But then he was struck by a Brilliant Idea which actually was so brilliant he wondered that he had not come up with it before.

"Actually Freddy," Juliette pointed out to him the next day when he presented her with his Brilliant Idea, "you *did* offer to set me up in my own shop before and I refused, graciously, of course. Don't you remember?"

"Yes," Freddy was unfazed, "but this is an altogether different sort of thing, don't you see?"

Juliette did *not* see, but she was far too tenderhearted to say so.

"Here is the thing. My sister has taken it in her head that she wants you for her dressmaker and no one else will do."

"That is very kind of Lady Georgiana, but she has not really seen any of my work," Juliette demurred, but she still could not help feeling gratified at the thought of her first real patroness.

"Apparently, she's seen enough of you and the carriage dresses you and Grace were wearing to make up her mind. And once Georgie makes up her mind, there is no stopping her." His heartfelt sigh told her that Freddy spoke from abundant experience with his sister's stubbornness.

"We can't have Georgie visiting you here and we . . ."

"Can't have me visiting her, I certainly agree."

"It's not what you think, Mademoiselle," Freddy flushed uncomfortably. "My mother and Georgie would find no fault with that, but Lady Lavinia . . ."

"Lady Lavinia? Surely she has her own modiste."

"She does, but she's deep, very deep, and if she were to encounter you at Claverton House she would not rest until she found out everything about you. *Everything!*"

"But surely she does not live at Cl . . ."

"No, but she concerns herself with its affairs as though it were hers. It will be some day," he finished gloomily. "So you see, if I were to set you up in a shop, everything would be all right and tight, no questions asked."

"But, my lord, I already told you, I cannot let you do that. I cannot be beholden to you, not that it is not all that is kind and generous."

"I understand, but here is the difference; you already have one customer, so you can consider it as a loan for fitting up Georgie in style. And you did say you have been saving to start a shop of your own someday. Why not sooner rather than later? Besides, I saw just the place in Burlington Gardens, Cork Street. It is not Bond Street, but still an excellent address, and a good price too."

Never mind Lady Lavinia discovering a *fille de joie* at Claverton House, Juliette thought, if she had heard the future Duke of Roxburgh talking of a commercial establishment to be had *at a good price*, she would have fainted dead away. Juliette, however, found it infinitely touching and sweet, and so like Freddy, bless his kindhearted soul

"It is not so very far away from here that you couldn't see everyone nearly as much as you do now," he added anxiously.

"Dear Freddy," Juliette laughed as she patted his arm. "You think of everything."

"I know you are devoted to Helen, naturally so; she is all that is admirable, but you know she wishes for you, all of you, to be established on your own eventually. You will think about it? And speak to Helen?"

"I will. And in the meantime, shall I sketch some ideas I have for Lady Georgiana?"

"Famous!" Freddy clapped his hands as excitedly as any lad who had just received his first cricket bat and ball.

After he had left, Juliette sat for a long time staring across the square in the direction of Burlington Gardens. Her own shop! She had dreamt of it for so long that now, when there was even a glimmer of possibility, she was suddenly afraid. What if she were not so good as she thought she was? What if Lady Georgiana were her only customer, or what if Freddy's sister had her way, returned to the country and had no further need for a fashionable London modiste? All were unsettling questions, none of which she could begin to answer. There was one person, however, who could, another woman who had gone into business on her own, taken on the fashionable world and made it beat a path to her door, the male contingent of it least, another woman with a vision who had made it come to life, and very successfully too, year in and year out. Helen could tell her what to do. With her head for accounts and her vast experience, she could tell Juliette in a moment whether it was the beginning of a whole new life or simply an impossible dream.

CHAPTER 30

Helen was cautiously optimistic. "Well you have been able to set a good deal aside in the three per cents to use towards rent for the first few months, and to purchase what you will need to start, but what does Freddy propose to do?"

"He will take care of the setting up of the shop in return for my designing a wardrobe for his sister. I shall use my savings to pay for the rent and he has agreed to lend me more should I need it in the first few months before I have attracted a regular clientele. I shall keep a strict accounting of it all, the value of Lady Georgiana's wardrobe, my expenses, and the interest I owe him on anything I borrow."

"That's my girl." Helen nodded approvingly. "No gifts. You want to know you can do this on your own, no matter what happens to Freddy."

"Of course." Tentatively, Juliette withdrew a packet of papers from her pocket. "I have drawn it all up, what I think will be my expenses, I mean. Would you be so good . . . I mean . . . could I ask you to look them over to see if they seem accurate and reasonable?"

Helen was silent for so long that Juliette was afraid that she had somehow annoyed or insulted her benefactress. Was she being ungrateful by leaving after all Helen had given her? Or was it that her leaving would affect the account books at their establishment more than she realized? Cursing herself for her insensitivity, Juliette began folding up the papers to put back in her pocket when Helen stopped her. Only then did Juliette dare look up at her.

To her utter amazement, the scornful green eyes were awash with tears, the ironic lips quivering. "Helen? I did not mean, I do beg your . . ."

"No, no . . ." Blinking rapidly, Helen patted her shoulder, then, reaching into her own pocket, she pulled out a handkerchief and, blowing her nose briskly, summoned up a watery smile. "It is just that I am so happy, so proud. This is my dream, Juliette, to have all my girls leave me for a secure future of their own making. It is what I wish for above all else, what I have worked for these past ten years. Truly, there is no need to look alarmed. I had no idea I would be so overcome; I had thought I buried all my feelings long ago, but yes, it does mean so much to me—everything, in fact." She squeezed Juliette's hand that was still holding the accounts. "I shall be delighted to look these over. Now go, start drawing up your sketches for Lady Georgiana. It is high time for you to fulfill *your* dreams now that you have fulfilled mine."

When Juliette rose to go, she found her legs shaking. She had no idea how much she had counted on Helen's approval for the project. If Helen Gerrard, hardheaded businesswoman of St. James' Square thought she would succeed, then Juliette knew she would. She could have received no higher vote of confidence than that. As she reached the door, Helen's voice stopped her.

"And Juliette?"

Juliette turned to find Helen beaming at her.

"Thank you."

"Thank you???"

"Yes, for being my first example to the other girls. Once you have established yourself, they will see it *can* be done. I can only give them a place to live and a way to earn money. *You* are showing them the next step."

Juliette was completely unprepared for the wave of pride that swept over her. Helen was right, she *was* showing them the next step. Instead of being a victim, she had become a leader. She had refused to give up and now she was winning her place in the world, or, at least she was well on the way to doing so. This decision made her feel strong and unafraid, bold even, and it suddenly occurred to her that this was how Adrian must feel on the eve of battle. Perhaps she had been too harsh in thinking it was only fame and glory he pursued; maybe it was a sense of purpose, a way of owning his own life.

Happier than she had ever been, Juliette raced to her chamber, taking the steps two at a time, just as Adrian did. She grabbed up her pencil and sketchbook, plopped herself in a chair and, calling up a vision of Lady Georgiana Claverton in her mind, began drawing furiously.

These same sketches arrived at Claverton House a few days later where Georgiana, tired of practicing the pianoforte, seized them eagerly and took them to the drawing room window overlooking Grosvenor Square. "Yes!" she breathed as she opened the brown paper wrapping to discover a simple slate-colored riding dress with smooth flowing lines and a businesslike hat to match. The solid color and total lack of fussy detail would make her less *gawky* as Madame Celeste would say.

The next sketch was of a ball gown, equally simple, whose compelling design and cut, rather than frills and furbelows drew the viewer's eye. Wearing it, she would not feel fussy and out of place the way she did in her newest gown which was awash in grape blossom and cockle shell trimming.

"What, no pianoforte practice?" Lady Lavinia's well-bred voice interrupted her absorption.

"I *was* practicing," Georgie tried not to sound defensive. After all, Lavinia was only her future sister-in-law, not Mama or her music teacher, but somehow one always felt defensive with Lavinia, "but some sketches just arrived from my dressmaker."

It was impossible to ignore the lavender kid-gloved hand thrust under her nose. Sighing, Georgie handed over the sketches.

Sniffing slightly, Lavinia frowned critically at the drawings. "They are not badly done. Rather elegant, in a severe sort of way for Madame Celeste."

"Oh, they are not Madame Celeste's."

Lavinia arched an eyebrow.

"It is a new modiste, a fr . . . a shop Freddy discovered."

"Did he now?" Lavinia's coolly elegant tones grew decidedly frosty.

"Yes on his way from Brooks's I believe. It is a new business, a Mademoiselle Juliette."

Lavinia's lip curled scornfully. "Mademoiselle Juliette, hrrmph."

"Yes. Do you know her?"

"Good heavens no! Undoubtedly she is simply a creature who is no better than she should be and therefore beneath one's notice and has decided to make a name for herself by calling herself a *modiste*, but she is *not* a modiste."

"Well *I* would say . . ." Georgie began and then thought better of it. She was not about to discuss Juliette with someone who dismissed her so callously. Lavinia's superior airs had always grated on Georgie, but now they were beginning to put her in a temper. Little as she knew Juliette, she had liked her immediately and was not about to expose her to further censure from a nastily sanctimonious ape-leader like her future sister-in-law. Actually, Lavinia wasn't precisely an ape-leader—she was engaged to Freddy after all—but she had the unfortunate temperament of one and she had not yet been able to bring Freddy completely up to scratch, Freddy who was generally the most obliging, most compliant soul in the world, which said a great deal, to Georgie at least, about Lady Lavinia's temperament.

"Very wise not to elaborate further. I should drop all association. A young lady should not know such things, much less speak of them."

"*I* was *not* speaking of them, Lavinia, *you* were. Now if you will excuse me, I shall go fetch Mama since I am sure she is the person you wish to see." And grabbing up her sketches, Georgie stalked from the room with all the dignity of her ferocious mother, leaving Lavinia open-mouthed.

"Well, I never! What do *you* want?" She rounded on the impressive footman who had materialized beside her.

"Lady Georgiana sent me to inquire as to whether you would like any refreshment." George was at his most majestic. Lady Georgiana had encountered him in the hall and instructed him to wait on *her future Grace,* as all the servants who disliked her hoity-toity ways, called Lavinia, "for I am sure she is in need of a restorative draft or something" she had added as she stomped off. Lady Georgiana had been a rare taking over something, the footman thought, but then *her future Grace* had that effect on people. So, hoping, in his own humble way to pay back *her future Grace* for whatever she had done to his young mistress, not to mention his young mistress' long suffering elder brother, George had straightened to the utmost of his six feet four inches and adopted his most lofty tone.

"Nothing!" Lavinia snapped. "I require nothing!" And she stalked out of the room, forgetting her errand entirely, which was not surprising since it had been largely manufactured anyway. Freddy had been even less in attendance than usual and Lavinia, though serenely confident of her place in the world and her glorious future as the next Duchess of Roxburgh, was growing uneasy, for what good did an engagement to the heir of a dukedom do if the heir was nowhere to be seen, or at least not hovering dutifully by one's side at the major gatherings of the *ton*?

Lavinia might not have been best pleased with the state of affairs, but her fiancé was in seventh heaven. In fact, his enthusiasm for his latest project was such that Juliette was constantly having to rein him in, in his plans for the shop. "I agree that silk drapes at the sides of the windows create an elegant effect, but the expense is ruinous. They will have to wait," she was admonishing him at that very moment.

Freddy's look of disappointment was heartrending, but Juliette held firm. "Helen has calculated down to the last penny how much I can safely invest in both the shop and supplies, as well as the scheme for paying you back, and I simply cannot afford it." She patted his arm encouragingly, "But when I am established I shall have income, and the drapes will be the very first thing I do with it."

Freddy brightened. "And the gowns for Georgie?"

"Coming along splendidly. She has approved the designs for all of them, but I am beginning with the riding dress." Juliette held out a sketch and a sample of the cloth.

"The color will go excellently with her coloring which tends to be a trifle high, what with her passion for riding, fresh air, and country pursuit, and I do think the ruching in the shoulders is quite cunning. It gives it a feminine air without being fussy. I quite like it."

"Coming from you, that is high praise indeed! I thought it best to start with something she will enjoy wearing; the ball dress will come later, much later."

"Our Georgie is a sad romp," Freddy sighed, "and there is nothing she detests so much as a ball. You are wise to wait."

CHAPTER 31

JULIETTE MIGHT WAIT, BUT HISTORY-IN-THE-MAKING COULD NOT, and the speed with which events were unfolding on the continent was alarming. Adrian was so involved with plans at headquarters that, despite his resolve to spend as much of the time he had left with Juliette, he was scarcely seen at Mrs. Gerrard's until one morning Juliette received a note begging her to reserve the entire next day for him.

When he arrived the following morning there was an air of suppressed excitement about him as he instructed her to bring a parasol and shawl in addition to the green sarsnet pelisse she was searing. "It is a surprise," he responded, smiling at her puzzled expression. He led her to the carriage, refusing to say anything more as they made their way along Pall Mall to Whitehall and the stairs leading down to the river. It was only as Adrian helped her out of the carriage that Juliette noticed the large wicker hamper the coachman unloaded and carried down to an elegant shallop whose curtained cabin in the stern offered luxurious protection against the sun or a possible chilly breeze.

"A boat!" Juliette let go of Adrian's arm to admire the exquisite craft with its long slim lines and velvet cushioned seats under the gaily striped awning.

A waiting footman stowed the hamper, climbed out, and then stood back as Adrian handed Juliette in and took his own place in the stern. "Everything all right, sir?"

"Yes, thank you, Sam. You may go home with John now," Adrian nodded to the carriage. "And I shall meet you back here at the time we agreed upon."

"Very good, sir. Enjoy yourself, sir."

"Thank you, Sam. I intend to." Adrian grinned conspiratorially at Juliette, then, leaning into the oars, pulled smoothly away from the landing.

"A boat!" Juliette repeated in wondering tones. "I have never been on the river, you know."

"What? Not even to Vauxhall?"

"The only time I went there, it was by carriage . . . .and of course that was at night. This," she looked around eagerly taking it all in—the scores of boats moving up, down, and across the Thames' vast expanse, the wavering reflections of the buildings in the silvery water, the gentle breeze blowing upriver, "is so much nicer. It is as though one has been transported into another world, familiar, but, at the same time, so very different."

"We *are* in another world," Adrian smiled at her, "*our* world, where nothing exists but the two of us, no rules of the *ton*, no looming battles, not even time itself. Now relax, lie back, and enjoy it while I explore it with you."

"How lovely!" Juliette sighed, sinking back against the velvet pillows. Turning her face to the breeze, she allowed her arm to dangle limply over the side as she trailed her fingers in the water, letting all the daily tensions of life slip away. The rhythmic dipping of the oars into the glassy surface was hypnotic, and the scenery gliding slowly by soon lulled her into a trance of peace and contentment which only lasted long enough for her to become aware of her captain's well-muscled arms pulling them along so steadily and swiftly. The day was warm and the sun beating down on them had caused Adrian to remove his jacket before they had even pulled away from the landing. Now the faint sheen of sweat that highlighted the angles of his face, the high cheek bones, forceful nose, and square jaw, and plastered the fine linen of his shirt to his body so every plane of his broad chest, every flex of his arm was outlined in exquisite, tantalizing detail.

Juliette drew a quavery breath, the gentle languor of the moment exploded by a sudden desire to hurl herself against that hard chest, to feel the power of all those muscles against her. Once again she found herself wondering that, after all the men she had known, she had never noticed anything about them, but *this* man . . . ! Every physical detail of Adrian, from his well-shaped hands with their lean strong fingers, to the bright blue eyes, the tiny cowlick on his forehead that gave him his a boyish, slightly raffish air, to the square shoulders and magnificent carriage took her breath away and filled her with longing—a longing to be closer to him, a longing to be part of him, a longing for, she knew not what—for everything, and for nothing, except him.Hardly daring to breathe, she sat transfixed by the irresistible urge to touch him, to feel the hard, smooth muscles in his arms, to trace his jaw, to . . . .Juliette shook her head as she tried to take herself in hand and re-establish control over these dangerous thoughts. Then, as the crowded buildings of the city gave way to fields and flowering trees, birdsong and the deep lowing of cows in the distance, she gave up. It was only one day, after all, *their* day. Nothing existed but the two of them, he had said, and tomorrow, or the next day, or the next, he would be gone, gone, perhaps never to return.

Gathering her skirts around her and keeping herself low in the center of the boat, Juliette edged forward. Tilting his head curiously, Adrian shipped his oars, watching her careful progress.

"Let me help you." She grasped the gunwales, delicately putting one foot ahead of the other.

"Help me?"

"There is no reason that you should do all the work by yourself. I can take one oar and you the other. It will be easier and faster with two." Juliette hoped it did not sound like the obvious ploy that it was to get closer to him.

Adrian grinned. "So it will . . . if you know what you are doing. If you don't, it will be a disaster."

"I have eyes in my head. I can see that we must be evenly matched. And I think we are, evenly matched, I mean. Do you not think so?" She raised a quizzical eyebrow.

"His lips twitched, but he answered seriously enough. "Definitely. Yes, Mademoiselle Juliette, in you I have certainly met my match. Here. Come sit beside me."

He was unprepared for the rush of tenderness as she sank carefully onto the seat beside him. She was so lovely, but with an impishness that was irresistible, and she wanted to help. What woman ever wanted to help, much less work? Every other one of her sex, Georgie and his mother excepted, wanted to be waited on hand and foot—not only wanted it, but demanded it. This woman wanted to share. The warmth of her thigh next to his as she settled herself next to him sent a jolt of something more than tenderness through him and Adrian nearly lost his grip on the oars.

"I can take it now." Her hands, small and delicate, but infinitely capable closed around the oar he was holding. She tilted her head to look at him, eyes glinting with mischief and knowing, both a playful girl and a worldly-wise woman in one potent mixture.

He drew a steadying breath. "Very well, on the count of two. One, two, one, two." And they were off, rowing smoothly upriver as though they had done it together all their lives.

They rowed in silence for a long time as fields glided by, coots darting back and forth in the water ahead of them, their black and white heads bobbing, and the occasional majestic swan glancing haughtily as if mocking their inferior and laborious mode of transport. Juliette kept up with him stroke for stroke, not betraying the least signs of tiring, and once again, Adrian found himself admiring her in a way he had never admired a woman before—her competence, her stamina—things he had only admired in his companions-at-arms. But then he would catch the scent of rosewater rising from her heated skin, glance down at the tendrils of golden hair clinging to the long smooth neck, and be struck all over again by her exquisite femininity and a hunger so intense it made him dizzy just to look at her.

They rounded a curve and came upon a deliciously secluded spot where an old willow bending over the water provided a green curtain of privacy. "If you will hold my oar, I shall drop anchor so we may stop awhile and refresh ourselves after all the exertion." Adrian once again marveled over a woman he could trust to remain calm and steady while he accomplished his task. It was actually rather nice to share a task with someone instead of relying solely on himself as he usually did.

"There now, Mademoiselle, this is your outing so please make yourself comfortable on these cushions while I wait upon you." With quiet efficiency, Adrian produced a cloth, plates, cutlery, and glasses and laid them out on a small folding table, followed by cold chicken, pigeon pie, strawberries, cheese, an assortment of tarts, and a bottle that he opened with a flourish before pouring its contents into a glass and handing it to her. "Lemonade. Or would you prefer wine?"

"Lemonade is lovely." Juliette's senses were already so overwhelmed by the warmth of the day, the mesmerizing glimmer of water slipping by, not to mention the exertion of rowing that she feared a glass of wine would render her completely insensible at a moment when she wanted every part of her alive to enjoy and treasure each moment of this perfect day.

As they ate, watching birds flitting in and out of the willow and the occasional fish jumping, Adrian told her all about his estate near Newmarket and his plans for raising horses. "After all his travails, poor old Caesar will be somewhat taken aback to share quarters with such poor creatures as race horses, but he deserves a rest after his loyal service. No man could have had a better companion. Many a time he has carried me on when I lacked the strength to do so myself."

"And now I count on him to keep you safe."

"Now, none of that, Mademoiselle Juliette," he laid a finger to her slips, smiling into the grave blue eyes, then, selecting the largest, juiciest strawberry he could find, stroked it gently over her bottom lip. When she opened her mouth in surprise, he popped it in. "Concentrate on the pleasures of today," he breathed in her ear before trailing warm kisses down her neck and back again to her mouth where he gently licked off a stray drop of strawberry juice. "Ah, Juliette!"

Juliette's head fell back against the cushions as her entire body seemed to dissolve at his touch. Ever since his lips had first touched hers, she had been dreaming of it happening again, longing for it, yet fearing it for the powerful responses his kiss had evoked in her. Now here, in this watery world apart, she gave up all thought, all consciousness except for desire, the desire to be loved and cherished. His arms stole around her, hands sliding up her back to cradle her head ever so gently as he pressed his mouth to hers, caressing, demanding. Her lips parted in a sigh of pure pleasure as his tongue swept across them, sending shivers down her spine and throughout her entire body. Gasping for breath, she wrapped her arms around him, feeling the hard ridges of muscle along his back as she clung to him, aching for his strength, his warmth, desperate to be part of him.

His lips devoured hers, his tongue tasting the warm flesh as it mingled with hers, filling her with heat and wanting. One hand slid around her shoulder to cup her cheek as he pulled away to look deep into her eyes. "I want you, Juliette," his voice was hoarse, his breathing ragged, and she could not help smiling at the thought that he seemed to be as desperate for her as she was for him. He held her with his gaze, alert for the slightest hint of unease as his hand slid down to the buttons on her gown, gently undoing them one by one.

Faintly at the back of her mind, Juliette wondered if, hoping that their promised last outing would be an intimate one, she had chosen this dress on purpose, a morning dress buttoning up the front rather than one of her usual carriage dresses with a high ruffled neck, but all further thought was obliterated as Adrian pushed aside the heavy lace trimming and cupped her breasts, claiming them. His touch was both assured and adoring as he stroked the tender skin, worshipping her body. Her head fell back as she reveled in his touch; she had never felt so cherished. Then he bent his head, sucking first one tight nipple and then the other and the dreamy reverence disappeared in a flash of fire.

"Please," she gasped, winding her arms around his neck.

"What, sweetheart?"

"Oh, I don't know, just please, I . . ." Juliette couldn't name the longing devouring her. She was dying of what felt like thirst, desperate for the drink that would satisfy her.

Adrian gazed down into her flushed face, the eyes heavy-lidded with desire and was nearly lost himself. Never had he wanted a woman so much, never had he been so unbearably aware that he held her happiness in his hands. Did she want him as much as he wanted her? Was it because she cared for him, ached with tenderness the way he did at every stray curl of hair, at the tiny frown between her eyebrows, the dimple at the corner of her mouth the delicate capable hands, the heartbreakingly beautiful smile? Did she feel the same way about him? Or was he just one among many?

"Adrian, please," she whispered.

And then he was lost. He plunged his mouth onto hers, sliding his hand up her thigh, the thin muslin of her gown slipping away like so many spider webs revealing warm firm flesh that he longed to bury himself in, lose himself forever. Slowly he trailed kisses up her inner thigh as her breathing grew more ragged until at last he was beyond thought, beyond concern for all the unhappy memories of her painful past as he felt the quivering response to his kiss.

"Aaaah . . ." The deep primal moan of pleasure told him that she too was beyond all conscious thought. Then her hands were pulling on his shoulders, sliding under his shirt to dig into his back. "Please, Adrian."

Never taking his eyes off her face, he reached into his pocket and pulled out a French letter, slipped in on and tied it with its gaily colored ribbon. "Are you sure?" He searched her eyes for any hint of doubt, but all he was passion, a passion mixed with a yearning that told him he, and only he, was the object of her desire. "Ah Juliette," he cupped her face with his hand as he kissed her mouth slowly and completely, then, unable to bear being apart from her for a moment longer, he buried himself inside her, losing himself in the welcoming heat.

She arched to meet him, pressing herself against him, giving herself to him, responding to every thrust with a feverish intensity that matched his own. Desperately he clung to the remaining shreds of sanity as he matched his pace to hers, moving to give her all the pleasure that was consuming him. He ducked his head to swirl his tongue around each taut pink nipple, slowly, round and round, matching every thrust as he felt the rising tension build within her, tightening, tightening until they both shattered in a single cry. Then, gently, gently, he pulled her to him, cradling her as she sobbed uncontrollably. "There, there, my love. Hush, my love, my precious Juliette." She could not say precisely why she cried except that it was all too much, an onslaught of emotions so overwhelming that there was nothing left to do but cry as she clung to him, the only solid thing in a universe that had just turned upside down. Her body, which had for so long been the enemy, the victim of someone else's lust, had somehow become hers again. Healed by his lovemaking, she lay protected, cherished, and content. For the first time in her life, she was not driven by a longing, by a striving for she knew not what. All her life she had been possessed by a need to prove herself, to make a place for herself in the world so that she mattered, so that people saw her as herself, Juliette, not the dutiful daughter of the house of de Fournoy, nor the potential lovely ornamental wife of some carefully chosen spouse, or Juliette the elegant, exclusive *fille de joie*, but Juliette, just Juliette. At last, looking up into eyes filled with tenderness and concern only for her, she was just Juliette, satisfied, happy, and at peace with the world.

"I love you, Juliette. *Come live with me and be my love.*" Adrian's lips brushed hers in the gentlest, most reverent of kisses as he pulled her close to his chest. She lay against him, the breeze ruffling her hair, the warm sun caressing her bare shoulder and thought that now she could die happy. If only this moment would never end. But even when it did, as it inevitably had to, it was hers to treasure for the rest of her life.

Juliette, being Juliette, could not completely ignore reality. Her life had been all too subject to its bitter lessons, and her practical nature soon reasserted itself, warning her that, as Helen had always maintained, love was a dream for other young women, but not those of Mrs. Gerrard's. "Sssh," she traced a soft white finger over those firm lips which had so tenderly and erotically evoked responses from her she had not even known she possessed, "let us live for today only, here in this world that is ours and ours alone. Let us forget everything else, but this." She reached up and kissed him, a long smoldering kiss that spoke of all her hopes and dreams.

"You will get no objection from me." Adrian grinned as he leaned down to suckle her aching nipples, and the fire between them burst into flame again.

CHAPTER 32

THE SUN WAS SINKING IN THE SKY as they rowed leisurely back downriver to the Whitehall Stairs and the waiting carriage. "St. James's Square, as slowly as you can," Adrian instructed the coachman before climbing in next to Juliette.

As the carriage began to roll off down Whitehall, he leaned forward, gathering her hands in his. "Today has been our special day, Juliette, and we have not talked of what is to come. Tomorrow the troops are to be reviewed and the next day we are off. This is the last time I shall see you for quite some time. I have Caesar and my own incredible skill and bravado," he grinned, "but events to come are likely to prove uncertain and hazardous in the extreme. They would seem much less uncertain and hazardous if I knew you were provided for." Her puzzled frown was infinitely adorable and he could hardly keep himself from kissing her, but what he had to say was too important. "I love you and I have loved you from the moment I first saw you. Please let me take care of you. I saw a wonderful little house in Marylebone. Please tell me you will let me buy it for you and you will wait for me there. Please let me give you all the comforts of life you so richly deserve and have never had. Please give me the thought of you waiting there for me as something to take away with me and sustain me in whatever is to come."

He saw the doubt in her eyes as he pulled her into his arms. "Please." Pressing his lips to hers he poured his whole soul into his kiss, willing her to want it, to want him as desperately as he wanted her. "We are one now, you cannot deny that?"

Juliette shook her head slowly. No, she could not deny that; he had taken possession of her soul and her heart as surely as he had her body, but no matter how much she longed to say yes, she held back. It was all a dream, too beautiful to be true. And dreams did not last; life had taught her that. What would she do when the dream died? Helen had taught her that one took care of oneself. It was the only way to be sure of the future. Depending on someone else, even someone as noble and kind as Major Lord Adrian Claverton, meant giving that up.

"Dearest Adrian," her eyes brimmed with tears, "I *do* love you with all my heart. You have given me so much—everything, in fact. You have restored my soul to me, but I cannot . . . ." She gulped down the sob that rose in her throat and struggled bravely on before she lost her nerve, "I cannot let you take care of me."

"But why sweetheart?" He pushed away a stray curl and gently wiped away the tears on her cheek with his thumb. "I *want* to take care of you."

"I know." She summoned up a wavering smile which quickly went awry. "It is a lovely thought and I thank you from the bottom of my heart, but I cannot let you take care of me. *I* need to take care of me."

He tilted her chin to gaze into her eyes, his own grave with love and concern. "But why? Why can't you let someone who adores you fulfill the wish of his heart and do that for you?"

"I am afraid." It was the barest of whispers before she buried her head in his shoulder and sobbed.

There was nothing to do in the face of such terrible distress except hold her close and stroke her hair. "Hush, my love. There, there, my love." Adrian did not completely understand, but his heart ached for her just the same.

At last she pulled away with a watery chuckle. "Not a very flattering response to an offer kindly meant."

One corner of his mouth quirked up. "No, but I am strong—battle tested and all that."

She sighed. "And very, very kind. I know you do not understand. It is all so sudden, and I am so accustomed to depending on myself. It is my only strength."

"No," he kissed her gently. "You have many strengths—talent, intelligence, humor, beauty, and self-reliance to a fault. Just know that I adore you and you will always be in my thoughts."

"And I love you." She buried her face in his neck, reveling in the warmth of his skin, his masculine smell of shaving soap mixed with sweat, the comforting strength of his arms around her. She would not allow herself to be taken care of by him as another woman might have, but surely, when he was going off to face the ultimate test, she could allow herself to admit that she loved him.

With a final searing kiss, he pulled away and climbed out of the carriage to help her down, escorting her in silence up the steps where the new footman was waiting to let her in. Even now, Tom Sandys was at home packing their bags. "Goodbye, my love. Hold me in your heart until I return." He lifted both her hands to his lips, kissing first one and then the other.

"I shall. And I will pray to *le bon Dieu* to watch over you and Caesar." Juliette's voice was so clogged with tears she could barely get out the words. Then, not wanting to make it worse by revealing her distress any further, she hurried inside.

Fortunately, no one was around to see her as she dashed up to her bedchamber, or so she thought. Through the open door in her office, Helen, poring over accounts, caught a quick glimpse of muslin skirts swirling up the stairs and shook her head sadly. Freddy had told her of Adrian's imminent departure and Dora had seen Adrian handing Juliette into the carriage that morning. It did not take as clever a mathematical mind as Helen's to put two and two together. She ached for her young charge. To Helen, all the women in her establishment were her daughters in one form or another, but it was best this way. There could be no happy ending for one of her girls and the son of one of England's most powerful dukes. Better to have the brief sharp pain of parting for a heroic cause than the long soul-destroying course of waning interest followed by marriage with a woman of Adrian's own social circle and children. Still, it was painful, and every single soul in her care had suffered too much pain already in their short young lives.

Helen sighed and nibbled on her pencil as she debated whether or not to go after Juliette. Intellect told her one thing, her heart another. Her heart won out. "Juliette?"

There was no response so Helen rapped on the door, more forcefully this time, and entered.

Juliette was sitting in the chair by the window gazing blankly across the square. She turned slowly as Helen approached. "He is gone."

"I know." Helen pulled the chair by the fireplace to face her and sat down.

"I love him."

Helen smiled sadly. "I know that too."

"You told us never to fall in love, but I could not help it. He is so . . . so . . ."

"Magnificent," Helen finished wryly.

Juliette nodded. "And I would rather have loved him despite the pain of his going than never to have known love at all. And besides," she lifted her chin with a proud defiant little smile, "even though nothing will ever come of it, I know he loves me—for now, at least. And being loved," the smile turned dreamy, "is worth all the pain of its loss. I would not trade it for the world."

This was uncharted territory. Helen, for all her worldly experience, had never been in love, and it was her fondest wish never to have the least, even the slightest brush with that emotion, but she could tell from the glow in Juliette's eyes that, for her at least, it truly *was* worth it.

CHAPTER 33

THE REVIEW AT FIVE FIELDS THE NEXT DAY was long and tiring and mostly, like all reviews, involved a great deal of standing around before they were dismissed to make their final preparations.

Adrian rode straight to Claverton House where he found Georgie in the drawing room perusing some drawings. "Carriage dresses and a riding habit, aren't they just bang-up designs?" She held the drawing out to him.

"What? Who has stolen my sister, Georgie, and who are you?"

She laughed. They are Juliette's designs and they really are quite handsome; they also look comfortable. I am so delighted that she is setting up her own shop so I will be able to visit her there. I *do* like her, Adrian. She *is* nice, isn't she?"

But the question was lost on her brother who stood staring blankly at the sketches in his hands. "Her own shop?" He asked hoarsely.

"Why yes. And Freddy is helping her."

But she spoke to his retreating back as he ran down the stairs, not two, but three at a time. In too much of a hurry to have a horse saddled up, he strode off towards St. James's Square, his mounting hurt and anger increasing his pace until he was practically running through the streets. Not only had Juliette not trusted him enough to care for her, she had not even told him her plans! And worse than all that, she had allowed Freddy, his own brother, the man who avoided responsibility like the plague, to come to her aid! Adrian could barely see the passersby for the red mist of rage and frustration that rose before his eyes.

It seemed an age before he arrived in St. James's Square just, as luck would have it, Juliette and Grace were descending the front steps on an errand. One look at the white set lines of his face and Grace suddenly remembered she had forgotten something inside.

"My lord," Juliette too was struck by his grim expression. "This is an unexpected pleasure?"

"How could you?" His voice was low. But there was no mistaking the fury as he propelled her back up the steps into the drawing room and shut the door.

"How could I what?"

"You *know* I wanted to take care of you. I offered you everything—my heart, my life—but you let Freddy . . . . Freddy, that . . ."

"Freddy is the kindest person on earth," Juliette responded firmly, but with a dangerous sparkle in her eyes, "and he is nothing but kind."

"Kind!" Adrian snorted. "Your protector, more like."

"No one!" Her eyes flashed blue sparks now. "*No one* is my protector!"

"What do you call buying you a shop?" His voiced dripped with scorn.

Juliette drew herself to her full height which, unfortunately was only enough to reach to his chin. "Freddy found the shop for me, but I put up my *own* money for it and he has lent me some more, at three percent, I might add, to stock it. I have the entire contract, witnessed by Helen, if you care to see it, along with my proposal for acquiring customers and paying him back. Now if there is nothing else you need to know, I have errands to do."

"I loved you. I offered to take care of you," he grabbed her wrist, pulling her to him and bringing his face close to hers so she could practically feel the tension in his jaw and the pulse beating furiously in his temple.

"I know, and it was very kind of you," she faltered as her own defensive anger sputtered from hot sparks of righteous indignation to the corroding ashes of sadness, "and I think you from the bottom of my heart. But you *know* why I could not let you."

"I thought I did," he hissed through clenched teeth, "until I found out that you can let Freddy take care of you, but not me."

"It is not the same thing. Not the same thing at all."

He dropped her wrist as he turned away, his face a block of marble, his eyes cold as winter ice. "All I know is that I loved you, offered you my heart, the only woman who has ever held it in her hands and *you* did not love *me* enough to let me take care of you."

He was utterly unyielding, Saint Michel unwavering in his purpose. She knew there was no explaining to him, no changing his mind, no making him see it the way it really was. "And *you* did not love *me* enough to trust me to take care of myself," she responded sadly.

"May *le bon Dieu* protect you, my love." She struggled to hold back the sobs as he stalked through the door, down the stairs, and out of her life. Then, sinking down on the nearest settee, she cried her heart out. Never had she felt so alone, but that, she thought grimly, was completely understandable, because never before in her life had she felt so loved. Never before in her life had someone's eyes lit up at the sight of her, never before had someone smiled just for her. Oh, her parents' eyes had lit, but never for her, only Auguste. All their proud smiles, even Jeanne's, had been for Auguste. As for her suitors and admirers, their smiles had all been for themselves, smiles of self-satisfaction and self-congratulation at the *bon figure* they cut with her on their arm, but never for her. Adrian had been different. He had loved her for her, Juliette, nothing more. And now he did not. She had killed that love with her own obstinate wish to take care of herself. What was wrong with her? No! Juliette shook herself, fished a handkerchief from her pocket, and wiped her eyes. No! What was wrong with love that it should make her give up herself? Helen was right. There was no such thing as love and they were fools even to dream of it.

Juliette would have been somewhat encouraged to know that Adrian, at least, was just as miserable as she was. His departure the next morning was a blur, even the farewell to his family, and he spent the entire crossing to Ostend staring at the sea whose gray blue swells were as cold and limitless as the emptiness corroding his soul. Other officers boasted and joked around him, making bets as to how long it would take them to drive Old Boney off the face of the earth and how much of that would be owing directly to their own valor and prowess. It all seemed so much vain foolishness to Adrian who suddenly no longer cared whether or not the world would be a better place without the Corsican monster.

What did it matter who ruled over mankind when even the closest of soul mates betrayed one another? Because that was precisely what Juliette Fanchon had done. She had won his admiration, enchanted his spirit, captured his heart, and then spurned him like the harlot she was. If he had been thinking clearly, Adrian would have realized that not accepting his protection was a most *unharlotish* thing to do, and quite the opposite of using him, but Adrian was not thinking clearly.

Fortunately, once they disembarked, there was no time to think about anything during the week-long march to their quarters in Ninove. Each day flowed into the next as they made their way to Bruges, then Ghent. The countryside, so flat and uninteresting, mirrored the dull lifeless cloud of betrayal that had turned his own life into an existence as featureless as the swampy lowlands surrounding them. The only good thing that could be said about it was that the exertions of the day tired him enough that he fell into heavy dreamless sleep every evening, only to wake up the next morning and do it all over again until they finally arrived at Ninove where they found lodgings as best they could in the simple peasant cottages which, despite the meager furnishings, were clean, their owners accommodating, and more than happy to abuse the French if given half a chance.

Adrian went through it all in a trance, a sleepwalker observing, but curiously untouched by the momentous events unfolding around him. Even the joint review of the troops by Blucher and Wellington himself failed to arouse anything but the most tepid interest. Fortunately, the rest of his comrades-in-arms were so agog with the glorious battle to come they failed to notice his silence. Only Caesar, when Adrian bedded him down each night, regarded him with sad sympathetic eyes, butting his master's shoulder in silent compassion. "I know, old boy," Adrian would sigh, rubbing his brow, "you liked her too, but we were both mistaken. Better luck next time, eh?" But Adrian did not want a next time. There had never been a woman like Juliette and there was not likely to be one ever again.

Chapter 34

Juliette might have been as miserable as Adrian, but she was more productive. Not for her the watchful waiting, the constant reviewing, always at the ready but never actually doing anything, always on the alert with no real knowledge of what was going on, of waiting to hear from leaders, who, if they knew anything more than their troops, were certainly not communicating it. On the contrary, Juliette threw herself into a whirlwind of activity.

The day after Adrian's departure, Freddy spent an ecstatic morning with her in Cork Street walking through every inch of the shop. "The first thing to go must be this window." Freddy waved a disparaging hand at the multi-paned window in the front. "Paltry, quite paltry. You must have a bow front with masses of candles in sconces on the walls on either side and, yes, a chandelier, I think."

"But won't that be ruinously expensive?"

"Quite possibly so, but think of the customers who will stop to look in."

Juliette nibbled her lip, not quite able to share his breezy optimism, endearing though it was.

Suddenly aware of the tiny frown wrinkling her forehead, Freddy patted her shoulder. "You will see, my dear, they will come in droves, but you *must* begin as you mean to go on, with éclat. Display beautifully colored drawings of your best designs in the window surrounded by swags of your most delicious materials. And always," he raised an imperative finger, "you will be in there, impossibly elegant in your own designs. The other modistes wear clothes to work which makes them look like the merest tradespeople. Humbug! *You*," he grinned at her, "will look like a queen! Your customers will be quite pea green with envy and purchase everything they can to outdo you. Yes," he chuckled at his own cleverness, "that is the way to do it—a new concept entirely!"

Juliette was more cautiously optimistic than Freddy, but she could not help being carried along on the tide of his enthusiasm and as she and Alice, freed from her duties at Mrs. Gerrard's to help Juliette, worked themselves to the bone scrubbing, cleaning, making draperies and supervising the glaziers installing the new window, and slowly, slowly, she began to trust his exuberance. It was shaping up into a fine looking establishment.

Georgie, who simply could not be kept away from such an intriguing project, found all sorts of excuses to drop by. "Just looking for Freddy," she explained airily the first time. "He was supposed to take me for a drive in the park." But not finding her brother, she was curiously uninspired to seek him out elsewhere. "I say, this is prodigiously elegant, much less cramped and dark than Madame Celeste's."

"Because it is in a good deal less exclusive locale than Bond Street. It is cheap enough for us to afford more spacious quarters," Juliette retorted, brushing away a stray curl with a dusty hand.

"It looks like a great deal of work." Georgie eyed Juliette's broom dubiously.

"It is." Juliette didn't mean to sound so sharp, but how was she going to explain all the conflicting emotions to this daughter of privilege whose every wish was someone's command? How to explain the thrill of taking control of one's own life, designing one's own future without having to consult anyone or ask permission or approval? To be sure, Freddy had provided money and inspiration, but he had been responding to something that was already there inside Juliette. He was assisting her, not guiding or controlling her, and there was a big difference.

"I could help." Georgie stripped off her lemon kid gloves.

"Whaaaat?"

"I know how to sweep." She pointed to the broom.

Juliette could only stare at her so Georgie took it from her nerveless grasp and began sweeping.

"There! Now you are free to consult with that workman there who looks in need of direction." She went back to sweeping vigorously and with a great deal more skill than Juliette would have thought possible.

In fact, Juliette quite forgot about Georgie as she explained the locations and special features of the counters and shelves to the carpenters who had been magically produced from one of Freddy's estates, and it wasn't until she turned around to discover Georgie ferociously attacking spider webs in a back corner that the full absurdity of the situation hit her. "Lady Georgiana, you should not be here."

"Why ever not? Freddy is helping you."

"But that is different. It is a business proposition."

"And I am one of your patronesses in whose best interest it is that this establishment become a raging success, and quickly." Georgie, whose face was now as dusty as Juliette's grinned broadly.

No proof against that grin, Juliette shook her head helplessly.

"Please let me help, Juliette. I am bored to tears here in London. There is nothing to do but parade around and show myself off, and I do not show to advantage. In the country I visit the sick, bring them soup, listen to their problems, do what I can to help. Here I am utterly and completely useless—until now." She cocked her head with a teasingly speculative look so irresistible that Juliette felt a tug of sympathy for her family who, as Adrian had pointed out, had long ago given up trying to control her. And, even though their circumstances were vastly different, she recognized a kindred spirit in Georgie who clearly wanted something more from life than to spend it as an ornamental cipher—a silent, dutiful daughter or an elegant, biddable wife. "Very well," Juliette, who had grabbed the broom again, relinquished her hold, "but you must promise me that you will not let anyone who could possibly recognize you catch you working here."

"I promise." Georgie went back to sweeping, then turned to Juliette, her face completely serious now. "And . . . thank you."

In the ensuing days, Georgie stopped by the shop regularly, always managing to produce some useful household article. "You need a teapot, you know, to refresh yourself. One thinks so much more clearly after a cup of tea," she greeted Juliette cheerily one morning, thrusting a paper covered parcel into her hands. The next time it was a small embroidered foot stool. "Everyone, especially a busy modiste, needs to put her feet up a bit, you know." But more importantly, she brought news of Adrian. "Lots of reviews and marching about, but they have not started on the invasion of France yet, or, at any rate, he is not at liberty to say."

Juliette gave a silent prayer of thanks. He was safe, for the moment at any rate.

Freddy was a frequent visitor as well, but he was too involved in the aesthetics of it all to discuss his brother. "Hmm, it looks a trifle severe," he frowned at the newly installed bow window. "Here," he grabbed a bolt of Pomona green satin and balanced it on the footstool Georgie had brought, then, draping a swag of it over his arm, he climbed onto the broad windowsill. "There!" He held out his arm and stood back so Juliette could admire the effect. "Does it not soften the lines while adding elegance and texture at the same time?"

Juliette could not help agreeing despite the sacrifice of one of her best materials. She had spent a blissful morning the day before at the Millard's warehouses selecting a few basic bolts of muslin from a wide array of weights and fineness and then in Leicester Square looking at silks and satins, one of which was now gracing her front window.

Dora, Grace and Helen were regular visitors as well, offering encouragement and practical advice, particularly Dora who continually remonstrated with her not to advance too much on credit to her customers, "particularly to those with impressive names. The higher they are in the *ton*, the more likely they are to take advantage of you because they know their connections can make you all the rage or ruin you in an instant, except for the Clavertons of course," she amended as Freddy sauntered through the door with a cheery wave to everyone.

"I've been making inquiries about looking glasses and I stopped in at Waring and Gillow, but to no avail. There is nothing for it but to have one made for it to be sufficiently elegant. I . . ." he smiled sheepishly as he pulled a crumpled paper out of his pocket and handed it to Juliette. "I thought something on this order might do."

"Perfect!"

The others crowded around. "Very elegant." Helen nodded approvingly. It will give just the right touch. Where did you find it? I would like to have something like that for myself."

"'Tis nothing, merely a little something I dreamed up," Freddy admitted modestly

"An extremely well-wrought design that would make even Mr. Chippendale and Mr. Hepplewhite pea green with envy, if they were still alive of course," Helen retorted.

"I like thinking of things like that."

It was a simple reply, but again Juliette heard the longing in his voice and felt a pang of sympathy. Freddy really would have been happier as a cabinetmaker than a duke's son. Suddenly, as she glanced around the shop with its newly hung chandelier and gleaming bow window, she felt incredibly fortunate. It was a risky adventure she was embarking on, but it was all hers. Bit by bit as she scrubbed and polished, planned and sketched and worked on Georgie's new wardrobe, Juliette felt she was on the road to reclaiming her life and her soul. She might be dead to her family, but Juliette de Fournoy was alive and thriving as Juliette Fanchon.

It was not only Juliette who had begun to take back her life. Several days after Mrs. Gerrard's ladies' visit to Juliette's shop an elegantly clad woman descended from a hired post chaise in front of an inn near Kettering, then, glancing around to make sure she was unobserved while the ostlers were attending to the horses, she crossed the yard and let herself into the side gate in the wall enclosing a rather imposing house next door. There she chose another side entrance and let herself in, then walked swiftly and silently down the hall to a room at the back.

"Dora, my dear, how delightful to see you. And here we thought you had vanished forever. It is gratifying to see that old friends are remembered after all." The fleshy-faced man behind a massive desk welcomed her with an oily grin, rubbing his equally fleshy hands together as if in anticipation of a particularly delicious morsel.

"Friends?" Dora snorted, pulling out her reticule and dumping a pile of gold coins on the desk. "Who said anything about friends? It is debts, I remember, debts with an exorbitant and constantly increasing rate of interest, debts that some people made it impossible to repay, but we Barlows *always* pay our debts. Consider this one paid!" She flung one last coin on the desk and turned to leave as swiftly and silently as she had come, but he stopped her before she reached the door. For a portly man he was remarkably quick on his feet.

"Now Dora, you know I offered you easy terms and I am willing to do so again, so you may keep your money." He redoubled his grip on her arm with pudgy, sweaty fingers.

"What, so you can break your word again? I think not." She raised her head to look him straight in the eye. "That was the repayment of my father's debt. *This* is the repayment of mine." Drawing back her fist, she landed a punch to his jaw that would have done Adrian and John proud. Then, smoothing her gloves as he crashed to the floor in an ungainly heap, she stepped delicately over his inert body, retraced her steps down the hallway, crossed back through the inn yard, climbed into the carriage, rapped on the roof, and settled herself back against the velvet squabs for the return journey.

"It worked!" she told her fellow students some days later as they arranged themselves in pairs for boxing practice. "He went down like a felled oak, well, not really an oak, he's too much a scoundrel to be compared to such a magnificent tree, but I dropped him with one blow!" She hugged herself in delight.

"Now, Miss Dora, these classes were meant to teach you to defend yourself, not indulge in blood lust," Lord John scolded her, but there was no mistaking the twinkle in his eye or the concern in his face when he detained her after the boxing lesson. "Are you certain no one saw you, Miss Dora? There is no end of trouble a powerful man can make when his masculine pride has been trampled in the dust."

Touched, Dora regarded him gravely for a minute. "Quite sure, my lord." Then her usual optimistic nature reasserted itself and she tossed him her saucy smile. "Besides, anyone who saw me would be cheering me on, not reporting me to the magistrate, and I dare say the magistrate wouldn't be half sad himself. The magistrate had been most sympathetic when the lovely Dora had appealed to him before. "I know he's a scoundrel, my dear, and his actions are highly unethical, perhaps even questionable, but not illegal so there is nothing I can do. My hands are tied."

Well, Dora thought with satisfaction, *she* hadn't needed the magistrate after all. She only wished her father had been there to see it, but for her own state of mind, she felt entirely vindicated, and she had done it all on her own with no one's help.

John was surprised at how gratifying it was to hear the pride in her voice and see the extra confidence in the way she carried herself. He and Adrian had done that for her. Who knew, maybe his boxing instruction would wind up saving more souls than all the sermons he delivered from the pulpit at St. George's? He only wished Adrian were here to see it.

The thought of his brother made him glance over at Juliette, another one who was standing straighter and taller these days. Though living over her shop now, she still managed to make time for her boxing lessons. Today she was the odd person in need of a partner. John crossed the room and sketched a mock formal bow. "If I may, Mademoiselle Juliette, I shall be your *victim*, er, partner today."

Her silvery laughter rang out. Lord, she was attractive. No wonder Adrian was besotted with her. As he studied her face, John's breath caught in his throat. There it was, the small crescent scar at the temple. His eyes fell to the slim gold chain around her throat and the unusual intricately wrought cross hanging from it. He had been right all along! Juliette Fanchon was no simple *fille de joie*, she was Juliette de Fournoy, only daughter of the Comte de Fournoy and descendant of one of the proudest names in France, a name that had been known and honored before William the Conqueror had set foot on British soil and way before the Clavertons had even existed. John could not wait to tell Adrian, and Freddy too, of course

CHAPTER 35

I T WAS A RELIEF WHEN WORD CAME that Napoleon had seized the initiative and crossed the border to steal a march on his enemies. Unlike many of his comrades in arms, Adrian had not gone to the Duchess of Richmond's ball. In fact, he had studiously avoided all the forays into Brussels in search of diversion and women only too willing to do anything they could to encourage the men about to engage in what was clearly to be the battle to end all battles. "I say, Adrian, old fellow," Captain Henry Braxton clapped him on the shoulder in what made do for the officers' mess, "This ball's the thing. All those young ladies dying to give us a proper send-off. Why even an old sobersides like Squiffy here is likely to get lucky with the ladies tonight." Squiffy blushed beet red, even to his protuberant ears. "Never mind, Squiffy," Braxton chortled, "you won't have to say a thing, no pretty speeches, don't even have to be light on your feet. You just stand there in your uniform and they'll throw themselves at you."

But no amount of urging could persuade Adrian who preferred to spend his time with Caesar, checking and re-checking his hooves and fetlocks, looking for any potential problems, going over the harness and girth, mentally preparing himself. No time to think of Juliette now, the silkiness of her skin as she had lain in his arms aglow with a happiness that lit up her entire being as she kissed him and admitted that he was the only one ever to touch her lips, the twinkle in her eye and the dimple at the corner of her mouth as she teased him, the feel of her body next to his as they had rowed slowly, magically on the silvery water. No time to think of anything but death and meeting it as nobly and courageously as possible. He did worry about Caesar, though.

Unlike Adrian, his fellow cavalrymen could not contain their eagerness for the impending battle. Responding to the general alarm raised at the ball, they had hurried back to the regiment and were saddling up as gaily as if they were heading off to a hunt instead of certain slaughter. "I am going to make sure I am next to Puffy when we charge," Braxton punched his fellow guardsman in the arm, "in addition to being so tall, he is as wide as a barn, a target not even a Frenchie could miss."

"Except for your nose, Braxton, which sticks out so far it is sure to draw more attention than my manly girth."

"No more than Squiffy's ears!" Henry grinned. "I shall be quite safe. And you, Adrian?"

"All of you nodcocks are so eager you'll be off through their lines and stuck on the other side without a thought of how to make it back," Adrian forced himself to retort knowing how much the banter and braggadocio contributed to the general morale, but for himself, he did not care. Somehow the zest and anticipation had leaked out of his life and the thought of coming home to his own estate and raising thoroughbreds did not beckon to him from the other side of the upcoming carnage as it once had. Nor did the prospect of covering himself with glory sing the siren song it had at the beginning before he learned that it was not courage, or necessarily even skill that carried one through the horror and confusion of battle, but sheer stamina and the stubborn will to survive that was at the core of all living things, and a very large amount of luck.

But suddenly there was no more time for reflection, and after what seemed like ages of standing around, the orders came to head toward Quatre Bras where, after a long march, made even more weary by a steady stream of wounded struggling toward them with tales of a surprise battle and retreat, they spent the night in a wheat field where they were awakened by gunfire in the early morning hours and were ordered to draw into battle order in front of a thick wood to protect the retreat.

Grumbling at the inaction and frustrated by their helplessness as their army fled from the victorious French, the guardsmen stood impatiently until at last a group of French lancers appeared in the distance, and barely waiting for the command, they charged, all exhilaration and pent up energy. Thundering down the hill they scattered the enemy right and left, clearing the village of Genappe of all resistance. Having cut a large and satisfactory swath in the enemy, they re-grouped and prepared to give chase when the orders came to retire.

"We could have beaten them! They were no match for us," Squiffy grumbled, disgusted, but Adrian, wiser in the ways of the supreme command, calmed him. "Relax, Squiffy. There will be plenty for you to do. This was only a small force. Rest assured there are battalions upon battalions somewhere thirsting for our blood, and Wellington is even now looking for the best spot for us to take up the fight against them."

A clap of thunder punctuated this pronouncement and there was no time for further discussion as suddenly the heavens opened and rain fell in torrents, soaking them all to the skin in a matter of minutes. There was nothing for it, but to find as much shelter as they could for the night. Adrian and the others dismounted, found what little corn they could for their horses from the fields torn up by troops, scrounged branches and straw to lay on the rapidly deepening ooze of mud forming around them, and, wrapping themselves in their cloaks and huddling together for warmth, lay down to grab as much sleep as they could.

Orders to mount up again came before dawn and they attempted to dry themselves out by lighting what fires they could from the damp wood which gave out more smoke than heat but at least gave them the illusion of doing something productive besides smoking the occasional cigar as they waited for further instructions. Unlike the previous morning, no one was inclined to talk. Too wet and hungry to do anything but wait in silence for the slowly rising sun to dry out the mud enough to maneuver, they sat staring at the horizon straining their eyes for a glimpse of . . . anything

Finally orders came to proceed towards the slight ridge above the road to Braine L'Alleud where they took up their position in the center, behind the infantry and a little to the right of a small ditch. From this slight vantage point they could see vast lines of troops and cavalry stretched as far as the eye could see, all waiting, waiting for the sun to rise, the ground to dry, orders to be given . . . they knew not what.

"By George," Henry whistled exultantly through his teeth, "you were right! The fighting yesterday was the merest of skirmishes. This, *this* is going to be a battle lads! If we don't cover ourselves with glory in this one, we shall only have ourselves to blame!"

Futility rather than glory, Adrian thought to himself as he caught the gleam of the sun on breastplates and lances. Thousands upon thousands of men ready to throw themselves upon one another, and for what? Their homelands, their families, their wives? They would fight so fiercely and for what, just so they could be betrayed by the ones they loved? It was all so fleeting—life, love, happiness—gone in an instant. What did it matter whether one earned glory or not, whether one lived or not?

Then came the sound of drums and the line of blue began to approach them steadily, relentlessly, their lances glittering in the sun. Suddenly, there was a roar of artillery, shouts of men, screams of horses, and smoke began to drift over the battlefield obscuring any perspective. All senses were obliterated in the din of cannon and musket fire and stifled by the smoke that stung the eyes and parched the throat so that the only thing real or solid was the man on either side of him and, at last, the order to charge.

Adrian raised his saber, and as the horses gathered speed, the world disappeared into a blur of blood red uniforms and muscles rippling under shining black hides, the roar of a hundred voices, one of which he discovered, much to his surprise, was his. They plunged down the slope and up the other side, then came the screams of agony as gaps opened up all around him. His muscles tightened, his head pounded, and the breath was squeezed from his chest by an iron band of fury, fury that mankind would do such a thing to itself, making life, which was precarious enough as it was, even more brutish and short, fury that even love, that best of human traits was even briefer than life, and less reliable. He had thought, for one brief shining moment, that he had, had love in his grasp, but that too, like glory, had been an illusion.

The shout turned into a roar of rage and despair as suddenly a breast-plated cuirassier loomed in front of him. The Frenchman rode furiously toward him, his sword poised to give a deadly thrust, but Adrian, veteran of years of fencing, parried automatically and, driven by the enormous anger and hopelessness of it all, rose in his saddle, slashing with all his might. The shock as his sword connected with his opponent's neck and shoulder nearly unseated him, but he hung on for all he was worth, no longer caring about winning or surviving, or even life itself as his enemy came crashing down against him. He hung onto the reins for dear life as he felt himself falling, and then the world went black.

There were cries and shouts all around as Adrian, flat on his back, struggled back to consciousness. A terrible weight pressed him to the ground and there was a thundering in his brain. His head swam horribly as he raised it to see what was happening. The thundering grew louder and a violent blow nearly split his head in two before he sank back into a darkness far more profound than before.

When he woke again, the shouts, the thundering were gone, only moaning everywhere, but otherwise a terrible stillness, no horses charging, no men marching grimly forward, weapons at the ready, just the stillness of total destruction, bodies everywhere—men, horses, gun carriages. The weight pressing on his chest was the body of the cuirassier whose life he had taken in that vicious burst of anger and despair. Gingerly he turned his head. To his left lay Harry, a bullet between his eyes, and next to him, his faithful and beloved Charger, his black coat slick with blood. To his right, Squiffy, dead eyes staring into space, a gaping lance hole in his chest, was propped against another dead cuirassier. Why? Why had he not died with them? Why was he forced to survive the carnage when they were the ones who had wanted so badly to live. A terrible thirst sharpened the despair, corroding his soul, a thirst so agonizing he barely noticed his throbbing leg or aching shoulder.

Then something soft and warm pressed against his brow. A gentle, yeasty breeze blew across his face. Caesar! Adrian twisted his head to see his horse standing beside him regarding him with sad, anxious eyes. "Caesar!" The pain was excruciating, but at least he was able to work a hand free to stroke the velvety nose. Another snuffle, this one stronger, blew his matted hair. "Caesar, my boy. Thank God you are alive!" His parched throat choked on a sob and hot tears rolled down his face as exhausted, Adrian sank back, welcome oblivion washing over him once again.

"Sir! Sir!" Disgusted to discover that oblivion had not taken him permanently, Adrian struggled to open his eyes. It was evening of what must have been a beautiful day, the pink sky darkening into a deep blue. His lips were cracked, his throat so dry he could not speak, and his body, the parts of it that were not numb, was a mass of pain. Everything was crusted thick with dried blood and flies. The weight was lifted from him and Tom Sandys face came into view. "Sir! You *are* alive! Thank God for Caesar or I never would have found you. Here, Sir." Strong arms lifted him and fire shot through his side and his leg, a fire so awful and consuming that even he, stoic that he had been raised to be, would have cried out except that his throat was too raw and dry to make a sound.

Adrian next awoke to a cool wet cloth being pressed to his lips. Water at last! Heaven! Perhaps he had died after all? But no. "Bevez, milord." A glass was held to his lips, and in spite of his longing for death, he drank, the cool blessed water sliding down his parched throat, softening the cracked lips so they once again felt as though they belonged to him. "Merci," he whispered, then turned his face to the wall, waiting for, hoping for the life to drain out of him.

CHAPTER 36

"AND THAT WAS THE WAY I left him, your Grace, asleep, but alive and in the good hands of the *beguines*. Begging your pardon, your Grace, but he is better cared for with them than if I were looking after him and I thought you would want to know as soon as possible so I took Caesar and we made as quick work of the journey as we could, him being tired himself and all, but I knew it was the fastest way to get you word."

The Duke of Roxburgh nodded, his teeth clenched so as not to give into the wave of relief threatening to unman him. "You have done very well, Sandys. I shall let the Duchess know immediately, and in the meantime, go to the kitchen and get something to eat, man. You look like a walking scarecrow."

"Yes, your Grace, very good, your Grace." Tom bowed and left the room, but not for the kitchen of Claverton house. Instead, he made his way to St. James's Square where he was welcomed with open arms.

Dora, glancing out the window of her chamber was the first to see him as he rounded the corner. "It's Tom!" She turned to Rose who was helping her mend some torn flounces. "Run to Juliette's shop and tell Alice her Papa is come home, and Juliette too," she added more soberly, wondering what news, if any, there would be of Lord Adrian. Then, throwing down her mending, she tore down the stairs and out the door catching him before he even reached their doorstep. "Tom! Tom Sandys you're home!" And oblivious to all possible spectators, she threw her arms around his neck, laughing and crying at the same time.

"Why . . . why . . ." Suspiciously red under his tan, Tom remained rooted to the spot before gently unwrapping her arms so he could look into her face. "Why Miss Barlow, of course I am home."

"It's *Dora*, you great oaf! Now come inside and tell us everything." Taking his hand she pulled him up the steps and back through the front door which Fenwick, grinning from ear to ear, held open until, recollecting himself, he hastily resumed his usual lofty expression.

"And . . . Lord Adrian?" Still gripping his hand, Dora hauled him upstairs to the drawing room where a bevy of ladies had now collected.

A shadow crossed Tom's face. "He is alive . . . .as good as could be expected."

"But?"

"But Miss B . . . er Dora, it's as though the light is gone out of him. He's alive, but he isn't, if you know what I mean."

Dora nodded sadly. After her father had lost the inn, his physical shell had lived on for a while, but the jovial, hearty man within had died. Before she could ask anything more, however, there was a commotion in the doorway.

"Papa!" Alice threw herself into her father's arms. Handkerchiefs were pulled from pockets and pressed to streaming eyes as Mrs. Gerrard's footman returned from war hugged his daughter as though he would never let her go.

Helen broke the silence at last. "Well, Mr. Sandys, from the little I have read of the battle, I expect you are ready to give up soldiering for good."

Tom nodded, his eyes fixed tenderly on his daughter.

"Then we shall be wanting our footman back."

He grinned. "Yes Ma'am."

It wasn't until some time later, after the congratulations and the thousand questions about the battle—was Boney really beaten, was it true that the Duke's horse had kicked him at the end of the long, horrible day—that he sought out Juliette.

She was sitting a little apart from the others, her smile at the joyous homecoming tinged with a sadness and worry that tore at Tom's heart. He had seen that same sadness in his major's eyes, even before they had left England, and guessed that something had gone very wrong between them. It had been only days before he left that Lord Adrian had been whistling under his breath, a smile in his eyes, brisk energy in his step, happier, in fact, than his batman ever remembered seeing him, and then it was as though a door had been slammed and a grim-faced stranger had emerged—silent, preoccupied and curt, even to Tom and his fellow officers, who, no matter how bad things got, had always before received a friendly smile and an encouraging word. A change in behavior that drastic could only be caused by one thing—a woman. And Tom had had no trouble in identifying the woman. There had only been one since his lordship had returned from the Peninsula-Mademoiselle Juliette.

"How is he, Tom?" she asked quietly as he approached.

"Not well, Mademoiselle."

"Will . . . .will he live?"

"Oh, he'll live all right, if you can call it that. It's not his wounds that are killing him," he responded to the question in her eyes. "To be certain, he's hurt bad, saber thrust in the side and the leg so badly broken and twisted he may never walk again. He wouldn't let them take it off though." A ghost of a smile flitted across the batman's sober features. "But he does not care about getting better, just lies there, his face to the wall. Begging your pardon, Mademoiselle, but he seemed so powerful fond of you, I thought you might could talk to him, and . . ."

Juliette shook her head sadly, "Believe me, he will not have anything to do with me, but someone must bring him home to his estate where he dreamed of raising horses. He needs the distraction of others around him, a reason to live. It may not seem like it, but these things help, I know!" she added fiercely as she looked around the room at her companions, her eyes glittering with unshed tears.

Freddy and John appeared later for one of the snug little suppers that were winning Mrs. Gerrard's almost as much renown as its beautiful women and challenging card games. Afterwards they repaired to Juliette's chamber.

"Never fear, Mademoiselle, one of us will bring him safely home, "John reassured her, laying a kindly hand on her shoulder.

"And I say, I should be the one to do so, John being essential to the spiritual welfare of his parishioners while I, I am nothing but a here-and-therian, and no one will even notice that I am gone. "Not true, Freddy, old boy; the tone of men's fashion would deteriorate drastically without you to lead us."

"I . . . .," Juliette began slowly, tilting her head to look at first one brother and then the other. "I think Freddy, for he will set the right tone."

"I will?"

"Yes. John is the very essence of sympathy and understanding with experience in the sufferings of the soul and the loss of faith. My guess is that his presence will only remind Adr . . . er, his lordship, of his own loss of interest in life. Better to have Freddy whose cheerful nature is the complete opposite of morbid soul-searching."

"I say, I rather like that, makes me feel a useful sort of person after all." Freddy beamed.

John stroked his chin thoughtfully. "You may be right about that, Mademoiselle Juliette, quite right, in fact. There is a certain *joie de vivre* about Freddy that is quite irresistible, and he certainly has the best sprung carriage and the most luxurious tastes of anyone I know which will make for the most comfortable journey possible for our wounded warrior.

But Juliette saw the worry in his eyes and knew that Adrian was in need of measures far more desperate than cheerful companionship. She had a sickening feeling that it would be a long time, if ever, before the Adrian they knew and loved returned to them.

CHAPTER 37

IT WAS OVER A MONTH BEFORE the anxious ladies at Mrs. Gerrard's were to learn anything more substantive than that Freddy had located Adrian at the *beguinage*, ascertained from the surgeon that he was fit enough for travel in gentle stages, and better off away from the pestilent confines of Brussels where every household was crammed to the roof with the wounded and the dying. He had dropped them a quick note to say that Adrian was as well as could be expected and they were coming home. And then they heard nothing for weeks upon endless weeks until Georgie suddenly popped into *Maison Juliette*, which had begun to build a slow but steady clientele consisting mostly of Goergie's acquaintances.

"Freddy has taken him directly to Ashbourne thinking the country air of his own estate will do him good. You would think that being away from that awful battlefield, which Freddy says is truly appalling, and home among his family would improve his spirits, but no . . ." Georgie's voice suspended on a sob and she blinked rapidly for a few minutes, ". . . but no, he just lies there, staring into the distance, refusing all the special delicacies Cook makes for him. He acknowledges us, but nothing more. It is dreadful, Juliette, as though he were already dead, and he very well might be if this keeps up. Mama is at her wit's end, and it takes a great deal to put "her there. Even *I* never did that."

Juliette's heart ached for Georgie, for all of them, but she knew that Georgie, least of all, with her ebullient enthusiasm and unquenchable thirst for life, would not understand. Even John, despite his sensitivity to the plights of others and his longing to administer to the sorrows of the world, though he might understand intellectually, had not lived the pain that Georgie described. Juliette had.

And that was precisely the argument John put to her the next day when he begged her to visit his brother at Ashbourne. "I know you have a business to run, Mademoiselle, and I know we have no right to ask it of you, but please come. You who have suffered, you who have lost your faith, your sense of who you are, you are the only one who can help him see the way to living again. And," he smiled his beautiful, gentle smile, "I know he loves you.

Juliette shook her head sadly.

"Something went wrong between you, I know. I saw it in his eyes right before he left, but where there is sorrow like the sorrow I saw, there is great love, and great love does not simply die from one misunderstanding, for I am sure that is what it was."

Again, Juliette looked skeptical

"I have not been in love myself, but I have seen enough of it to know that where true love is concerned, there is no right or wrong, only misunderstanding. I saw enough of how my brother felt about you to know it was true love. Please, Mademoiselle Juliette."

"Very well. I shall ask Dora to manage the shop, and the others to help as much as they can." In truth, Juliette had been longing to be with Adrian from the moment she had heard he was still alive. If Freddy had not gone, she herself would have journeyed to Brussels and searched until she had found him, just to see his dear face again, those brilliant blue eyes, no matter how desolate, the square jaw, the firm lips, just to wipe his brow and spoon healing broth through parched lips, cleanse torn flesh, anything just to love him, to be with him, to care for him, even if he did not recognize her at all.

And so it was that a few days later, after giving final instructions to Dora and Alice who were taking over the brunt of running *Maison Juliette*, Juliette climbed into Freddy's elegantly appointed, beautifully sprung traveling carriage and began the journey to Suffolk.

They made excellent time, but it was still very late in the evening when the carriage came to a halt on the gravel drive in front of a classical brick and stone façade. Ashbourne Hall was not large by many standards, but its lines were well proportioned and gracious, promising comfort and welcome inside. The entrance hall was as elegant as the exterior and the sight of a grizzled servant holding open the massive oak door with something like a look of approval warming his blunt features, went a long way to reassuring her that she had done the right thing.

"Mademoiselle Juliette!" Freddy, rising eagerly from a chair by the fire even before the servant had fully ushered her into the drawing room, put all further doubts to rest. "Thank you for coming, my dear," he held out his hands, warming hers in his pudgy clasp. "You had a smooth journey, I trust?"

"Yes, thank you, my lord." Juliette allowed the servant to take her pelisse and sank gratefully into the opposite chair, too tired to think or respond while Freddy sent instructions for Cook to prepare her some refreshment.

"He has gone to sleep at last, and perhaps you too should get some rest before you see him." The troubled look clouding his usually sunny features warned Juliette that this was the wisest course of action, even though she longed to fling her arms around Adrian immediately and promise to do anything, everything, whatever it took to bring him back from whatever dark place he inhabited, which John's plea gave her some hope to believe she might be able to do.

So, taking Freddy's advice, she allowed herself to be fed and led by a solicitous maid to a snug little chamber, undressed, and helped into bed where, despite the fears plaguing her over the meeting with Adrian, she succumbed to the exhaustion of the journey and fell into a deep, dreamless sleep.

But once Juliette awoke, anxiety overtook her and she was barely able to swallow her breakfast chocolate before sending word to Freddy that she was ready to see the patient. He was waiting for her in the hall as she descended the broad marble staircase. "We put him in the library over here," he pointed to the left front corner of the house. "It has a view of the drive and the paddock, both of which John and I hoped would provide some distraction, but to no avail, he barely looks out the window. In fact he barely looks at anything." Freddy sighed gustily.

Juliette laid a hand on his arm, giving him an encouraging smile she was far from feeling. "I shall do my best." Then, taking a deep breath, she crossed the threshold.

Freddy was right, large palladian windows gave ample views of the drive on one side and green fields on another, not to mention plenty of light, so much light that she barely saw the figure in the bed next to the windows overlooking the pasture.

Since he had cast her hand away on the steps of Mrs. Gerrard's at their last meeting, Adrian had filled Juliette's thoughts, almost to the exclusion of all else. She remembered every detail of the tan, chiseled features, bright blue eyes, teasing smile, not to mention the long powerful legs. It was mostly the half tender, half admiring gleam in his eyes and the broad chest that turned her legs to water and caused her breath to catch in her throat every time she thought about them or dreamt about them, reliving every touch, every kiss, every glance during their time together. Ever since they had parted, she longed to be with him again, to feel him hard and strong against her, loving her, holding her, and . . . She glanced down at the slight lump under the blankets, a lump so small that it hardly seemed as though it could be a man, much less Adrian, under all those covers, except for the gaunt head resting on the pillows, ashen face turned to the wall.

Again she was overwhelmed with a longing to fling herself against him, but not for comfort this time. She wanted to hold him, warm him, breathe the life back into the skeleton of the man who lay there so still and hopeless.

If he heard her footstep on the threshold he gave no indication, nor did he move or turn his head when, choking out his name, she sank down on the chair next to the bed. "Adrian," she whispered taking one lifeless hand in hers.

"Why are you here?" His voice was so thready she barely made out the words.

"I came to see you. I am worried sick about you and I want to help you get better.

"You have your shop to run."

"That doesn't matter. The only thing that matters is you." The tears were flowing fast now, choking her voice so she could barely get the words out as misery squeezed all the breath from her body."

"Nothing matters."

"Yes it does. *You* matter. *Life* matters. *Love* matters."

"No," his voice, usually so strong and confident, was listless, toneless, dispirited, "none of it does."

"Then why did you not die?"

"What!" The blues eyes suddenly fixed on her with an intensity Juliette had not thought possible. They were still bleak and dark, hostile, even, but at least they were alive she told herself.

"You could have, you know, lain there, bleeding, allowing the life to seep out of you, given up, given in to your injuries. I know about that. I have been there, lying weak and beaten, knowing that all I had to do was give in to the darkness, the sweet oblivion of forgetfulness and death."

His were still fixed on her, still angry. That was good. Anything was better than hopelessness. "I thought oblivion was what I wanted. My mind wanted it, but my heart, my spirit, call it what you will, clearly wanted something else because it did not let me die, and here I am, glad that my heart or my spirit was right."

"Because you got your shop." His mouth twisted bitterly. "But I have nothing—a broken useless body."

"No, not because I got my shop, because I found love, *your* love. *You* gave me love. Because you cared for me, I came to care for myself. My heart and spirit would not allow me to die, but it was not until you came along and loved me that I truly began to live. And I love you the same way, no matter what you feel about yourself. I see the real you, the one who fights for the good and the right at any cost, and *that* is the man I love."

"That may be *your* fairy tale, but it is not mine." He turned his head back to the wall.

"We'll see," Juliette muttered to herself. "We'll just see about that."

CHAPTER 38

"HE SPOKE TO ME, HE ARGUED WITH ME. THAT IS A GOOD SIGN," she reported to Freddy and John that evening. John and Tom Sandys had journeyed together later to Ashbourne in order to relieve Freddy, in John's case, or, in Tom's case, to return with news to those anxiously waiting at Mrs. Gerrard's.

"I hope you are right." Freddy shook his head gloomily, as he absently swirled a glass of port. "I agree with Juliette, though, anything is better than this terrible listlessness." He smiled at her apologetically. "I am sorry you are the one to bear the brunt of his anger."

"I am hoping that the anger comes from great hurt, which I never meant to cause, but at least it means he is not indifferent to me . . . I hope." Juliette tried unsuccessfully to stifle a sigh.

"John reached over to squeeze her hand. "You are a wise woman, Mademoiselle Juliette, and a good one."

"I hope so. And now, gentlemen, if you will excuse me, I have a patient to attend to." She rose and returned to the library where the fire appeared to be the only living thing in the room, and settled herself next to Adrian's bedside to wait for anything, even the tiniest thing, she could do for him.

At first he would not let her wipe his brow or give him water or food. "Go away." He muttered it, he sighed it, even shouted it, but she always shook her head no.

"Very well." At last he gave in, but he did not betray by the least response, not so much as the flicker of an eyelid, that he was aware of her presence, much less accepted it.

Several days later as Tom and Freddy were preparing to return to London, Juliette waylaid the former batman in the hall. "Was there a veterinary surgeon attached to your regiment, Tom?"

"Yes, Mademoiselle, a Mr. Dalton, he was."

"And do you think you could get a message to him?"

Tom grinned. "O' course I can. And if I can't, his lordship," he nodded towards the drawing room where Freddy was deep into a discussion of drapes and carpets with the housekeeper, "will know how."

"Good. Then make sure this gets to him." With something of her old impish smile, Juliette thrust a note into his hand.

The following days passed in endless monotony. John traded shifts at Adrian's bedside with Juliette, but even he was beginning to lose hope. "He is wasting away and the surgeon says he can do nothing more for him. He has done all that he knows how," John reported when Juliette came to relieve him one evening. "If he were one of my parishioners, I would have a better idea what to do, but Adrian was never one to have much faith in our Lord."

"No, only in his strong right arm, his skill on a horse, and his own courage." Juliette smiled sadly. "And now he is punishing himself for having lost it. That, oddly enough, is a good thing, this self-punishment, because it is an act of will, a show of purpose, destructive though it may be, because without it he would have gone long before now."

"Punishing himself?"

"Because he could not fix it all: he could not fix my life for me, he could not save his fellow companions-in-arms and their horses from the terrible carnage, and now he thinks he cannot fix himself, on his own, at any rate. Once he realizes that he needs the help of others, once he allows them to love and help him, then he can heal. I know of what I speak because I am only alive now because of the love and concern of other people who took care of me when I no longer cared for myself."

John frowned thoughtfully at his hands clenched in his lap considering silently for a long while, but when he looked up, a hint of a smile brightened the weariness in his eyes. "Once again, I say, you are a wise woman, Mademoiselle Juliette, either that or a witch."

She chuckled. "Neither one, just someone who has seen a great deal more of life than she would have preferred."

He rose, laying a firm hand on her shoulder, and smiled deep into her eyes, a gentle smile full of comfort and appreciation. "And may the wisdom it has given you save us all."

"I hope so. I hope so," she whispered as the door closed quietly behind him and she was left alone in the dancing firelight with the motionless figure in the bed. Carefully, ever so carefully so as not to disturb him, she took Adrian's skeletal hand in hers and pressed it to her cheek, willing into it all her vitality and hope.

Clop, clop, clop, the regular hoof beats woke him to another day of endless drills and review as they whiled away the time until the clash between the two unstoppable forces poised to go at one another's throats. Adrian reached for the reins to throw himself into the saddle and got nothing but linen sheet. Sheet? He opened his eyes. Yes, he was here, crippled and helpless in his bed at Ashbourne.

Clop, clop, clop. Still the dream persisted. A warm breeze caressed his cheek and it smelled of oats? He turned his head towards it to find himself transfixed by the dark serious gaze of . . ."Caesar!"

Without thinking, he sat bolt upright, grimacing as the lancing pain in his side and leg reminded him why he was there. "Caesar?"

The big horse rubbed his nose ever so gently against his master's cheek, whuffling his pleasure at seeing him at last. "Whatever are you doing here?"

"He was pining away, so much so that he overcame his good breeding and the certainty that horses belong only in stables to seek you out." Juliette appeared at the stallion's side.

Caesar nudged him again, this time with a little of his own former playfulness and snorted delicately, but so deliberately that Adrian was left in no doubt of his equine companion's joy and relief at finding him safe and alive. As he reached up to stroke the velvety nose, Adrian felt a drop of water on his hand and realized that hot tears were streaming down his cheeks. "Oh Caesar!" Reaching both arms to his horse's neck, he buried his face in the glossy black coat and wept as he had never wept in his life.

He wept for all his fellow soldiers who had fought and suffered, for the loss of so much life and the ruin many others, for the disillusionment and destruction of it all, the shattered dreams of valor, glory, truth and righteousness and love.

"Ah, there, I knew he would be happy to see you."

Finally, he looked at her, her pale careworn face made even paler by the bright golden curls framing it, the eyes huge and anxious in her thin face, and his heart shattered. She did love him, enough to ignore his brutal rejection of her, his cynical refusal to heal, his rejection of life itself.

"Caesar has something to show you." Gently she led the horse to the other side of Adrian's bed by the window.

Inching forward, Adrian looked out. There in the paddock, his paddock, were eight black horses contentedly munching apples that had fallen from a nearby tree. "Where did they come from? Who are they?"

"Survivors of Waterloo, just like you. And only a survivor of something that terrible can help another survivor heal."

He shook his head slowly, and suddenly he was overcome with the oddest sensation; a chuckle rose from somewhere deep from within him and turned into a laugh—shaky and barely discernible, but a laugh, nevertheless. "You are, as the French would say, Mademoiselle, *Incroyable!*"

Joy surged through her. He's alive! He's alive, her heart sang as she sent a silent thanks to *le bon Dieu* watching over her. "Thank you sir," she tossed Adrian a curtsy before, turning serious again, she lifted his hand from the coverlet and looked deep into his eyes. "And now you must rest. Mr. Tripp will be calling on you this afternoon."

"Mr. Tripp?"

"The veterinary surgeon from Newmarket."

I *know* he's the veterinary surgeon from Newmarket, and the best there is, but how do you know him and why is he coming here?"

"From Mr. Dalton."

"Dalton? But . . . ." He broke off as an impish smile tugged at the corners of her mouth. "Clearly you have all the answers to these questions."

"Tom Sandys furnished me with Mr. Dalton's name and direction. It was Mr. Dalton who sent these wounded horses he has been caring for," she nodded toward the window, "and recommended Mr. Tripp. The horses are healing beautifully, but they still need expert care. He is coming to look at them this afternoon and you too."

"Me!"

"Yes, Freddy ordered a bath chair for you so we can wheel you out to the paddock, but then Mr. Tripp is going to take a look at that leg of yours."

The spark died out of his eyes. "It's useless! The surgeons all agree I shall never walk again."

"The surgeons that wanted to cut it off to save your life in the first place?"

"Yeeees." He glanced up at her curiously, but there was no reading her expression.

"Well, veterinary surgeons don't have that luxury. If they cut off a leg, their patient dies, and if the patient can't use the leg, the patient dies, so perhaps they are more committed to fixing legs and knees and things than their human counterparts."

Perhaps there was something to what she said, Adrian reflected. The surgeons he had known were all a bit of a sawbones, but then, they had had to make their way through thousands of wounded in a very short time. "We'll see."

He sounded skeptical, but at least he wasn't rejecting her idea out of hand. "And now, "Juliette raised his hand to her lips, "you must get some rest."

Her lips were soft and warm, silken, like a rose petal. As she pressed them against his skin their warmth flooded through him. Adrian hadn't realized until this moment how cold he had been, cold and frozen into lifelessness until now when her touch melted the ice that had been in his veins and he slowly relaxed, every muscle giving in to a soothing languorousness as he drifted off into sleep, a comforting, healing sleep, free of dreams and the nightmares that had haunted him since consciousness had first dragged him back to reality on the shattered, horrific battlefield.

It seemed like no time at all before he woke again, curious for the first time in months about what the rest of the day would bring. His room was oddly bright and pervaded by the smell of ham and eggs which also, for the first time, seemed amazingly appealing.

"Good morning."

Adrian looked up to find John at his elbow, a cup of chocolate in his hands. "Morning??"

"Yes, you slept right through the night." John looked as pleased as though he had just been told he was to minister to the poorest parish in the entire kingdom.

"And a good part of the day before the night. Damn and blast! I missed Mr. Tripp."

Now, *that* sounded more like his brother Adrian. John gave a silent prayer of thanks. A man who expressed himself that forcefully was a man on the mend. "Don't get yourself into a pucker, my lad, he comes every day and will be just as happy to see you this afternoon as he would have been yesterday, more so, because you look rested for the first time since last May, and after you've had breakfast, you will be even better."

Surprisingly enough, he *did* want breakfast.

"And, oh, Mademoiselle, he ate everything on his plate," Cook later confided to Juliette. Reaching into a capacious pocket, she fished out a handkerchief and swiped viciously at her eyes, sniffing loudly. "It's that pleased I am!"

"And I too. Thank you for all you have done to get him to eat the little he has." Her own eyes wet, Juliette patted the loyal retainer on the shoulder before hurrying off to see the patient.

John sat with Adrian while Wilson shaved and dressed him and then helped the valet get his brother into the new bath chair a stable boy had wheeled in for him. It was quite a process, and Adrian was pale and panting from the unusual effort by the time that had him settled in and swathed in blankets, but the look on his face told them all that it had been worth it, Wilson being so overcome he had to leave the room in a hurry to maintain his dignity.

"She loves you, you know." John took the handles of the chair and began pushing Adrian toward the door.

For a long time Adrian did not respond. "I know."

The whisper was so faint that, not sure he had heard it, John leaned down to catch the words, but caught his breath instead at the pain in her brother's eyes.

"I hurt her badly, John. I did not believe in her and now," he waved at his useless leg, "even if she did forgive me, which she is far too spirited and independent to do, I have nothing to offer her."

"Nonsense! Even you, pagan that you are, know that *Love hopes all things, believes all things, endures all things*. And she is determined enough for both of you. You wait and see. She'll have you back on Caesar before you know it."

At that moment the subject of the conversation appeared in the doorway clad in a bonnet and pelisse and clearly eager for their excursion. At her side was Mr. Tripp. "Good morning, my lord. I am glad to see you up and about and ready to visit our lads in the field, but first, if I may, I should like to take a good look at that knee, if you others," he nodded briskly to John, Wilson, and Juliette, "will excuse us, I shall wheel him out when we are done."

"Now then, let's have a look." The veterinary surgeon helped Adrian free himself from the blankets and lap robe, casting a sharp assessing glance first at his patient's tensed lips and weary eyes, knowing full well that in all of his patients, spirit made all the difference between healing and inevitable decline.

"Yes," he felt the knee gently, but firmly, "you took rather a beating. I dare say, with the sawbones wanting to take it off rather than spare the time for regular fomentations, and ordering laxatives and a succulent diet, not to mention exercises. We treat our animals better than our human patients by walking them around rather than confining them to a bed, thereby rendering the poor humans weaker and more helpless than they were when first confined. Here," he grasped either side of the knee, "let us see if we can make it bend at all."

Adrian grimaced and clenched his teeth as pain shot through his entire body. There was no way his knee would ever bend again, much less bear weight.

"Aha!" The surgeon took out a jointed piece of wood and laid it against the knee, then held it up for Adrian to see the barely invisible angle it made. "See? There is some play in your knee. With regular flexing of the joint we can strengthen it. Are you ready to work with me, sir? It will entail a fair amount of exertion, not to mention a good deal of pain, but I should think a soldier like you would be up to it. What do you say?"

It was a challenge, an insurmountable one, in all probability, but suddenly Adrian found himself welcoming the chance to do *something* besides lying there helplessly, hopelessly. "Yes, Mr. Tripp," he took a deep breath, "I am."

"Good lad! Now let us see to your horses." And wrapping him back up, the surgeon wheeled him out into the warm autumn sunshine where the others were waiting.

CHAPTER 39

As they approached, John and the others crowded around the fence
waiting for them, there was a whinny from the far side of the paddock and
Caesar came trotting up and thrust his head eagerly over the fence. "Hello, old
boy." Adrian reached up to stroke his nose. "Yes here I am, really and truly. These
people," he nodded ruefully at the little group who were all observing him with
various levels of anxiety, "are not about to let me become a slugabed. Now let us
see your fellows." Forming his lips in a way he thought he had long forgotten,
Adrian whistled. Eight glossy black heads rose, sixteen ears flicked, and, gathering into formation, his new-found responsibilities hurried over to the fence.

"Hello lads." He reached out a hand to pet each in turn as Mr. Tripp wheeled
him along the fence. "Mr. Tripp says we all have a lot of work to do, but he
thinks we're up to it. What do you say?" A whicker here, a head toss there, and
he knew he had his answer. "Very well then, you are all dismissed." As a group,
they wheeled and trotted off. Hot tears stung Adrian's eyes. Lord, they were
magnificent. In all his nightmares he had forgotten just how magnificent they
were. He turned to Juliette whose encouraging smile was belied by the worry
darkening her eyes. How truly she had stuck by him in spite of his lack of faith,
in spite of his total rejection of her and everyone, everything else. He reached
out a hand. "Thank you for saving them."

"How could I help it? I love you all."

And that was the thing, she loved her fellow creatures, not just him, but
Freddy, and Grace, and Dora, and Alice, and she worked hard to make all of
them happy in spite of the cruelty she had endured. It was that life force that
had first drawn him to her, it was that warmth and sensitivity, so clearly evident
the day she met Caesar and his sister that made him love her. And he did

love her. He knew that now, and that was why he had felt so betrayed when she had rejected his offer of protection. He had never loved anyone before, never offered himself before, and she had turned him down. But now it appeared that it was not he whom she had rejected so decisively, but the state of dependence, and who could blame her? He was wholly dependent now on her and his brothers, and much as he loved her, loved them, he hated it. A wry smile twisted his lips. What was it she had once said about the past, experience, and learning? Not only was she a loving woman, she was a wise one. Again he looked up at her, seeing her relax as she saw him smile. How she had worried for him! Adrian glanced around. They had *all* worried about him, not the least Tom and Freddy who had rescued him from that hell hole of human wreckage, Waterloo, and the makeshift hospitals all over Brussels teeming with the wounded and the dying.

"They are doing well," Mr. Tripp remarked, eyeing his patients as they went back to grazing. "A few more bullet extractions and my work will be done. I didn't like to do it all at once for fear of overtaxing their endurance, but you," he favored Adrian with a piercing look softened by a crooked smile, "with you, I have only just begun. I have instructed all of them," he glanced over to Juliette and the others, "to foment that knee twice a day and bind it at least four times a day. In the meantime I shall send Mr. Smith to measure you."

"The farrier?"

"He is also an excellent smith, hence his name from generations of blacksmiths, and he will fit you for a brace. Your knee will be too weak to support you, but I think," his craggy face twisted into a thoughtful frown, "yes, I truly think that in time, you should be able to walk on it without a brace, though, mind you, you will probably always need a cane."

"A cane!" He was not doomed to life as a helpless cripple! Already Adrian felt some of his former energy slowly seeping back into him. He glanced at the anxious faces around him. They actually thought he had given up! Well, he admitted to himself, he almost had. If it hadn't been for their faith in him, *her faith*, he amended as he observed their significant smiles in Juliette's direction, he would have. Now it was time to show his gratitude.

"Very well. Do your worst, Mr. Tripp. Let us go back to the house and you will show us how to proceed."

And thus began a strict regimen of the succulent diet, fomentations and exercise that Mr. Tripp prescribed for all knee injuries, whether his patients had four legs or two. It was a grueling and painful process, and there were days when Adrian, sweating and gasping from the pain and exertion of it all nearly gave up.

"Relax," Juliette would soothe, bathing his brow. "*Rome was not built in a day*, as they say, and you have no strength left in you after lying in bed for over two months. Once your stamina returns, it will be easier."

Adrian did not believe her until one day he was able to lift himself from his bed into the bath chair without collapsing from the effort and then to balance on a crutch without the support of Juliette on one side and Wilson on the other. "A miracle," he breathed as he remained upright on his own without his head swimming uncomfortably and his knees buckling under him.

"No, just hard work and nature," Mr. Tripp replied briskly, but Adrian could see that the surgeon was pleased. "No more bed for you, my lad-a couch perhaps, and chairs. The longer you are upright, the better your balance will be. My other patients do not have that problem, but we two-legged creatures, we are oddly equipped at best, and deeply inferior to our four-legged brethren. And speaking of our brethren, I know of one who has been waiting to ride with you this age."

"Ride?"

"Certainly. Your knee may still be stiff as a board, but there is nothing wrong with your thighs, man. Oh, a little weakness to be sure, but there is only one way to cure that—practice. Caesar is waiting."

And without further ado, he and Wilson, John, and Juliette led Adrian to the gravel drive where Caesar and another horse waited patiently. Adrian glanced at his companions. John was dressed in his customary garb and Wilson clad as usual. Mr. Tripp's gig stood nearby so the rider for the other horse remained a mystery until . . . . Adrian was so attuned to every emotion that flitted across Juliette's expressive features he had not even noticed her costume until now, a handsome slate-colored riding habit whose muted color emphasized the deep blue of her eyes. It somewhat severe lines, softened by a high collar topped with white lace, showed off her elegant figure to perfection. Blond curls clustered under the jaunty high crowned hat—a vision that left him oddly breathless with a weakness in the knees that had nothing to do with his injuries. "Mmm . . . ademoiselle Juliette," Adrian stammered like a raw youth besotted by his lady love, something he had not done since his salad days. "I did not know you could ride."

The delicious lips curved into her enchanting dimpled smile. "The English are not the only equestrians in the world, you know."

"No need to point that out to someone still recovering from his last meeting with Frenchmen on horses." The answering gleam in his eyes made Juliette's heart sing. He really was on the mend.

"In truth, French women are not so horse-mad as their English counterparts, but my brother taught me to ride at Juniper Hill." It was out before she even knew it. Juliette fought the urge to clap a hand over her mouth, but that would only have called attention to her slip of the tongue. Her parents would have nothing to do with the crowd at Juniper Hill whose urging of a constitutional monarchy had failed to save them from the wrath of the revolution, but

Auguste, with all the fire of youth, had been attracted by the intellectual vigor and flashing wit to be found there and had taken his sister along on many occasions to sit wide-eyed as Talleyrand and Madame de Stael exchanged clever remarks. The energy and vitality, so different from the gently mournful company of her parents' friends, was profoundly inspiring; there people were thinking of the future, not focused firmly on the lost glories of the past. The Comte and Comtesse de Flournoy had been horrified by the new friendships, but Auguste was their only son, and Auguste could do no wrong. Juliette, on the other hand, was another matter. One admiring reference to Madame de Stael, and she had been prohibited from returning to Juniper Hill, but not before she had learned to ride.

Juliette was glad of her riding lessons there now as Adrian and Caesar, the groom trailing at a watchful distance, led her around the estate pointing out new paddocks here and the soon to be location of a magnificent stable there. They made a slow circle of the fields closest to the hall until Juliette could see that Adrian was tiring. His seat was a little less erect, and he had slowed his pace, his features sharpened by the pain and exhaustion of his ordeal, but his eyes were alert and intent in a way she had not seen since he had left for France. The relief of seeing energy in him after weeks of dull lifelessness nearly overwhelmed her. Even the furiously angry Adrian who had flung her away on the steps of Mrs. Gerrard's had been preferable to the listless stranger who had lain so quietly on the bed by the window.

"You look happy." Adrian turned to her now, his eyes searching her face.

"I am. You are returned to us, and that is all that matters."

"And your shop?"

"*You* are all that matters." Oddly enough, Juliette did not even feel a pang as she uttered these words. Weeks ago she had bargained with le bon Dieu, *Let him live and I will stay by his side no matter what it costs.* And it was worth it to see him like this. A shop could be for later, or not at all if it could not survive her absence, but love, well love was forever.

Slowly, imperceptibly, asking questions about his prospective thoroughbreds and their training all the while so that he would not notice that she was ending their ride, Juliette led them back to the drive.

"What, returning already," Adrian teased when he finally realized where they were, "I thought you were made of sterner stuff!" But she could see the lines of weariness around his eyes as the groom helped him dismount and was glad she had ended their ride when she had, leaving him enough strength for another day.

"It was a fortunate thing you tore your right knee and were wounded in the left side, leaving you strong enough to mount and hold the reins." Mr. Tripp hurried over with the bath chair and Adrian sank into it gratefully, overcome with exhaustion. But it was a good sort of exhaustion, a productive sort of exhaustion that meant he could look forward to a good night's sleep, a sleep without dreams, if he were lucky.

CHAPTER 40

IN FACT, IT *WAS* A DREAMLESS SLEEP, and Adrian was astounded to awake to a day that had dawned many hours earlier.

"Not quite cavalry hours, but it's good to see you looking none the worse for wear." Mr. Tripp stood at his bedside, an oddly shaped concoction of metal rods and leather straps dangling from his hand. "Sorry to haunt your bedside, but Smith, here, could not take much time away from his forge and he wanted to see his handiwork in action in case it was in need of adjustment.

A hulking form, cap in hand, emerged from the shadow of the doorway. "Good morning, my lord. Apologies for arriving all unexpected like, but I've left Tim minding the shop. He's a good lad, but it's a lot to ask of a mere boy."

"Certainly." Adrian shook off the last remaining grogginess and shoved aside the bedclothes. "I take it I am to put my leg in that thing?"

"I have made a hinge here, my lord," the blacksmith opened the contraption, laying it on the bed next to Adrian, "so you can fit your leg into it and then we can use these straps with the buckles I have attached to tighten it. I hope it is tight enough to fit now because of course you will grow all that muscle as you exercise and will be wanting to loosen the straps pretty quick, I expect."

Adrian thought the man was being extremely optimistic, but he nodded politely, not wanting to seem in any way critical of what the blacksmith obviously considered his *chef d'oeuvre*. Raising his leg, he managed to fit it into the brace and, with some help from Smith adjusted the straps to fit snugly.

"There!" The blacksmith stood back to admire his creation. "Now Mr. Tripp and I will help you up, give you this here crutch, and you'll be off and away."

Again, Adrian sincerely doubted the accuracy of the man's words, but again he nodded politely, only to be proven wrong a few minutes later as Mr. Tripp and the blacksmith took him under each arm and raised him to a standing position. His left leg felt horribly unsteady after lying useless for so long, and he didn't dare put weight on his right, but when, with a knowing look between them, the two stepped away, leaving only the crutch under his right arm to support him, Adrian was left with no choice but to stand on his own . . . .or fall.

Gritting his teeth as pain, weakness, and the nausea of fear washed over him, Adrian hung on doggedly until it all passed and he was able to catch his breath and feel the steadying strength of the brace around his leg and the reassuring sturdiness of the crutch.

"Excellent!" Mr. Tripp rubbed his hands together as though it were the merest nothing at all, as though the outcome had never been in doubt for a moment. "Now take a step toward me."

"What?"

"Come, come, man. Mr. Smith did not go to all this trouble merely to see you stand there like a great lump; he wants to see you walk."

"Walk?" It came out as a hoarse croak

"Yes, walk. Put one foot in front of the other, you know, *that* sort of thing." Then, seeing his patient's incredulousness, the surgeon relented, softening his usual brisk tone. "I would not ask it of you if I were not sure you were perfectly ready, perfectly strong enough to try—not to run, mind you, but to try. Just a few steps. You'll see."

And Adrian *did* see. Taking a deep breath, and gripping the crutch as though his life depended on it, which it did, his face twisting with concentration, he put the crutch a little in front of him, swung his left leg forward, wobbled precariously and then put the tiniest bit of weight on his right leg to steady himself. Nothing happened. He did not fall. The dizziness vanished, and he felt reassurance beginning to seep back into him. His body still functioned on its own after all. Just to make sure it was not an illusion, he took another step forward, this time smoother with less wobbling, then one more so he knew without a doubt he could do it.

"There! That's enough for one day." Mr. Tripp trundled the bath chair under him and Adrian collapsed into it.

"Excellent work, Mr. Smith. You are a craftsman of rare skill, and now you had better get back to your shop before Tim burns it down. I thank you for your time."

A grin and a bob, and the blacksmith was gone, leaving the two men to check the brace for any signs of rubbing and discomfort.

"Is there a Mrs. Tripp?" Adrian asked.

The surgeon raised a bushy brow. "Yes."

"I don't suppose she is in need of a dashing new costume to impress all her friends."

The brow rose higher.

"I only ask because, in addition to being an excellent nurse, Mademoiselle Juliette is a modiste of some talent, my sister's modiste, in fact, which is how she came to be here. Lady Georgiana knew that Mademoiselle had successfully nursed members of the émigré community and asked, as a favor to her since no one is in town at the moment and business is slow, to attend to me." Adrian, who had not told a lie since he had been caught stealing Cook's tarts when he was eight, excused this bald-faced untruth in the interests of repaying Juliette in some small way for her devotion.

"Now that you mention it, she could use something new to wear to next winter's assemblies." Mr. Tripp rubbed his chin thoughtfully as, not being entirely truthful himself in this particular moment, he appeared to believe an explanation that in no way accounted for the tenderness in Mademoiselle Juliette's eyes every time they fell on her patient, or the adoration in Adrian's as he followed her every movement. True, the veterinary surgeon was more skilled in reading horses than humans, but to his mind, this was a case of true love if ever he had seen it.

"Thank you. Mademoiselle will be delighted to hear that. Her talents have been too long wasted on me; it is time she pursued her own interests.

Mr. Tripp smiled broadly and said nothing.

CHAPTER 41

TAKING A BRISK WALK AROUND THE GARDEN to clear her head, Juliette was coming to much the same conclusion though, oddly enough, it didn't make her as happy as Adrian might have expected. Anxious and upsetting as her time at Ashbourne had been, there was a special magic to it that she had never experienced before, nor was likely to ever again. For once in her life, she had been needed, no, more than needed, she had been absolutely crucial to someone's existence, someone she loved with her entire being. She could not have imagined how rewarding, how fulfilling it would be, more, even than seeing her most exquisite creations admired by one and all. In all those quiet evenings she had sat by Adrian's bedside, smoothing the hair on his forehead, bathing his face with lavender water, giving him hot milk, anything to soothe his troubled sleep and ease the pain, she had been able, with every gesture, even the simplest of reassuring touches on a clenched hand, to show her love without ever having to say it out loud.

And, she could gaze at him as long and as lovingly as she wished without being observed, touch his feverish cheek, even press her lips to his without anyone's seeing her, without having to explain herself. She had been free to love unreservedly, without having to think of the consequences or what the world would say. Loving Adrian when he needed her was as natural and uncomplicated as breathing. But now that he was healing it was altogether different, and every day that Adrian grew closer to his normal self, the more halting steps he took on his own, the more reality crept back into their quiet, isolated existence.

Oddly enough, it was Adrian's thoughtfulness that brought reality crashing back with a vengeance. "I have a project for you," he announced one morning with a little smile after he had practiced walking unaided the length of the library and the entrance hall, "and for once, it does not mean me."

"Oh?"

"The Newmarket assemblies are fast approaching and Mr. Tripp confided in me that his wife longs to cut a dash." Once again, Adrian was stretching the truth. What was wrong with him? Perhaps his wounds were not healing as well as he thought. "And I told him that London's most fashionable modiste was actually here in Newmarket nursing a cantankerous war veteran. He was much struck and . . ." Adrian paused as he saw the wariness creep into her eyes. "What? I thought you would jump at the chance to show your talents."

"I would, but . . . it's so very kind of you to think of me . . ."

"But?"

"But what will they say about an unmarried young female who is not only your nurse, but a seamstress as well . . . as well . . . as a hundred other things she could be. Please do not mistake me, it is the dearest thing of you to want to help me, but have you thought of the consequences? I should not be here. You are healed. You no longer need me. It is time for me to leave you to recover on your own."

"There will be no consequences. I love you." He took her hand in his, looking deep into her eyes dark with worry. Then, without thinking, knowing only what he wanted, Adrian drew her into his arms. His right leg wobbled, but held. It was the rush of joy, rather than any physical weakness that nearly made his legs buckle underneath him. She was here at last, in his arms, something he had never thought would happen again, something he had not in his wildest dreams dared to dream after he had pushed her aside and gone off to war.

"Oh Adrian," she whispered, lifting her lips to his, soft, yielding, loving, sweet, and full of life and promise. His hands slid down to her waist, pulling her close so he could feel every gentle curve, every beat of her heart. She was his once again, his guardian angel, his love.

"Marry me," he murmured, tracing the column of her neck to the sensitive private spot behind her ear.

"What?"

He had said it without thinking, but now he knew it was so right. The mention of her leaving had suddenly put everything in perspective. Soul destroying as it had been, his recuperation had shown him what it was like to share his life with someone, and he knew now, with a flash of absolute clarity, that it was what he wanted for the rest of his life. Before, he had been Adrian, adventurer, warrior, driven to prove himself against the world, but even though he had done this as part of a highly trained similarly motivated band of comrades, he still had been alone. Now he was not, and he liked it that way, wanted it to be that way forever, for them to live together at Ashbourne, raise their children, and grow old together—a dream that a younger, less experienced Adrian would have dismissed with a cynical shake of his head.

"Yes!" There was absolute conviction in his voice as he pulled her even closer to him and brought his lips down hard on hers, claiming her, making her feel the unbreakable bond between them. A quiver ran through her. He knew she felt it, as he had always felt it, but was only now acknowledging it. They belonged together, just as he had known it the instant he had seen her that first day at Mrs. Gerrard's with the light from the window turning her curls into a golden halo framing her beautiful face with the intelligent knowing eyes whose depths were shadowed with a sympathy born of a secret sorrow.

"Oh Adrian!" Juliette gave herself up to his kiss, pretending for one delirious moment that she could actually say yes. In the past few days she had begun to admit to herself how much she loved him, from the slight cowlick on his forehead that gave an endearingly boyish touch to his rakish good looks, to the firm mouth that set in such determined lines as he struggled to walk, to claim his life back, to the broad shoulders which, despite their recent spareness, were squared proudly against his weakness, to the warmth that glowed in his eyes whenever he looked at her.

Her heart turned over in her breast at the very thought of him, and more than once, she had toyed with the idea of letting him take care of her as he had once begged to be allowed to in what seemed a lifetime ago before he had gone to war. But now, after their days struggling together to bring him back to life, after sharing the place he had dreamt of making his home, after fighting to preserve the life he had planned for over the years, she loved him too much to ruin it for him. He would be mingling with country families at assemblies, and horse fairs, race meetings, and discussions of local affairs. A man like that needed a wife above reproach, a wife whose own respectability upheld his position in the community. In London his friends might envy his connection with a beautiful *fille de joie* from the exclusive Mrs. Gerrard's, but here they would condemn it, and she could not allow that to happen to the man who had given her so much joy and happiness, the man who had given her back her very self.

But oh, how it hurt, like a knife to the heart, the thought of never seeing him again, that bright, teasing smile that was only for her, the look in his eyes that told her he knew everything about her and loved her all the more for it.

"You know I cannot, but I am honored . . ."

"Why can you not? You are honored? What rubbish! I love you. You love me, I know you do!"

"I cannot. My shop . . . I . . . ." In truth she had not thought as much about her shop as she had expected to, but now, at least, it gave her something to cling to as she threw away her chance for a lifetime of love and sharing, of happiness.

He was suddenly still. "I see."

The words were barely even a whisper, but the pain resonating through them brought her head up to see once again the bleakness in his eyes, the horrible emptiness she thought she had chased away forever haunting them once again. He thought she was rejecting him as a man, a man who was now a shadow of that bold, perfect warrior who had swept her off her feet—Saint Michel, now a broken, fallen angel. No, she would *not* let that happen!

"No, *mon brave*, you do *not* see." Tears stung her eyes as she reached up to kiss him, a love slow kiss, as her mouth explored his, tasting his lips slowly, caressing the square line of his jaw, the firm, proud column of his neck to the opening v of his shirt and the hard plane of his chest. For a moment she rested her head there, reveling in its solidity. As she wrapped her arms around him, pressing her body to his, melting against him, she felt him hard with need, and a hot arrow of desire ran through her. Weak as he was, he wanted her and, miraculous gift that it was after all she had been through, she wanted him. Helen had been wrong, falling in love was a good thing. No, they could never be together; yes, her lonely soul would cry out for him forever, but today they would be one. Today they would both be healed and whole again.

Carefully, ever so carefully, so as not to threaten his frail balance, she inched backwards toward the bed, drawing his shirt gently over his head and then, her arms still around him, sank slowly onto the bed, pushing him back against the pillows with a playful shove before she knelt next to him, leaning down to plant butterfly kisses on his forehead, each side of his mouth as she slid her hands down along the square shoulders and then back up his neck to cup his face. The, looking deep into his eyes, she smiled, a slow, intimate smile, full of mystery and promise as she pressed her mouth to his, hot and full, sealing herself to him, mingling her breath with his as she parted her lips and traced his mouth with her tongue.

"Aaaah." Adrian sighed as pure pleasure laced with desire, a desire that ignited her own with a heady sense of power and a fierce pride that she could bring pleasure to a body so battered and broken, restore the joy of being alive to a soul so deadened by sorrow and loss.

Juliette trailed her fingers across his chest, lightly, ever so lightly tracing the angry red scar on his side before pressing her lips against it. "Oh Adrian," she whispered, her heart squeezing with love and sorrow at the sight of such a grievous wound on his perfect body and the thought of all he had suffered, all that she was going to suffer, the prospect of losing him piercing her own soft flesh just as the lance had pierced his.

Adrian reached up and pulled her to him, fiercely, hungrily, no softness now, but with the desperation of a starving man as he thrust his tongue deep into her mouth, tasting her, mingling with her. His hands slid down her waist, cupping her buttock, warm and strong as they pressed her against the pulsing hardness that seemed to take over his entire body, consuming him with the need to lose himself in her warmth and softness. He ached for her so much his hands were shaking, but again with that teasing little smile, she read his mind as, lifting her skirt, she rose and settled over him, hastily undoing his breeches in one quick motion before surrounding him with heat and desire. With a longing as desperate as his own, she drew him into her, riding the wave of his passion with a rhythm that matched his own so that he hardly knew where she left off and he began. He fell into the vortex consuming them deeper and deeper, tighter and tighter until she seemed to ignite with ecstasy and, as she tightened around him he felt the rush of life and love sweep over him with a fierceness and power he had never known before.

With a sigh of pure bliss, Juliette collapsed against him. Adrian twisted his head so he could gaze at her, the long dark lashes lying against flushed cheeks, her entire face aglow with love and passion, a soft satisfied smile curving her lips, and he wanted to lie there forever with their arms wrapped around one another, to fall asleep with her and wake up again with her beside him in the morning, and for all eternity.

They lay together as the sun that had bathed them in its warm early morning glow climbed higher in the sky casting soft shadows around them. Gently Adrian pressed his lips against her forehead. "My Juliette. There is only one word—*incroyable!* I would never have believed it possible, none of it, any of it, that I could ever be that man again."

Juliette rose on one elbow, propping her chin on her hand. "You were always *that* man. You still are." She was silent for a long minute, regarding him with an intensity he felt right down to his toes. Then, in one swift movement, she was off the bed and standing next to him smoothing her dress, twitching the skirt to make the trimming fall just so. "As to the rest, it is simply the stock in trade of any *fille de joie* worthy of the name. With a lift of her chin she turned on her lemon kid slippers and was gone, her skirts swirling around her.

CHAPTER 42

ADRIAN LAY STUNNED, UNABLE TO CATCH HIS BREATH from the shock of it. Life had come back to him more exciting, more joyful than it had ever been, with a future that for the first time in his life seemed real enough to touch, and then, just as quickly, it had been wrenched from his grasp. The suddenness of it all left him reeling with no idea what to believe so he simply lay there with the world whirling around him and the shadows deepening into utter darkness.

"Adrian?" It was John, a taper in his hand. "Why did you not ring for light or a fire?" He peered anxiously at his brother lying so still and pale.

"She has left me."

"I know." Carefully placing his candle on the table, John sank into the chair, *her* chair, next to the bed. "I am sorry. I could not stop her. I tried, but she . . ."

"Is as independent and stubborn as . . . as only Juliette can be." One corner of Adrian's mouth twitched into a semblance of a smile then dissolved into a sigh. "I asked her to marry me."

"I know that too."

"Brother John, forever the omniscient one." But there was fondness in Adrian's tone as he at last looked up. "And after that she dismissed me as nothing more than one of her clients. But I . . ." his voice was growing stronger now as he reviewed the entire scene in his mind, taking it apart piece by piece, moment by moment, gesture by gesture, "but I think she was . . ." Now that he thought about it, that quick turning on her heel was not dismissive, but so he could not see the tears in her eyes, but he had seen them, just before she turned totally away, even as they had quivered and fallen from her lashes. The hard, cynical edge to her voice was to mask the quaver underneath it, but he had detected it anyway. The decisive snap of the door was to cover up a sob, but he had heard it, "but she was lying to save me from myself," he concluded triumphantly sitting bolt upright in bed. "She *loves* me! And I love her. She worries about my reputation. I have never cared about my reputation. I am proud to marry someone as strong and loving and kind and as . . . .well *everything* as Juliette and I don't give a fig *who* she is!"

"As well or better born than you are."

"What?"

The look on his brother's face was so comical John could not help laughing. "She is the daughter of General le Comte de Flournoy."

"Even *I* have heard of that old battle axe, and he retired from Louis' army before I had my commission and paid attention to such things. How do you know this, oh omniscient one?"

John grinned. "A hunch, and then I visited my friend the Abbe Carron who confirmed it for me, but it was too late to tell you; you had already left for the continent."

"It wouldn't have made any difference anyway," Adrian frowned thoughtfully as he gazed off into space, "but now . . . now, it just might. A secret smile tugged at his mouth as he nodded. "Yes, it just might do the trick." And throwing his legs over the side of the bed he grabbed his crutch. "Here, be a good fellow and help me up."

"Not until you assure me that you are not going off somewhere half-cocked. You need supper and a good night's sleep first."

"I've been in the cavalry; I know the importance of preparing for a campaign. The last one I fought was on an empty stomach with very little sleep and look where it got me! This is a battle I intend to win thoroughly and completely. Now, lead on to supper brother John."

Juliette was fighting a battle of her own as the coach rolled on down the road toward Newmarket, then Cambridge, and on to London, and she was losing. In spite of her absolute conviction that what she was doing was best not only for Adrian, but for herself, she could not stop the waves of sadness washing over her.

She had managed to hold back the tears after closing the library door behind her until she reached her bedchamber and then they spilled over like the agony in her soul. How dear he was—marriage—without a thought for the blemish on his name. Who would have believed such a thing could happen to her, disgraced, and disowned by her own family, offered a place of honor in another family with an equally proud and ancient lineage?

And it had not only been Adrian who offered her this. John had been waiting for her in the black and white marble entrance hall as she descended the staircase clutching her valise. "Wilson told me you asked for a gig to take you into the village." He took the valise from her listless hand and set it on the floor. "I wish, *we* wish you would not go."

"I have to." Her throat was so tight she could hardly get the words out.

He searched her face trying to read the expression she was struggling so desperately to maintain. "Leave only if it is good for you, but otherwise, please stay. I know we have no right to ask; you have already done so much good here that we are forever in your debt."

The kindness in his eyes squeezed the last drops of blood from her aching heart. "You are very kind, but I cannot. He asked me to marry him!"

"And there is no way you can see to do that?"

Her eyes flew open. "No! Of course not! The family, your family . . ."

"Would be honored to have you join it." He took both her hands in his. "Truly."

Tears stung her eyes. "How could I, a *fille de joie* . . ."

"A brave woman who has endured much hardship and become a person in her own right, but" he released her hands ever so gently, "I understand that you want to establish that person completely on your own, truly claim your own life before joining it with another's. You are wise, I suppose, but we shall miss you, and I personally shall pray that someday you will feel you can join our family. Now, I have dispensed with the gig and ordered the traveling carriage. You are here at our behest; there is no reason you should not return home in as much comfort as we can provide."

Home. Juliette leaned her head back against the velvet squabs. She could not help feeling just the faintest flush of pride at the thought. Yes, the shop and her rooms above it would be cold, deserted, dark, and lonely, but it was *hers*—not yet quite a home, but hers, and hers alone. She was not dependent on the kindness of anyone for the roof over her head, and that was a good feeling, lonely— she shoved the thought of Adrian ruthlessly from her mind—but good.

But Juliette was wrong. Her shop was *not* cold, deserted, and dark. As she fumbled to fit the key into the lock, she saw the sudden flicker of a candle in an upstairs window, heard the padding of feet, and Alice, clad in a dressing gown, met her on the staircase at the back of the shop.

"Alice!"

"Welcome home, Mademoiselle. It will be just a moment I shall have the fire lit in your bed chamber and some tea brewed. I also have a bit of cold ham if you like."

"Thank you, Alice. I am not hungry, but I could use some tea." In a daze, Juliette followed her upstairs, allowed her to take her pelisse, and sank into a chair. In no time at all, a fire was blazing, more candles were lit, and hot tea was on the table next to her. She took a restorative sip. "How ever did you know to be here? Not that I am not forever grateful, but this is too good to be true." Smiling, Juliette glanced around the cozy room, still finding it difficult to believe it was hers, all hers.

"Mrs. Gerrard said that you might come home at any moment and we should have it all ready and welcome when you did. Tomorrow I will show you how the gown is progressing for her ladyship. Miss Grace and Miss Dora have been helping, and of course, her ladyship is here most every day."

"And has sent over some cast-off furniture, I would guess." Now that she was somewhat revived, Juliette was able to study the unfamiliar writing desk in one corner and a looking glass in another.

Alice looked sheepish. "Well, she said as it had all been sitting in their lumber room this age some use should be gotten from it. And you know her ladyship, once she puts her mind to a thing . . . ."

Juliette nodded. Like her brothers, Lady Georgiana was generous to a fault, and possibly more stubborn than any of them, except Adrian. No! She would not think of him, of the love glowing in his eyes when he had asked her to marry him. He was not just being kind, he truly *did* want to marry her, and oh, she wanted to marry him—or at least her heart did. But her head kept saying *What about later, when the world casts him out as surely as it cast you out.* No! She would not think of Adrian. "Yes, I should like to see how you are doing on her ladyship's gown."

"Now??"

"Now!" There was no time like the present for taking up where she had left off, and grateful for the life she had managed to create for herself, along with the help of Helen, Freddy, Dora, and Grace, not to mention a lot hard work on her part, she followed Alice down to the workroom and welcome distraction.

"Excellent!" Juliette examined the tiny, almost invisible stitches. "And the French work at the flounce is very smoothly done—elegant, not fussy, just as Lady Georgiana will like it." She pored over the gown, inch by inch, for all the world as though it were midday instead of well past midnight after the endless carriage ride and the soul destroying scene that had preceded it, a scene she wished she had not been forced to enact. To her dying day, she would never forget the look on Adrian's face as she had tossed those casually cruel words over her shoulder at him, *As to the rest, it is simply the stock-in-trade of any fille de joie worthy of the name.* All the love and admiration glowing in his eyes had gone out as surely as if she had tossed a bucket of water on a blazing fire, his dear face stricken with betrayal, *her* betrayal when she would have given her life to make him happy. Well she *was* giving her life to make him happy because she would never again feel whole and complete as his love had made her, never again feel that at last she belonged somewhere in the world. She hoped it was penance enough to condemn herself to a lifetime of loneliness so that in time he could be happy as he deserved . . . with someone else, the right sort of woman, a woman of his own rank with an unblemished reputation who would make Ashbourne a home where the entire county would gather, where people would come from near and far to admire his stables and blood stock, who would add to her husband's standing in the community instead of diminishing it with a sordid past.

"We should have it finished by tomorrow. Lady Georgiana will be glad to know you are returned. She spoke of needing a pelisse and mentioned that an acquaintance had admired her carriage dress so much that she wants to order one just like it. Miss Dora told her straight out that it would not be *just* like it for of course, no two creations from Maison Juliette are ever alike, but she did assure her that you would create something in her acquaintance's own personal style that would suit her as well as your creations suit Lady Georgiana.

Juliette smiled faintly. "And as usual, Dora was right. Thank you, Alice, and thank you to everyone who has looked after Maison Juliette so well. Now, go get some sleep.

Juliette's own body longed for sleep itself, but her mind would not stop going over every moment at Ashbourne, every look, every gesture of Adrian's, the pain and despair they had fought through together, and the triumph they had shared. She must be content with that, with the memories and the knowledge that she had coaxed him back to himself, to his former life, albeit not so steady on his feet, but engaged and purposeful again, and that was no small thing. She would have to be content with that, and she *would* be content with that . . . in time.

CHAPTER 43

JULIETTE PLUNGED BACK INTO HER OWN LIFE with, if not with great enthusiasm, at least with great determination. The enthusiasm, she kept telling
herself, would come later.

Freddy and Georgiana were delighted to see her, Georgie to ply her with
questions about Adrian and his plans for his stables, and Freddy to discuss
some new design he had for a slightly different cut of sleeve and an idea for
using net in flounces. All this was very flattering, but painful in its reminders
of Adrian—Georgiana's restless energy which was so very like her brother's,
Freddy's kind smile and blue eyes, not so dark or admiring as Adrian's, but
warm with approval and encouragement that made her feel important, valued
for the talent she possessed and what she had accomplished, and helped her
forget what she had been.

Dora and Grace visited every day, stopping by the shop for a quick cup of
tea nearly as often as they had stopped by her chamber at the Mrs. Gerrard's,
and they talked of everything: Tom's safe return and his gratitude to Juliette
for hiring Alice, to Grace's new music teacher who was both encouraging and
challenging her in such a way that for the first time she felt someone besides
herself was taking her singing seriously, and the growing pile of Dora's savings
that were going to allow her to purchase a small inn of her own in the country,
far away from London, of the new customers Lady Georgiana had introduced
to Maison Juliette, Juliette's latest designs, and even Lady Lavinia who had been
seen giving poor Freddy a tongue-lashing in the middle of Bond Street, everything in fact but Freddy and Georgiana's youngest brother.

Juliette was grateful for their forbearance though it was obvious from the
sympathy in Grace's eyes and Dora's bracing manner that they were taking

great care to avoid all mention of Lord Adrian Claverton. At last, one day, Dora could stand it no longer. "And he let you go so easily after you nursed him back to health? I must say, I thought he was made of sterner stuff."

"He is," Juliette defended her lover, "but I am sterner still, and I cannot run my shop and entertain a gentleman at the same time."

"Very true," Grace agreed sadly, "and your shop has been your dream forever."

"Precisely."

But Helen, who had accompanied them on this particular visit was not fooled. "Nonsense! You're a clever woman, you could run your shop and still have plenty of time for Adrian, but you are in love with him and you're afraid."

"For both of us."

"With good reason." Seeing the anguish in her protégé's eyes, Helen reached out and took her hand. "It hurts now, but you made the right choice, for both of you, as you say."

"Then why do I feel so lost?"

It was the softest whisper, but it cut through Helen's heart like a knife. "I don't know. I have never been in love so I don't know what losing it feels like, but I have suffered the loneliness of losing my parents. I imagine it feels something like losing one's arm or the ability to walk."

Juliette nodded sadly.

"Well, you know from your recent experience that even the crippled can learn to walk again. It won't ever be the same, but you will manage. That's the thing about us, all of us," she nodded at Dora and Grace deep in conversation as they examined a length of the latest French silk, "we've lived through pain and loss before, overcome great odds and succeeded in spite of it all, and you will again, in time. But it will take time. You will never be the same, but," she smiled, nodding wisely, "you will be stronger, and strength is what matters."

Juliette was not so sure about the strength part; at the moment she would have preferred love. Helen was right; it took a long time, sleepless nights, days of backbreaking work, leaning over her sketchpad or head bent in concentration as she stitched furiously, hoping to lose herself so deeply in her work that she could not spare a thought for anything else, hoping to exhaust herself with her effort so her worn-out body would overpower her with the dreamless sleep she craved.

Oddly enough, it was the customers who provided the most distraction, and thanks to Lady Georgiana and Olivia Childs, they came in increasing numbers. Olivia had been the second customer after Georgiana and had been most impressed with the shop. "It is vastly elegant. Your sense of style extends far beyond mere clothing, my dear."

"Actually, it is Freddy who is responsible for the entire décor.

Olivia had heard about the Marquis of Wrothingham's manifold interests already. "Such a pity he is a peer. What a waste of a wonderful talent, being the heir do a dukedom when he could accomplish so much. Ah well, at least you are giving him an opportunity to indulge his creative genius." She broke off to admire a bolt of striped French silk that Alice had brought to the window. "What a magnificent piece of fabric!" She sighed luxuriously as the shimmering material slipped through her fingers. "I should love a gown of this, but it is far too dear for my purse, I am sure."

"No, this is a gift from Maison Juliette. Now come look at the design I have drawn up for you."

"Juliette, this is far too generous a recompense for the little . . ." Seeing the proud smile hovering on her friend's lips, Olivia hesitated, understanding that this gift was as much about affirmation as it was about gratitude. "Very well, my dear, if you insist; I shall be so grand I shall hardly know myself, but you can be sure I shall insist on telling everyone it is from Maison Juliette." Though she reveled in the fabric, the opera singer barely glanced at the design, "because I trust you implicitly" and chatted instead with Grace, who had stopped by while doing errands, about her own new singing master. "He is excruciatingly critical, but so inspiring that he gets my voice to do things I had no idea it could do. You must come to one of my lessons, Grace and see how you like him and how he compares to yours. But I must fly for he is expecting me this very minute. I shall send you a note when I have the next lesson." Then, turning to Juliette, Olivia gave her a quick fierce hug. "I am so glad for you, and so proud. You must let me pay . . . No? Very well, then, but truly the way to repay me best is not to give me a gown, but to save some other lost soul who is at the point of desperation. You will find them at any one of London's coaching inns and you will know the moment you look into their eyes which ones need your help."

Another quick hug and she was gone leaving Juliette quietly thoughtful. Yes, she would do that. As soon as the shop was earning enough to afford another seamstress, she would do just as Olivia had suggested and save some poor lost soul from all those in the city who preyed on their misery and helplessness.

Olivia's visit was quickly followed by Lady Georgiana and her mother. Georgie had come to beg Juliette's help for a school friend who was *not particularly taking in a way that one would notice, but just a good sort of person a man should want for his wife-sensible, intelligent, no-nonsense and a good friend.* "But she is not particularly comfortable in society, so I rather fear she will not show to advantage, or worse still, be entirely ignored," Georgie confided. "But you could create some gowns that would give her enough confidence to be appreciated as she ought, couldn't you?"

Juliette was flattered by Georgie's utter faith in her abilities and touched by her devotion to her friend. Once again she reflected on the Clavertons' generous spirit, though the duchess looked to be something of a dragon when Georgie brought Juliette over to be introduced to her mother who was frowning critically at a piece of shot green and white sarsnet. "Very pretty, but rather fussy, in my opinion." The duchess laid it down as her daughter approached.

"Mama, this is Mademoiselle Juliette whose designs I showed you."

"Your Grace." Juliette sank into a graceful curtsey.

"Hmmm." The Duchess looked her up and down with an appraising eye. "Seems to be a good sort of gel, Georgiana." Then, turning her sharp gaze directly on Juliette, she nodded briskly. "And if you can interest my daughter in something besides horses, then I commend you. Mind you, no daughter of mine would be allowed to fill her head with frippery nonsense, but a Claverton cannot turn up at Almack's looking like an ape-leader. I, myself, cannot be bothered with such things which is why I turned Madame Celeste loose on Georgiana, but my daughter would have none of her. I am glad she seems to have taken to you." The Duchess shook her head sadly, "Georgiana was stubborn from the day she was born, never would take to a bridle."

"Thank you, your Grace." Juliette did her best to hide her smile. Georgiana had warned her that her mother was something of a tatar, but clearly she was fond, and perhaps even a little proud, of her daughter.

"Then I may bring my friend Verena to see you?" Georgie returned to business.

"Most certainly. I shall look forward to it."

"Lady Verena Carstairs, sensible sort of girl, sweet natured, not too biddable," the Duchess mused, "would have been much better for poor Freddy than that Gorgon he has, but there's no help for it; Clavertons always marry Harcourts. Well, good day to you." And with that, she was out the door leaving Juliette to recover from the visit as best she could. No wonder Georgiana was such a force of nature; she was the image of her mother, albeit prettier and more mischievous. It was fortunate for the Harcourts that Freddy had been the sacrificial Claverton because even Basil, slimy scoundrel that he was, would have been no match for Lady Georgiana.

The shop felt strangely silent after Lady Georgiana and the duchess had departed in the whirlwind of energy that seemed to accompany all the Clavertons. It was that energy that had first drawn her to Adrian with a force so strong that it had overcome all reason on her part. And it was the loss of that energy after he had been wounded that had torn at her heart and made her feel so needed, so valuable for the first time in her life as she saw that energy slowly return under her care. Was it still there, that zest for life and doing things, that passion to make things better, or had her deliberately cruel words destroyed it along with his desire to marry her?

Marry! Adrian had wanted to marry her, give her his name, share his life with her. Madly unrealistic as his proposal had been, Juliette hugged it to herself like a talisman. She was worth something to someone. A proposal not accepted was not much compared to a life of companionship and love, but just the memory of it would warm the loneliness for the rest of her life. And it could be worse; she could be like Freddy, tied forever to a woman who would make him miserable and slowly stifle that creative spark that gave him such joy. Better by far to be living her own life, alone, on the fringes of society than sacrificing her very soul as poor Freddy was.

Juliette picked up the shot green and white sarsnet the Duchess had been admiring and smiled over at Alice who was stitching a flounce for Helen's new carriage dress. "Well, we have our marching orders—the most exquisite gown we can create for Olivia and designs that will give a deserving young lady some éclat during her first Season."

"Yes, Miss." Alice smiled back. She loved the shop with all its beautiful silks and laces, the companionship when the ladies from Mrs. Gerrard's called on them. and the excitement of being around important people like Lady Georgiana and the Duchess who was actually more like a real person than she could ever have expected. With her father home safe and happy in his duties at Mrs. Gerrard's, Alice was happier than she could ever remember, except for the vaguest memory of her mother being alive and well, but then her father had been away for the war and there had been the constant fear that he would never return and the destitution that would face them if he did not. The only thing marring Alice's complete happiness was her mistress. Mademoiselle Juliette was still the kindest, most understanding mistress a person could have, always teaching Alice new stitches, how to cut the cloth to best advantage, describing the peculiar qualities of every fabric along the way and sharing her sketches and ideas *so you will be ready to open a shop of your own one day*, Mademoiselle Juliette always said, but Alice did not want a shop of her own. She was perfectly content to help Mademoiselle Juliette who clearly liked the challenge of making her own designs and executing her own idea of how things should be done. That sort of responsibility was more than Alice wanted to take on, preferring to anticipate her mistress' needs, fill them to perfection, and be rewarded with her grateful *Oh, well done, Alice! How did you know that was just what I wanted?*

But while Mademoiselle Juliette was kind as ever, she had lost the sparkle about her. She still smiled, but it was a sad sort of smile, without the playful dimples. And Alice often caught her staring into space, her sewing untouched in her lap. Everyone knew it had to do with the Major. It had been this way ever since he had left for the war which was natural enough for who knew if he would come back. But he had come back, and Dora and Grace had told her that Mademoiselle had nursed him back to health again so why wasn't she happy about it?

"I thought they were in love," Alice confided to Dora one day as she was sweeping the floor and Dora was looking at a bit of silver lame that had caught her fancy.

"I did too." Dora sighed.

"Then why is she so quiet. Why isn't she happier?"

"Love doesn't always make people happy, especially people like us. Love is a luxury for people who have a place in the world. We do not. We live outside it. Mademoiselle Juliette knows that. She can take care of herself in our world, but the Major has family, friends. If he were with her, he would have to give them up. She knows what that is like and she would never ask him to do that. He will thank her for it in the end and she will be glad for the choice she has made, but for the moment, she suffers."

"Oh. That *is* sad."

Dora nodded. "But at least she has us, and Mrs. Gerrard's ladies are no small thing to have at your side.

Alice smiled. How well she knew that! Dora, wise in the ways of the world, spoke the truth.

Chapter 44

B UT IN THIS CASE, DORA, for all her worldly wisdom, was wrong.
Several days after the discussion between Dora and Alice, as Alice was
stitching and Juliette was going over accounts, the bell over the door rang and
a broad shouldered shadow fell across the spring sunshine streaming through
the doorway.

"Adrian!" The pen dropped from Juliette's nerveless fingers as she rose to
her feet. For a moment she remained transfixed with shock and a sudden wild
joy, a joy so irrational that it refused all her efforts to subdue it. Oh the happiness of seeing that dear crooked smile, even that determined limp once again!

"Well, Mademoiselle, this is quite an establishment you have here." He
glanced around, a curiously proud smile hovering at the corner of his mouth.
"You have done a most excellent job, an excellent job, but I am come to convince
you that you are desperately needed to do an equally excellent job elsewhere."

Juliette's stomach knotted as cold reality washed over her. "You . . . .you
know I can't."

"I know nothing of the sort. I do know that you gave me a list of misguided
reasons in a rather roundabout, but brutally honest way and I am come to
prove to you that they are just that—misguided—generously and lovingly motivated to be sure, but misguided, nevertheless."

The shop bell rang again and another shadow, smaller, with a slightly taller
one behind it blocked the light.

"Maman! Papa!" Juliette could feel her knees begin to give way as all the
blood rushed from her body. She clutched her chair for support. "I . . . I thought
you were in France," she babbled idiotically.

"This gentleman," the Comte de Flournoy nodded in Adrian's direction as

he helped his wife into a chair, "convinced us that it was our duty to return."
"Duty?" Juliette gripped the back of her own chair to keep the world, which was
beginning to tilt dangerously toward the realm of the fantastic, from turning
completely upside down.

"Yes," the comte continued, calmly stripping off his gloves as though he had
just ridden over from Manchester Square instead of half way across France, the
Channel, and a good bit of England. "He has pointed out that in order for the
illustrious house of de Flournoy to continue, the line, if not the actual name,
there must be heirs and he has volunteered himself as a means to ensure this."

Juliette caught the slow wink Adrian flashed at her over the heads of her
parents, a wink which suddenly, and against all reason, made the world glow
with possibility. Stunned though she might have been by the recent turn of
events, she was not too stunned to guess the real reason behind her parents'
astonishing materialization in her life. "Auguste?"

The comte shook his head. "A noble sacrifice for his king and his country."

"Oh Papa!" Juliette's heart went out to the frail old man who held himself so
stiffly even as the tears ran down his cheeks. What it must have cost them, these
two frail old people, to make such an exhausting journey!

The comte held out his hand and she flung herself against his chest, her own
throat too tight to say another word. Awkwardly the comte patted his daughter's shoulder while his wife took her hand and pressed it to her wet cheek. "We
have been wrong to disavow our own," he acknowledged at last. "This gentleman, this milord Adrian, has made us see that. He has shown us that the pride
and courage of the de Flournoys flows in your veins as well, just in a different
way. You have fought and survived, triumphed over adversity as de Flournoys
have always done down through the ages."

Juliette's eyes flew to Adrian who shrugged modestly, but the grin tugging
at the side of his mouth grew wider.

"But Papa, the Clavertons, they too have an important family and I . . . well,
what will people say?"

"You are a de Flournoy; they will say nothing. And if they are so ill-bred
as to open their mouths, you will raise your head high and have nothing to do
with such *betise*."

"She will do nothing of the sort!" The Duchess of Roxburgh strode in,
Georgiana in tow. "The world will welcome my daughter-in-law with open
arms or I shall know the reason why."

Adrian's grin now stretched from ear to ear and even Juliette could not suppress a tiny smile at the thought of anyone daring to act in any way, but the one
the duchess commanded.

"You are outnumbered, you know," a voice whispered in her ear, the warm
breath caressing the sensitive area just below her earlobe. How had he done

that? One minute Adrian had been standing behind her parents, and the next he was at her side, limp, cane, and all, his arm stealing around her waist to pull her hard against him. What would her parents think of such a display?

But the look on the Comte and Comtesse de Flournoy's faces had nothing to do with their daughter standing in a man's arms in a dressmaker's shop and everything to do with the joy of finding her again. Adrian had done that for her. He had believed when she had not. He had hoped and dared when she had given up long ago. Who could not love a man who would cross an ocean, well the Channel, at any rate, to make her happy?

Slowly he turned her around so she was facing him, so she could not help looking up into the bright blue eyes blazing with love and something else the brought the blood to her cheeks at the thought of her parents seeing that look and she struggled to keep from giving herself up to his kisses right then and there. The teasing smile was daring her to do just that, but Juliette was made of sterner stuff. After all, the blood of the de Flournoys ran in her veins. *No one*, not even Major Lord Adrian Claverton, was going to tell her what to do. She opened her mouth to respond to the question on everyone's lips, but Adrian forestalled her. His face drawn in concentration as he clutched his cane, he carefully bent his good knee, sliding his injured leg slowly out behind him so he was almost kneeling before her. "Mademoiselle Juliette de Flournoy, will you do me the very great honor of becoming my wife to have and to hold from this day forward, until death do us part?"

What was a girl to do? They were all looking at her, Alice, her parents, the duchess, and behind, Dora, Grace, and Helen who had simply materialized in the doorway. It was Helen, once again, who came to her rescue. Her green eyes, so often glittering with cynicism, were soft and warm with approval as she nodded ever so slightly, her emerald earrings glinting in the sunlight. Juliette sighed inwardly. She wanted this so desperately that she was afraid to trust herself, or even Adrian, but Helen, clear-eyed ironist that she was, did not believe in love and marriage; she could be relied on to discourage someone from a blindly fatal step and she was not doing so—quite the opposite, in fact.

Juliette smiled down into the blue eyes fixed so intently on her, but being Juliette, she could not help hesitating just for the slightest moment to prove to herself and to him that she was making her own, and no one else's choice. Cocking her head, she raised a quizzical eyebrow. "Ah . . . yes. Yes, I think I will."

And then she was in Adrian's arms that felt so right and so perfect around her that she wondered at herself for ever having doubted that this was the place she wanted to be, the place she truly belonged. "My love," he whispered, pressing his lips to hers and claiming her for all the world to see. "Your father has assured me that the word of a de Flournoy is sacred; you are well and truly committed. No second thoughts of driving me away with manufactured excuses."

"No, Adrian." It was frightening and wonderful to be so completely understood and loved in spite of it.

"And I have it on the best authority that Maison Juliette will continue to make my daughter presentable until some poor fool takes the baggage off my hands." The duchess shot a minatory look at the comte before he could even think of objecting.

"You do?" Juliette was as stunned as her father

"Adrian has assured me that he will not distract you to the extent that you leave off designing, though he may demand so much of your attention that you might need someone else to manage your shop. I dare say you will find someone competent enough among your friends here." The duchess eyed Dora, Grace and Helen. "They are a very capable looking bunch."

"That they are." Adrian chuckled.

"Yes, your Grace," Juliette replied meekly enough though she wanted to hug her ferocious prospective mother-in-law for completely outflanking her father who, military man though he might be, looked to be completely cowed by his relative-to-be.

Lady Georgiana fortuitously recalled a pressing appointment at the milliner's, and she and the duchess offered Juliette's parents a place in their carriage as far as the rooms Adrian had booked them at Pulteney Hotel. Dora, Grace, and Helen vanished as mysteriously as they had appeared, and Alice discovered a great many things to be attended to in Juliette's chambers upstairs.

"I do hope you will forgive me for the crowd of reinforcements, but, like the Iron Duke, I do my best to influence the outcome of my engagements with thorough preparation, and I could not bear the prospect of an unfavorable outcome." Adrian was completely serious now. "I was too afraid to leave it to chance, more afraid than I have ever been before, that you would insist on condemning me to a life without you for all those foolishly generous and utterly mistaken reasons. That is why I had to bring them, your family and mine, to prove you were wrong, to prove that all that matters is that you are Juliette, just Juliette, with no past to haunt you, only a future for us to love and care for one another forever. Yes?" He leaned his forehead against hers, looking deep into her eyes.

"Yes."

At last as his lips pressed against hers, taking her slowly, thoroughly, completely, the healing that had begun the day she had shared herself with him in their magical private world on the river was completed.

EPILOGUE

"WE ARE GATHERED HERE, DEARLY BELOVED . . ." As John spoke the sacred words, he realized with something of a shock that at that moment he was actually happy in London's most exclusive church. For once, the rector of St. George's Hanover Square was truly doing God's work instead of preaching to a fashionably bored and inattentive audience. Seeing the joy and love reflected in Adrian's and Juliette's faces and the happiness of the expressions of the select few invited to the ceremony, he knew he had been part of the sort of redemptive work he longed to make his calling.

The marriage had brought hope and faith to the cynical. Helen looked as radiant as he had ever seen her, and Dora, Grace, and Olivia were unabashedly dabbing their eyes with lace handkerchiefs exquisitely sewn by a beaming Alice. It brought comfort to the grieving as the Comte de Flournoy stood proud in his uniform, unbending only slightly to smile at his wife as he gave his daughter to his new son-in-law. And it brought friendship and understanding to those who, despite their exalted position in life, needed it; both Freddy and Georgie were smiling as proudly as if they had brought about the happy event single-handedly. And it brought the hope of a new generation to those whose duty bound them to carrying on ancient names—even the duke and duchess' characteristically stoic features were softened with joy.

As Adrian, his new wife on his arm, walked proudly down the aisle, planting his cane firmly with every step, he nodded gratefully to all those who had helped him win his stubborn bride. How many people had contributed to this day of happiness! And if one person was conspicuously absent, so much the better. Lady Lavinia had discovered a pressing engagement for precisely that day and hour, but, as Freddy had pointed out, it was no loss; no one wanted such a Friday-faced creature putting a damper on the festivities anyway.

As the happy couple drove off on the first leg of their journey home to Ashbourne, Adrian glanced down at the head resting contentedly against his shoulder and smiled. "Happy?"

"Oh yes!" Juliette looked up at him, her eyes shining, and for the first time, he noticed that the tiny wrinkle of worry that usually hovered between her delicate eyebrows was entirely gone. His arm tightened around her as he pressed his lips to hers, reveling in love, their future, and the fineness of the day.

But back in London, two people sitting on either side of an empty fireplace in a dark paneled library had no appreciation for love, the future, or the fineness of the day. "You needn't have taken such a risk after all," one of them remarked waspishly. "It was reckless and in the end, unnecessary. Mademoiselle Juliette is disposed of after all."

"And as usual, you are a spineless fool," the other retorted, "relying on luck to save us when our entire future hung in balance, leaving me, as usual, to take matters in hand in case your notoriously fickle luck failed us."

Even before studying eighteenth-century literature in graduate school, Evelyn Richardson decided she would have preferred to have lived in England between 1775 and 1830. Now living outside of Boston, she enjoys access to the primary sources that allow her to explore the details of the period and immerse herself in the same journals her heroines enjoyed which for her, as a longtime reference librarian, is the best of all possible worlds.

CPSIA information can be obtained
at www.ICGtesting.com
Printed in the USA
BVHW071658100321
602114BV00006B/608

9 781603 816175